PERFECT CIRCLES

The Sequel to *Two Wheels*

a novel by

GREG MOODY

VELOPRESS • BOULDER, COLORADO

ISBN: 1-884737-44-7

Printed in the U.S.A.

Library of Congress Cataloging-in-Publication Data:

Moody, Greg, 1952 –
Perfect circles : a novel / by Greg Moody.
p. cm.
"The sequel to Two Wheels."
ISBN 1-884737-44-7
1. Title.
PS3563.05525P47 1998
813' .54--dc21

98–11485
CIP

VeloPress
1830 N 55th Street
Boulder, Colorado 80301-2700
USA

303/440-0601
303/444-6788 fax
e-mail: velopress@7dogs.com

To purchase additional copies of this book or other Velo products,
Call 800/234-8356, or visit our
Website at www.velocatalogue.com

Cover illustration by Matt Brownson

Acknowledgments

My thanks go first to those friends and family who gave of their time to read and criticize and make this happen. I will always appreciate that.

Also, my thanks to Dr. Dave Hnida, who helped with the medical aspects of the story, Ron Kiefel, whose experience at Le Tour de France was invaluable, as well as the staff at VeloPress, including John Wilcockson, Charles Pelkey, Amy Sorrells, Mark Littrell and Tim Johnson, who encouraged and laughed and criticized constructively.

Deep thanks also to Stephen White, who never failed to support, encourage, or buy lunch.

And yet, my greatest thanks of all must go to Becky, Devon and Brynn. They make me laugh, they make me love, they save my life.

Dedication:
To Becky

CONTENTS

Prologue vii
1 Back in the Saddle Again 1
2 S.O.B. 15
3 Les Misérables 37
4 Death be not Colnago 47
5 In Mourning 65
6 The Next Time I See Paris 75
7 Once More, Dear Friends, Into the Breach 81
8 Dancing at the Rascal Fair 101
9 Parry and Thrust 121
10 Into the Lion's Den 125
11 Digging 143
12 Lab Rat 147
13 Reach Out and Tag Somebody 151
14 Rest Day 177
15 Liquid Courage 189
16 One-Hundred-Sixty-First Man on the Mountain 207
17 The Rough and Ragged Edge 233
18 I Did It My Way 247
19 Given an Out 269
20 Under the Volcano 279
21 Death Wears a Bowler 293
22 The High Price of Visions 301
23 Night Train to Paris 313
24 Home Again, Home Again... 321
25 The Timely Visitor 331
26 Duck and Cover 341
27 The Old Man and The Sea 349
28 Is Paris Burning? 351
29 The Party's Over 369
30 Leaving on a Jet Plane 375
Epilogue 383

PROLOGUE

Today was the first day of the end of his life.

Henrik Koons pulled the red-white-and-green Lexor Computer jersey over his head and stiffly brushed it down along his sides. This was still a good body, he thought. Rough hewn, gone to freckles, but a body that could still get the job done, whatever that job had become. He turned, first this way, then that, in the half mirror of the dingy apartment on the outskirts of Eindhoven, near the Dutch-Belgian border, and admired the view of himself.

At 26, Henrik had seen the life of a professional cyclist from the rear. Four years in the pro ranks had meant four years of looking up the ass end of every other rider in the pack.

That, however, was going to change. And change soon.

Henrik glanced outside. It was a miserable day, wet and blustery; just another mid-June afternoon in the Netherlands. Still, miserable days had lately given themselves to be great riding days: brash and cool and full of a headlong flight down the road.

And a great riding day this would be, Henrik grinned to himself, for he had found the secret. His body hadn't changed. He was still tall and stringy, the muscles of his chest and legs serving only to fill out his Lycra uniform. His training hadn't changed, nor his diet, but now, he knew, he had discovered the key to the winner's circle; not some ancient Teutonic secret of life, but a modern chemical equivalent that was easy to take, easy to mask, easy to hide away. It was his new drug of choice and he wasn't letting anyone else in on the secret. He had a source, a cheap source, for an unknown, completely unregulated miracle. Perhaps it would stay that way if things went well and he kept his mouth shut for once in his life.

Only a dim light cast through the thick yellow fluid hanging heavily in the tube of the classic glass syringe. This was the ultimate: a career in a bottle. Henrik tapped the side of the metal fitting and watched, fascinated, as an air bubble floated slowly to the surface. "Don't want you in there, my friend." He depressed the plunger and released the bubble through the needle. He stood, pulled down the back of his riding shorts and poised the needle over his right buttock. It was beginning to look like a connect-the-dots game, he realized, the small red and brown marks of the needle meshing with his freckles and moles to form intricate patterns and shapes on his ass.

When I am a champion, he thought, I shall have beautiful women, perhaps two at a time, draw lines between the dots.

He took a deep breath and drove the needle home, injecting 6cc's of the heavy fluid into his cheek. He waited for a second to feel the familiar burn, but it didn't come this time. He was relieved. His miracle drug was an uncomfortable task master, unusually tough to accommodate. Surprising, though, this was a much higher dose than he normally took, perhaps by three. "A little be good, a little more be better," according to the wisdom of Granny deKuyper.

He expected more of a reaction. It made no sense.

Henrik sat on the edge of his bed and continued to wait for the first rush, already slightly behind schedule, that heralded his new found power and influence on a bike.

TRULY.

This was the day.

This was the way.

Henrik Koons flashed down the right edge of the lane, cut to the middle, then back again to the edge. His bike-handling had improved, along with his power, his drive, his confidence on a bike. Lexor Computer would never again be able to relegate him to the back of the peloton, to the role of domestique, water carrier, for the Dutch and Belgian stars who rode at the head of the team. This time, this year, was his and his alone, and he knew it. He felt it.

He approached the rear of the Fiat and cut to the middle of the road, passing on the driver's side, tapping the old man's elbow with the flat of his hand as he passed, easily.

"*Olé! Eh, Toro!*" he shouted and slammed past the startled senior, cutting back to the inside. He heard the screech of brakes and a honk and a muffled, startled, curse, but, what the hell. The road was his as it had never been before. It only promised to get better.

Soon, the asphalt would turn to gold and the gold would turn to fame and the fame and the gold would turn to women, spread out before him like this country road, reaching out in an endless line for just a minute, a moment, with him. He could almost see them. Feel them. Hear them. Smell them.

Henrik cut back to the middle of the road, once more startling the ancient driver of the even more ancient Fiat and drove himself harder, faster, than he ever had before. Beautiful, he thought, this was simply beautiful.

The tires hummed. They were beginning to actually form a tune. Henrik sang along for a minute at the top of his lungs, startling more of those he passed. The town of Bakel passed in a blur. The villagers, young and old, watched in stunned fascination as he shot past the church, the shops, the cafés, all a wave of images that crashed over him. Their eyes were on him, while his eyes, his thoughts, his focus lay ahead. This — this — was the ride of a star, a king, the next Merckx, Indurain, Anquetil, Colgan, he thought.

What had taken an endless amount of training and effort before, now came without price on himself or his lungs or his legs. Every part of him felt marvelous, as if there weren't an ounce of pressure to bear on each pedal stroke.

This was the birth of a champion.

He had only watched them in the past, riding with them, but not *of* them. They were the ones who were made for this sport, who sat in the middle of the pack, riding easily, waiting patiently, watching with amusement as team managers sent the riders like Henrik ahead, too early, stupidly, to clear the road, to change the pace, to draw off anyone too anxious to wait for the proper break, late in the race, that would finally decide the winner.

Despite the futility of it all, Henrik would throw himself into his job with all the power he could muster. The photos of the race rarely captured him, but when they did, they always showed a man on the verge of collapse. The legs that had made him the local amateur champion of Eindhoven had left him long ago, or, to be honest, were never truly good enough to bring him here in the first place.

He struggled, he gasped, he agonized as *they* rode past, as if on rails.

Indurain and his fellows would flash by, a spotlight shining on them and them alone, the champions fresh and comfortable, showing no effort in their style.

Damn it. He was a mouse and had been a mouse, all along, sent to draw out the cat, to play with the cat, while the cat played with him until the cat struck suddenly, without warning, leaving him one dead, damned mouse.

First the leaders, then the lieutenants, then the sprinters, then the domestiques, then the rest would pass, and Henrik could only watch them go, the colors of the cycling rainbow flashing beyond him on titanium rings, as he fell back behind the cars and the trucks and the motos of the passing parade.

And, yet, even then, he would find himself in a race again, with the final dozen riders, roster fodder for each and every team, who were fighting to be something other than dead last. It used to be a bizarre, sought-after honor, Henrik had been told, to be last, dead last, the *lanterne rouge* of Le Tour, but now, it was nothing more than simply last. Finis. Kaput. No honor. No trophy. No nothing. Simply last. Out of 23 races he had finished so far this season, he had been last only twice, if always in the final group.

But no more. Not again. Not last. No mouse. Henrik Koons had been reborn.

He smiled and thanked the gods of modern chemistry.

The road narrowed ahead and he aimed his bike between two approaching cars, one passing the other. He smiled at the startled faces of the drivers and actually closed his eyes for the last few feet. He felt the roar and the rush of the engines as the cars shot past, the drivers panicked into holding their lanes. Henrik exploded out the other side, a look of triumph on his face. The head wind that had held him back, in life, as well as on the road — was behind him now, pushing him on toward a triumphant finish to his career.

Henrik picked up his pace, again, and found still more power in reserve. He was controlling the road, like an Indurain, without effort, without wobble, with nerves of steel. He could feel his heart pounding in his chest and it only drove him on toward more. Harder, faster, longer. This was the training ride of his career, he thought, the one to which all to come will be measured.

The tires hummed. The crankset sang. His legs were pistons, driving hard, churning toward a bend in the road that rose upward and screamed at him as the blacktop tore itself free of the earth and leapt up like a snake, whipping back and forth across the sky as he rode toward a head with no eyes, his legs pounding out an unstoppable staccato and his heart shuddering in his chest with each powerful beat.

Henrik squeezed his eyes shut, waited a second, then snapped them open again. The road was back where it was supposed to be, along the green and flowering earth in the middle of a Dutch summer, heavy with the scent of wheat and wet grass and blooming flowers. The trees on each side of the road reached over to build a rich green cathedral over him as the pace, even now, continued to grow. In this moment, he realized, he had passed the realm of the common athlete and had become a star, stepping into the rarefied atmosphere that reached from deep within him and gave him yet another burst of speed and power and control.

Wait until Le Tour, he thought. Wait until then. He would not hang his head in shame this year. He would not be a part of the laughing group, the last, uncaring, riders of the race. He would be on the podium. He would be in yellow or green or red polka dots. Or best of all, all three at once.

A car approached in the distance.

Henrik set himself in the middle of the road. Watching. Daring.

His pace continued to increase. His heart began to hurt from the exertion, but he drove himself on toward the car, approaching on the horizon, that now moved to the center of the road, the vision rippling in the reflected heat.

The Americans, he knew, called it chicken. This, he knew, as life on the edge.

Henrik focused on the lights and grill of the small car. He squinted his eyes and thought his way through it. The colors of the world around him began to darken as the one spot in his vision grew. The trees smeared. Sound passed in a rush of unrelated noise. His vision converged on a spot directly between the two headlights. Just one spot. A silver spot. As the spot grew, he noticed a blue dot with letters in a scripted hand centered within. Ford. American. Perfect. He hated American cars. He concentrated on the dot. On the grill.

On the car.

Chicken.

And he knew he would win. He would split the car in two, leaving each half by the side of a country road in the Netherlands, the driver dazed and confused and stunned by what had happened to his American roller skate. He would tell the story for years to his friends in the bars of Amsterdam, always wondering aloud: who could it have possibly been who split his car in two? Who was that all-powerful rider?

"It is I," raged Henrik, "Thor, God of Thunder."

Henrik laughed, the burst of sound echoing from him and sending a shiver through his entire body. The colors of the day were now bright and fantastic, a fluorescent explosion of light. The Dutch countryside had taken on the look of a Van Gogh painting done in garish neon. As much as he wanted to look, though, he couldn't, wouldn't shift his focus from the oncoming car, the two headlights still dead center in the road, as was he. The lights flashed off and on, off and on, in warning, in dare, incredible.

Somewhere, in the distance, he heard a horn. His focus did not shift.

Harder and harder, increasing the pace until his heart felt nearly to explode from his chest, Henrik arrowed toward his challenge. Closer. And closer. Harder. And harder.

Ten meters.

Eight.

Five.

Two.

Contact.

With a roar of flame and sound, Henrik felt the rending of metal around him, the scream of the driver as the car and bike connected, the shearing edge of the bike tire cutting through the car like a razor through silvered holiday paper. Henrik shifted his focus quickly only once to see the demon driver stare at him in shock, his plans of driving a bicyclist off the road gone forever, along with his cheap American car. Through the back seat. Henrik raged. A stuffed children's toy caught in the wheel, then tore into felt and feathers as he rode through the trunk, the bumper, then gone. Henrik heard the satisfying sound of metal screaming along the tarmac as the two halves of the car careened into the stone fence along each side of the road, then merged into a heart-pounding silence. He left the scene as if shot from a cannon.

The road rose up before him and he pushed on, harder, faster, more vicious than ever before, his heart tearing itself from the foundations of his chest, the world around him smearing away in a vague distortion of the dark end of the palette, browns and dark blues, blood reds and greens, the road rising up again, a beast, enveloping him in a dark fold.

His heart beat furiously and he drove his pace on, his head snapping down, down, down, down.

His head snapping down.

He convulsed once, twice and yet again. He fought to raise his head, to see farther, a bit farther, down the road. The prize was within his reach. He had found his key to the podium, to stardom and a world that lay just beyond, once hidden from his view, now his for the taking.

And so he pedaled on.

Once, twice, again.

His legs moved in circles, perfect circles, perfect technique. Even as he began to die.

Perfect circles.

His legs turning perfect circles.

His eyes snapping back and forth, gauging a road that did not exist.

Turning perfect circles.

His chest convulsing, his life pouring from his mouth in a white froth.

Turning perfect circles.

On the floor. Of a dingy apartment. On the outskirts of Eindhoven.

Perfect circles.

Perfect circles.

Perfect.

THE TURN-OF-THE-CENTURY PATENT LEATHER SHOES STOOD JUST BEYOND THE leading edge of the vomit, part and parcel of a brown, plaid, turn-of-the-century suit, edged by a stark, white, turn-of-the-century collar and a blood red tie on a sharply defined turn-of-the-century neck, rising up to a lined and hardened face, a visage of too many days in the fields, a face that Norman Rockwell would have softened for mass consumption. The sharp, aquiline features were framed by a shock of unruly white hair topped by a black bowler.

Gingerly, the figure stepped around the muck and gore that spread across the floor and tapped Henrik Koons on the shoulder with the sharply edged point of his shoe.

"Come along now," he whispered.

CHAPTER ONE:

BACK IN THE SADDLE AGAIN

He swam forward to the edge of consciousness, first rising through the warm dark and into the muted light, past the crisscrossed red lines that sat just behind his eyelids. He didn't want to open them. Too much homemade red wine in the little café just off the Rue de Rivoli had left chunks of grape floating around in his blood stream, just waiting to plug up important parts of his brain pan. Anquetil could live like this during training, he thought, why can't I?

Anquetil is dead, he remembered. Keep that in mind.

There was a headache the size of Cleveland sitting just behind his right eye, running behind his ear to whatever that thing was called at the back of his head. A quick, self diagnosis and he opened the pain-free left eye, only to gaze upon a small map of Rhode Island. No, that can't be right, he thought. On all the maps he remembered from grade school, Rhode Island was pink. Rhode Island was pink, Connecticut, blue, Massachusetts, green, and, what state was brown?

He opened the eye a little wider and refocused. The great state of Rhode Island, dressed in an unnatural brown, disappeared to be replaced by an unusual, Rhode Island-shaped rust stain on a dull white ceiling. He contemplated it for a moment, as you don't often find bas reliefs of Rhode Island in this corner of France, and considered reporting it to his landlady; then, realizing it hadn't grown in the six weeks he had lived here, decided it wasn't worth the trouble or the psychic energy he was now spending on it.

Will Ross rolled to his right. He looked across the bedroom of the small Senlis apartment, some 40 kilometers north of Paris, as the morning sun slowly began to stream into the room and pick up bits of dust floating through the thick air. He tried to find a pattern in them for a moment, then, refocused again, through the partially opened door of the bathroom.

My god, he thought, rather dreamily, but she has a nice ass. He smiled, drew the sheet tight around his neck, then frowned. I hate that, he thought. Ass. There's no romance in such a word for such a nice one. Butt. Bum. Rump. Derrière. No — this was more like the golden, sunflower covered hills of — where — the rolling hills of—.

He smiled.

Cheryl Crane saw Will looking at her in the mirror. There was a momentary flush of embarrassment, then a smile. She turned and looked across the room at an unshaven face, covered with scars, staring dreamily, if drunkenly, at her nakedness from under a Pocahontas sheet his mother had sent him.

"Yes? May I help you?"

"Believe me," he replied, sounding like a four-pack-a-day Marlboro man at the bottom of a 50-gallon drum, "you already have."

"Whatever you're thinking about, forget it. You're in training."

"Aw, that's crap."

"What?"

"That 'Rocky' crap," he mocked, dropping his voice into a growl, "Remember Rock — 'women weaken legs.'"

"No, it's true," she replied. "We sap the vitality out of you so that all men have got left is the energy to drink, belch, watch TV and not listen."

"What?"

"See?"

Will rolled up into a sitting position and swung his legs off the edge of the bed. An early-morning erection was giving John Smith a big chin.

"And good morning to you, too."

"Reveille for one and all."

"How romantic. You just know how to sweep a girl off her feet, don't you?"

"Women love it. I'm a smooth-talking, debonair kind of guy with all the right moves and a face as smooth and pink as a baby's behind. What's not to love?"

For emphasis, he belched, then waved his hand frantically in front of his face to dissipate the noxious smell.

Cheryl dropped her head against the mirror with a 'clunk,' then turned back to Will, now stretching, languidly, on the edge of the bed. He had a heavy five o'clock shadow that made him look like Satan's take on Fred Flintstone. The scars from his face plant into the back of a team car earlier this season had created the effect of the Martian landscape on what had been an attractive, if not handsome, face. At the moment, Will was unshaven, whiskers poking out at odd angles from the brightly glowing pink scars, mouth belching wine, seafood and Caesar salad into the humid air of the tiny apartment. At that moment, she knew that she loved him.

He smiled, sheepishly, his hair askew.

Cute, she thought, definitely cute.

He scratched himself.

Pretty much cute, she thought.

She left him and turned back to the mirror. She had a team to run. That wasn't her job, of course, as it would be simply too outrageous if anyone really knew, but after a season and a half as a soigneur, a female soigneur, no less, for Haven Pharmaceuticals — masseuse, gofer, mother confessor and jack of all trades to one of Europe's top cycling teams — she was quietly calling the shots. The directeur sportif, the team director, had gone and gotten shot in the leg a few months back and there was no one else to step into the administrative role, mainly because it was one of Carl Deeds's assistants who had done the shooting. After a great internal hue and cry from the board, Henri Bergalis, the prince regent of Haven, had taken the plunge and put her in charge. Quietly, of course. Very quietly. So quietly, in fact, that most of the team was completely unaware of who was the head "man."

A woman, a young woman, managing a European team. *Mon dieu.* The sport, the teams, hell, France itself, would collectively expel bricks the size of Renaults, even if she were doing little more than setting training schedules, playing travel agent and pushing papers of various sizes to different points of Carl Deeds's desk a couple of times a day. Given the possible reaction, no one knew. Even the UCI, cycling's international governing body, called and sent their mail directly to Henri Bergalis himself. And no one would know. She'd be out as soon as Carl Deeds returned from rehab. Then, she'd be gone.

No matter what she had done or was doing, Cheryl knew it was time to go, it was time for her to get back on the bike herself. She had learned from this team, about tactics and power climbs and placement in the pack. She had also learned from the all male, mostly European, team about discrimination and grudging acceptance, but now it was time to get back on the bike and rediscover the power, the rush, the adrenaline high of blasting down a mountainside at dawn with the wind in your ears and the bugs in your teeth. She had to do it for herself, even if it meant leaving Will in the process.

He had fallen back onto the bed, his early-morning hard-on morphing a cartoon rabbit into a unicorn with big ears.

She sighed. Even if it meant losing Will in the process. She had to get back on the bike. She had to ride.

What she hadn't meant to do was fall in love with him again. Cheryl Crane had loved Will Ross, desperately, 16 years before, when he rode with her brother through the fields and farms of Michigan. Then, her brother, Raymond, had been killed during a race by a drunken farmer running barricades in his pickup truck and Will had simply lost it, running away from racing and Stewart Kenally, his coach and mentor, and Cheryl's family and Cheryl herself. Her mother had been desperately hurt by Will's abandonment, which had filled Cheryl with a deep and lasting hatred of the man. And, yet, meeting him again this spring, watching him ride, watching him grow, watching him win, and, yes, damn near getting killed with him once or twice, had pulled her back toward him, until now, she thought, as she closed the brassiere, here we are: lovers in Paris in the middle of June. She gazed at herself in the mirror and smiled. You can't get much more romantic than that.

"HhhhhAcck. God. Agh. I feel like shit."

She barked a deep, satisfying laugh. Yep, you can't get more romantic.

Cheryl pulled the black Haven team polo over her head and hand smoothed her hair. "Are you still riding to the track with me?"

Will sat up quickly and looked around him. Morning had broken and Woody had disappeared. His hand moved up to a scar running under his right eye and he followed it to the corner, wiping some sleep away. Will nodded.

"Then, get a move on, will you? I'm about ready to leave."

"Clear the bathroom and be amazed." She looked at him. "Truly," he said, walking in and gently pushing her toward the door. "Are you done?" She nodded. "Good. You get dressed out here and I'll be right with you."

Cheryl crossed to the window and opened it wide, hoping to catch a breeze through the apartment. She heard the shower start and went back to her dressing. She wanted to be on the road in 15 minutes, even if that meant she'd have to wait in the soggy velodrome office for a few minutes before beginning the team meeting. If there was anything about her family, they were prompt. Prompt, hell, early. Early as hell. Her uncle had been so early for one job, she remembered, that he landed in jail for two years. She pulled on her Levis. They were just a shade tight. Too much riding in cars, she thought, not enough on bikes. We'll change that soon enough. She bent to tie her new K-Swiss sneaks. Work clothes. Most people used to dress in high fashion to work, she pondered as she looked at herself in the mottled full-length mirror, now they dress like they're going to clean the garage.

She grinned, turned from the mirror and jumped. Will was — done. He stood in the doorway of the bathroom, showered, shaved and sporting a fresh red, black and yellow Haven team jersey. Short hair slicked back, teeth shining, he looked, except for the glowing pink scars on his face, like an ad for the team.

"How do you do that?"

"Do what?"

"How do you get yourself together so quickly? I mean, you frighten me, sometimes."

"Hey …" he smiled and touched her chin as he walked past, "fastest stripper in the seventh grade. You either did it fast or found that somebody had thrown your clothes out the gymnasium window. I never lost it."

"It is a talent."

"Definitely."

Will walked over to a two-story brick-and-board book rack loaded to groaning with one mystery and endless piles of racing gear and pulled out what he would need for the day: shoes, jackets, a shirt and pair of jeans. He stuffed them all in a Haven back pack. It may have been true that even the French didn't care about professional road cycling anymore, or, at least, their national fanaticism had diminished, but he still loaded himself with logos. He was a salesman, a walking billboard for Haven Pharmaceuticals and the team. Who knew? It could mean the difference between another season on the road with good facilities and strong backing, or wrapping up his career with a two-bit American outfit that had reluctantly signed off on a team because of a bike dweeb in marketing and, now, couldn't wait to get out from under it. He turned, picked up his bike, a battered white Colnago frame with brand new everything else, turned to Cheryl, still dumbstruck beside the bathroom door and said, quietly, "Shall we?"

"I'm not ready yet."

"Get a move on — you've got a bunch of guys to push around."

FORMER POLICE INSPECTOR LUC GODOT CAREFULLY LIT THE CIGAR. CUBAN. HE rolled the Cohiba between his fingers as the flame kissed the edges of the wrapper, so sweet, so early, so luxurious.

He could afford them now.

Some 30 years with the Paris police had led to a dead-end office in a dead-end hall with a dead-end career. Here's your watch, thanks for your help, get your sorry, sagging ass out of here.

He had been saved by Henri Bergalis and Haven Pharmaceuticals.

I could be a testimonial for the company, he thought.

'Haven Pharmaceuticals gave me a life. Let them give you a life, too.'

Godot, the newly installed Chief of Security for Haven Pharmaceuticals, laughed quietly as he took a long draw on the cigar and spat a stream of rich, blue smoke toward the ceiling and the exhaust fan that carried it out into the morning sky of Paris.

Godot's office had become the smoker's haven in the corporate headquarters. For some reason, the board of directors had come to believe that a company dedicated to the health of the world should not be filled with people packing their lungs full of tar, nicotine and other assorted carcinogens.

Too bad, Godot thought, that another American fetish descends upon the Continent. But the fan had been a condition of employment, Godot recalled with a smile. Certainly I'll be your Chief of Security, certainly I'll take the job and the salary and the perquisites, *but* … you will not — *will not* — take away my cigars.

It hadn't happened that way, of course. Godot had been too shocked by the job offer and salary to worry about whether he could smoke in the building or not. Henri Bergalis simply knew his people. He looked the other way and quietly had the exhaust fan installed, and, without an official pronouncement, employees soon began gravitating toward Godot's office at all times of the day and night to puff away merrily without the morality police chasing them down with a fire extinguisher.

One room of the building was in a continual blue haze and everyone was happy.

Godot sent a series of smoke rings wafting toward the ceiling, watching for a moment as each held itself together in a perfect circle, only to be stretched and pulled, one at a time, toward the fan and the world outside.

Perfect.

He turned back and faced the morning tabloid. It was thin, both journalistically and ethically, but it found the stories he truly cared about reading every morning. Today, his eye had been drawn to the graphic and gory story of a cyclist's death in the Netherlands.

'WHEELS OF DOOM!' the headline screamed.

He flipped the pages of the paper open to the jump and was greeted by a gruesome black-and-white photo of a young man, in cycling clothing, curled into a fetal position on a dirty wooden floor, his life spewing out both ends.

"God, what a mess," he said aloud to the empty office.

He could see the feet of one of the investigating officers just off to one side of the photo.

Better you than me, pal.

Better you than me.

CHERYL STARTED THE TEAM CAR, AN AGING PEUGEOT WITH ENOUGH LOGOS stamped across its body to qualify it for circus wagon status, and reached for the gear shift. She paused, then turned off the car and turned to Will.

"I have an offer."

Will grinned. "As long as I have a mattress, you'll always have an offer," he said, making a great display of licking his lips.

Cheryl froze at the joke, turned and restarted the car.

"I'm leaving."

"*What*?! Just because of one shitty joke? Jesus, you're touchy. Come on — let's talk about this."

Cheryl turned off the car again and stared out the windshield.

"No," she said, quietly. "It's not that." Her eyes snapped toward him and burned through his jersey. "Although that was a particularly shitty thing to say."

"I'm a particularly shitty human being. I'm sorry. Don't leave."

"Why?"

He froze. She had thrown her cards on the table and called his bluff. If he didn't say anything, once she left, he'd never see her again or smell her or touch her or tell her, and yet, he felt anchored to the seat, as if the gray, brown faux leather of the Peugeot held him tight with Krazy Glue. He watched her stare at him, then turn to stare out the windshield at some meaningless point in the distance, the rolling hills of —. God, don't let this happen, don't let her walk out of your life, don't let this happen, damn you, *say something*!

But he didn't.

His brain sounded the alarm.

Tilt. Tilt. Tilt. Tilt.

Cheryl finally broke the curtain of tension that had dropped between them.

"Remember Stewart Kenally?"

Will shook his head as if to bring a wandering memory up to a point where he could deal with it. Of course he knew Stewart Kenally. Stewart Kenally had taught both him and Cheryl how to ride and race and survive on a bike, road or track. Now, with the changing focus of the marketplace, Kenally was supposed to be building quite a reputation with mountain bikes back in the States.

"Stewart is creating a team. He needs riders, plus somebody to run it. He needs somebody to lead it. I've been with Haven for a year and a half now, ever since I mangled myself at Nevegal in a downhill blaze of glory. I've got to get back, Will. I've got to get back on the bike."

Will felt a ball of gas the size of William Howard Taft build just behind his tongue and pull his chest tight. Cheryl riding again. It got her back on the bike, but left him out in the cold.

She watched his eyes click back and forth, desperately searching for a conversational direction.

"Relax. You could come along," she said quietly, hopefully.

His shoulders dropped and he laughed. "Oh, no. I'm a road rider, you know that. Maybe track. That mountain stuff just ain't for me. You rode World Cup for, what, two years and survived? That takes a different kind of person."

"A person with balls."

"Or," he said, "a person with ovaries."

"Hey," she smiled as if a great victory had finally been won, "you're learning."

"It takes me a while, I'll admit, but I'm not a complete dolt. No, I just can't see the attraction of hitting 30 on an irregular track running through a forest on a mountainside ski run masquerading as a bicycle course."

"Ah, but that's the joy of it."

"I wouldn't call it joy."

"It's no different from shooting down a mountainside at 60 miles an hour on a narrow road in heavy traffic with a driving rain in your face — is it?"

"Maybe — but I can trust the peloton — it's like racing in a school of fish. You can sense where everyone is going, but mountain biking — man — that's like amateur night with a mechanical bull. Everybody's heading down the mountain like a pack of cartoon dogs chasing Bugs Bunny. It's nuts."

"You just don't have the bike-handling skills to ride the mountain. Admit it."

It sort of rankled Will to hear Cheryl put it that way, but it was true. It was a different world, riding a mountain bike, and took a different kind of rider: a rider with different skills and a different outlook and a different set of muscles, both mental and physical. Some folks could cross back and forth, like Tomac and Furtado, but most stood by their chosen style, roadie or mountain, without a backward glance.

Will was a roadie, pure and simple. Cheryl was a granite grinder. He'd have to live with that.

"It's my chosen line of work," she said quietly, breaking into his thoughts and dispelling the never ending war behind men and women, road or mountain, home or away.

"Yes, and for that, we now offer up the body and soul of our soon to depart Cheryl Crane. Say hello to your mother."

"So you won't come along?"

"I'd love to," he said, lying as smoothly possible on such short notice, "but they need me here."

Cheryl expected this. And yet, as her eyes carefully examined his face, she decided to push.

"I know that. I understand that. And, I know why you're here and what you have to do, but I have to know that you know something about me. And that is that I love you," she said, almost under her breath.

"And I … and … and I…." Will felt his face start to flush, the pounding in his neck growing to the point where he could literally not hear anything around him other than the sound of his own ragged breath. He felt like he was climbing L'Alpe d'Huez in a snowstorm, his face suddenly hot, his eyes stinging, his hands wet and cold. He went into cranial vapor lock again, his eyes blank, his mouth open and dry, his brain buzzing over and over again — tilt, tilt, tilt, tilt.

Cheryl searched Will's face for his reaction, then, reached up and stroked his cheek with the tip of her fingers. "I know. I know where you've been and what you've done and what's been done to you. But that's in the past. This is now. The now is — the reality is — that I love you, Will. I've told Henri."

"That you love me?"

"No, that I'm going home after Le Tour and he's got to find someone new by then." She paused for a moment, then added, quietly, "I'd like you to come along."

She took a deep breath and started the car for the third time.

"And I just want you to know it."

"But I have a career here."

"I know. But it doesn't have to be now. It can be when you decide you're done."

"You think that's soon, don't you?"

"No," she said quietly, putting the car into gear, "just whenever."

They looked at each other for a moment, with only the quiet murmur of the Peugeot filling the compartment. Then, she pulled the car quietly into traffic, turned a corner and was swallowed up by what passed for rush hour on a mid-June morning in Senlis.

PAUL VAN BRUGGEN HATED THE DRAFT THAT BLEW THROUGH THE DOOR NEXT to his work station. As the low man on the police lab totem pole in Eindhoven, he had the lousiest schedule and the worst seat in the house. Lab work, he knew, was more than just tests and computer readouts. It was looks and hunches and reactions and smells; and whatever smells were generated in the entire lab usually blew toward the lab station next to that damned door, his lab station. The right time of the year and it smelled like the open air fish market in Copenhagen.

He replaced the lid on the plastic tray holding Mrs. Juergens's kidney and speared another piece of chicken out of the plastic tray holding his lunch. He popped it in his mouth and moved it around a bit, trying to pick up a flicker of flavor. He cooked like his mother, he realized, boiling everything until there was no taste remaining within a mile of the meat.

He replaced her tray in the refrigerator and made the final notation on the report. Cancer. He turned to the side and spit the chicken into the wastebasket next to his stool. Mrs. Juergens was only 24. Damn.

Life is too short for crappy food.

He flipped the manila cover closed on the life of Eva Juergens and tossed the file lightly into his "out" basket. Sad, he thought, it's not heaven or hell where we all end up, but some civil servant's "out" basket.

His boredom was reaching critical mass. Van Bruggen rubbed his forehead, then closed his eyes and reached into the pile next to his microscope. He dug around a bit, running his fingers up and down the edges of the files, hoping to pull one that might just catch his interest. No, not that one, it was too fat, meaning there were years of previous files to go through, a long history of illness and concerns leading up to the inevitable meeting with the angel of death. Not this one, there are too many tabs, meaning that somebody else had started the case, noted a lot of indications and high signs that led nowhere and only confused the issue, tabbed them all and tried to palm it off on him.

Find your own way out of your own damned mess, van Bruggen thought.

And, then, he found it, if only by touch and intuition. He ran his finger along the spine of the relatively thin folder and felt an intuitive need to read it. This, he thought, this is my file. This is the case that will move me up the ladder of the laboratory bureaucracy until I stand tall as the undisputed head of a mediocre department.

He pulled the file and placed it carefully in front of him, paused, and then flipped open the cover.

The top sheet read, in a smeared blue ink, Koons, Henrik.

Koons. He squinted at the label.

"I remember this one. She mentioned him."

✷

CHERYL MOVED THE SMALL, GAILY DECORATED CAR SMOOTHLY THROUGH TRAFFIC. She concentrated on the road while Will stared out the side window. Hell of a way to start a day, he snorted. First, you lose her to the States, then you lose her heart because you let her go and freeze up like a 1929 Whippet. An odd pressure remained just behind Will's eyes. He tried to shut off his mind, but Cheryl was there, and her scent happily filled the car. Goddamn it! Why hadn't he said something? Fear of losing her forever? Fear of commitment? God, what a cliché. God, how true.

Will hadn't really dated since his ex-wife, Kim, had become his ex-wife, Kim. The divorce had knocked him for a loop, both personally and professionally. He had been living in squalor in a little Belgian apartment, while Kim rose to the top with Haven under its previous management, and, brother, had she been under the previous management. He snorted a laugh and blew snot across his lips and chin. Kim's connections with Haven Cycling had gotten him this job on the team, after which, he had spent most of the spring trying not to be killed by her or her friends, part of some dandy corporate takeover scheme, only to see her blasted out of existence by a 175-pound Russian sprinter hitting 45 miles an hour on the flat and snapping her neck like a dry twig at the finish of Ghent-Wevelgem, a single-day classic in Belgium.

Baggage? Enough to fill a cargo ship. Fear of commitment? He'd come by it honestly.

But Cheryl. Man, she didn't deserve what he had done to her today.

By now, she had negotiated the late-morning traffic of Senlis and was now aimed toward the velodrome. Each town in France had its own velodrome, it seemed, with each town in France trying to decide what to do with it. Many were abandoned, or even being used as junkyards, as fewer raced bikes and more simply watched other people living life on a television set. In Senlis, the town race track had found a new life. The track itself was ridable, if only just, while the tower and buildings had been converted, with little money, most supplied by Senlis, into a sort of training center for the Haven cycling team.

It was an unusual arrangement in France. Most teams functioned more as independent conglomerates of riders than actual teams. They lived apart, split after races, then came back together only at the next starting line. But Haven was different. The late, great corporate puppeteer, Stefano Bergalis, had decided to use an American model and keep the team together as much as possible during the season for training, meetings, practice and travel. This then, was the result, an aging velodrome with peeling paint festooned with a bright red-black-and-gold Haven logo. This was the physical center of the team.

This, then, was home. Home for one hell of a dysfunctional family.

Cheryl pulled the car into a parking spot and stopped. She turned off the engine and glanced Will's way. She smiled.

"Do you think, by tonight, you'll be talking to me again?"

"Perhaps," he said, with an embarrassed smile," if — it's a very good day."

"Oh, piss off," she said with a laugh and stepped from the car. "Come on — you've got work to do."

"What," he said, pulling himself out of the sagging leatherette seat, "no more surprises?"

"No more. Promise. I'm done for today. One's my limit."

Together, they stepped into the cool darkness of the main building, and Will could actually feel the tension lift. She was amazing that way, able to twist his feelings into a hundred different shapes in a moment's time, like a clown with baloon animals.

Will rolled his right ankle, then stretched it back and forth a few times. He had inflamed something. His Achilles tendon felt tight as hell. Careful there. Don't want that to blow.

"You okay?" He could hear her more than see her. His eyes had yet to adapt to the darkness.

"Yeah, it's just gimpy."

He turned, focused on a tiny point of light at the end of the hall and flinched instinctively. Will was already pushing Cheryl to the side when he heard the *whoosh*, before dropping his head back and away from the sound and the dark stick that slashed past his face in the shadows and slammed with a *snap!* into the wall beside him.

Will shut his eyes and opened them wide. He focused first on the rubber tip of the stick, then down its polished brown length to a hand, then across the hand and down the arm to a shoulder, then off the shoulder and up to a face.

There was a cartoon he remembered called "Life in Hell."

It had nothing on this moment in time, this place in the universe.

Satan was alive and well and standing in front of him.

Carl Deeds had finished rehab and rejoined the team.

"Hello, Willie, Cheryl. Nice you could join us today."

Will suddenly felt sick.

"I thought you said you had no more surprises."

"I did. If I knew I had a surprise like this, I would have brought more underwear."

CHAPTER TWO:

S.O.B.

Carl Deeds stood before them looking every inch a Kennedy politician straight out of the '60s, except for the sweat. He was tanned, rested and ready to go, wearing a powder-blue nylon polo shirt that looked about as comfortable as a Saran-Wrap tuxedo. And — for a guy who had his left knee badly wrinkled by a gunshot blast only months before, while standing up in a car at Paris-Roubaix — that certainly wasn't a bad way to look. Modern rehab was amazing. Damn it to hell.

"You're both late," Deeds grunted.

"Hi, Carl." Will said with mild, manufactured enthusiasm. "Howyadoin?"

Cheryl merely smiled.

Deeds twisted his head slightly to the side and smiled. He said, quietly, almost under his breath. "I'm fine, Will. Nice win at Roubaix. I never got to tell you."

"You sent me a letter."

"I did?"

"Yeah, very nice," Will replied, "although you misspelled my name a few times."

"Oh. Pain pills. Pain pills really screwed me up."

"Must have. You don't spell 'Will' with a 't', and my nickname isn't 'Dorothy'."

"Sorry. And Cheryl. Henri Bergalis tells me that you've pretty much been the boss around here."

"Yeah, well...."

"Not any more. I'm back. I expect you to fulfill your contract as written."

"In other words, once again, I am a glorified gofer."

"Check your contract. It reads duties as assigned and I'm assigning you the duties of my assistant."

"Without the title, of course."

"Let's not be greedy. You'll get the money. You'll get the duties to slam on your résumé after you leave, but it has got to stay quiet. You understand?"

She stared at him blankly, not with bitterness or frustration, but simply with the weariness of another day with all the work and none of the glory. "Yes, I understand. We've understood for centuries."

She ran her fingertips along the back of Will's arm in goodbye and turned and walked down the darkened hallway in silence.

WILL AND DEEDS MOVED DOWN THE MUSTY, MURKY HALL TO THE CAVE THAT had been designated as the team meeting room. Will turned and smiled vacantly. "Well, as you can see, Carl, this is a bit of surprise. Glad you're better. Glad you're back," he lied. The team had functioned very well without the energy or insights of Carl Deeds along for the ride.

"Thanks, Will — we've had our problems…."

"Excuse me. I hate to interrupt the Old Soldier's Parade," said the voice from behind the paper, "but I have a date this afternoon — and — could we get on with this?"

Tony Cacciavillani hadn't even made the effort to look over the edge of *L'Équipe*, he simply shouted his request while buried in a story of his latest conquest: the sprint he had nearly lost while eyeing the 18-year-old girl with the stunning black hair at the finish line in Luxembourg. She was now a part of the furniture in a far too expensive Paris apartment and would soon learn a very hard lesson of life: everything in Tony C's life was expendable, except, of course, for his bike, his mother and the fabled Roman Warrior.

Deeds turned and looked at the open copy of the French sporting paper as if the paper itself had spoken, rather than Cacciavillani. Will waited for the explosion that never came.

"Yes, let's get on with it," was all Deeds said quietly in reply. "Will," he turned and smiled, showing really nice dental work, "find a chair and let's do this...."

Will nodded and looked around the room. Ten riders were here, including himself. Tour teams were made up of nine. A cold thought wandered idly through his head. Who would be dead by Lille?

The paper, representing the hidden Tony C., was there, he was safe, along with Riccardo Paluzzo, a first-year pro from Sicily who hadn't lost his enthusiasm for much of anything. Paluzzo's energy and coltish behavior had made him a favorite on the team and with the public. Miguel Cardone, a Basque, sat darkly to one side, his ego overreaching his talents as a super-domestique, a strong utility player, by over two-to-one. John Cardinal, an American, fell in with Cardone and matched him easily in the ego-to-talent ratio. He could be on the edge.

Heinrich Friel was new to this part of the team, a German known for his fierce climbing ability and a razor sharp focus on the bike that was damned near hypnotic. He'd need that on Mont Ventoux when he'd be climbing in the heat and praying for a slow and painful death while throwing up onto the slopes of an extinct volcano.

The team needed a climber.

Edouard Meerbeeke was here as well. He and Friel had ridden together on the Haven 'B' squad, doing quite well in the secondary races that peppered Europe. He was an unknown to Will. Haven's Fearless Leaders had brought both Friel and Meerbeeke up to see if they could meet the challenge of the big team and the big race.

Henri Bresson, an aging rider who had shown the light of greatness over the past years, only to see it dim with age, was in the room as well. A nice guy, thought Will, who showed him Haven's version of the ropes early on. It would be a tough Tour for him, if he made the cut, but even if he did it would certainly be a last summer in the sun for Henri Bresson.

I hope I can go out with as much class, Will thought, realizing that his own exit from this rolling enclosure of Spandex and Campy gearing wasn't too terribly far down the road.

"Allo, Weeell," Bresson over-pronounced, sounding like a cross between Edith Piaf and Kermit the Frog.

"Good morning Ahnri," Will countered in his best Jacques Clouseau, "ah believe you have a mith in your rheum."

Bresson barked a quick laugh. "You wait. I am working on John Wayne."

It was Will's turn to laugh. "Get it right — that could be damned un-American of you." Bresson smiled and went back to his paper.

Sitting quietly in the corner was a new kid, strangely familiar to Will, but yet to be introduced. Will thought about wandering over to say hi, but realized quickly that company and conversation were not what the new guy was looking for at the moment. Was he the odd man out for Le Tour?

And there was Richard, Richard Bourgoin, the team lieutenant who had overcome his Dixie Cup full of grief at the tragic death of that monumental asshole Jean-Pierre Colgan five months before, to take command of the team and make it his own. He was quite a guy, and, likely, the best friend Will had in the peloton. He was safe in his job. And, as long as Richard was safe, Will was safe, as Bourgoin would ride with no one else.

"Good morning old man," Richard said from a ragged couch. He was sinking in ever so slowly and would soon disappear from the view of the world. "Join me."

"Oh," Will chuckled, "not on your life. That thing is quicksand. I hear there's an entire Brazilian soccer team lost in there."

Bourgoin smiled, then shifted a bit on the couch, suddenly uncomfortable with the thought of what might be lurking below him.

Will kicked a small circle of rug over to the edge of the couch. The rug was cleaner than the carpet and he was willing to sit on it. No telling what you could get from that carpet. Bugs the size of ponies regularly presented themselves from the folds of the thing for inspection. He leaned back on the front edge of the couch and looked toward Deeds.

"By the way, Carl. Nice shirt." John Cardinal's face grinned brightly as he looked around the room for reaction to his comment.

Deeds stared straight ahead for a moment, then turned his head slowly and very deliberately toward John Cardinal.

"No … really. I mean it." Cardinal's face went from amusement to panic. No one in the room reacted. He flushed a bright crimson and shifted uncomfortably in the metal folding chair.

"Oh, man," Will thought, rubbing his eyes in a vain attempt to hide, "you don't want to piss him off and you don't want to do it this early in the day."

"Yes, Mister Cardinal — it is a nice shirt."

Ooh, Will thought, he called him 'mister.' This is not good.

"It is a new shirt. It is a nice, new polyester shirt that replaces the 100-percent cotton polo shirt with the embroidered Haven logo that is sitting in a suitcase of mine somewhere in Kennedy Airport, either chewed to pieces or simply lost forever. I spent much of last night shopping at a Bas Prix and replacing most of my wardrobe with miracle fabrics of the 1970s. If you want to discuss my wardrobe later, we can discuss it ... if ... of course, you have any energy left to discuss much of anything."

The hidden meaning in the veiled threat shot around the room like a 220 line dropped into a bucket of water. Today was supposed to be an off-day. Light training, early release, all followed by an evening in Paris. It was quite obvious that, given the return of Carl Deeds, it was not to be — at least today.

Cacciavillani heard it. You could see his hands grip the edge of his newspaper tighter and tighter, slowly balling up the entire broadsheet. He leaned forward to hear the other shoe drop.

"You guys have been training like Bill Murray in 'Stripes.' A little here, a little there, a little 'Doo-wah-diddy.'"

Will scanned the room quickly and smiled. The Europeans had a singularly blank look, as if someone had just shown them the blueprints for a fast breeder reactor.

"Well, today, that changes." Deeds swung his wooden cane down against a wooden box. A hollow 'Thh-Whack!' gave the line emphasis.

"We have national championships and the Tour de France coming up in about two weeks. Somehow, you talked management into skipping the Tour of Switzerland, which I have *never* missed, and beat up on a bunch of second-raters for six days at the Midi-Libre. That's not training. That's not focus. That's just plain crap. Bad planning crap. We should have been aiming at this point for months, but, due to circumstances beyond our control, you've been left on your own — sort of Spanky and Our Gang trying to decide whether to go fishin' or go to school. Well, kids, Miss Crabtree's back and she ain't got no damned ice cream with her. I've brought you back to this dump to prepare you for a race I'm going to win. Today, is the first day of your month in hell. None of you are getting off the bikes until we hit Paris and the finish line of Le Tour. Any questions?"

His tanned face had gone pale, while beads of sweat defined the upper edge of his eyebrows. Deeds had, obviously, rushed his return, and yet, he didn't pause.

"Any answers? Any problems, besides what I've seen in the results of every race? No? Fine. In 30 minutes, we do 200 kilometers. Suit up, boys — hell awaits on two wheels and the devil himself is once again running the show."

Carl turned on his right leg and, using the cane for increasing balance, walked unsteadily out of the room. He pivoted on his heel in the hall and stomped toward his office. A strange rhythm followed him down the hall, click-clunk-stomp, click-clunk-stomp. It grew faint, then ended with the slam of a door in the distance that echoed through the building.

Every eye in the room turned to Will. There were questions that had to be answered, and now, by the team lieutenant, the keeper of all knowledge, the father confessor, the inspiration, the nose wiper, the guy who oughta know.

Will sighed.

"'Stripes' was a movie — an American military comedy. 'Our Gang' was movie kids. They were always skipping school to fish and Miss Crabtree was their teacher."

No one moved for a moment, then heads began to nod, slowly, with understanding.

THERE ARE THOSE WHO SAY THAT FRANCE HAS LOST ITS PASSION FOR CYCLING — forgotten the sport of Jacques Anquetil and Raymond Poulidor, Bernard Hinault and Louison Bobet — but the rolling enclosure that was Haven still stirred something in all it passed: the brilliant white of the Colnago frames, the whirring perfection of the Campagnolo gears, the knife-edge hum of the Mavic wheels, a flock of black-red-and-gold jerseys, all in rhythm, speeding, as one, down a French country road, north of Paris in the middle of June, stopping one and all, controlling the pavement like an army on maneuvers.

Jean Jablom stepped out of his bicycle shop as the caravan sped past. He eyed Richard Bourgoin, the French team leader, and waved at Will Ross, the American lieutenant — a regular in his shop, for conversation more than gear — then watched the team disappear over a hilltop, then reappear in the distance, then disappear and reappear again before losing themselves over the horizon.

Jablom turned back to his shop and reached for the door. He stopped. Inside, a group of French teenagers was looking at mountain bikes. The few road bikes Jablom still stocked were virtually ignored. The passing of Haven, the premier cycling team of France, had not caused a stir among any except the faithful. And there were far fewer of the faithful today.

As he watched the teenagers spin the wheels of the mountain bikes, a tear ran down the wrinkled moonscape that was Jablom's face. This year, it will change, he thought. This year, a Frenchman will win Le Tour de France.

And you, he silently raged, looking at the teenagers, just missed him.

THE HAVEN PHARMACEUTICAL BOARD MEETING HAD TURNED INTO A HAVEN Pharmaceutical bored meeting for Godot. He looked down the polished table toward Henri Bergalis, his savior and boss, trying to keep an interested look in his eyes and sleep out. The financial report droned on and Godot's eyelids took on another 40 kilos. Meanwhile, in the back of his head, a thought kept rattling around. He wasn't sure what it was, something nagging at him from this morning's paper. It had nothing to do with him, nothing to do with the company, but was simply a bee buzzing around the mind of a 30-year police vet.

He slammed his hand on the back of his head, as much to wake himself up as drive the idea forward to a place where he could get a handle on it. He slapped the back of his head again. He was waking up enough that, as he looked around the board room, he realized that he was now the wide-eyed center of attention of the suit-and-tie set.

Each board member sat stiffly in his high-backed, heavy leather chairs. Before them, on the table, each had his own miniature office: today's report, a pager, a cellular phone and a pen. Except Godot. How, thought Godot, would he be able to do battle without his weapons of war? How would he be able to do his job without the right equipment?

"Luc?" Henri Bergalis spoke quietly from the head of the table.

Godot didn't hear. His mind had suddenly and silently frozen on one thought. His eyes shot back to the faces around the table. Rochon. And Bieber. And Fleming. And Gardone. And Sansabelle. All with their equipment. All ready to do the job.

And that rider. What was his name?

Exactly.

How would he be able to do it … without the right equipment?

"Luc?"

Godot stood slowly and carefully as if not to jog the thought free and send it skittering aimlessly around his head again. He walked from the room as a man in a daze, to the silent stares of the Haven Pharmaceutical board. Bergalis watched him go, smiled and returned to the business of the meeting without missing a beat.

Godot, meanwhile, marched toward his office with quick determination. This thought had been a long time coming and he didn't want to lose it now.

"Isabelle," he said to his secretary and lover, "please be so kind as to call the Eindhoven police district in the Netherlands and ask, if you will, for a copy of the police report on one…." he paused, trying to remember the name. "Just ask for a copy of the police report on that cyclist who just died."

"Why should they give us a copy of a police report?" she asked, jotting down the request.

"We are Haven."

"They are the police."

Godot paused for a moment, scratching the stubble on his chin. She was right. After three decades on a force, he knew the attitude and knew it well.

"Just tell them that Luc Godot of the …" he paused, "… Paris police wants a copy of the report — everything — including photos. Tell them," he stopped for a moment, trying to find an answer in the carpeted wall of his secretary's office," tell them I have a case, possibly related. Give them this address, but leave Haven out of it."

"You could get in trouble."

"They have to catch me first."

"And they won't?"

"Isabelle, my love," he said, looking deeply into her eyes, "if there is one thing I learned on the force, it is this: we never caught them as much as they got caught."

Isabelle Marchant gave him a puzzled look.

Godot smiled.

❂

THE FIRST 10 KILOMETERS OUT OF SENLIS HAD BEEN LITTLE MORE THAN A WARM-UP, an easy pace of 30 kilometers per hour with little or no discipline within the ranks. Keep up, that's all that was required. For the team leaders, that was no problem. Will and Richard had found a symbiotic relationship through the spring, beginning with Paris-Roubaix and then crystallizing in the Giro d'Italia. That, Will remembered fondly, had been a great race. Haven hadn't controlled much of the race, if any, but it had always been in the fight. From what had seemed to be a position of weakness at the start, the team had challenged the leaders constantly, on the flats, in the sprints, in the mountains. No matter what was happening, or where it was happening, Haven had been there. Rominger and Indurain and Jalabert couldn't turn around without a black-red-and-gold jersey reminding them that this was, indeed, a contest.

Haven had proven a lot at the finish line. Richard was second on the podium. Will had finished high in the pack. The team was strong and the unpleasantness of the winter and spring had only served, it seemed, to create a world beater.

A turn into the wind brought Will back to this moment in time, on a road, on his bike, sucking up exhaust from the Peugeot that led the way and cleared a path for the team.

"No one said anything about wind," Bourgoin complained.

"You've been at this long enough," Will reminded him, "there is always a wind and it's always in your face, no matter what direction you're heading in … and … it always gets worse on the way home."

Bourgoin cursed quietly in French, then shifted gears. The pace was growing faster. Will shouldn't have been paying so much attention to the conversation. In that moment, Deeds had Cheryl pick up the pace in the car and was setting the tone for the training session with fast intervals, set to burst out the top end of each rider's aerobic conditioning, in the hopes of building endurance for the mountains that sat only three or four weeks in the future. It was Will's job to sense the change in pace, to know when, where and how the pack was attacking and lead Richard into it, not the other way around. He had missed a step. When he had finally reacted, it was more as if the bike had made the move than he, anticipating the problem and setting up the pace that solved it.

Deeds would discuss it with him later.

Will shifted his focus forward, watching the small car speed away in the distance. He could hear the team around him, and by the sound alone, he knew it was beginning to stretch out. He placed himself first, ahead of Bourgoin, then waved Paluzzo to the front.

"Lead us out, Riccardo. Set the pace."

The first year Sicilian pro nodded and, like a kid filled with too many candy bars, leapt to the front, reaching toward a pace that could pull the team back up to the disappearing team car.

No need to worry about losing the car, Will thought. With all the logos and stickers decorating its sides, it would be like trying to lose Ken Kesey's psychedelic bus in a white linoleum airplane hanger.

Haven, as a team, surged ahead.

❂

PAUL VAN BRUGGEN SIGHED HEAVILY, AS IF BURDENED BY THE ATMOSPHERE OF the Eindhoven police lab.

This one was a challenge, he thought, a true testament as to what Dutch society had become. When Paul was a boy, no one, it seemed, anyway, ever died. People lived to a remarkably old age, the young were polite and motivated and the world seemed bright with light and colors. Now, with the legalization of drugs, this world was nothing but shades of gray. If crime had not dramatically increased because of the strict administration of the drug trade, it certainly had become more a staple of Dutch life. And death, it seemed, was always just around the corner. Despite quality controls, there was forever a junkie death wandering through his lab, even a lab as off the beaten track as that in Eindhoven. He knew from experience that the offices in Rotterdam and Amsterdam ran a regular assembly line when it came to drug deaths. It was simply a fact of life in the new Netherlands.

This, however, was something new.

He prodded the burgundy lump of liver in front of him for the 20th time. It was puffy at one end, a sure sign of cirrhosis or steroid use, but the other end had shrunk in size and was showing an incredible amount of short-term damage. Plus, it was almost off the scale in terms of weight. Size had decreased — but density and weight had increased? It was like a dwarf star collapsing in on itself.

He leaned forward again, bringing his nose almost in contact with the gelatinous skin of the organ. There was a strange spicy scent, vague, ill-defined, something he couldn't quite put his finger on. Van Bruggen took a deep breath and sat back on the high lab chair, cocked his head to one side, unconsciously hoping that the thoughts from one hemisphere would spill over into the next, reached out with his right hand and speared a piece of cheese with his pen. Popping it into his mouth, he pondered the liver of Henrik Koons.

Steroid damage. That much was obvious, but the blood work-up showed nothing. If he was masking the steroid, the masking agent should show up in some obvious or altered form.

Nothing.

He tapped his pen on the side of the tray, beating out a march cadence.

So … the blood said no steroids, but the look of this liver did — he pondered — in spades. Enzyme levels were off the map, showing damage. Natural steroid use would show itself by elevated levels in the blood work, but none of the standard tests for steroids gave a positive.

This is damned peculiar, he thought.

Elevated levels of liver enzymes and heavy liver damage … but no masking agents, no road signs, no gas chromatograph indicators. Internal damage only. That was it, along with a heart that literally burst from its moorings inside Koon's chest. That sounds like amphetamines, like … what did his brother in the States call it? Crystal meth. But that would be easy to find. No, this was something new. New and exotic. His eyebrows lifted as he read the profile again: professional cyclist. Makes sense. This fellow was looking for the fountain of money that amateur and professional athletes around the world have been chasing for the last century: the perfect boost — effective, undetectable and sustainable.

And, in this case, deadly.

"Eventually" deadly, like steroid abuse, like amphetamines. But this, this had been quick, if the liver was any indication. The organ was in the midst of rapid deterioration. He poked at another piece of cheese and leaned over to look again at the death pictures of Henrik Koons. Ugly way to die. Certainly won't win Death Mask of the Month in the commissary.

He sensed her before he saw her. The scent. The feeling, almost ethereal, that somehow the atmosphere in the room had changed, grown lighter, perhaps more colorful since she entered the room.

"Hello, Magda."

"Paul, you always know. How do you always know?"

"I know because my world becomes better every time you enter it."

"And mine." Magda Gertz reached around his shoulders and smoothed her hands across his neck and down his chest until they found the warm and growing lump at his crotch. She massaged it, once, twice, then pulled her hands, slowly, back up to his shoulders.

"And how does it go?" She scanned the notes he had scribbled on the page.

"My work today? Fine. Mr. Koons is giving up his mysteries. Slowly. But giving them up."

She playfully picked up the report. "And who is our mystery guest today?"

"A cyclist with a drug problem. Your cyclist. The one you saw in the paper."

"I'd love to hear," she whispered, "but, can't he wait?"

"Ah, he can wait forever, I fear."

She smiled, subtly, coldly. "Then lunch. Let's have lunch. A long lunch. Together. Alone. And then you can write your report. How important is this?"

She waved his notes in the air. He swiped at them once, in fun, then grinned ear to ear.

"Not so much — but I've had lunch. I've been nibbling at some cheese."

"How about dessert, my mouse?" She said the last words, quietly, with warm breath, into his ear. Paul felt himself stiffen and the blood begin to rush from his brains to his pants.

"Lunch," he said, his voice just slightly ragged, "lunch is good. With dessert, lunch is good."

He pulled a lab cover over the pan carrying the assorted body parts of Henrik Koons and walked, with some discomfort, over to the refrigerator. He pulled open the door and slid the tray in, closed it, then turned to wash his hands at the lab sink. He pressed his erection against the counter and thought of German soccer games in an attempt to make it go away.

Paul heard her say, quietly, "Don't lose that. I want to see it again."

Van Bruggen blushed and involuntarily shuddered. Oh, you will, he thought, you will see a lot of it this afternoon. He wiped his hands quickly on a towel, tossed it aside and walked briskly toward the door. He offered his arm, which she took with a smile, snapped off the lights and pulled the door closed behind him. The door locked with a hard "clack."

For a fleeting second, van Bruggen thought about his report and the notes he had made that morning. He should have put them in the locked filing cabinet.

Then again, the door was locked and as he looked at the sleek and beautiful profile beside him, framed in an almost outrageous shock of naturally blonde hair, he thought to himself that some things in this world are far more important than the death of a junkie. What could possibly be more important than a woman who drove all the way from Rotterdam to see him for a little love in her afternoon?

He reached over, ran his hand down her back to her derrière and gave it a playful squeeze. She returned a wicked smile.

Ah, yes, he thought. This was far more important.

✵

PERHAPS THEY HAD TAKEN THEIR VACATION FROM CARL DEEDS A LITTLE TOO EASILY.

The pace of the Haven Cycling Team had kept up, but it was becoming more ragged. Shifts were missed. Pacelines were loose. The power of the group began to fluctuate.

"Goddamn it! I knew it," Deeds shouted from his perch through the sunroof of the car. "You've been playing *kids' games* all the time I've been gone!"

The voice rose and fell with the road. A hundred-fifty kilometers into a 200-kilometer ride and the team was beginning to fray at the edges. Tempers were short, especially among the domestiques near the back. They were new members, some of whom hadn't trained for the A-squad of a major team; nor had they worked together as a squad lately or enough to make for a truly cohesive unit. Will felt a certain amount of guilt, for as team lieutenant, it was his responsibility to make that happen. He had fallen short.

"Pacelines! Pick it up — Goddamn it, Cardinal, keep it tight! And if you can't keep up, Bresson, then give it up! Give it up!"

Will shot a glance over his left shoulder and, in that split second, captured the pain and end-of-the-road agony that spread across the face of Henri Bresson. Bresson had been good, to be sure, in his day, but too many years on the bike had taken their toll and the man was reaching the end, far sooner than Bresson himself had planned. Will knew it was coming for him as well, he only wondered if he would be able to recognize it. It was clear that Bresson had not.

The exhaust-belching Peugeot shot ahead again, and Bourgoin responded to that and Deeds's insults with a fresh kick. Will looked quickly at Paluzzo as Bourgoin streaked away and shouted, "Keep up with him … and watch the pace." The young rider nodded and followed the team leader, the rest of the pack falling in behind like obedient baby ducks.

Will slid back through the pack, checking his speed, then picking it up so he pulled in cleanly beside Bresson without a break in the pace. Bresson was having a hard time of it.

"Howyadoin'?"

Bresson didn't answer at first.

"Henri…."

"Can't … talk … must … focus…."

"Come on, Henri. Climb up tight behind the kid there," Will looked ahead to the young Spaniard, barely out of his teens, riding strong, "get in tight, man. It doesn't do you any damned good way out here. Use the paceline — I'll drop in behind. Remember, life is easier in the middle."

Bresson pushed himself forward to within centimeters of the youngster's back tire while Will tucked in tight behind him. Head up, mentally focused on where he should be, Will felt the immediate tug of the paceline, as if he were being pulled along by a gigantic magnet. It was mental and it was wind resistance, he knew; but, Will laughed, at his age, he had to use every trick in the book.

The line of riders shot across the gap that Bourgoin had opened to the pace car, gathering speed on the long, straight stretch of narrow blacktop, while the colors of summer opened on either side. Bourgoin popped off the front and slid back down the line, tucking in behind Will at the end.

Even tucked in the middle, sandwiched in the midst of the machine, Bresson continued to struggle.

Will knew what Bresson was feeling. He had felt that kind of physical emptiness before — and he was beginning to feel it again today. This was a lot of work for a 32-year-old, even a 32-year-old in great form — something Will had found over the last five months.

There was something about riding that peaked right about 30. Then, your physical powers diminished rapidly. Not so much that you couldn't ride and you couldn't win, but nothing was easy any more, and the fun quotient of it all was dividing itself exponentially.

Haven raced along, cutting an almost metaphysical wedge through the countryside, through the smell of manure and the green swath of the wheat fields, the day swirling in a vortex behind the rolling caravan and quickly settling back into its own bucolic rhythm.

It had always been that way for Will, even back when he and Raymond Cangialosi raced along the back roads of Michigan for the Two Wheels Bike Shop out of Romulus, Michigan. With each pedal stroke, he remembered, he could feel the air that was almost thick enough for a name wash around him, first with protest, then yielding, a bit of the humidity always staying behind, sticking to his face, his eyebrows, and his woolen jersey, suddenly heavy with sweat. The green rows of corn would shoot past, sometimes close enough to the road that Will could hear the 'thup' 'thup' 'thup' of each line, before he hurtled through tight, blind corners at 45 degrees, inner knee up, head dangerously close to the long grasses along the side of the road, then, just before disaster, curling back into the tuck and sprinting away in a flash, pounding hard down a back road of memory. Strange. His legs and lungs never felt the work, the pain, the effort, like they did — now.

"Ack." Will reached down and rubbed the cramp in his right calf for the fifth time. This was happening too often. It was his own damned fault. His right leg was giving him fits because he wasn't doing enough stretching. Riding easy for the first three kilometers just didn't cut it anymore.

God, this time it hurt.

The paceline had risen and fallen twice. Will was now close again to the front and his pull. Three riders ahead, he could see Cardone taking his pull at the front, six to eight meters behind Deeds. Will gave his calf one last squeeze and put his head down to focus on Bresson's back wheel, perhaps an inch-and-a-half from his, with Deeds slowing the pace in the team car before the next interval session.

Will's head shot up in reaction. He had reacted almost before he felt the ripple run through the pack, as if someone had dropped a heavy stone in a pond. Something wasn't right. Cardone was no longer at the head of the pack. At first, Will thought he had slid back to the end of the paceline, his pull at the front finished, but he would have sensed his passing. Will aimed high and saw Cardone pumping the bike hard, in an exaggerated back-and-forth swing, past the team Peugeot and a wildly gesticulating Deeds. Cardone, without looking back, raised his right arm in an insulting salute to Deeds, the car and, perhaps, the team itself, and shot away down the road in a perfect, completely unexpected attack.

The paceline slowed unconsciously, the focus of an entire team shattered by the unexpected turn of events. What had been a knife edge of 10 riders slicing through a June afternoon in northern France became nothing more than a jumbled pack of riders, aimless and without focus, looking to the colorfully painted Peugeot for direction. The pace slowed quickly: 45 … 40 … 30. The team car sped away, then hit the brakes, hard, the trunk rising off the road as if it wanted to leap over itself in a perfect somersault. Deeds stuck his head out the sunroof.

"Gentlemen," he said, in a voice loaded with sarcasm, "as many of you may notice, he is getting away!!!"

Will understood immediately what was going on. "Clean it up — let's go! *Allez vite*!!" He shouted back at the team, breaking into their individual states of confusion, then kicked it into a big gear and began the chase.

As Will raced past the open window of the car, he could hear Deeds shouting at him in Doppler Shift, ".... *Jesus God in hell*, it certainly took you long enough...."

This was the stuff he *knew* he'd have to be watching for in Le Tour, just as he had in the Giro and the short, thank you God, Tour of Luxembourg and Midi-Libre they had just finished. Analyze the threat, know their strengths, catalogue their weakness, guess their strategy, watch for the break and react accordingly. Either ignore it all because it's not a real threat, or get Bourgoin's butt up there, right there, right now. Will had to know what to do and when to do it.

This was a time to move Bourgoin's butt forward, and quickly.

The question that leapt into his mind, along with the metronome that clacked, continually, almost brutally, in the back of his brain pan, was, "is this Deeds's idea of a game? Set up, then break it up with something outrageous?" It didn't fit his style, really — nobody with any sense ever attacked from a paceline.

Click. Click. Click. Click. Click. Click.

Will increased the pace. The chase group, which, in most cases, would have been only a few riders, was now the entire team. The team car was out of it now, trailing the group. Will was almost thankful for that. A lungful of exhaust was no help at a time like this.

Click. Click. Click. Push it. Click. Click. Clickclickclick....

Cardone had timed his jump perfectly, and, given the surprising power he had generated, it was a great race move, almost a sprint. Will aimed high down the road and could see Cardone cresting a hill in the distance. In the pack's moment of confusion, he had already gained a half-minute, perhaps a few seconds more, on the team. The man was flying, despite the fact that there was no way in hell he could keep it up for 25 more kilometers.

Will slid off the tip of the line and fell back. Bourgoin was being sandwiched, for the most part, his pulls at the front shorter than anyone else's. If this were a sprint, Will's job was to keep Cacciavillani, the team sprinter, up near the front for a little boom and zoom. Bourgoin could never match the sprinters in a nose-to-nose shoot out, so at that point, Will simply had to guarantee that Bourgoin would finish high enough in the pack so he didn't lose any ground on the race leaders.

The wave that was Haven surged ahead toward the escapee. The pace was a killer now, clickclickclickclickclick, and Will was loving it. The cramp in his leg faded and the wind, a gentle breeze in his face that had turned into a maelstrom of their own creation, roared in his ears. This was power, this was joy, this was life.

This was racing.

The big gear turned perfectly, and, aside from the sounds of the breathing, almost in rhythm, and the hum of the chains, Will could hear only his heart, pounding out a back beat with his crankset. The power of the road raced through "The Beast" and into Will, turned and headed back again: a perfect circle, a perfect electrical loop. Each rider kept up the pace, never slacking, never falling off — except ... Will felt another ripple, turning down the pace a notch for a split second, throwing each rider off, even if just a bit, before regaining the rhythm, a step down, a note off the original.

From six riders back, Will glanced up to see Cardinal taking his pull at the front. This wasn't right. Something like that three weeks from now could mean disaster at Le Tour.

They'd have to talk.

God, Will thought, he hated that. Confrontation wasn't his style. Expecting everybody to do their own work and pull their own load was his style.

Cardinal fell off the front and the new kid dropped in for his pull. Immediately, Will felt the shift again, an electrical surge running through the pace line as new blood restored the higher pace. This guy was good. He knew, instinctively, what had happened and rectified it immediately.

They'd have to talk.

Will smiled.

Cardone was in sight, now, within, reach. His gap had been eaten by the snaking pace line in a little over 10 minutes. Ten minutes, 10 kilometers closer to home. With help, from another team or another teammate, in a race,

Cardone might have been able to hold out until the finish, as the pack rose up and tried to gobble them alive. But alone, it was next to impossible. Even if you won alone, you blew yourself out for the next day or the rest of the race.

"Hey, I won! Hey, I'm dead!"

Will took his pull at the head of the paceline and decided then and there to reel Cardone in. He snapped the Ergo lever and felt the immediate drag in the gearing. His legs, the prettiest legs in the family, his mother used to say, responded in kind, kicking out the energy needed to boost the pace and drag the now-hooked fish back into the Haven boat.

Fifty meters ... 40 ... 30 ... 25 ... 22 ... 25, as Cardone tried desperately to stay clear. Twenty ... 15 ... 10 ... 5. Will could sense the heat rolling off the exhausted rider ahead of him. Sweat and exertion and — something else — something he couldn't quite place.

Will and the paceline roared past like a train passing a kid on a knobbly skateboard.

"Back of the pack, pal."

Cardone shot him a glance that would have stopped a toaster, but fell back quietly, his day at the front finished, without glory. Will watched Cardone drop to the back out of the corner of his eye, then decided to keep the pace high. The outskirts of Senlis approached, and there they'd have to maneuver in traffic; but for now, Will figured to work them out. Besides, the higher the pace, the faster to the showers and Will had had just about enough of this ride for the time being.

✵

CLEATS CLICKED AND SCRAPED THE CONCRETE AROUND THE VELODROME TOWER in Senlis, to the point where you had to shout to make yourself heard above the din.

Will couldn't hear what Deeds was saying to Cardone, across the pavement, but it didn't look good. Deeds was red in the face, as was the Basque, and, that finger, that damned finger of Carl Deeds, was beating out a tattoo on Cardone's chest, reminding the rider that it was Deeds, and Deeds alone, who called for a breakaway.

God, Will thought, I bet he's lovin' that. Both Deeds and Cardone.

Will took one more glance at Cardone's face and saw murder in his eyes. Will then looked to the side and saw Cheryl, collapsed in the front seat of the team car. The pressure of driving, setting the pace and dealing with Deeds had obviously drained her.

Will felt a tap on his shoulder and turned to meet the eyes of Richard Bourgoin. God, he thought, how could one man who looked so horrible at the end of every ride, ride so very, very well? Bourgoin's eyes were red and runny, his face a shade of gray that Will hadn't seen since Uncle Bill took one last drag on a Camel straight while plugged into a hospital respirator.

Still, Bourgoin could ride like the devil's own, no matter how he looked.

"Dinner, Will?" He looked into the car. "Cheryl?" She didn't move.

"Sure. That would be great. Call it."

"The place — how about Costes?"

"Naw. Someplace else. How about Il Fiore?"

"No. No way." Cheryl slowly, painfully, pulled herself out of her funk and into the conversation. "I don't want to spend my evening in a smoke-filled room with a bunch of unpublished writers eating pastries and crabbing about the literary world."

Bourgoin nodded in agreement and thought for a moment. "I know — Au Cochon d'Or. Nice place, real food. On the Rue du Jour."

"Sounds good."

Cheryl smiled. "That's fine. Let us ride into the city with you and we'll take the train home tonight. It's gotta be early."

"Ah, yes," Will said, pointing back toward Deeds. "Hell has returned and he drives a Peugeot."

"Hey, I drive the Peugeot," Cheryl said defensively.

"Sorry, I knew that — but I'm too tired to come up with a better joke."

Bourgoin smiled, his face lighting up and the color restoring itself to his features. This guy was a French matinee idol when he wasn't riding, thought Will. No wonder he never allowed the team to release race pictures. No one wanted to see cycling's Richard Gere gray-faced with snot running down his lip.

"In a moment, then." Bourgoin waved haphazardly and clacked off toward the showers.

"You better get out of those clothes yourself and into a shower," Cheryl said. "After a ride like today, the little bacteria must already be chewing on something vital."

Will laughed and nodded. He was beginning to really feel the ride. The adrenaline rush of the last few kilometers was wearing off, leaving only a rusted framework within.

"And you?"

Cheryl kicked her head over in the direction of Deeds. "Mein fearless leader is needing me. Probably kick my butt for letting Cardone jump."

"Call if you need help."

"Don't worry," she whispered, stroking one of the scars that lined his face, "I can handle a one-legged fat man."

Deeds's head shot around.

"I heard that. I have two legs, only one knee. Come on, Crane. Let's go over the paperwork and see how you've screwed up my team in my absence."

Her fingers drifted off Will's face like clouds off the face of an Irish hill. He closed his eyes and savored the moment. When he opened them again, she was already in the building with Hopalong....

Will kicked off his riding shoes, and, picking them up with one hand, picked up "The Beast," his aging, white Colnago, with the other. Even with the addition of the Ergo gearing from Campy, the weight hadn't increased all that much, maybe an ounce or two. Damn, this company made great bikes. Four years old and this bike was still as sharp as his grandfather's straight razor.

He felt a presence beside him and started as he turned. Henri Bresson looked at him with eyes that spoke of sheer exhaustion.

"Will," he wheezed, "Will, thank you. Thank you. For what you said. I app ... re ... ciate it. Very much."

"No problem, Henri. You'd do the same for me. Especially when you get your rhythm back."

"Yes," Bresson gasped, "when I get, when I get," he turned and rolled his bike toward the open door of the shop, "when I get, when I get...."

The voice whispered itself into silence.

Will shook off the image as he carried "The Beast" to the mechanic's door and put the bike down, rolling it ahead to Luis. "An extra bag of oats, pal, she was great today." Luis Bourbon looked at Will as if the rider had just fallen off a turnip truck. The analogy was completely lost on the mechanic.

Will turned toward the shower room. Behind him, the young rider who had restored the paceline tinkered with his bike. From the looks of things, he knew exactly what he was doing.

The rider ignored him.

"You caught the change in pace and brought it back up — nice instincts."

Will felt the hairs on the back of his neck start to rise, a flop sweat when what you're saying, how you're reaching out, is having no impact at all on the person you're trying to reach.

"Yeah … well. Good job today. Good job."

The rider kept tinkering with his cables.

"Uhh, by the way," there was an uncomfortable pause, as the rider refused to look up from his bike. "I'm Will Ross." Nothing. "And you are…."

The youth looked up slowly, irritated by the interruption.

"I am ..." he said, very quietly and deliberately, "… Prudencio. Prudencio Delgado."

Without thinking, Will blurted, "Delgado. Any relation to Pedro?"

The line hung in the air like a fart the size of the Hindenburg. Will began to turn bright red. The line had been a joke between himself and a friend, a friend who had died, brutally, at the start of this season, a friend he desperately missed, a friend who understood the joke, and appreciated it, unlike the boy who crouched beside the bike in front of him now.

"No," the rider said. "I am not related to Pedro."

"Sorry, man. Bad joke."

"I am related to Tomas. Remember? The man you killed in Milan?"

Now, the joke was on Will.

And it wasn't funny at all.

CHAPTER THREE:

LES MISÉRABLES

In the weeks of Deeds's absence, the team hadn't been slack in its race preparations or its training, and, yet, in the two weeks since his triumphant return to Senlis, Deeds had made everyone feel, if not slack, then pretty damned close to it.

Will had never experienced this kind of training crunch before: sprints, climbs, intervals and long-distance hauls. The only thing missing was traveling to the U.S. to train at altitude, a decision which caused no end of complaint.

"Carl, I could win this race," Cacciavillani squawked from the dinge of a shower stall, "if only I could train in Vol."

"Where?"

"Vol."

"Vol?"

"Yes, Vol — in the Colorado mountains."

Deeds paused for a second, then looked at Will, who didn't even look up from drying his feet on the shower-room table.

"He means Vail. Train at altitude in Vail."

"Yes, Vol," Cacciavillani agreed from the stall.

"No. No 'Vol' this year. I spent the entire training budget on these fine accommodations here in Senlis. We win this Tour and every team will have a velodrome to train at around France. Think of that," Deeds said with a smirk. He turned, and, using his crutch, strode off with the clack, slap, clack, slap, that was becoming his trademark.

Cheryl, who had turned flush with the grind of chasing after Deeds, heaved a devastatingly deep sigh and followed him down the hall. Under her breath, Will knew, she was muttering her mantra: "Six more weeks. Six more weeks. Only six more."

Tony C. ran his finger down the wall of the shower, coming up with a gray plume of mildew. He looked from that up to the ceiling, covered with some sort of flying dust bunnies and spider webs, then turned to Will.

"Everyone will soon have a place like this — I am grown afraid."

Will smiled. He pulled on his sweats and wandered down toward a couch, grabbing an orange and a copy of *L'Équipe*, the French national sports paper, along the way. He had already been on the bike for three hours today and would have rather just stayed on the bike and ridden for seven hours straight than ride hard for three, take two off, then ride for another four. Nobody in the sport trained like that, but Carl Deeds did, saying he got the idea from American football two-a-days.

Great, thought Will, something else we can thank the NFL for as it makes tons of money and rides roughshod over every other sport in the world. Two-a-days. Will hadn't hated anything quite this much since freshman football practice in high school when big Tom Dykstra had passed out and fallen on him, driving Will's helmet into the ground and damned near suffocating him before the three other members of the freshman team were able to roll "The Beef" off the short and scraggly body of one Will Ross.

His football days had ended there.

Will took a towel and rolled it up behind his head: The couch's ancient leather covering, with its soon-to-be-exposed springs, stuck to your neck like crazy if you didn't take some kind of precaution. He sank down into the sofa and opened the paper.

Le Tour. Le Tour. This paper owned Le Tour. Cycling always had a section here, but for five weeks every summer, it owned this paper. Today, it was, very nearly, the entire thing.

Team profiles filled the pages, along with insights and details on the favorites and the sponsors. Sponsors paraded through the paper in both copy and advertising as if they owned the world, which, perhaps, was not too terribly far from the truth. The international spotlight was on sponsors today and for the next month. This was their time to shine, this was their chance to reap all the millions they had sown with bicycle teams over the past year.

Will flipped through the paper. He already knew the course, right down to every pebble on the hell that he knew as Ventoux. He already knew the competition. As for the rest, he'd learn it all, first hand, over the next few weeks, so there was no sense filling his brain with it now. The soccer scores were socked away on an inner sheet. The soccer fans would have to deal with it, just as cycling fans had to deal with soccer the rest of the year.

The item was stuck, down in a corner, right on the border between cycling and soccer. Four centimeters to one side and Will would have mistaken it for a report on yet another full stadium brawl at a European Cup soccer match.

Will translated it with his high school French, which left out a word or two here and there, but usually found the gist of the article.

"Dutch rider … natural causes," read the headline.

Will knew he was missing something here, because there was an "n'" attached to a verb in the long headline. Was it: he didn't die of natural causes? No, the negative seemed to be directed toward the subhead on the investigation.

His French had improved, dramatically, over the past few months, but Will was still no Maurice Chevalier. Which, in its own little way, was fine with him. He considered that being incomprehensible gave him an air of inscrutability.

Will picked through the article.

The police autopsy on Henrik Koons had been completed. The autopsy was — inconclusive? Check with Bourgoin on that one. Cause was heart attack brought on by drug use. What drug? Yet, no *narcotique* was found in his system. Police lab in Eindhoven found physical evidence. Yet, nothing in l*e sang*, the blood. Man, must have been long-term damage. Taking it for years, tries to kick, body just shuts down.

Henrik Koons.

Koons. Henrik Koons. Will furrowed his eyebrows and tried to squeeze an idea out of his memory and into that small section of his head designated for full conscious thought.

Koons. Jesus. The Dipshit.

Will knew him. Koons had been kicking around the circuit for years, picking up a ride wherever he could, playing off old friendships to get another shot. What team had they been on together? God, that Brit team. What, four years back? Now, that was a horrible team. No support. No management. The weather was crappy. The bikes were worse and they only got to the Continent for three races that year. No funding. No riders. No equipment. No joke.

But there was a joke. It was the team.

Will shook off the memory of the team and a dismal flat just outside London and dug around for a mental picture of Henrik Koons. Obviously the guy had made one hell of an impression. That was years and many bottles of wine ago, but Will was able to rustle up one thought, one flash, one piece of a memory, not even a full picture, only a sense of a person.

Henrik Koons was, quite frankly, a jerk. He was one of those guys who always thought he was better than he was and spent the majority of his time trying to convince anyone and everyone of that fact. If you listened, you learned he deserved more than he was getting in money, position and power.

One memory led to another and yet one more, until Will realized he had retained a pretty good picture of fellow rider Henrik Koons.

God, what an asshole.

Will could not abide prats and Koons was a certifiable, Grade A, No. 1 prat. Given his determination to be taken seriously, his quest for stardom, if anyone in the sport was sure to find drugs a pleasing trade-off, it was Henrik Koons.

Yes, indeed. What a jerk.

Dead jerk.

Back of the pack.

For eternity.

What a pisser.

The paper crumpled in Will's hands and curled into his lap like a Westie finding the perfect spot to sleep, following the example of its master.

MAGDA GERTZ SWEPT HER ENTIRE HEAD AROUND, THROWING HER HAIR IN AN arc away from her ear to make room for the phone. In the golden sunlight of the afternoon, it was a very sexy move and she knew it.

"Yes?"

Paul van Bruggen was taken aback by the sharp urgency in her voice.

"Hello, gorgeous," he said, drawing out the greeting almost as if he were calling to her across an alpine field. "How are you today my sweet?"

She paused for a moment, thinking as to who this might … "Paul … Paul. How are you? I'm fine. I'm packing."

"Packing? What? A vacation without *me*? How could you?"

"It is work, my love. Work that keeps me away."

"Hmmmmph."

"Anything new? What about that drug death — the cyclist — what have you learned?"

"What? Oh my, you have taken him to heart, indeed, haven't you? Yes, this was a tough one. We had to go through a number of layers of testing to find this one. Sneaky. Very sneaky. Surface testing won't find it. Doesn't turn up in urine. Doesn't turn up in blood. Turns up in autopsy — which makes it difficult to find in a living person."

"Where in the autopsy?"

Van Bruggen felt smug. "It took me a while, but I realized there was one place folks never really looked…."

"Where, Paul?"

The sharp edge to her voice broke his concentration and the joke fell shattered on the ground like a full gravy boat dropped from the table.

"You don't want to know."

"Ah, Paul, you know how your work fascinates me. Especially this one. Tell."

Despite the wires and walls and distances between them, he felt himself growing hard at the sound of her voice.

"The eyeballs, sweets. I found it in the eyeballs. Traces of certain substances can stay there longer than anywhere else, caught up in the fluid and tissues."

"What substances?"

"Nothing I recognized. That's the thing. I'm still trying to identify it."

"What are you guessing?"

"Some synthetic. Maybe carried out of a research lab. Has all the earmarks of big company protocol. It's very clean. I'll bet a janitor heard about it and snuck it out for a pile of cash for his friend, Mr. Koons."

"The late Mr. Koons."

"Eh, he took the ride … he paid the price."

"That's awfully cold, Paul."

"I am awfully cold, my love. When are you coming back to warm me up?"

"I'm going to Paris."

Van Bruggen paused, waiting for the other shoe to drop. "And ... what, you're not coming back?"

"No. I'm coming back, but it won't be for about a month. I'm thinking about going to a race for a while."

"No offense, my love, but what are you talking about?"

"Le Tour de France. You know I used to work with cycling teams."

"No, I never knew that."

"Really? I could have sworn I told you. I used to work for the Haven team years ago, part of its medical team."

"What did you do, love, warm their hearts?"

Magda Gertz snapped, her voice tinged with anger and resentment, "You know, I hope, that I have two degrees in research chemistry and an advanced degree in medicine, don't you? You do know that? You do know that I have more degrees than you?"

Van Bruggen frantically backpedaled in his conversation. "Oh, love, I am sorry. It is only … it is only…."

He tried to change the subject: "Must you go?"

"No," she said, suddenly calm, "but I want to…. Who knows? Maybe I'll find your synthetic. If one rider has it, other riders have it. If other riders have it, they will use it over the three weeks of Le Tour. And if they are using it — then we will have collapsing riders along the course. And if we have that, we can pinpoint effect and source and substance."

"Why should you care, my darling?"

"I care Paul, because that is my job."

"BioSyn works you too hard, love. But … if that's your job, what is your pleasure? Perhaps a stop in Eindhoven, an afternoon? You can catch the night train for Paris. A few hours here — nothing lost — you have … what … three weeks to catch up with the race?"

"No time, Paul." She leaned conspiratorially into a corner and whispered, "but just think how it will feel in a month — eh? Just think"

She could hear him shudder, in relief, in anticipation, on the phone.

"I'll call you with my number in Paris, Paul. I need … I'd like to know anything else you find." The huskiness in her voice had excited him to the point where she could almost hear him climb into the phone.

"Keep working, love — the time will pass quickly."

She kissed the phone and heard a sort of strangled gurgle on the end of the line. She hung up the phone and looked at the wall. The art deco neon clock said 3:45.

Plenty of time to catch a train.

Magda Gertz strode to the bed and opened her shirt, climbed up and threw her leg over his waist.

"I have 20 minutes. Get to work."

She laughed with the sound of a thousand angels.

SPINNING.

That's all he was doing at the moment.

Spinning.

Will hadn't been this far off the pace in months. It hadn't been the morning ride, that was a wash. It hadn't been the nap. That was necessary. It hadn't been dream inside the nap. That had been a bother, but merely that and nothing more.

It had been lunch.

Or lack of same.

Will should have been eating from the moment he got off the bike in the morning until the moment he threw his right leg over the saddle in the afternoon. He knew this game and he should have been playing it, but the nap had captured him and carried him off, to the point that, now, while he was awake, he was dying on the bike.

Stomp it, pull it around, stomp it, pull it around. He was off the rhythm and it was killing him.

Bonk. He was bonking. Haven 'Le Surge' energy bars weren't giving him anything. They might give you a boost, but you couldn't make a day out of them, you needed real food inside the furnace. The energy bars were like throwing gasoline on embers. They blazed for a moment, but left things lower than before.

GoodGodI'mdyinghere.

They're going to find me along the road, he thought, nothing but a puddle of goo in a Haven jersey, my bike standing over me like a Greyfriar's Bobby, baying at the moon over such an unfortunate death. Will snapped back into focus, pulling himself away from Bourgoin's wheel at the last instant. They would have touched and that would have been the day, for them and whatever string of the paceline that sat just behind them.

Damn. Focus. You can't make mistakes like that.

Not with Bourgoin. Not at Le Tour.

His pace was still up, but the struggle to keep it there was becoming overwhelming. His rhythm was gone. Like Fignon at the '89 Tour, struggling into the center of Paris to find that one last ounce of power, that one last flash of speed, he destroyed himself in the search, losing his rhythm, losing his power, and, in the end, losing his race.

He rolled off to the side of the road near the outskirts of Betz, the rest of the team, shooting past in formation, Henri Bresson, struggling himself, bringing up the rear. Will squeezed his eyes shut, then opened them wide again. This was serious. He was seeing designs in the gravel by the side of the tarmac, patterns of colors that made no more sense than anything else around him. He dug in his jersey for anything that might help. He looked up for a moment as the Haven team Peugeot rolled slowly past. Deeds took one look at Will's face then jerked his thumb back, back toward Senlis. Cheryl looked sympathetically, paused a moment, then gunned the small car, choking it for just a second, before speeding off in pursuit of the team.

Will dug in the back pockets of his jersey and found a box of sport drink, Haven Formula 45. He hated this stuff with a passion. It had the consistency of warm snot and tasted something like sweetened library paste, but it gave you a boost like nobody's business for maybe 20 minutes before it crashed you hard to the deck like Leaping Larry Shane doing a number on Gorgeous George.

Will downed the Formula 45 and turned the bike into the wind to begin pedaling toward Senlis and the end of this day. "The Beast" fought him for a second, as if wanting to turn back into the fight. He wrestled the bike back and pedaled slowly toward home.

Jesus, he thought, one day like this on Le Tour and he was done. There was no turning back in the middle of the race, there was no turning off. No matter how bad it got, there was no letting go. If you did it, you did it only once, and then you went home.

This was it, he thought. This is my one vacation for the next month. A whole damned afternoon. Some vacation. He dug deep inside his chest and hawked up a lougee the size of a '55 Buick. Half was phlegm, half was Formula 45. The stuff kicked in his gag reflex.

The bike continued west, toward Senlis, perhaps 20 kilometers away. Over the past six months, he had ridden this road any number of times, to the point where the horse knew the way. Once through Nanteuil, he could catch the farm roads and sail along unhindered. Slowly, but unhindered.

Will put his head down and cranked. The day was beginning to close in on him, the clouds growing heavier, the wind, or breeze, or whatever it was hitting him in the face, becoming steadier and thick with the possibility of rain. He put his head down to cut the resistance, if just only a bit, and tried to ignore not only the weather, but the scenery and the town and the growing traffic that signaled Nanteuil.

He focused on the crankset and his feet, his little feet, wide but short, in the Look shoes. He cranked … and around. And cranked … and around. And cranked and saw his dream again.

Tomas. Tomas Delgado. Sitting in the distance. On a crate of Italian oranges. Tossing one up in the air, watching it hang for a split second, then drop back down into his hand. Spinning the wheels of a bike that hung in the air. A battered, white Colnago. Saying nothing. Tomas. His best friend. An ace mechanic. Dead too soon in a courtyard in Milan, the victim of a corporate hustle. A bomb meant for Will in the seat of a bike.

Tomas. Sharing. Never judging. Never blaming. Unlike his brother Prudencio.

Will stared at the crankset. Once, twice and again. He could feel the stiffness in his right calf. It was a tickle, annoying, more than anything else, but now it was there more often than not. Around again. As the energy drink took hold, his power didn't increase, but his form did — the circles weren't quite as ragged. They were cleaner, smoother, not forcing the issue. Around. And again. The stiffness in his calf began to evaporate. Around. And again. Around.

Circles. Perfect circles.

It was all a circle, he thought. A perfect circle.

The farm fields sang a slowly gaited staccato as he passed between them, cutting the heat of the day with his movement.

He felt the humidity swirl around him like a stump in the middle of a tepid stream, which, he knew, was what he had become. At 32, he knew, he was coming to the end of his circle.

A perfect circle.

CHAPTER FOUR:

DEATH BE NOT COLNAGO

His collapse on the road three days before was nothing that Will had ever worried about before. People crash and burn all the time. Riding wasn't a machine function, it was a human function, and, as human function, was subject to all the vagaries of humanity: power, drive, motivation and lack of same.

It happened to LeMond. It happened to Hinault. It happened to Colgan. And Indurain. And Fignon. It happened to Eddy Merckx.

On second thought, it never really did happen to Merckx, now, did it? Ahh, but there was human and there was completely over-the-top, butt-in-the-air super space alien.

It was to be expected on occasion: a rider, any rider, finding everything necessary to life except the will to stay on the bike, the will to keep the pedals turning, the will to see the finish line.

It was an occupational hazard.

For some reason, though, it wasn't playing out that way. Not this time.

He had reached, through luck and drive, and, it seemed, the right people blowing up their apartments, the step below the top of the pyramid. He was not the team leader, but he was the team lieutenant, second in command of the powerful Haven Pharmaceuticals racing squad to Richard Bourgoin, a long-time talent who was considered, if not a favorite, then, certainly a possibility for the podium in Paris at the end of Le Tour.

It was said and it was so. *L'Équipe* would have it no other way. Bourgoin would be the first French possibility for a win since Hinault in 1985, if, it went unsaid, others could be convinced to lose.

Still, there seemed to be an undercurrent running through the team. Will's last few days had been particularly unspectacular. Dropped once, he had spent the next few rides missing his pace, losing his rhythm, riding back to the velodrome more on a wing and a prayer then two wheels. Deeds had said nothing. Cheryl, on the other hand, was concerned and vocal about it.

"Have you thought about a physical?"

"I'm in great shape."

"You're exhausted."

"I wasn't exhausted last night."

She chuckled. "No. But I think you could be woken from the dead for that. Your recovery is way off. You're just not picking it up like you used to."

"I'm fine. I'm just off peak."

"Hell, you're not just off peak, you're in a crevice."

"Crevasse."

"That's even worse. And that's not the way to be, especially now."

Will couldn't argue with that.

This was not the way to be going into Le Tour, 4000 kilometers around the edge of France, through some of the worst mountains God ever devised, for three weeks with only two days off along the way.

This was not the way to do it, Will thought, not the way at all and others, besides Cheryl, were noticing as well, especially Miguel Cardone.

Cardone was angling for something — what, Will wasn't quite sure. But there was an angle nonetheless. Did Cardone want this job as team lieutenant? Have it and enjoy, Will thought. It was much more fun to simply ride a race and listen to somebody else give the orders than have to think your way through the day, never missing a beat, a look, a move, a tactic. Maybe Cardone wanted to be team leader. Good luck, he thought. Bourgoin had waited too long and worked too hard to give up the gold star simply because Veruca Salt came along and wailed "I wan' it Daddy … I wan' it NNNnnOOOOWW!" And beyond those two jobs, there weren't many others where Miguel could really shine. Sprinter? He was mediocre at best. Climbing? Four others on the team had him beat there. Super domestique? That was pretty much his job description already. So, given the facts at hand, it had to be Will's job as lieutenant. That would explain the talk.

No one had spoken to Will directly, but he and Cheryl had heard the chatter running through the team: a word here, a word there, a four-man conversation stopping in mid-sentence as he or she walked into a room. Still, words were caught. They said Ross is off the pace, Ross is holding up the team, Ross cannot lead us in Le Tour.

Only Bourgoin and Bresson — who until recently had been farther off the pace than Will, and suddenly had been riding better, stronger, with more confidence than he had in months — stood apart from those spreading the acid. Bresson was peaking for Le Tour, it seemed, and had no time for such foolishness.

Through it all, Will held his head high and scuttled off into his shell.

He had hidden away from Kim during the divorce, and now, years later, with Kim dead and buried, he still studiously avoided confrontation with her or with just about any discomfort he faced in life. In a way, Will wished his parents had taught him how to argue, but somewhere along the way he had missed the barge and could only key into the emotional extremes. Explode or shut it away. Here, in Senlis, he shut it away, even from Cheryl.

Until now. Will had to find some answers. The volatility of the situation, with Le Tour right around the corner, was tearing at his ego, his heart, his very soul.

"Hey, Henri," Will called down the hall to Bresson. Whatever had been passing for air conditioning in the building had long ago given up the ghost. The humidity from the outside air and the showers had turned the hall into a rain forest. Bresson stood dripping sweat, his jersey open to the navel, his dark brown arms and neck leading to a fish belly white chest.

"Yes, Will...."

Will paused for a moment, wondering how to open the conversation on this particular subject without appearing paranoid. There was, he felt, no way to do it comfortably, so, he just did it, quickly, blindly.

"What's the deal?"

"Deal?"

"The deal with me. I have a bad day on the bike — a few weak ones on the road — and suddenly, I'm headline fodder on the jungle drums around here."

Bresson looked at Will blankly.

"I'm No. 1 on the Hit Parade."

Again, Bresson shook his head.

"I'm the primary topic of conversation around here, most of it is concerning how I can't do the job anymore."

"Ahh," Bresson nodded in sudden understanding.

"You've been there, you've heard. What have you heard … and … what do you think?"

Will realized in saying it that he wanted an answer to the first question, but, not, necessarily, an answer to the second.

"I've heard things…."

"Like…."

"Like nothing." Bresson held up his hands to slow Will down. "Things. Just talk."

Will looked at him expectantly.

"Will, my friend," Bresson said gently, "you've got to remember something." He put his hand on Will's shoulder. "Remember where you are. Remember who you are. Remember what you have done."

Will shook his head, missing Bresson's meaning.

"You are a part of Haven. You are an important part. You are second in command. You have earned it, just as I have earned this — my chance to ride. You have paid your dues."

"Okay, so?"

"In all the world, Will, there are only 30 … maybe 40 … jobs like yours? And while some may pay more, none have the support and the freedom and the facilities you have…."

Will looked slowly around as if to punctuate Bresson's obvious joke. These were facilities to die for, no doubt about…. Bresson grabbed Will's face and twisted his face forward again.

"I'm not joking, Will. This is a sport made up of champions. Amateur champions from all over the world. Champions who, as professionals, have had to take second, or third, or last place on the team for years and now feel that it is their time, their due.

"You, my friend, are only in their way."

Will nodded slowly. In the dark and dank tunnel, smelling vaguely of mildew and wet towels, only days before the start of Le Tour de France, Will's own personal hell, he was beginning to grasp a sense of understanding. After riding at the back of the pack for so many years himself, feeling that frustration, he was now near the podium and, being there, realized that others felt his old frustration — especially those who were close before and now had to take a new back seat to him.

"What do you say, Will — they are gunning for you?"

"Yes, they are gunning for me."

"Just as they were for Richard Bourgoin last year, when he was the team lieutenant. And Jean-Pierre Colgan four years before. And every other lieutenant or team leader that has ridden Le Tour or the Giro or the Vuelta or any other race, big or small, that exists in this world of riding. Remember, Will — this is a sport of egos. No race would ever be worth a damn if it wasn't. This is a sport that calls for people to use their minds as well as their legs. Their spirits as well as their lungs. Their pride is, quite often, the only thing that brings them across the finish line."

"And when they smell blood in the water…."

Will left the sentence unfinished.

"They strike," Bresson said quietly, then smiled.

"They strike."

With the thought of some Spielbergian monster swimming through the sewer pipes underneath the decaying velodrome of Senlis, they both began to laugh, heartily, which would give the gossips on the team fodder for at least another afternoon.

"And you," Will said, "you're riding well."

"The magic of old age. God always gives you one more shot before he kills you."

"Don't say that. I've lost too many friends already."

BIEJO FORTUNA SPUN THE HEAVY GOLD COIN, AGAIN, ON THE MIRRORED SURFACE of the table. He was playing a waiting game and he hated to wait. To pass the time, he spun the coin, despite the fact that each spin, playing itself out in a hum, then rattle and desperate roll to find the power to right itself left a trail of micro scratches on the polished African ebony.

What did he care?

It was his wood. He could afford to cut down a rain forest, if need be, to get another one.

He spun again, but this time, spun his chair as a bored and restless four-year-old might, kicking a table leg with each turn, watching the summer night settle over Paris. He spun again and again, until a building in the distance caught his eye.

Fortuna looked out through the golden light of late afternoon in the city. The building began to glow as floor upon floor of the massive office structure lit with reflected sunlight, preparing for the end of another day.

What are you working on, he thought, in your little cubbyholes and pristine laboratories? What are your computers telling you?

And how can I steal it?

He smiled. If I haven't already.

A small console on the desk next to his chair buzzed once, then twice again, almost in a pattern. Fortuna leapt to the button. This was what he had been waiting almost 20 minutes to hear. He grabbed the phone and slammed it to the side of his head.

"Yes!?!" he blurted.

"Cytabutasone, darling," she purred.

"What?"

"Listen closely. They're about to find it. Isolate it. Cytabutasone. The synthetic steroid, based on testosterone and adrenaline? The undetectable one?"

"Yes," he said, with a slight tone of exasperation, "I remember it." He tapped the coin on the table for a moment and asked, "Masking agents?"

"Still unnecessary."

"Performance?"

"Performance enhancement in the test module was apparently double — or even triple — normal physical function," she said, with unvarnished excitement. "It worked in some ways like an amphetamine in low doses, to boost performance, then the steroidal function kicked in to aid recovery."

"Recovery?"

"It was actually rebuilding muscle tissue — almost overnight — just as you predicted."

Fortuna began to smile. This was good. This was so very, very good. This was going to be worth a fortune in the legal — or illegal trade.

"Downside?" he asked.

"Minor — apparently. True downside is unknown at this point. Perhaps some liver damage, but that may be from an abnormally high dose taken just before death."

"Death?"

"Yes, the test module has … died — overdose."

Fortuna let the thought work its way around his brain for another few moments, felt a peak of emotion and sighed.

"Then, I suppose," he said, "we need a new test subject."

The line was silent.

"When are you here again?" Fortuna asked.

"Soon. You owe me money, my love."

"Not until I see the data."

"You will see data."

"And I want the report. The medical report. Coroner. Police lab. Whoever that damned boyfriend of yours is."

"How and when?"

"Immediately. What about the test?"

"Over the next few weeks. I'm setting up a full field test. By the way, who, might I ask, will be paying for all this?"

"Not to worry. Haven Pharmaceuticals will pick up the tab."

"Really? The Bitch Goddess of us all? How can you be so sure?" she asked.

"Oh, I know. I know."

"When will you pay my end?"

"Your end. Your end is always on my mind."

"I miss you," she whispered.

"Keep me informed," he said, breaking the banter with a straight-edged command, "and keep an eye on a rider named Ross. He might be one we can use."

Biejo Fortuna could have sworn he heard a chuckle in the background, then the click of the receiver. The line was dead. He hung up his phone and leaned forward, spinning the heavy gold coin on the mirrored surface of the conference room table. Spinning. And spinning. And spinning.

Leaving a trail of microscopic circles wherever it went.

Spinning. And spinning.

And spinning.

"FOR THE LAST TWO WEEKS," DEEDS BELLOWED, "WE'VE BEEN WORKING PRETTY HARD."

(*You* working? Will thought. You've been riding in a car.)

"And I know a lot of you are wondering when we're going to get some time off."

(Many have been offering up prayers and novenas.)

"And the answer is: today."

(Which only proves that prayers are answered and the Blessed Virgin is listening in at novenas, even if she knows you're only there so your mother won't turn over in her grave — after she dies, of course.)

"Many of you have late travel arrangements home for your national championships this weekend. The team has people in from Paris — from Haven — so, I've got meetings."

(Thankyouthankyouthankyouthankyou.)

"Although...."

(Here it comes....)

"I think you should get out and do 30 to 50 easy kilometers."

"Yyyeesss! Dodged the bullet!!!"

Will froze in the middle of the room. All eyes, he realized, were turned on him. His thoughts given voice, he was the Homer Simpson of international professional cycling.

"Yes, Will?"

"Nothing, Carl. Just thrilled, that's all."

"Perhaps Will should do the 50 — or more," Cardone spoke with a quiet menace from the back of the room. "He certainly needs it."

Will closed his eyes and waited for the shoe to drop. Yes, he did need it. But more than needing the road, he needed the rest. Maybe everybody did, as if Deeds's harsh rhythm on the road had caused the team to peak too soon.

But the gauntlet had been slapped down with glee, and with no intention of it ever being picked up, Will turned toward Miguel Cardone, sinking slowly deeper into the couch that ate Cincinnati.

"Hey, Mig — wanna do 50 with me?"

All eyes turned toward Cardone, who blushed, slightly, his bluff called.

"Well?"

"Yes," Cardone said stiffly, "yes, I'll do 50 with you, but it will be my 50, a hard 50, not old-man 50 with time to look at the flowers."

"I'm not big on flowers. A beautiful woman might slow me up for a moment, but I'll stay with you — boy."

The word hung in the air, with the warm acceptance of road kill, an insult in any language.

"Call your time Miguel. I'll meet you on the line."

"One hour, old man. One hour out front."

"O-tay, Spanky. I'll meet you at the clubhouse door."

Cardone pulled himself, with difficulty, from the soft and sunken couch and stomped from the room, followed by Cardinal, who was quickly turning into Cardone's squire, valet and toady. It was not a graceful exit.

Will turned, his eyes making a slow circuit of the room and coming to rest on Deeds and Cheryl standing off to one side.

"Sorry to ruin your meeting, Carl."

"I was done."

"Good. Glad I could provide the after-meeting entertainment."

Deeds leaned forward and whispered, "Look, Will, finish this clown and get back here. Bergalis wants dinner with you and Bourgoin and me."

Will smiled.

"Thanks, Carl."

Deeds spun on his heel and clunked his way out the door.

Cheryl looked at Will intently.

"Just do it. And do it quickly."

"You looking for a lesson?"

Cheryl Crane lost her conspiratorial smile.

"No, I'm looking for dinner. I'm dying here."

❁

IN THE MIDST OF WILL'S FIVE-MINUTE DOZE, TOMAS DELGADO STARED AT HIM, not a word said, not a breath taken. The orange, a huge, brightly colored fruit, was tossed in the air and slapped down, up in the air and down, up in the air and down, hitting the dead mechanic's hand each time with a loud 'thwap.'

Thwap. Thwap. Thwap.

The sound of a flat on a hot asphalt road. The sound of an orange in a dead man's hand.

Meanwhile, the wheel of the battered, white Colnago spun endlessly.

Will could hear the hum.

❁

GODOT WAS STRETCHED OUT ON HIS OFFICE COUCH FOR THE FIFTH TIME TODAY. It had taken the Eindhoven police district 10 days to get him the additional reports on the death of Henrik Koons. Embarrassment, he'd wager. They'd missed a major aspect of the case. Walked over, under, around and through and never did find the damned thing. The method. Boy looked like a pin cushion and there were no pins to be found.

Then again, he thought, he hadn't won the prize. It had taken days of wracking his brain before he was able to, quite literally, knock the idea forward to the front of his consciousness, days of searching his mind for what had been missing from the autopsy reports of Henrik Koons. It was right there, he knew, right before his eyes, and as it became known to him, he'd felt remarkably stupid, because it was so very, very simple, so very, very basic.

The junkie and his junk.

The junkie without his junk. The needle man without a needle.

Someone had done a little housekeeping after Mr. Koons pedaled to his final reward. Someone who wanted to create more questions and buy himself a little time.

With Godot's help, the Eindhoven police district had cleaned up its report, rechecked the apartment and effects and, then, promptly, refiled the investigation under "Overdose."

Gone and, yes, forgotten. Goodbye and good luck, Henrik, you're messing up our filing system.

Godot's eyes slowly slid back over the new pages of the police report from Eindhoven, stopping first at the edge of a black-and-white scene photo, then across to a paper clip, then onto the final chemical analysis, stopping at the letters in bold faced type that read: UNKNOWN.

Now, what did that American TV detective say in this sort of situation?

Ah, yes.

"This is a *pissoir*."

Or, words to that effect.

WILL HAD DRIFTED OFF FOR ONLY A FEW MINUTES, BUT IT WAS ONE OF THOSE naps where five minutes seems like forever, lost in a sleep that simply defies time. He shook himself awake and suddenly felt the emptiness that the death of Tomas Delgado had carved inside him.

Oh, pal, you shouldn't have died.

I should have died. That bomb in the saddle of the bike in Milan was meant for me, courtesy of an ex-wife and a corporate boyfriend with designs on the company and the death of a cycling team.

Should have been me. That's sure as hell what your little brother Prudencio thinks. Should have been you, Ross. Should have been you.

A vicious thought rattled through the tin can of his brain.

Glad it wasn't though. Sorry, Tomas. I'm really glad it wasn't.

He stood, wiped the sleep from his eyes and walked toward the mechanic's room. Luis Bourbon, the leading team mechanic since Milan, pulled Will's ancient, though upgraded Colnago, affectionately known by the entire team as "The Beast," from the wall rack.

"It's very good, Will."

Will paused for a second. Bourbon had not said three words to him in the past six months. Now, there was not only words, but feeling behind the words. He didn't know how to respond.

"Thanks, Luis."

Will smiled, then let his mind drift elsewhere.

That elsewhere was still waking up. Will hadn't thought about the 33-mile challenge ahead or Cardone or the very real possibility of losing. He thought about Tomas and beyond him, Cheryl, and the very real fact that death and distance had often taken his friends outside his reach.

He desperately wanted to skip the ride and race home and make love with Cheryl again, the horns at the top of his head starting to curl backward in on themselves, until soon he'd look like Princess Leia out of "Star Wars" with two huge circles at his ears.

Yet, more than that, he wanted to talk. He was beginning to feel the weight of his own thoughts and feelings start to bear down on him again, as they had at the end of last season, when, out of luck, out of work, out of chances, he had begun to drink himself to death, quite slowly, in a dirty little bar in Avelgem.

Cheryl and Tomas and Haven had released all that, and now, the burden was coming back again, heavier than ever, with no opportunity to let go. It was all on him this time. Will gritted his teeth and rubbed his chest. Damn it all, he thought. I've just got to get rid of this stuff. He laughed. Why can't I just dump it and let somebody else deal with it?

He took the bike and rolled it toward the door.

"C'mon doctor," he said under his breath, "we've got some problems to solve."

The bike answered with a thrum through its spine that Will felt through his gloves and hands and arms.

Damn, he thought, I love this bike.

THE FIRST 10 KILOMETERS HAD BEEN A THROWAWAY, ROLLING, CATCHING THE rhythm, warming up, one rider not paying attention to the other. Mentally, they were gauging and sensing and feeling out each other's intentions, short and long term, but outwardly, it was all silk and style, spinning without a care.

Will took the inside of the country road, northeast of Senlis. He had taken this course endless times before, as it was a cheap and easy training ride, nothing more than a little something to stretch out the knot that had set up housekeeping in his right calf.

Today, however, it was for the marbles. Maybe not all the marbles, but some of the marbles, and maybe not real marbles, but the unconscious marbles that everybody on the team thought were in the circle of his mind waiting to be grabbed by a steely...what the hell was he talking about?

In his momentary wandering, Will realized he had blindly dropped left and crossed to another road, the second leg of the 50-kilometer course, and picked up the pace. Cardone had experienced no lack of focus and had sensed Will's move, dropping in cleanly behind him, hugging the rear wheel of "The Beast" so tightly that Will could almost feel the additional drag shoot up through the tire and the crankset and the seatpost and his butt.

Shit. First blood. And it's mine on the floor.

He spun out hard, slowly building up his speed in the big ring. He never rose out of the saddle, but concentrated on a point in the distance, focusing his mind there and his legs on the pattern of the pedals.

Perfect circles.

Push and pull in perfect circles.

Watch the rhythm. Watch the rhythm. Make it smooth. Suck him in.

Cardone tucked himself in directly behind Will as the speed increased. Over the next five, then 10, then 15 kilometers and through the turn around at 25, the cadence never slackened.

Will knew he was taking a chance at the front, as Cardone was already setting himself up for the final sprint through Senlis. Stringing it out this long could easily prove to be Will's undoing. He had to watch the pace and keep it high, but too high and too long and he'd be burned out before he could throw the switch on the bastard.

Will hunkered down and felt a new surge from "The Beast," almost as if the bike was taking up the slack left by his own, aging legs. The pace increased again as the pair of riders, almost as one, shot down the road back toward the outskirts of Senlis. Thirty kliks out and Will had held the rhythm for nearly 40 minutes. His lungs felt the burn, while his legs, especially the right, called out for a new pace, some kind of relief.

As if in answer, a truck approached on the left, in the distance. His hands low and deep inside the drops, Will could feel a solid and distinct tug to his left.

Damn, he thought, I've got a bad bearing in the headset. The tug disappeared for a second, then pulled, ever so slightly back to the left, almost as a hint. Deep inside his gourd, a mad hatter of an idea began to grow.

Sweet Jesus, this was stupid.

Will looked ahead and judged speed and distance and danger.

One wrong move here, pal, and you're dead, with little body parts fertilizing the asphalt, the kind of thing that makes a momma's womb collapse in a dead faint.

And yet his eyes continued snapping back and forth, back and forth, gauging, measuring, calculating, praying.

Will realized, in a flash of understanding, that a number of things had to happen all at once: the driver of the truck had to touch his brakes; Cardone couldn't follow him, or, slacken his pace; and, there couldn't be any traffic coming up from behind, because Will couldn't take the time to peek back and check without giving it all away.

This wasn't trusting to luck. This was making it up as you went along.

Good Lord, he thought. What am I doing?

The light blue truck approached, hitting at least 75 kph on the flat and empty country road. Will stared at the odd apparition of a gigantic plastic fly on the roof top, then shifted his gaze down to the engine cover and the black grill and the chrome Mercedes logo shining out from its center. That was his focal point.

Concentrate there, shut it all out around you.

One-hundred-fifty meters.

Keep your head canted forward, don't twist to the side. Don't telegraph the punch.

One-hundred-twenty-five meters.

Keep the rhythm steady. Don't jog it. Lure him in. Put him to sleep.

One-hundred meters.

Around. And again. Around. And again.

Seventy-five meters.

His eyes shot to the far shoulder. It was paved maybe a foot into the gravel. His eyes shot to the truck. The driver was riding the center line. Still, it was going to be tight.

Fifty meters.

Watch the logo. That's your mark. Watch the logo.

Twenty-five meters.

Time it. Time it.

Twenty.

Time it.

Ten.

It all happened at once.

Without a twitch or change of rhythm, Will shot across the road at a 45-degree angle. For a blinding second there was nothing before his eyes but black grill work and a silver three-pointed star in a circle and the sound of an air horn wailing in panic, then the edge of the truck appeared with a mirror racing directly at his head. Will ducked and felt the bottom edge of the chrome mirror plate brush over the top of his helmet with millimeters to spare. The edge of the truck blew him back just a bit, turning his speed down a notch while he kept his cadence high, in a whirlwind of dust and gravel and screaming tires. The vortex from the rear of the van pulled him back toward the centerline and he followed it, hard again, right across to the right shoulder, right across to Cardone, who, in his shock at such an apparent suicide had not slackened his pace. Will tucked up tight, right onto the back tire of his tormentor, now taking the pull, fast, hard and even, the pull he had so completely refused for nearly 35 kilometers.

Will's blood was up, the mounting agony of a few minutes before now blown away with a shot of adrenaline, the blast of a trucker's horn and the cool taste of chance taken without a moment's thought of death.

He could ponder the move later and shudder in his bed under his Pocahontas sheets, hugging Cheryl tightly and mystified by his own stupidity, but now, there was nothing but a brain-freezing focus on the wheel and shoulders of Miguel Cardone. Watching his rhythm. Watching his moves. Watching for the twitch that almost always came before the jump — unless, of course, you had a coach named Stewart Kenally who bred it out of you with a stick across the shoulders that burned like an afternoon in the third level of hell.

Cardone was stuck, and he knew it, until the sprint inside Senlis. Somewhere inside the city limits, at a turn, in an intersection, on a turnaround, he'd shake Will, this aging visage of grim death hanging just off his ass.

They turned back onto the main road leading into Senlis, two riders, two bikes, one mechanical creature. The fury of the attack stopped people on the streets and forced them to stare in disbelief. There was no possibility of looking away, they had to watch, and, as the pair turned a distant corner, there was a sense of loss in each passerby who would not be able to see this force of nature resolve itself.

Will hit some gravel on a hard right turn and sensed, for a split second, his tires losing their grip, but then, felt the bike respond, almost by itself bringing him back into line, directly behind Cardone.

He loved his bike. Oh, bless you Ernesto and your little elves in Colnago-ville.

He could hear the effort now, Cardone wheezing in the rhythm of the crankset, the effort of the first 35 kilometers, in Will's slipstream, and the last 15 in the pull, finally taking their toll. For his part, Will's move with the truck had saved him. He felt revived at the rear, torqued high and tight with adrenaline, despite the high focus he'd had to maintain in the rush through the streets of Senlis.

Five blocks, now four, to the turn into the cul-de-sac and the velodrome. Watch for the sprint. Watch for the sprint. Four blocks, now three. Suddenly, Will caught the move, not through the shoulders, but through Cardone's ass. Through the middle range of his vision, he sensed Cardone's butt rising, almost imperceptibly, off the saddle. Will took it for all it was worth, jumping to the left, on the inside of the turn to the cul-de-sac, forcing Miguel out and wide and off his pace, the sprint already lost, though Cardone would never admit it.

The bike was alive in Will's hands, charging, flying, absolutely electrified. Together, man and machine sped toward a nonexistent finish line to win a race that meant nothing more than the shuffling of egos on an imaginary chart.

Will put his head down and felt the bike shiver between his legs. The wind of his own efforts roared in his ears. His heart soared. The road slid magically beneath him.

Head down. Race won. On the inside lane.

He never saw it.

He never saw the car.

He never saw the black limousine pull out of the velodrome parking lot.

He never saw himself hit the left front panel head on, the bike exploding beneath him in a scream of metal and almost human agony.

Time slowed.

He felt himself, almost outside himself, sail over the hood of the car. Slowly, Will turned his head and watched the panic of the driver as he soared, without effort, in a bubble of silence, past the windshield and over the street, curling himself into a ball, by instinct, before hitting the gravel with his shoulder and rolling, ass over teakettle, thinking not of the pain shooting through his shoulder, but of the new jersey he was wearing and how the thing would be torn to shreds before he even got a chance to make it really stink.

Damn.

His shoulder felt like somebody had just bashed it with a 36-inch Rocky Colavito Louisville Slugger. The pain raced down to his fingertips then up again and down to his gut, making him nauseous. Will turned to see Cardone riding circles in the cul-de-sac, his arms up in a victory salute. Whatever finish line he had set in his mind, he had crossed it first and Will would have to settle for sloppy seconds. Very sloppy.

Cardone looked at Will with a sense of triumph and disdain.

Great, Will thought, I had the bastard beat.

For a fraction of a beat, time stopped.

And then — oh, Christ — a thought grabbed Will by the throat and turned him away from Cardone and back to the car, past Cheryl and Deeds and the people who were now running to him across the velodrome grounds. Will charged toward the car, ignoring the pain in his shoulder, grabbed the sharp edges of the bodywork to pull himself, on his racing cleats, around to the driver's side, where he found his shattered bike.

The wheel, the fork, the frame itself, were broken into pieces like the shards of his mother's favorite crystal on a concrete floor.

The front wheel, leaning up against the front panel of the limo, slipped to the ground with a screech and a rattle of shattered metal.

And in that instant, Will knew.

His bike had died.

CHAPTER FIVE:

IN MOURNING

Every time the door opened in the small restaurant three blocks from the velodrome, the change in air pressure blew a cloud of cooking smoke and aromas out and away from the oven hood and across the 15 tables that were packed into a space hardly large enough for a magazine rack and an aspirin display.

Will watched the cloud waft across the room of tile, ancient wood and brass, then rose up out of his chair just a bit to drink it in. The food was wonderful here, but you lived for the sensation of falling through a cumulonimbus of olfactory delight. Cheryl, worried that she was starting to lose him, pulled him back down into his seat.

"How do you feel?"

"I feel like crap. How do you feel?"

"I feel fine, but you were the one who had the accident."

"It was no accident."

"Oh, Jesus, Will," Cheryl sighed, "it wasn't murder."

"It was velocidc, surc as shit."

She barked a short laugh, which made Will smile. He turned to watch the cloud above him move toward the next table and went back to his dinner, lost in his own fog. He picked at the steaming plate of pasta that sat motionless, for the moment, on the table in front of him. Who knew? One more pill and anything might be possible, from a reality overload to watching the pasta dance across the table.

Will picked at some strands of noodle and turned them slowly, then flicked them over and back onto the mound of food. Even such minor exertion made his right shoulder throb with a dull ache. His shoulder, his hip, his knee, his ankle, his entire right side was pretty much a wash. And that calf, he knew, even in the middle of his brain cloud, was dangerously tight. No matter how tired he might be at the end of this evening, he had to remember to stretch it out.

Somewhere, in the distance, he heard the buzz of the conversation, so constant for the last few minutes, stop, and felt the eyes at the table turn to him.

"Will, are you still with us?"

Will's eyes cruised the table, beginning with Cheryl then moving past Deeds, to some weasel Will didn't know and Henri Bergalis, then back to Bourgoin, leader of the Haven team, sitting on his right.

Bourgoin had put up with Will's mood swings for almost six months now, and had grown so accustomed to the line between sullen silence and euphoric chatter, that he glanced at Will for a moment, shrugged, and went back to his dinner without breaking stride.

Henri Bergalis, the head of Haven Pharmaceuticals, however, did not recognize the signs and worried about one of his leading riders, and, perhaps, if you stretched the definition a bit, one of his friends. He cared about Ross for a number of reasons. Will was, in his own way, a good rider: tough, resilient, uncompromising. He was fun to have around, capable of outrageous behavior both on and off the bike, today being a prime example, as few riders would take on the dangers of a challenge race only days before the start of Le Tour. And, finally, Will Ross had, quite unintentionally, put Henri Bergalis at the top of an international pharmaceutical corporation after years of standing in his brother's shadow.

That was certainly worth something to Henri Bergalis.

"Will. You haven't said a word all evening. Haven't eaten. That's not good. You need your carbohydrates."

"I need a drink."

"Is that wise?"

"I've never been known for my wisdom."

Deeds turned and blew out a sigh. "Jesus with a hangnail, Ross, that's for damned sure. Did you land on your head, today, or what?"

"Carl," Cheryl said, quietly, "give him some room. His shoulder is torn up and he's full of pain pills at the moment. Let's just give him some room."

"You forget — I've been there, done that. Nobody gave me any damn room."

Cheryl remembered. She had been driving the car when Deeds was shot. The bullet had been meant for her chest. Then again, she didn't feel a twinge of guilt and wasn't about to put up with his bitterness.

"You're alive, Carl. That's all the room we had in the car."

Deeds looked ready to argue the point, paused, sighed, and went back to his dinner.

Mentally dancing on the edge of the conversation, Will felt the sudden tinge of mother-based guilt associated with any sort of anti-social behavior.

"Sorry," he mumbled, for a mumble was about the best he could manage, "it's not that. The shoulder's fine."

"I should hope so," Deeds cackled, "the way you're eating pain pills."

"Haven 22/15s," said the bookish little man sitting to the right of Henri Bergalis. "Haven 22/15s. You exceeded the dosage by a good 85 percent."

"You took 'em away before I even had a chance to really get started," Will said with an edgy smile.

"You were irrational in your dosage," said the little man.

Will smiled with an aching dreaminess. The pills did work, he thought. He couldn't feel his shoulder, for the most part, and he was beginning to not really care about the vague, almost phantom, pains he could feel. Nor did he care much about the voices at the table that rolled in and out of his consciousness, like people talking at the bottom of a tin can.

Will started to slide off into his own little world.

"Will … Will?" Bergalis asked quietly, then turned to Cheryl for an answer.

The table was silent for a moment, until she looked up from her nearly empty plate of spaghetti and realized that all eyes, except the two ping-pong balls with dots belonging to Will, were turned in her direction.

"Urrg … umph." Cheryl swallowed her bite as politely as possible, quickly washing down a straggler of pasta with a swallow of red wine. "Urrg. Um. Well." There was a long, uncomfortable pause. "What?"

"What's with Will? How hard did he fall on his head?" Bergalis seemed genuinely concerned. Unusual, Cheryl thought, for the chairman of a multi-national industrial giant, especially one who was still concerned that she wound up with Will instead of him.

Cheryl looked over at Will, whose eyes were doing a drug-induced tango at the moment, and pondered her silent friend.

"Well, gentlemen — it is not his shoulder and it is not his head."

"Well, then, what's wrong?"

Bergalis and Deeds leaned forward for the answer.

"What, bad news from home?" Deeds asked without a trace of sympathy.

"No, it's not head or shoulder or his family, Carl — it's his bike."

"His bike?"

"Yes, his bike."

The little man beside Bergalis began to chuckle.

He was alone in doing so and, quickly realizing that fact, swallowed hard and grew quiet.

Bourgoin spoke up, his quiet voice edged with ice.

"I know it sounds silly to you, Monsieur Engelure, but it is very real to us, who ride for a living. We come to know our bicycles, many times better than we know our wives. We know their strengths, their weaknesses, their moods — yes, their moods. And to some —" he looked at Will, still lost on his own personal road to Mandalay, "— to some, they become even more, an — extension — of themselves. A part of their personality, their riding style."

"But a rider, is it not true," argued Engelure, "has many different bikes, for many different things — different races, terrains?"

"True, true." said Cheryl. "But for some, there is one and maybe only one bike that … well … talks to them. And this bike talked to Will."

"He's psychotic, then?" Engelure asked.

Quietly, as if rising slowly from the darkness of a mental swamp, Will answered in a thickly blurred voice.

"Maybe so, Monsieur Engelure. Maybe so. Maybe we're all a bit psychotic. But, anyone who has ever ridden a bike, a bike they can truly, truly call their own," he muttered, swinging a finger in the air, "would know immediately what happened today."

"I rode a bike. I never felt that." Engelure looked around the table, quickly, for support and found none in the eyes of Deeds or Bergalis.

"You felt it. Once. You lost it as you grew up and found cars and women and all the things that seem special in the adult world. There's magic in a bike, a magic of seeing and riding and, hell, just being free. Most people grow up and lose that magic. But we don't."

Will looked at Engelure with dark, empty eyes. "We don't."

"Because you ride a bike every day. That is your job."

"It's more than a job." Will shook his head, trying, in vain, to clear the pain-pill logjam from the argument he was trying to make. "It's not a job. It's...."

Bourgoin quietly interrupted.

"It's life."

Engelure snorted. "*Certainement.*" The table ignored the sarcasm.

"That bike was as alive for me as Franklin Roosevelt," Will said, distantly.

Cheryl looked at him quizzically. "He's dead."

Will paused for a second and thought. "Then, Eleanor."

Cheryl sighed. "She's dead, too, Will, but," she patted his arm, "we get the point."

Bourgoin nodded.

"So today, after the ride that bike gave me, after all the rides that bike gave me, to see it flattened on the side of a car — *your* car," he pointed hard at Engelure, "it hurt. It hurt like hell."

"Yes, but the bike didn't give you the ride. *You* ..." the little man pointed hard back at Will, "... gave you the ride."

"Really? Did I? When I was looking right, who pulled left to avoid a lateral drain I hadn't noticed? When I missed the jump, who tugged to get my attention? When I was descending at 100 kilometers per hour, who held turns that I, alone, certainly couldn't have held?"

Louis Engelure stared ahead as the speaker babbled on, keeping a slight, faked, smile of understanding on his face. This man was obviously mad, he thought, and yet, the rest of the table was silent. Perhaps they're all mad.

Cheryl, Bourgoin, Deeds and Bergalis all nodded quietly. Engelure suddenly realized that he was in the midst of a cult that had seen the light, a light that had passed him by completely.

"Well, I'm sorry about your bike. Haven will buy you another one I'm sure."

Will sighed. "Yes, I'm sure," he mumbled with quiet resignation.

Henri broke the heavy atmosphere that hung over the table: "Louis is here for a specific reason. And ... I'll let him explain it to you."

The little man nodded toward his boss, looked around the table with the attitude of a burned-out teacher at the start of another year teaching sullen teenagers, and said, "I am the head of research and development for Haven

Pharmaceuticals, and we are in need of a field test."

Deeds and Bergalis didn't move. They knew, already, the storm that was coming.

Bourgoin, on the other hand, shot up like a fully loaded Roman candle, while Will dropped his head and began to swing it in a drunken back-and-forth motion.

"What?" Bourgoin bellowed, "we are to be lab rats?"

Engelure waved his hands frantically. The sudden tension and anger in Bourgoin's response had diners in distant parts of the restaurant turning and pointing toward the Haven table.

"No. No. No. No lab rats. The clinical testing has already been done. This … this is a field test of a series of performance-enhancing…."

Will interrupted like a drunken sailor. "What … drugs?" Will looked at Henri Bergalis in shock. "Henri, Mr. Clean himself, doing the drug number?"

"Stop! No." Engelure sat back heavily in his cane chair and wiped his forehead with a handkerchief. "No. Please. Just hear me out."

Will and Bourgoin settled, and around them, the diners went back to their meals, so rudely interrupted by the clowns at the noisy table.

"Fine. Now…."

Henri Bergalis raised his hand.

"Let me."

"Fine." Engelure looked at the two riders with an ill-concealed disgust.

"Research and development has come up with what Monsieur Engelure believes is a performance-enhancing vitamin. Not a drug. Not amphetamine, not hormone or steroid or EPO or anything like that, but a vitamin that keys into the system in such a way that it increases performance — naturally."

"No such thing." Will said, suddenly realizing that he sounding like Fred Mertz in the bottom of the Grand Canyon. "Vitamins unlock food or muscle storage, but they're notoriously inefficient delivery systems."

Will blinked his eyes hard. The effort of sounding at least somewhat sober had caused him to break out in a sweat.

"Yes, there is such a thing, Mr. Ross." Engelure trembled, just a bit, with a defensive anger. "Yes, there is — and we have developed it."

"Well, what does the French government think about this?" Cheryl asked,

"And how much has it been tested ahead of time and who has it been tested on and why should the team just drink down whatever little cocktail the boys down at R&D have devised?"

"Because you are employees and employees do what they are told."

"Not good enough, chump." Will rose out of his chair and leaned unsteadily across the table toward Engelure, staring at him through red, rheumy eyes, the scars on his face glowing like shuttered neon in the half light of the brasserie. "Not good enough by half."

"And why not?"

"Because," Will said, falling heavily back into his chair with the exertion, "if this stuff doesn't work ... I'm hung out to dry, not the company. If this stuff has long term damage, it's my ass, not the company's. If, in all your drink mixing back at the ranch, something illegal wanders into the mix to boost the test results and keep development on schedule, it's my career, not yours."

"Funny coming from a man who had to be pulled away from a bottle of 22/15s this afternoon."

Will settled deeply into his chair, fully accepting the accusation.

"That was different. That was today. That was training. That was accident recovery. What you're talking about is a race — a big race. *The* race."

"Henri...." Cheryl said in a pleading tone.

Bergalis nodded and touched Engelure on the arm. The little man grew quiet. It was an amazing trick, thought Will, like a kid soothing an agitated pet lizard.

Cheryl turned to Henri Bergalis, who quickly changed the mask of his face from business to pleasure as he looked at her. Cheryl blushed momentarily, then asked, "Are you sure you should be doing this — now? I mean, it is Le Tour de France. Should you really be screwing around with untested formulas at Le Tour?"

Bergalis shuttered his eyes just a bit, then, gently whispered, as if to a lover, rather than an employee, "We are Haven, *cheri*. This is what we do. This is where my father tested all his drugs, good and bad, legal and illegal. This is the reality of Haven and it always has been. This is why my father built this company and stayed in racing. The difference is, we are not testing drugs, we are supplying vitamins. That is all."

He touched her hand and broke the spell. She drew it back quickly and shook her head.

"Will," Bergalis said quietly, turning to address not only Ross, but the entire table, "this is a company project. It is done with the knowledge and support of the French government. We have done extensive research on it so far, but not in the realm of world-class athletes. Such as yourself."

Will smiled. Yeah, right. World class. His shoulder was beginning to make its presence known again through the wine and the pills.

Henri Bergalis smiled back. A little flattery, he thought. It goes a long way.

"Do you feel comfortable with it, Henri?" Bourgoin asked quietly.

Bergalis nodded.

"And you, Uncle Carl?" Will said, pointedly.

Deeds nodded, but without, Will noticed, quite the same confidence shown by Bergalis.

Will turned to face Louis Engelure.

"I'm not even going to ask you."

Engelure's face slowly collapsed in on itself, rolling into a bright red ball with two beady eyes, no nose and an angry slit for a mouth.

"Don't hurt yourself." Will smiled at his drunken wit. He wondered if he'd be embarrassed about this when he sobered up tomorrow.

Bourgoin remained silent, pondering what, for him, was the most important question of all.

"Pill … or … needle?"

All eyes turned to Henri Bergalis.

"Louis?"

Engelure brought himself up to his full height, which wasn't all that much, and said in a voice filled with undisguised and rather gleeful venom, "intravenous."

Now, it was Will's turn to collapse.

"Swell. Just swell."

Bourgoin knew exactly what he was thinking. "Fine, then," Bourgoin said, wiping his face angrily with the ancient, red napkin, "fine — I.V."

Engelure smiled with triumph. "It is a more efficient delivery system."

"But …" Bourgoin continued, his voice quiet, his manner sure, "… I want *strict* controls on the vitamin supply. Storage. Accessibility. Quality control. I do *not* want this team damaged, either physically or in reputation, by a less-than-adequate product."

"We don't want another TCN," said Will.

"No," Bergalis agreed, "We don't want another TCN."

"TCN?" Engelure looked quizzical. Will answered his look quietly, dredging up what seemed an almost painful memory.

"Entire team. Dutch team. Strong. They said," he pointed out, "that it was liquid vitamins stored at the wrong temperature. Not necessarily sanitary conditions. *Everybody* got sick. *Everybody* was out of Le Tour."

"That will not happen here," Bourgoin stated flatly.

"It will not," Bergalis agreed.

"No shit," said Will and Deeds at the same moment in time.

Screw you all, thought Engelure to himself.

"WE HAVE PLANTED THE MARK."

"Who?"

"Not who … what."

"So, what, then?"

"Haven."

"The company?"

"The team."

"The entire team?"

"The entire team."

"What about medical control?"

"If we can't see it … *they* can't see it."

"So it's in?"

"It's in."

"Marvelous."

Magda Gertz hung up the phone without saying goodbye. When you stood to be as rich as she was going to be by the end of the month, you could afford to hang up without saying goodbye.

CHAPTER SIX:

THE NEXT TIME I SEE PARIS

Paris still lived for him.

Despite the onrush of the modern world, Paris retained much of its centuries-old charm and atmosphere, a matter of intense pride to the French as the center of their world. New York might sink into a morass of crime and garbage, London into a sea of bad attitudes and worse architecture, but Paris, even with all those things, continued to resonate with its own rhythm, its own personality, its own *je ne sais quoi.* The look, the feel, the sense of the city remained unchanged, despite wars and crime and garbage and strikes and rampant development and greed and municipal corruption and far, far, far too many people.

Will felt a bump from behind and instinctively checked his wallet.

Still there.

He brushed a pigeon from the edge of the bridge with his rolled copy of *L'Équipe* and snapped the paper open, glancing at the pre-Tour coverage. American papers had nothing on this, amazingly detailed stories on each team, rider, manager, mechanic, soigneur and team doctor. Vitamins, bikes, team cars, jerseys and sponsors also got the run up, more detail than even the company accountants ever knew. The course, the peaks, the sprints, the time trials, Will had been living with them all on a daily basis since Paris-Roubaix when it seemed obvious to everyone other than himself that he'd be a member of the Tour squad. For the past week or so, the Tour "race bible" had been his only reading. Too bad. He had a Stephen White mystery that was burning a hole in his bookcase and it would be a month before his eyeballs had enough energy to focus on the words.

Without a break in mental stride, he gazed off the edge of the bridge and down the length of the Seine, toward Ile de la Cité and Notre Dame. The humidity and heavy bitter scent of the river embraced him, forcing him to take deep breaths to clear his mind. God, he thought, I love this city and I can hardly wait to see it again, because that will mean it's over.

He carefully thought around what lay between the visits.

Will and Cheryl were pretty much on their own this weekend. Everyone else on the team — the Europeans — had rushed home yesterday for their national championships. The U.S. Pro Championship came earlier, though Will was never really interested in riding it. It was tough to pull up stakes in Europe, travel across the Atlantic and ride your heart out against a U.S. team that trained for this event all year. Will laughed cynically. Who was he kidding? He had never even been invited to compete, so what was all this righteous indignation? Until this spring, he had been little more than European roster fodder, Ameri-trash wandering the Continent. About all he would have ever been allowed to do in the States was hold the checkered flag at the end, to signal another win by Lance Armstrong.

Will checked his watch. He had only about an hour today, to walk, to wander, to touch the city and restore himself. When that hour was gone, he'd try to scratch up the money to hit a hot restaurant, like Lasserre, then pack his last bags for Lille, catching a late train. Sunday, he'd ride the prologue course once or twice and keep up on Bourgoin's efforts in the French national championship. Early Monday, the photo sessions for the company publicity push would begin. That would be followed by a late team meeting, and, then, three final days of team training, working the prologue and the first few stages of Le Tour, leading to Haven's Friday media party and introductions, infused with carefully scripted appearances by team members between light training rides. Friday night would see the official team presentation for a live French TV show. Then it was Saturday and the start of 3978 kilometers Tour through northern France and the south of England, from Normandy to Brittany and Poitou, through the Dordogne region and into the Pyrenees, two fast stages, then up Mont Ventoux and into the Alps. In the end, whatever might be left of the field would limp home to EuroDisney for the final triumphant ride into Paris before a swelling and fanatic hometown crowd and an international TV audience. In the States, Will knew, that crowd wouldn't know the glory of the sport if you bashed them over the head with a cast-iron bust of Victor Hugo. No, they'd be watching from the comfort of their faux leather recliners, munching Cheetos and waiting for Championship Bass Fishing, up next on ESPN.

He shook off the image.

Ah, this, then, was the life he had chosen, one step above rugby, but four steps below monster truck rallies in the American ranking of sports. Who was he kidding?

He rolled his shoulder and felt the distant pain of the deep bruise. That might aggravate him over the next few weeks, but it shouldn't hinder him.

Will snorted.

Shouldn't hinder him.

He had never been able to perform in Le Tour. He had only completed it twice and both times he was most assuredly in the lower end of the pack. Now, he was high on the roster and expected to be high in the standings.

Amazing what a little murder, death and destruction could do for a man's career goals. He stared at the river flowing under the bridge for a long, humid moment. He was sweating, not from the summer day in Paris, but from his own anxiety.

This was it. This was the one race at which everyone and everything had been aiming all season. The Tour of Flanders, Ghent-Wevelgem, Paris-Roubaix, the Giro, every classic, every stage race in the world took second chair to Le Tour. It was as if the meaning of life, the path of human existence, all boiled down to this one race, the Super Bowl, the World Series and the Stanley Cup, but more, the event that teams had been discussing and planning and dreaming of since the moment the last one ended, if not before the last one ended. This was the capstone, the key, the top of the pyramid, all jammed into three weeks of intense riding, bad roads, mediocre hotels and worse food, all for the greater glory of Haven Pharmaceuticals, and Le Société du Tour de France and its sponsors.

Good God. What the hell was he about to do?

Again, he shook off the thought. Plant it in reality, pal. The race was a killer, no doubt about that, a no-doubt-about-that, damn-it-to-hell killer, which had killed him in the past, quite handily.

Still, he found himself standing on the bridge over the Seine, feeling like a kid at the start of a new school year, at that moment when all the failures of the past crystallize into a moment of promise that screams: "This year, I'll study … this year, I'll work hard … this year, I won't screw around in class."

This year.

Never worked out that way, but you always hoped.

This year, he thought, I won't screw up. I'll ride hard. This year.

He let out a long, ragged sigh.

His hour, alone, with Paris, was over. It was time to begin the long uphill climb to get back here, in one piece, one month from now down a long, nasty road.

Cheryl would be waiting for him back at the hotel. Maybe Deeds would spring for dinner at Lasserre. He had the company Gold Card. Maybe they could ask Godot and Isabelle. They were an item now. Will could use the company, as well as Godot's thoughts on this vitamin business.

That damned thing still stunk.

Will's hand shot up, followed by a sharp whistle. The cab dropped smoothly across two lanes of traffic and pulled toward the curb. A small group of young teenagers, laughing, giggling, enjoying the city, flowed around him like a fast stream avoiding a stump. Will turned with them and laughed. As he stepped to the curb and pulled open the door of the cab, he instinctively felt for his wallet.

Gone.

He smiled.

The empty wallet he always carried in Paris was gone, while his money, papers and keys were still safe in his inside jacket pocket.

"God, I love this town," he thought.

Will reached into his newspaper and drew out the heavy billfold he had stripped from the leader of the pickpocket flock as the kid was stripping him. Will snapped out a 200-franc bill and passed it to the driver. "Royal Monceau, if you please."

The driver pocketed his good fortune and pulled smoothly into traffic.

Will settled back for the last comfortable ride he'd have in a month and remembered what his mother had always told him.

It's good to have a talent you can fall back on.

Tonight, Lasserre. And he was buying.

❁

PAUL VAN BRUGGEN SLICED THROUGH THE LIVER SAUSAGE AND SPEARED IT with the end of his pen. Slowly, he chewed the edges off like a giant might chew off the edges of a parasol. He normally didn't work Saturday at the police labs in Eindhoven, but protected his weekends from the clutches of his bosses. Otherwise, he wound up working them all. "We need this. We need that," van Bruggen nattered, with a sarcastic smile. The bosses could wait until Monday. The magistrates could wait until Monday. The dead can wait until Monday.

But this, this was something *he* needed.

He sat staring at the reports fanned out in front of him: his notes, his files, his results, his analysis, and, the liver of Henrik Koons.

The index finger of his right hand poised on his lips, the fingers of his left twirling a tiny liver sausage umbrella, he stared at the effluvia that filled the table space in front of him.

"Speak to me," he whispered.

"Speak to me."

Nothing was said.

"Speak to me."

The room was silent.

"Say something!"

The phone rang beside van Bruggen, shocking him out of his alpha state, causing him to fling the liver sausage across the room. Off balance, he toppled from the stool, kicking the lab table and upending the tray containing the last above-ground mortal remains of Henrik Koons.

His head broke the fall.

Van Bruggen's eyes fluttered open, flicking away the drops of preservative and congealed blood that dripped onto his head from the white enameled tray that sat cockeyed on the table above. It was, he thought, as his mind rose up toward the surface, like sitting through a rain in the midst of a charnel house.

He smiled. Then, realized where he was. Frantically, van Bruggen scrambled out from under the gory waterfall and crawled toward the lab sink, gagging and retching along the way. He spied his wheel of liver sausage in a corner and heaved again. Without any clear view as to where he was racing, he slammed the top of his head into the bottom edge of the sink, filling the room with a hollow ring. He sank to the floor, feeling a deep, distant nausea.

And, then, the thought hit him, working its way through the threat of vomit and past the threshold of pain. He was aware of all the legal protocols from the major drug companies. He was aware of the illegal drugs that hit the markets. They were all in his computer search. But — what would *not* be there? What would not be in the police files? Something new, of course, but something more. Something freshly brewed in a basement kitchen — or — something old that never made it out of some multinational's testing phase.

This magic bullet that had killed Henrik Koons was new, but it was simply too clean for a homemade protocol. This was big business at work, with a lot of money and research behind it.

Van Bruggen pulled himself up on the edge of the laboratory sink, casually threw up into it and stumbled to his computer, settling into his chair for what he knew would be a long and difficult search.

CHAPTER SEVEN:

ONCE MORE, DEAR FRIENDS, INTO THE BREACH

Will leaned his head back and pointed his nose at the sun. He could feel the stretch at the base of his throat, then along the muscles across the back of his collarbone as he slowly twisted his head to the right, to the left and back again, slowly, very slowly, the crisscrossed road map of veins on the back of his eyelids warming and cooling as the hot spot of the sun crossed back and forth. The day was clear and starkly bright, which was good in a way, as clouds would have flattened the light and made the contours of the streets of Lille vanish within themselves. A sharp sun today would at least give those contours some definition. The blue polarizing sunglasses he wore were designed to provide even more shadow and sweep to the streets, and keep him from squinting his way through the five hard turns and the one sweeping turnaround of the prologue course. In the end, what bothered him most was the humidity, as July 1 in northern France was something like riding at the bottom of a swimming pool.

He twisted his left arm up and glanced at his watch: 4:15 p.m. Five minutes to his turn in the barrel, his start on the ramp, the beginning of his three weeks of personal hell in Le Tour de France.

Out of the 198 riders, he was slotted almost exactly in the middle of the prologue pack. At 2:50 p.m., the first rider began his solo time trial. He was a rider from the last of the 22 teams, after the order of the teams was determined by their previous year's Tour finish and/or current UCI world ranking. Then, one minute later, a rider from team No. 21 was slated to begin in the 197th position, then 196, 195 and so on, leading up, some three-and-a-half hours later, to numero uno, last year's winner.

The weaker riders usually began the parade, although a directeur sportif might give an early start to one of his faster riders, perhaps a sprinter, to grab some excitement, charge the crowd, throw off another team's strategy and grab a top placement if the weather went to hell and speeds were cut dramatically later in the day.

Still, it was usually with the top 22 riders that things truly began to get interesting in the prologue. Richard Bourgoin was listed at 14th, conforming to Haven's ranking. After a disappointing finish last year — a fast fade in the final four stages — Bourgoin had been working on his time-trialing technique, and his climbing and sprinting skills, leading him to tell Will the night before: "This year, I will make it a show."

As for Will, he didn't care about a show, he simply wanted to survive.

Don't crash. Don't lose focus. Don't go slow. Keep your focus. Watch your technique. Keep it smooth. Watch your focus. Don't daydream. Make it fast.

Will stretched his neck again and thought his way through the 7.2-kilometer course, weaving his way, like an exotic dancer, through dreams of the layout. Sprint off the ramp in the Grand Place. Short sprint to a hard right turn, short sprint to a harder left, long, flat straight to a hard left, long sprint to the halfway turnaround, keep the rhythm, keep the rhythm, right turn, back on the long straight, rhythm, sharp right, and into the long final straightaway. All flat — little, if any climbing.

Keep the rhythm. Keep the focus.

He took a quick glance at his watch. Five minutes. This close, you had to watch. In 1989, Pedro Delgado, the '88 winner, had missed his starting time by two minutes and 54 seconds. Rumor was that he was stuck in the can. That was added onto his time for the entire race and he wound up, 4000 kilometers later, in Paris, 3:34 back. Without the mistake, he would have been only 40 seconds off the mark going into Paris, a whole new race.

Quelle tragédie.

The lesson being: don't miss your start time.

Forty minutes before, Will had waved Prudencio Delgado off the ramp. The kid's hard, black eyes had burned a hole through Will's head. Not a word was said, not a damned word. You'd think that the excitement of riding Le

Tour for the first time would have overcome some of the hatred he obviously felt, especially since Prudencio was here only by a stroke of strange, good fortune. Two days ago, Prudencio was odd man out until Edouard Meerbeeke had decided to go wide on a blind turn and run flat out into a Coca-Cola machine that was sitting in the street for a reason no one had yet to completely explain to Deeds. Now, Prudencio Delgado was in his place, riding hard, riding fast and stepping up in the general classification of Le Tour de France.

Perhaps, over time, Will thought, Prudencio's hatred of him would fade. Perhaps, over time, a friendship could develop. Perhaps, over time, Atlantis would rise from the sea and EuroDisney would make money.

Perhaps, over time — over time. Time.

Will flipped his arm up again and glanced at the watch. Five minutes.

Time stood still when you — time stood still?

"Where the ... where the hell — Ross! Ross, goddamn it!"

Will froze for a split second, then swept up his bike with one hand, the urgency in the voice of team manager Deeds breaking into his last-minute musing and sending him, in a dead, yet, clumsy, run, toward the starter's ramp.

"Goddamn it, Will — you're up and you need every goddamned second available to you if you're going to help Richard and wind up someplace other than the back of the goddamned broom wagon!"

He could hear somebody else calling his name, somebody on the P.A. system, calling his name as if, as if, *shit*, as if it was his starting time. He had started counting it out to himself as soon as he swept up the bike: 8-9-10-back of the starter's box ... 11-up the stairs ... 12-13-leg over the seat, right foot into the cleat ... 14-short breath ... 15-push off. He was on the road, Le Tour had begun, at least 15 seconds late and more than a dollar short.

His left foot found the pedal without thinking and he was up and out of the saddle, pounding hard toward the first turn, 500 meters ahead. He was pushing, pumping, harder and longer than he had planned. That 15 seconds. Have to make up the 15 seconds.

Watch the rhythm, watch the ride.

Will tucked in on the drops of the handlebars, ignoring the aero' bars stretching out ahead of him. There were two tight turns coming up and, despite years of riding with the things, he didn't trust laying out on the bars during a tight turn. He needed the low center of gravity and the control of the drops.

Coming up. Hard right. He was doing well, he thought, rhythm was good. Watch the line. Watch the line. He dropped in close on the turn, bringing his right leg up to the top of the stroke and holding it for a split second during the peak of the turn.

As he pushed the stroke through, the force brought his lean back up to center and righted the bike. A half-kilometer down and another turn, this one to the left. He stayed in, tight on the drops, tucking in to cut the humid weight of the air as much as possible.

Damn, this stuff was thick. It was like riding in a steam room.

Watch your focus. Don't lose sight. Watch your focus.

The turn came up quicker than he expected, very hard to the left, almost a hairpin. He tucked in, found the line and brought his left knee up the to the top of the stroke. Will dropped into the turn, tight against the barriers and started to come out wide, too wide. The rider before him, one minute out front, had obviously misjudged the turn. He had flown across the street and driven himself, full force, into a metal barricade covered with nothing more than a thin Credit Lyonnais banner. No one had been around the corner to warn Will or the motorcycle cop that preceded him; and now, in panic, the rescuers and the rescuee were scrambling to get out of their way. Will nailed his rear brake and threw his weight to the side, sliding the wheel out and bringing him safely through the turn. The problem now was that his rhythm had been shot in the foot. He rose out of the saddle and began to pump hard, trying desperately to bring the force of his legs, his waist, his chest, his entire body down on the crankset, rather than throwing it side to side in a futile and wasted pumping motion on the bike.

He glanced up as he began his sprint down the longest straightaway of the course, only to find one of the course gendarmes dashing in front of him, so panicked by the crash and the sudden appearance of Will and his police escort that he couldn't find any escape from the course other than a straight line down the Boulevard Vauban.

"*Bougez!*" was all Will could think to say: shift it!

And shift the gendarme did, taking one giant step to the right, just enough for Will to slide past on the left — and clip him, hard, with his shoulder, which exploded in a burst of deep-seated pain.

Will swallowed hard, forcing a wave of nausea back down into his lower depths.

Damn, he raged. Rhythm off. Pain in his shoulder. Off the pace, late out of the gate, off the pace. Damn. He rose out of the saddle and drove hard for the next turn, still more than a kilometer away.

"Where were the damned officials!" he cursed aloud, using a rising anger to fuel his speed. His mind began to race away from the moment at hand, to rage at the broken watch and the late start and the heavy, wet heat of the day, and the....

Will moved into the stretched-out awkwardness of the aero' bars. Keep your arms narrow. Watch your focus. If you lose your focus, you lose your race. Pay attention to where you are and what you're doing.

Next turn, left turn, onto another long straight. He stayed up in the aero' bars for it, taking the chance. He had never been a master of control on the damned things.

Left leg to the top of the stroke, pause, lean, whoosh, through, shift from the top, fly, now, damn you, fly.

The crowd, he sensed, was huge, even now, midway through the seemingly endless field. It had to be six- to eight-deep in some spots and solid through the course. He was riding on a gray ribbon of asphalt and cobbles through a sea of humanity, as if it were Moses on the motorcycle just ahead who had split humanity in two.

He realized, suddenly, that except for the few moments when he had raced down the ramp at the start, and as he chased the gendarme down that first, long straight, there was no sound. Those two moments had only intruded into his internal watch, as if his hearing had turned itself inside out. He heard nothing more than himself, and that, only at a distance, his breath and his heart holding the focus and staying with the road, even if his mind refused.

He was in a bigger gear than he needed now, trying to build his cadence and keep the pace up to a point where he could make up what he had been losing all along the route. A spot of rage continued to burn within him, deep inside, as he worked over the missed start and the control mistakes.

Force it back, he thought, force it back.

The sweeping turn around a traffic circle approached.

He shifted himself back to the drops, clicked down a couple of gears, coasted smoothly around the long turn, and then rose up out of the saddle sprinting to regain the rhythm. He slid the bike back and forth beneath him and began to feel the power build. He was finding the focus, finding the pace. Yes, indeed, finding the power.

He stayed tucked in tight, now, on the drops. This was the ride he had been looking for since the start of the day. He had finally found it. The faces rushed past in a blur of color, his eye reaching down through the waves of people, sharp right back into the Boulevard Vauban and its long straightway, then the final smooth right turn and the finish just beyond. He couldn't hear his heart or his breath anymore, nothing other than the wind, the wind he was generating himself. He was in the pipeline. He was part of the road.

Drop right, smooth through the turn, never losing the line, he could hear a rising cheer from the crowd in the back of his mind. He held a tight line and hunkered down on the pedals, in the big gears, for the burst to the final turn. The front line of barricades and the people leaning over them were only inches from his right arm. The excitement they felt was filling him with a renewed strength and a rising hope for a great finish.

He brought up his right leg for the final turn and felt, rather than heard, a roar from the crowd. A white-blue-and-red form appeared tight on his right, a Banesto jersey, the rider who had left the box seconds after Will. The shock and surprise of seeing him appear so suddenly, so unexpectedly, threw Will for a second and he rose up out of his tuck, losing his focus, losing the top end of his pace.

"*Shit!*" he yelled, and immediately bore down on the drops of the handlebars. Now, what had been a mental walk in the park to the finish line became a desperate challenge for Will. Whatever had come before in today's race, he was already a minute down from this guy, and God only knew how far down from the leaders. This was horrible. He was starting a 2500-mile race from the back of the pack. From the back of the damned pack. From the back.

A small voice rang from behind his ears, "Where you always start it. Where you always finish it."

He shook off his own voice, his own doubts, and tucked in behind the

Banesto rider in a sprint for the finish. Ignore the rest of it, man, now it's a race. Now — now, it's a race. But the rider for the Spanish team was already up and starting to fly. Will missed the move and jumped late, forced to play a last-minute catch-up game in the rush toward the line. His spirit broken, Will drifted lazily over to the right and crossed the line a full second behind the Spaniard.

Will braked and coasted through the crowd at the finish toward the Haven enclosure and the relief of a chair and a bottle of water that he knew were waiting there for him.

Oh, god, what a mess. A 7.2-kilometer course and he had been passed. Between his late start and shitty ride, the guy had made up a full minute on him. You needed 20 kliks for that, usually, unless, of course, you were riding like a complete *putz*! Now, a new rage replaced the momentary relief of having crossed the line. Somewhere, somehow, he had completely botched the prologue. He had lost a full minute!

God, it must have been like watching some kid on a damned tricycle!

He braked to a stop before reaching the crowd barriers and stepped off the specially designed time-trial bike. His rage got the better of him and he picked the bike up and held it over his head. The crowd around the enclosure leaned forward in anticipation. Cameras snapped and buzzed, their motor drives trying to catch the moment when the American drove the 15,000-franc bike into a car windshield or the ground or some reporter who just happened to be walking past at the moment.

But that moment passed, as Will's anger subsided and he realized that it wasn't the bike at all. It was him and his own lack of power and his own lack of talent and his own … lack.

Will lowered the bike, climbed back on the saddle and started to weave his way through the crowd at the finish toward the Haven bus. He couldn't stop sweating. The crowd closed in on him, not to congratulate him, not for a quote, but just, there. There were hundreds, it seemed, many unwashed, and the humidity was making it all seem so close, so tight, so unbearable.

Will couldn't catch his breath. He had to make it through this crowd to the orange plastic fencing that blocked off the huge Haven team bus from the rest of the world. He kept working his way through the patch of people that had gathered at the finish, but they were all working against him.

"Come on! Come *on*!" he bellowed, angered not only by his work in the prologue, but the fact that he couldn't get to the damned team bus.

Now, he was getting nasty about it all. His temper was up, along with his blood pressure from the ride, and he was losing his patience with this mindless wall of faces that just wouldn't let him through!

He pushed people out the way and finally burst through the crowd at the gate to the Haven enclosure.

"Here …" he almost threw his bike at Luis Bourbon, the team's lead mechanic. Luis looked at him with understanding. "Thank you for not cracking the bike."

"*De nada*."

Will was panting hard and sweating more than anything he had felt on the course. He could feel the blood pounding in his ears and the pressure on his jaw as he clenched his teeth.

Then, he felt the calf.

His right leg jammed up like a knot of Silly String. The pain exploded in his calf, his stomach, his chest, his head. It took his breath away. The crowd that had ignored him, even as he pushed angrily through, now turned as he, at first, squeaked in pain, then, roared, clutching, blindly, at his right leg.

He couldn't move. He couldn't walk. He hung there, on the orange plastic fence post, trying to take the pressure off, trying to catch his breath, desperately trying not to throw up.

Will began to hobble toward a plastic folding chair set on one side of the bus. He hopped on his left leg, desperately gasping, trying to slide his right leg behind without stepping down on it. The calf muscle exploded to nearly five times its normal size in pain.

"Here."

He felt the hands take his left arm and pull him over toward the chair. Instinctively, he put his weight on the shoulder of his Good Samaritan and felt the glory of pulling up the right leg. The pain didn't go away, but it subsided to the point where he could actually breathe again. The chair, now, was only a meter away. Will hobbled one more step, then spun off his savior's shoulder and landed heavily down in it. For a second, a split second, he thought the damned thing would burst beneath him; it would just be his luck this day, but the chair held.

Finally, he thought, life is going my way. Life, hell, the last five seconds, are going my way. Let's not get carried way with this life nonsense.

His head back, his eyes closed, he tried to center himself and catch his breath, again, for the second time since his had crossed the line, when he felt two powerful hands kneading his contorted calf muscle, breaking down the rock hard knot and freeing him from the explosion of pain that had brought him to the point of collapse.

He kept his head back for a moment, his eyes closed, and concentrated on releasing the knot mentally. The phantom masseuse had already broken the top layer of the knot, now it was up to them both to break the internal mass that was making him want to spew breakfast all over the Place de la Republique. The fingers found the trigger. Will jumped a bit, then felt the immediate release. He took a deep, lingering breath and slowly lowered his head, opened his eyes and gazed at two, deeply tanned and absolutely amazing breasts. He gasped, involuntarily, then choked, and leaned forward as if to stand.

Magda Gertz placed her right hand on his chest and pushed him back into the chair.

"Not yet — you're not done."

Oh, yeah, thought Will, I am. I am now, at this moment, completely and totally fried.

She smiled at him in a delightfully crooked way and looked back to her work on his calf. Will felt somewhat ashamed. Her breasts weren't talking to him, but his stare would make you believe that he and the two of them were lost in a deep discussion as to how to save the world. He looked to the side, took a quick glance back, thank you God, then leaned his head back, stretching himself out along the chair.

Magda Gertz smiled.

Mine.

She found a knot, dead center along the soleus, about half to three-quarters of the way up the leg. She positioned her finger and pressed in — hard.

Will bolted, trying to rise up on his left leg and pull the right away, struggling desperately for some safety from the pain. She had found the real trigger, deep inside his muscle, that one spot, sometimes the knot itself, sometimes not, where the fibers and the nerves had bunched together in an internal form of red-meat gridlock. She was the cop on the scene and she made it flow again, but she had to kill some drivers to make it happen.

Magda Gertz held tight to Will's right leg, wrapping her fingers around from the front and increasing the pressure of the dig. Will's eyes began to fill with tears. Magda turned him, slightly, back toward the chair and he lowered himself into it, slowly, as if the pain might go away if he were careful.

And it began to fade.

"What the … what the … did you … do?" he croaked.

"You can't recover if it's all bunched up like that. Can't recover at all. And if you had gone walking on that — just the wrong move and you could have split that muscle, heel to knee. Do you want that? I don't think so."

"No. No," he wheezed, out of breath.

"I don't think he'd want it, either." She cocked her eyes to the side and let go of the trigger. She went back to a deep massage of Will's calf.

"What in Jersey Joe's shorts are you doin', woman?" Deeds slid up to the side of the injured rider.

Without changing the rhythm on Will's leg, she looked up at Deeds for a moment and smiled.

"You should work on the rhythm as you walk, Carl. It will increase your speed, your comfort and your attitude."

"What the … Gertz. Goddamn, Gertz. What are you doing here?"

"Saving this rider's Tour. Maybe his career."

Deeds stood by the side, obviously expecting Magda Gertz to drop everything and stand to give him a hug. She remained focused on Will's leg and it annoyed Deeds no end.

"This boy might not have a Tour after his performance today. Tell me, Will — getting to the line … on time … mean nothing to you?"

"My watch stopped, Carl."

"You prepare for that, Will. We were looking for you."

"I'm sorry, Carl. I only lost 15 … maybe 20."

"I'm sorry, too, Will. You lost 40. And that wrinkle on the turn set you back another four or five, and then your breathtaking speed and stellar smoothness lost you even more."

"How much more?" Will asked, the enormity of already being 40 seconds down before his Tour even started, before he even stepped on the bike, making him sick to his stomach.

"A minute from what was seen as the average pace — about 8:45. You did it in 9:40. The guy who passed you did it in 8:39. There are still …" he glanced down at his start list "… 30 riders to go. The fast ones. You should be well off the leader board by bedtime. Hell —" he croaked out an angry laugh, " you are *now*! You never even made it close. God, Cardone was right!"

"What right?" Magda said, making herself a part of the conversation.

Deeds shot her a glance, weighed the question quickly, then opened the door. "Miguel Cardone made a pitch last night and again this morning. Lightning Jack here peaked at the classics — Paris-Roubaix. Not just season peaked, *career* peaked. The Giro was the top end of his downward slide … Midi-Libre was a *joke* … and now, this — Mr. Champion misses his *goddamned start*!"

The words hung heavy in the air. Will couldn't think of anything to say. His mind was blanker than a summertime school blackboard. He stared forward, finding a spot on the tarmac just ahead.

"So?" It was Magda Gertz, pushing the conversation.

Getting no response from Will, Deeds turned his attention completely to her.

"So, after today's performance, I might just take Miguel up on his suggestion and let him ride shotgun for Bourgoin. Might help you learn to stay on time. Hell, Cardone started 22 spots behind you and is a full 45 seconds ahead. Fascinating, ain't it?"

"Which means, that without his late start, without having to pick his way through the accident at the Boulevard Vauban and then having to reestablish his rhythm, that Will and Cardone had nearly the same time. Fascinating. One man rides without problems, does his best, does well, what he sees as 'good,' while the other rides a course filled with barricades of his own and others making all along his way and still performs — despite …" she said, holding up one hand to staunch Deeds' next argument, "what the clock says — and you say … hey … you're no damned good, maybe I'll replace you like the man with the noisy ambition wants. Carl," she whispered conspiratorially, "you're better than this. Don't let your ambition blind you to what is real around you."

Will never thought he would live to see it. Carl Deeds cornered in an argument. Deeds stewed for a moment, then, took a huge, deep breath as if to reset his temper.

He turned slowly to Will.

"Sorry, Will. It happens to everybody at one time or another. I … suppose. We'll meet tonight at the hotel." He stole a glance toward Magda Gertz. "But your lawyer isn't welcome."

She made a face and laughed.

Deeds smiled and quickly gave her a glance, up and down, lingering in no one place on her body.

"Lookin' good, Magda. Looking good."

She smiled. "Thank you, Carl. Always nice to see you."

Deeds turned to head back to the team car, in which he'd follow Bourgoin. Over his shoulder, he shouted, "As for rubbing his legs, Magda, we have hairy, ugly men to do that — don't ruin him for us."

Will watched his directeur sportif, the team director, climb into the brand new white Fiat, supplied by the organizers.

Will had been a part of the conversation, but not, necessarily, of it. He sensed a real connection between Deeds and this woman, to the point that, oddly enough, Deeds was walking with a little more style, a little more rhythm, a slightly smoother gait.

Will turned back to Magda. She flipped her blonde hair to one side, out of her face, and smiled. A very warm, very winning, smile.

"Thanks."

"It was nothing," she said, starting to walk away.

"Wait, wait," Will hobbled after her, gingerly beginning to reintroduce his calf muscle to the real world. "We, uh, were never really … we never met."

She turned back to face him.

"Magda Gertz. Tour fan."

"I'm Will Ross. Uhhhh …"

"And what is it you do, Mr. Ross?"

He laughed, suddenly at ease with this Nordic vision.

"I … uhh … cause problems for my bosses and make them lose sleep wondering why the hell they would hire me to ride bikes."

"A pleasure."

"Yes, a pleasure."

They shook hands and Will felt a surge of excitement run through him. Wow. This woman was charged.

Positively.

"How, uh, how do you know, uh, Carl?"

She laughed, throwing her head back again. "Carl and I go way back — I used to do medical for a few of his teams."

"Control? Drug testing?"

"It was testing — but it was product testing. Research and development work. Nothing spectacular. Just out of school. I was the new girl on the street."

"New kid on the block."

"What?"

"Nothing."

"I left that … but I come back. I like the riders. I like the sport. And I like to help out where I can."

"Well … thanks. My leg feels better than it has in weeks."

"Work it. You're setting yourself up for a big muscle tear if you don't. Every night and every morning." She turned.

"I, uh, can't really do it alone."

Magda Gertz stopped and turned for effect. She turned from the waist, one quarter of the way around, accentuating her ass and her chest. Her head came a bit more, throwing her hair to the side in a long, slow and glowing arc.

"You don't have to …"

"You'll be around?"

"There are hairy, ugly brutes who can do it for you. Supplied by Haven."

Will deflated, visibly.

Magda Gertz turned back and began to walk away.

"Don't worry," she called over her shoulder, "I'll be around."

She smiled to herself, no one else a part of it.

As if on cue, Cheryl Crane walked up, a billboard of Tour passes and credentials. The humidity of the day had worked a number on her hair and makeup. Will turned to greet her and started visibly.

"Thanks a hell of a lot." She watched the crowd ebb and flow around the departing Magda Gertz. "Who was that?"

"I dunno, really," Will answered blankly, "some friend of Carl's."

"Well, can I give you an important safety tip?"

"What? Yeah, sure."

She leaned closely and whispered in his ear: "They're not real."

And then she bit down. Hard.

PAUL VAN BRUGGEN WIPED A PIECE OF SLEEP FROM THE CORNER OF HIS EYE and casually flicked it toward a corner of the hall. It was biodegradable, he mused, so it's not really littering. He was late. The schedule he had been trying to keep, clearing the police files for the district of Eindhoven as well as searching for his mystery drug, had brutalized his schedule. Today, it was almost noon as he dug in his pocket for his key chain.

He rattled the keys in his hand, trying to find the one that fit the lock of the laboratory. There, the blue one. He blinked twice, and again, trying to clear his eyes as he fit the key into the lock and turned.

There was no resistance. The door was unlocked.

He quietly turned the knob and pushed the door open, slowly, following the edge of the door with his head to peek inside the laboratory, set to spring down the hall toward the safety of the police officer's break room if he was surprised by an intruder.

The room was empty. The room was quiet, with the exception of the computer fan whirring quietly in the corner.

He had left at 10:30 the night before after another 15-hour day, the computer running on alone, continuing the search for his missing formula, digging through the files of the regulatory agencies of Belgium and Germany, the Netherlands and France for something that had been registered for testing but never made the market for one reason or another.

Obviously, he had failed to lock the door behind him.

And yet, as he thought back, he could see the blue key in his hand last night.

Ach. He was losing his mind. Too many long hours in a poorly ventilated room filled with exotic chemicals and decaying flesh. It could happen to anyone.

He dropped the bag containing his lunch on the main lab table and walked toward the computer station, flipping the lights on in the laboratory as he passed and peering quickly into the corners just to make sure he didn't, in fact, have any last-minute, unexpected company.

Obviously, he was losing his mind. The lab was empty. The vials and files were untouched. The computer sat alone in its corner patiently blinking an answer to his query.

He sat in the hardwood office chair and stretched his eyelids one more time. He took a deep breath and reached for the mouse. It was his personal moment of truth.

Just above the bottom of the screen flashed the words: 'Search Complete.'

He moved the cursor from the "BACK" icon to the "FORWARD" arrow and clicked twice. The screen went blank for a moment, then brought up a page from a French registry, the first of nearly 500 in the report.

The title line caught his eye: 'Cytabutasone/HP.'

As did the next, in a thick, red type: 'Discontinued.'

WILL STARED AT THE CEILING OF THE ANCIENT HOTEL ON THE SOUTHERN outskirts of Lille. There were better hotels in the world, and there were better rooms in better hotels in the world, but Deeds had told the Tour organizers not to place the Haven team in any of the modern chain hotels, such as Ibis or Novotel. Deeds was a traditionalist, if, in fact, the word traditionalist referred to someone who liked staying in hotels that Napoleon would have refused. So, instead of lying on a king-size bed, watching cable TV, here he was, in Le Tour de France, searching the water stains of a plaster ceiling for pictures of the Madonna.

Will slowly refocused on the blue bag and watched the I.V. drip, drip, drip, then run down the long, plastic tube into his forearm.

"I hate this stuff."

"Hate what?" Henri Bresson rolled over, pulling the I.V. closer to the side of his bed with the movement.

"I hate I.V.s. I hate needles."

"I don't mind the needles," Bresson said, almost dreamily. "What I mind is Monsieur Engelure digging around in my arm searching for a vein. Once, twice, three times rooting around. I wouldn't mind if he were a nurse with *grande* tetons, but it is just him with his scraggly beard and bad breath. That … is what I hate."

"I understand."

But, in fact, he didn't. Will couldn't understand how anyone could look forward to the needle, no matter how it helped in recovery, both for muscle or energy output. It was necessary in Le Tour now, as the stakes were simply too high to rely on nothing more than homeopathic medicines or straight, out of the bottle vitamins, or good nutrition and a decent night's sleep.

Will glanced over at his roommate. The tensions of the past few weeks had faded into memory as the Tour team had been posted. Will was assured a slot, but Bresson had been riding the rough and ragged edge. Meerbeeke, Cardinal, Delgado and Bresson had all been waiting for the word to come, the axe to fall, and, when it fell, it fell on Delgado. Chance had put Prudencio back in the field, and, chance had brought Bresson to one more starting line.

Would he be at the finish? Will looked up the tube to the I.V. bag, a slow drip, drip, drip sure to keep him flat on his back for another 30 minutes.

"Enough," Will said, sitting up and pulling the needle from his arm. He jammed a piece of cotton down on it to staunch the blood that dripped from the hole in his arm.

"Engelure will have a fit."

"Indeed, yes, indeed. But I raced for nine minutes today."

"A bit more than nine."

"A bit more than nine minutes today."

"A bit more like 10."

Will began to laugh.

"Yes, indeed a bit more like 10. It would have been less than nine but I was busy looking at a broken watch for 40 seconds and then came around a corner determined to run a Michelin up some official's Sans-a-Belts. But … it was less … *less* —" he emphasized, poking a finger toward Bresson, "— less than 10. And because of that — I don't need no damn drip tonight."

"Engelure wants a full test. Right from day one."

"Yeah, and I want a Porsche and a Blaupunkt and a woman named…."

Will froze and stared at the window.

"A woman named…."

"A woman is all I want," Bresson said, a dreamy air in his voice. "I don't care what her name is."

Will stared at the window and felt a grip tighten around his heart like a tennis ball in a vise. He was about to say Cheryl.

But the face in his mind had been someone else altogether.

DINNER HAD BEEN INCREDIBLY UNSPECTACULAR.

Whatever contributions the French had made to the world of food, they sure as hell hadn't come from this chef, this hotel or this meal. The food was bland, soggy, overcooked in the case of the pasta and undercooked in the case of the meat. Will sawed into the steak, a pale brown on the outside and a deep, cold blue on the inside. The thought that only hours ago this had been one cold cow turned his stomach.

He twisted his face into a Brando look and said, with a voice that crossed the line somewhere between Brooklyn and Jersey City, "Hey, Cheech, it's all fatty."

Bourgoin looked up from the plate of spaghetti he was devouring. In a muffled voice he asked, "Is that, smack, another movie?"

"Yeah, it's 'Serpico.'"

"Never saw it."

"You ought to."

"Good?"

"Naw, but Pacino's beard is great."

Bourgoin barked a laugh and sprayed bits of pasta across the table at Miguel Cardone.

"*Augh*! *Jesucristi*!"

It had been a perfect shot, thought Will, catching Cardone full face. He'll be picking those off for days. It could have only been better if it had been planned.

"Oh, lighten up, Miguel. You're likely to get sprayed with all manner of stuff in the next few weeks."

"Rain."

"Mud."

"Little tiny rocks."

The table seemed to come to life in the home version of "Can You Top This?"

"Coca-Cola."

"Wine."

"Cow manure."

"Sheep shit."

"Field run off."

"And that's just from the riders," John Cardinal cackled at the end of the table, breaking up the crowd.

"Road kill."

"Skunks."

"Frogs."

"Dogs, cats, birds."

"Grease."

"Oil."

"Exhaust."

"Vomit."

"Piss."

"Diarrhea."

"All manner of gas — farts, burps, belches — with hitchhikers and without."

"And little bits of pasta. You should be happy. You've already got one down."

"Delightful."

"Well, Miguel," Will said, leaning forward, "you see a bit of everything on the Tour, a little of this, a little of that — and a lot of shit. You name the shit and you see it."

"And you, I suppose, see it all from the back, eh, Ross?"

The chatter at the table froze and hung in midair, replaced by a collective intake of breath as the entire squad turned to face Will and catch his reaction.

Will paused, slowly lifting his eyes to meet Cardone's. The smile that had been part of the fun only moments before now had an edge to it, a cold and somewhat brutal edge that no one had seen before. They leaned forward. Only those closest to Will and Cardone could hear what was said, and later that night, they talked about what it would mean to the squad and its chances in Le Tour. Bad karma, they thought, with two team members so openly antagonistic toward each other.

"Not this year, asshole," Will had said, sotto voce. "I may not win, but I'll sure as hell be ahead of you."

Cardone didn't react.

He didn't need to.

He had gotten what he wanted.

THREE A.M.

Will stood at the window, his head leaning against his arm, leaning against the cold plaster surrounding the frame. It was, tonight, about the only cool thing in the room.

For all the money that Haven had thrown at the race, and the team and the riders, you sure as hell didn't find much of it in the choice of accommodations. The rooms were small, spare and very cold, if only in atmosphere. Without air conditioning on a hot and humid night like this, they were unbearable.

The heat of the day had simply moved inside, leaving the outdoors still and heavy and a few degrees cooler.

Will wiped his eyebrow, which had grown thick with a bead of sweat.

He had to get some sleep, but the heat and his own anxiety were getting in the way.

He had to be up in a few hours, on his way downstairs for a team meeting and 7:30 a.m. breakfast — and more of that hideous pasta. Then, after a 9 a.m. departure from the hotel, he faced a 10:30 start in Euralille and the 234-kilometer stage one to Armentières.

'Mademoiselle from Armenteers, parlez-vous? Mademois....'

He felt a bit guilty about Cheryl. She had called and left a message. They hadn't connected tonight. Now, she was likely already up and moving through her lists, picking off the nuts and bolts of today's stage. Strangely, though, it was this Magda on his mind, more of a fantasy than a real woman, but what a fantasy.

"Back off, monkey girl." Will laughed, then quickly tried to cover it. He could hear Cheryl. He could see her. She wouldn't take an ounce of anything from this Magda dame. Will smiled. The image of Cheryl grew in his heart, replacing the zipless fantasy form that Magda Gertz had taken on during the course of the long, hot evening.

Wonder how well she knew Deeds?

His focus changed from the stars to the half-moon hanging dully over the French countryside ... to the few clouds that ranged idly by, to the steeple of the church and the sharply domed houses of the town, to the industrial-styled roof of the brasserie across the street, to the lamppost, to the window, to the sill of the window, when he realized that, finally, after a night of tossing and sweating and worry, he was dropping off. He slowly shuffled to his bed, so as not to break the spell, and slid between the rumpled sheets, asleep before his feet reached the end of the bed.

Henri Bresson was still awake.

He had listened with interest to the argument of Ross and Cardone at dinner. He had been in the midst of arguments just like that throughout his career. There's always one rider in your face, he thought.

Bresson reached under his bed and felt for the black leather pouch. Running his finger along the edge gave him a sense of cool security, something far more than any other piece of luggage he had ever owned.

It was a race. It was a career.

It was one more season in the sun.

CHAPTER 8:

DANCING AT THE RASCAL FAIR

The knock came about 7 a.m. One of the new soigneurs, there were three now, not as cute as Cheryl, but rather short and round instead, gave two knocks and some sort of grunt, then wandered down the hall to hammer on Bourgoin's single room. It was too damned early as far as Will was concerned. He hadn't been able to fall asleep until somewhere around 3 in the morning, and everything preceding that had been fitful tossing and turning in the turgid atmosphere of the cramped room.

He knew he would dread it.

For the next three weeks, he knew he would wake up, fully awake, 30 seconds before the soigneur got to his door and would dread the knock that started another day. It would be no different from elementary school, when his mother would stick her head in the room and chirp, "Rise and shine — daylight's in the swamp."

He came to hate that, too.

Henri Bresson snored quietly over on his side of the room. Will padded over and kicked the side of the bed, somehow hoping, deep inside, that he might break a toe and wind up on the sidelines for the next few weeks, in a somewhat less traditional hotel, with air conditioning and room service. No such luck. Bresson grunted, rolled over toward the window, and began snoring again.

"Go ahead," Will mumbled. "I leave you to your fate."

He gave the bed one last kick. Sharper. No luck. His foot was fine.

Bresson belched and grunted. Will kicked the bed one more time.

"Come on," he whined.

Bresson belched again. Interesting reaction, he thought.

Will stumbled into the lavatory and peed. There was a tub, but no working shower. Rather than go through the entire ritual, he simply rubbed himself down with alcohol, wondering if Jean Jablom's old saw that it toughened your skin was true, dressed in a Haven parachute-cloth training suit — "So light you can almost fly!" — and wandered back into the room. He would put on his race uniform after breakfast.

Bresson sat on the edge of the bed, looking far more the worse for wear.

"Morning."

"Uh huh."

"Better get a move on, once we've got a quorum assembled, Deeds likes to start his morning meetings."

"Uh-huh."

Will knew Bresson would be there. Henri hadn't missed one yet.

Entering the restaurant, more of a lobby nook, Will took a bowl off the sideboard and filled it with muesli — a combination of cereal, raisins, nuts, wood chips and whatever else the kitchen help had sitting around. He tossed some strawberries on top and poured on a bit of milk.

"*Café, monsieur?*"

"*Oui, café. Noir, s'il vous plait.*"

The coffee came and Will stared at it for a second before sipping. Gawd, it was wretched. For a country that was supposed to be so damned concerned about cooking, it really did hate food, didn't it?

Will looked up from his small, black cup of hell and let his eyes wander around the table. Bourgoin looked worse than he did, as least as far as he could tell from the inside of his own face. Cardone looked grumpy. Deeds was immersed in paperwork, wearing enough logos and passes and Tickets of the Day to look like an explosion of subscription cards from a fashion magazine. The others wandered in looking shell-shocked. Nobody slept well in the heat. This did not bode well for the next three weeks.

Only Tony Cacciavillani looked wired for sound, still tanned from the Giro, rested from almost two weeks of light training after dropping out of the Midi-Libre on stage three and ready to go. He was ready to fly, ready to win.

He must have gotten laid.

"*Buon giorno*, teammates."

"Why're you in such a damned good mood?"

"Life, my American friend."

"You sound like somebody out of the movies."

"I am somebody out of the movies. I am 'The Flash,' the fastest man on earth."

"Flash is out of the comic books."

"That is the movies."

"That is the comic books. I know The Flash. I owned The Flash. My mother threw out a pile of The Flash that would have made me rich. You, sir, are not The Flash."

"You wait until this afternoon … my slow, late, friend — then you will see The Flash."

"No, some teenaged girl in Armentières will see The Flash, or would it be, 'Little Flash?'"

"That is a horrible thing to say." Cacciavillani stuck out his lip in an exaggerated pout, then burst into laughter that filled the room.

"Perhaps I will call him Flash from now on."

"I'm not sure you want to — you might scare them off."

The table came slowly to life.

More of the team arrived, including Bresson and Delgado. The room began to fill with the sounds of chatter without direction, crossing the table, crossing the room, loud and full of life.

"I'll leave you by Le Cateau, today."

"Do you know anything about Banesto's new sprinter?"

"By Le Cateau? I'll have you waxed by the top of Avesnes."

"What … because I'm Italian, I should know every Italian in the world?"

"What? That's Category 4 — that's barely a bump in the road. No, you'll be watching my ass today."

"Well, you'd have a better chance of knowing the Italians in the race than I. Do you know the guy?"

"I would not be betting on that idea."

"Yes, I know him."

"First to Seclin buys."

"And...."

"Buys what?"

"And what?"

"Dinner."

"Jesus! Is he any good?"

"Dinner's free."

"Yes. He's Italian."

"Is that all?"

"Is that all?"

"Yes."

"Yes."

"Jesus."

Deeds raised his hand to end the conversation, but the chatter continued apace, the room filling with sound, the volume on the upswing.

Magda Gertz then stepped down the two tiled steps into the room.

She was dressed as one might be for a tourist's vacation in the Greek Islands: peach slacks, a matching halter in a slightly lighter hue and her blonde hair pulled back in a tight ponytail, tied off by a peach scarf. She wore a black lanyard around her neck that ended in a Tour pass laying across the top of her breasts.

Tony C. muttered aloud, "Oh, if only I were that piece of plastic."

Will snorted, then realized that he, too, had stopped talking and was staring.

He also realized that everyone else at the table had stopped talking and was staring.

Magda Gertz realized it as well.

"Good morning, boys."

And the boys, caught in their wide-eyed stare, turned with embarrassment back to the table.

"I should bring her along," Deeds mumbled to himself, "for effect, if nothing else."

Cacciavillani had heard him. "There is, dear Carl, always something else."

"Give it up, Tony. She's at least 20. She's too old for you."

"Put her in the back seat of the car and drive ahead of us, would you?"

Deeds turned his attention back toward the team.

"A housekeeping note: Monsieur Engelure is most annoyed. Two of the vitamin I.V.s were pulled by the riders rather than the med techs. That could cause infection and knock you out of the ride. Bourgoin and Ross, don't do it any more. Also, Engelure is reminding us how important it is to take your entire I.V. every day. Otherwise ... you will not get the full measure of wonderful Haven vitamins that will propel you across the line at a very high rate of speed — at least, that's what the ads say."

He looked around the table at the riders, some nervous, some excited, with some of the younger riders, Paluzzo and Delgado, fearful of what lay ahead.

"Eat up. Eat wise. Remember — you've got a long stage today and a long way to go. This is only the start."

"Yesterday was the start," Cardone said, "and Ross missed it."

Will wondered when it would come up, and now it had. He waited for the explosion from Deeds, the hoot from the team. It never came.

"What was it, Will? Watch?"

"Yeah. Battery died."

Deeds dug in a bag and tossed him a small, leather case.

"Henri Bergalis sent this over for you. Thought you could use it."

Will opened the case to find a new training watch. An Ogden. Top of the line, from its sleek lines down to the two stopwatches on the face. The Haven boss liked the finer things in life, which made his friendship with Will Ross all the more questionable. Will smiled.

"If I break my watch, can I have one, too?"

Deeds ignored the crack from Cacciavillani and went ahead with his description of the first stage.

"What we've got here today is 234 kilometers, lots of flats, some rollers, and two climbs, both category fours, nothing much to worry about."

"Yes! Sprinter's day!" Cacciavillani grinned and shoved his arms in the air.

"God, don't you ever wind down?"

But Will knew the answer: Tony C. couldn't wind down. It wasn't a part of his makeup. The sprinters were a breed unto themselves. The beginning and the end of the Tour were about the only times they'd be able to shine or have a chance to spend a day in yellow, building up points for the green jersey, the sprinter's prize. Once they were in the foothills of the Alps and the Pyrenees, into the mountains, the sprinters would begin to splinter, fall back, and work toward nothing more than simply maintaining their points position and avoiding elimination on time.

"The category four climbs — what have they got?"

"Glad you read your race bible, John. One's about 150 meters off the flat, the other about half that. Shouldn't be a problem. Gentlemen — and I use that term loosely —" Deeds said, staring hard at Cacciavillani, who, moving his head slightly back and forth, seemed to be undoing the snap of Magda Gertz's brassiere with his eyes, "you are responsible for knowing what you face here today and every day. I'm not your mother."

Cacciavillani continued to lose himself in the chest of Magda Gertz.

"Tony, I'm not your mother."

"Yes, mama. No, mama."

Deeds slapped him on the back of the head.

"We've got the start in Euralille at 10:30, then a ceremonial one in downtown Lille at 10:45. Then, about eight-and-a-half kilometers of neutralized riding through the town before we actually hit the official start a few minutes after 11 a.m."

"Why all the ceremony?"

"Because it's the first massed-start stage of the Tour, and the Greater Lille Chamber of Commerce spent over a million bucks to be a part of Le Tour and le television. You listening to me, Ross?" Deeds said.

Will shook his head and feigned shock, "Geezo-peezo, Carl. I was the only one who was listening to you. Everybody else was scoping the dame."

Across the room, Magda's eyes shot up. She wasn't used to being called a dame. She wasn't used to being called much of anything. In fact, it was she who usually did the calling.

The Haven table leapt into a chorus of voices, 20 conversations from 10 people.

"Enough," Deeds waved his hands, "*Enough*!" It quickly settled.

"You've got three sprints during the day and one feed zone. You've got two guys to think about today. I want Richard competitive and I want Tony up front. Tony, you know where you'll have to be...."

"I have sprints at 36, 160 and 220 kilometers, then the final sprint in Armentières."

"Ah, so you have read the book."

"Carl, I am a pro."

"Indeed." Deeds said sarcastically. "Will, keep tight to Richard. You've got the radio today. I'll be in your ear."

"We still only have one of those? How did I get so lucky?"

"Good living and that's your damned job. Besides, it's a new one, with a transmitter that fits in your pocket, so not only will you be able to hear me, I will have the distinct pleasure of hearing you respond to my orders, Mr. Ross."

Will saluted.

"The pack will likely split and reform before and after each sprint, with some possible attacks on the bigger of the two climbs, that's just after 90 kilometers. But I don't expect anything spectacular and I don't expect anybody to be out there killing themselves. This is day one and it's a long way to Paris. You're not going to win anything today."

"Who's in yellow?"

"Newcomer. McReynolds … Brit. The guy who went after the hour record on the washtub bike. He wants to still be in yellow when we cross the Channel. Matter of pride."

"He's got three days to get there, a lot can happen," Will remarked.

Cardone couldn't resist the opening. "A lot can happen, Ross, in 40 seconds. What are you now — two minutes out of the yellow?"

"He's out of the yellow, Miguel," Bourgoin said coldly, "but so are you. Without Will's late start, he's still five seconds ahead of you. And you — had no problems along the way."

The room grew uncomfortably quiet.

Deeds let it linger for a second, then, then picked it up.

"Tony, I want you in the middle of that sprint when we hit the finish. I want Richard up and close behind. We lose no time here — nada. This is the best year we've had … since last year anyway. And this year, none of you has to deal with Jean-Pierre. So let's get out there and do our jobs and make Haven proud and win this race. I am convinced — convinced — we can do it. This year, more than any year. Right. Any questions?"

"Can I get some new muesli? Mine's all soggy."

The room exploded.

Deeds looked at Will with frustration. This wasn't going to be easy.

Will froze.

Two hands had slid onto the back of his shoulders and up to the top. The hands were smooth and silken and moved with a gentle grace. He could sense her before he heard her, before he smelled her.

Magda Gertz leaned forward, over Will, and looked at the Haven table. The laughter froze in mid guffaw. Even Carl Deeds was silent and staring.

"I just wanted to say," she said, in a slow and quiet search for the proper English, "that I wish you the best of luck."

The back of Will's head was alive with nerve endings, each hair follicle searching the air desperately for a brush, a touch, a graze. He stared straight ahead, stiffly, hoping that he wasn't turning to a raspberry blush before her and the team.

She smiled and squeezed Will's shoulders, then turned to leave, brushing her cotton halter against the back of Will's head. His scalp was suddenly electrified, as if he had just kissed a 220 line.

Now he was blushing.

"You will be around, won't you?" Tony C. called after her.

"Oh, yes," she said, over her shoulder. "I'll be around. In your dreams, Mr. Cacciavillani."

Tony C. smiled. "I am ..." he said stiffly, "... an 'appy man."

The entire team watched Magda leave the room, with the exception of Will. He didn't need to watch her leave. He could feel it. The back of his head had sprouted eyes, like an atomic potato.

The blush began to fade from his face, leaving only the pattern of scars that he had won in a crash at the Ruta del Sol at the beginning of the season glowing red. His face looked like a map of the Martian canals.

Tony Cacciavillani looked over and grinned.

"And how, my friend, is your 'Little Flash?'"

It was Will's turn to laugh.

NINE A.M.

Will finished suiting up. No need to pack his suitcase, as they'd be returning to the hotel after the stage — the stage was one big loop, and the finish in Armentières was only 20 kilometers away from Lille. He stretched in the gloomy hall and zipped up the new Haven jersey. This was Le Tour. Nothing old. Everything new. Everything bright. Everything shiny.

He felt the tug of his right calf.

Everything except the rider.

He stepped back into the room and began to stretch the leg again for the third time. He felt it pull, almost fighting him, as he worked his foot forward and back, forward and back. He'd have to watch this. There was a time when he could just loosen himself up on the bike, but that was long ago and far away. He was bustin' to flinders in great, grimpen chunks. Old age was a bitch. Thirty-two years old and he was ready for the home.

Bresson was turning his head in lazy circles, loosening his neck and shoulders. They hadn't said much today, as there was nothing much to say. The breakfast meeting had laid out the jobs of the day and Henri's was little more than housecleaning. Watch the pack, be ready to jump, to pick up the pace or slow it down, to gum up the works or carry a message, sacrifice and self discipline, the world of the water carrier.

Will had been there and should still be there, he supposed. He knew where Henri's head was living today, and it wasn't at all a jolly place.

"You coming? Team van is ready downstairs."

There was a loud crack of a vertebra in Bresson's neck, and his shoulders sagged.

"There. Got it. My neck was giving me fits."

"Ready?"

"In a minute. I've got a few more things to pack in my race bag."

"Okay." Will turned to leave. "Henri — ride with me. We're the old men of the team. Let's ride together and keep each other's spirits up."

"As much as possible," Bresson said, never turning away from the window. "You ride with the big fellows, now, Will. I am not really a part of that world."

Will understood the feeling. It was a class structure to be sure. Will picked up his gloves, helmet, sunglasses and race shoes and stepped out of the room, quietly closing the door behind him.

Bresson waited for a moment, then reached over and pulled the faded cotton sheer across the window. Instantly, the small, gray room grew more stifling, as the last trace of a morning breeze was blocked.

He reached under the pillow and pulled out the rolled leather pouch. Unfurling it, he reached for the classic glass syringe, needle ready, filled with the heavy yellow liquid. Just 1 cc to start, just enough to take the edge off the ride.

After all, Henri Bresson was still a virgin. He had no idea where this would take him.

Or for how long.

Or at what speed.

Or what might await him at the finish line.

THE PELOTON, THE MAIN PACK OF RIDERS, WAS STILL NORTH OF VALENCIENNES. Just beyond the city, the climbs would begin, toward Avesnes-sur-Helpe. These climbs weren't much, really, hardly more than speed bumps, but a rider could feel the drag on the ring unless he was buried inside the pack, using the power and pace of the group to lift him up and over.

These same riders were already thinking ahead to the two stages in the Pyrenees; then the Alps, where the climbs would kick up and over 2000 meters or 2200 meters, day after day after day. Ventoux. L'Alpe d'Huez. Val-Thorens. God himself couldn't help you there. It was the simple reality of mountain and man and machine.

Mountain wins.

Every time.

Will had stayed close to Bourgoin for the first 50 kliks, waiting for a word from Deeds that never came. No reason for it. Nothing was happening. There were no attacks, not even from the rookies looking for a taste of first-time Tour glory and media exposure. Not a peep. It was a quiet ride in the country at a steady, monotonous pace, the danger coming, not from the speed, but from

198 riders packed like coleslaw on roads far too narrow for their safe passage.

Bourgoin faded to Will's right and took up a conversation with Willard Kruse, one of the other Tour favorites. It had often been a battle between Kruse and Indurain over the past few years, with Miguel the Machine effectively crushing competition. But this year was different. Kruse had been training at altitude in Colorado, and Bourgoin wanted to know about life in Vail.

Will already had been there, done that and, so, drifted away. Bourgoin was safe for now. Will slid to the middle of the pack and glanced around, looking for a familiar face. He saw one up ahead, wearing the colors of Lexor Computer.

"Hey, Webster."

"Hey, Will, how you doing?"

Will knew Chris Webster from a year on a British sponsored team that was more of an embarrassment than a contender. Only Webster had survived the bloodbath at the end of the season with something even approaching a promotion. While the rest of the team, Will included, had found themselves sweeping up for the peloton, roster fodder for weak teams at best, Webster had nailed himself a prime slot with Lexor, even going as far as making a run for the Giro d'Italia this year.

"How're the wife and kids, Chris?"

"Growing. Thrilled that I'm away — thrilled when I come back. It's a good life. You oughta try it."

"Tried it once. That's enough."

"Sorry to hear about your wife."

"What do you mean 'hear' about it — it happened right in front of you. If you hadn't broken left, you would have met her face to face."

"You know what I mean."

"Yes. Thanks." Talk of Kim — his recently departed ex-wife, run down in a high-speed Belgian sprint this past spring when she wandered onto the course without looking — scratched sharply over the recently formed scab. It was time to change the subject. "Hey — how about that rider of yours — the drug death?"

"Who? Koons? Don't know if it was a drug death. No one is quite sure what happened to him. Found him dead in his apartment. Cops said it looked like drugs, smelled like drugs, walked, talked and quacked like drugs, but nobody found a duck."

"So what did they call it?"

"Drugs. Unofficially. Officially, it was the Dutch equivalent of 'death by misadventure.' I've always liked that term."

"I've always been fond of 'death by old age after a great meal and marvelous sex.'"

"Good luck."

"Then or now?"

"Both," Webster said with a smile, rising up on his Time pedals to push through the crowd and back to his team leader.

The brush with Valenciennes, which was also on the route of Paris-Roubaix, had already passed, quickly, smoothly. Will heard the radio crackle in his ear. It was the first contact he had had with Deeds and the lead team car since before St. Amand-les-Eaux.

"Yeah, what's up?"

"Find Bourgoin. You're approaching the first climb. You'll want to stay with him in case he needs anything or if anybody jumps."

"What do you mean if anybody jumps? This group is about as aggressive as a tour group in Cozumel."

"Will, there are times I just don't understand you."

Will laughed. "Is that supposed to be some sort of code?"

"What?"

"Never mind. Hey, Carl, we just passed Valenciennes."

"Yeah, so?"

"Wanna go visit your knee cap?"

"Fuck you."

"Maybe you can get your shoe back."

"Like I said...."

"I know."

The static grew, then faded in the midst of Deeds's message. "... Bourgoin and stay with him."

"Aye, aye, skipper." Will had fallen back a bit in the pack through the radio conversation, so he rose up on his pedals and scanned the crowd of 130 riders ahead of him to find Bourgoin. He found McReynolds easily, the man in yellow riding high out of the school of barracuda surrounding him. They were waiting for his move, his insight, his break, hoping without hope, that some of the magic would rub off on them.

Kruse. Pantani. Jalabert. Bresson.

Bresson was riding strongly near the front. Interesting. Great. Good for him. The Haven team leader was behind and to the left of Bresson, using the Breton's strength to pull him through to the front on the now ascending road. The pace was slowly beginning to grow, as much as to simply get to the feed zone and the finish line as quickly as possible, as to deal with the upcoming climb and end the madness. This was Le Tour, the greatest race in the world, but the hard reality was: this was a six-and-a-half-hour day on the bike, and everyone pretty much wanted to get it over, done and out of the way. The only one with any real stake was Winston McReynolds, hoping to hang onto to the lead and the yellow jersey for another four days until well into his home territory of *Angleterre*.

Will picked a line and began to follow it through the pack, working his way up to Bourgoin's rear wheel. There, he'd evaluate the situation and either pull Bourgoin or Bresson along in his slipstream or simply ride along. Whatever. It was time to go to work.

Will's new bike was a slick piece of machinery. Fresh out of the box from the Colnago bicycle works in Cambiago, geared with top-of-the-line Campagnolo Ergo levers, it damn near sang on the road. The problem being, it didn't sing to him. Not yet, anyway. It was a bike, simply a bike. Great bike, to be sure, but merely a bike.

Will pulled up to Bourgoin's wheel, then pushed a bit harder to bring himself alongside. He wished, somehow, that it was "The Beast" beneath him.

"Hello, boys — how's tricks?"

Bourgoin, over the past few months, had slowly loosened up, even on the bike, even in the midst of a crisis or a blast for the line, to enjoy sparring with Will.

"She is fine."

"Ha! Nicely done. Didn't expect that from you."

"Henri … *ça va*?"

No response. Will started to say something again, but noticed quickly that Bresson's focus seemed sharp and total: his form was great, his technique smooth, his reflexes top line. He was obviously in another world, and talking would only break the spell. Will could only figure that today, for whatever reason, Henri Bresson was in the pipeline. This was his day, his stage, his race, just as Will had felt at Paris-Roubaix three months before. Best to sit back and let him lead the way.

Bourgoin tucked in behind Bresson, with Will behind the team leader. Their wheels came within centimeters of each other as the pace increased. The first of two climbs lay just ahead, with half the stage left to go beyond the peak. It was subtle, but Will continued to feel a gradual increase in speed, as if they were actually on a slight descent rather than an incline.

Bresson was slowly, almost with quiet deliberation, beginning to roll away from the pack, taking Bourgoin and Ross with him, like two twigs caught up in a wave. The wind-up was so quiet, so slow, so unobtrusive, that most of the pack didn't notice anything. It looked from the back as nothing more than repositioning.

As the three riders drifted from the pack and formed a tight paceline, Will said one word into his microphone: "Breakaway."

THE HOTEL IN LILLE HAD QUICKLY GROWN QUIET AGAIN, FOLLOWING THE team's departure to the start. The summer heat had put an end to all unnecessary movement and chatter. All that remained of the Haven team at La Punaise Couchez was a pile of post-race bags that Cheryl and two soigneurs were loading into the back of a van, which they'd drive straight to the finish in Armentières. So many people had been in and out that Monsieur Lucher had stopped watching and was napping behind the counter.

He never saw the person in the lobby.

He never saw the rolled-up black leather bags.

He never saw them being slipped, quietly, carefully, into two of the rider's parachute-cloth satchels.

All he saw was the movie playing on the inside of his eyelids, while all he heard was the sound of his own, rhythmic breathing as the heat and humidity of a summer day rose to their peak.

THERE WAS A CRACKLE OF STATIC IN HIS EAR, AND THE SOUND OF SHUFFLING, as if someone had keyed the microphone in a panic, then, lost grip, bobbled it and finally came up with it, only to have nothing to say.

"Who? Who?" The tone in Will's ear was frantic.

"Us." Will whispered.

"*What*?"

"Us. Damn it, us."

"Goddamn it, Ross — you and these goddamned out-of-the-book breakaways. If I could get you right now I'd wring your goddamned neck!"

Will slid back a bit and struggled to keep up with Bourgoin's rear tire.

"Jesus, Carl, it's not *me* — it's Bresson. The guy is nuts!"

"Shit. Shit. Shit. Shit. You got company?"

Will took a quick glance behind him. One Lexor rider ... one Banesto ... and two from the Lotto team were reacting, bridging the widening gap up to the Haven break.

"Yeah. We've got company. Four, maybe five taking notice."

"Settle Bourgoin back in. You've got 130 kilometers to go. Hold Bresson if you can. He's jumping too damned early."

"He's not listening, Carl."

"Goddamn it, everybody thinks they're Eddy Goddamn Merckx on this team! When is somebody going to listen to me!?!"

"I listen, Carl."

"Shut up, Will."

Will gave a short, sharp whistle that caught Bourgoin's attention. As the Frenchman looked back, Will gave a short, sharp drag of one finger across his neck. Bourgoin understood immediately. Kill the break. Bourgoin turned and whistled ahead to Bresson, who never reacted, but continued in his steady staccato drumming toward the crest of the climb and the finish line 130 kilometers beyond.

Slowly, Will and Bourgoin fell back into the peloton, which had looked upon the last few moments as a feint, while Bresson and four other low-level riders disappeared up the road. Bresson was alone at the front. No one was there to help him. No one was there to take a pull at the front. Henri Bresson was doing it alone.

Too soon was right, Will thought. He had jumped too soon. Bresson was looking at 80 miles at the front of a killer paceline.

Not even God could stay out that long without help.

THE BUZZ OF THE INTERCOM STARTLED GODOT. WITH LE TOUR NOW IN FULL swing, the corporate offices of Haven Pharmaceuticals had become as cold and quiet as a mountaineer's boot. The sharp buzz of the intercom made him jump, in such a way that an infant smoke ring leapt out of his mouth at an angle and was pulled toward the exhaust fan, looking more like a map of Montenegro than a perfect circle.

He pressed the button and coughed, loudly. "*Oui*?"

"How attractive," came the disembodied voice of Isabelle Marchant, his secretary and lover. The speaker cracked once and hummed loudly. "How much longer are we going to be here?"

"What do you have in mind?"

"I could use an early dinner and a show."

Godot smiled. There was romance in the air tonight.

"What kind of show?"

"A good show. And an expensive dinner."

"It is still an hour until quitting time."

"The cats are away. Isn't it time for the mice to play?"

He smiled to himself. Indeed. Every manager of Haven Pharmaceuticals was in Lille, supporting the team and schmoozing with other sponsors and clients, enjoying an all-expense-paid vacation while trying to impress Henri Bergalis that, yes, indeed, some work was getting done. Some vacation. Besides, Godot couldn't stand cycling. It demanded exertion, and everybody involved in it was a flake. He had learned that lesson this spring.

He pushed the intercom switch. "Any ideas for this evening?"

"Not a one. Which makes it exciting, wouldn't you say?"

Indeed.

He crushed out the end of the Cohiba and turned the exhaust fan to high. By tomorrow morning, it would still smell of cigars, but at least the blue haze would be gone. He opened the door and flipped out the lights of his office.

"Ready, my dear?"

Isabelle didn't even look at him, but in what seemed to be one smooth and swift motion, turned off her computer, switched off her desk lamp, covered the computer with a plastic sheet, turned her phone to voice mail, snagged her purse and stood up.

"Yes."

Luc Godot laughed and offered his arm. Isabelle took it, then scrunched her nose at the cigar smell wafting off his jacket.

"I'll change. Five minutes. Five minutes at home. I'll change."

"I should hope so."

They moved toward the door and he reached for the light. Just as he flipped the switch, he noticed a thin manila envelope sitting on the edge of his "in" basket.

"What's that?"

Isabelle turned back with a glance and shrugged. "Late mail. I'm not sure."

He sighed. He glanced at the envelope, then at her, then back at the envelope. She tugged on his arm and he looked back at her. "It will wait. It will wait, I think, until tomorrow."

She smiled wickedly. "Who says we'll be coming in tomorrow?"

"Indeed." Luc Godot laughed. "Indeed."

They stepped out the door and drew it shut with a deep "clack." The slight breeze created by the door made the overnight envelope, balanced on the edge of the mail basket, sway, then fall, face down, on the deep ocher carpet, obscuring the initials "P.V.B." typed neatly in the corner over the legend, "Laboratory. Eindhoven Police District."

THE MAIN BODY OF THE PACK WAS ONLY EIGHT SECONDS BEHIND THE SPRINTERS at the arrival in Armentières. The entire peloton had picked up power and speed on the rush into town, gathering up those rude enough to try and get a jump on the crowd. The sprinters had worked their way to the front and began to break, sweeping past the vulgar interlopers and sprinting toward the line. With such a flat and easy stage, no one had really been working all that hard, no one had really considered the race to be truly started. A few early breakaways were nothing to worry about.

Yet, as the top five sprinters crossed the line, the first with both arms up in a victory salute, they had failed to notice that one rider had stayed away, one rider had stayed out, one rider had stayed clear.

Bresson, breathing hard and sweating heavily in the heavy July air of northern France, was already off the bike and gulping down water when the second place finisher took his empty victory salute.

Somehow, Bresson had slipped the net of communications and spotters and checkpoints. He had never been taken seriously. Now, it was far too late. McReynolds was still in yellow, but the shock of seeing the communication in his ComNet team fall apart so utterly and completely, was almost too much for him to bear. He watched Bresson mount the podium for the stage win and turned to flay his team manager, his directeur sportif.

Will had brought Bourgoin in early, pulling him up toward the front in the main field sprint. They'd all get the same time for the stage. Nothing much would change in the general classification.

Except, of course, for Bresson, who was playing leapfrog through the standings, much to the dismay of some of the greatest riders in the world, much to the delight of the international cycling press. The reporters had been writing for weeks about the favorites and the tactics and what would happen when. Here, then, was someone and something new, a face out of the back of the pack rushing forward to claim his prize much to the shock of those around him.

What a story.

Will rose two spots in the general classification. He had gained 10 seconds on two hapless riders. Bourgoin dropped to 11th, due to the jump of nearly 50 positions by Bresson, who was now in fifth.

It had been, by all accounts, a spectacular day.

A little too spectacular.

❂

LOUIS ENGELURE STOOD BY AS THE HAVEN TEAM DOCTOR EXAMINED BRESSON'S eyes, his heart rate, his blood pressure. Deeds leaned into his face.

"What the hell is going on here, Bresson? You suddenly get deaf?"

"No. I suddenly got strong."

Engelure moved between them, protecting his charge, one of the few on the team who would listen to him and had actually been enthusiastic about the vitamin regimen. Deeds kept moving to one side, then the other, trying to see and talk around the sweating research director.

"Is there something here I should know about?" Deeds asked with an edge.

"Like what?"

"Like … help?"

"The help is vitamins — my vitamins," Engelure barked.

"Shut up, you."

Bresson looked surprised, then insulted by the question.

"Nothing. Nothing at all. It was simply…."

"What?"

"It was simply my day."

"You don't have a day. Not when I'm running this show. You completely ignored me."

There was a knock on the van door.

"Medical control. Bresson and Bourgoin."

"No randoms?"

"No. Not today."

Deeds turned back to Bresson.

"Time to pee in the bottle. You better be telling me the goddamned truth here, Bresson. I run a clean shop. You do this shit — get me in trouble again — and I'll rip your lips off and use them for doorstops." He was nose to nose with Henri. "You got me?"

"*Oui.*" Bresson gently pushed Deeds to one side and rose, stepping toward the door of the bus. He looked at Engelure and smiled, giving him a thumbs up, before stepping out into the heavy sunshine of Armentières and walking over to the medical control van.

Engelure smiled and watched as Bourgoin followed Bresson toward control and the golden bottles full of answers.

"You see? You see? They won't find anything because there is nothing to find. No banned substances. You ..." he pointed harshly at Will, "you ... and Bourgoin decided that you wouldn't need any I.V. You wouldn't *need* my vitamins. You *see* what it did *today*? That could have been *you* on the podium."

Will wasn't listening. He was too busy scratching his nuts. He had to get out of these shorts, quickly, or he'd have all kinds of problems down the road, the itch, or mushrooms or saddle sores the size of a duplex. The damned shorts, after hours in the saddle, were a jungle breeding ground for every hideous bacterial organism known to man.

Engelure kept talking, blindly, while Deeds fumed and Will stood in the back of the well-appointed, yet already messy, Haven team bus, furiously digging at his naughty bits like a spaniel who just discovered he had the ability to do so, when Magda Gertz stepped onto the top step of the bus platform.

All three men stopped what they were doing and stared, Will with his hand still deep inside his riding shorts.

Magda Gertz smiled.

"Is it an itch you have ... or are you happy just to see me?

CHAPTER NINE:

PARRY AND THRUST

Cheryl Crane stomped heavily into the cool of the Haven team bus, a day on the road, in charge of a variety of difficult and minuscule details having taken its toll on her. She was worn out, frankly, and didn't care who knew it. She wore the flushed complexion and the slightly dirty sheen of someone who had been in the dust pit all day.

She stepped up off the steps and stared at Magda Gertz, tall, blonde and beautiful, not a hair out of place, then swung her attention to the men of Haven, Deeds and Engelure hovering around Gertz like flies on a dead wildebeest. Will, meanwhile, danced maniacally in the background, his shorts around his knees, an open bottle of isopropyl alcohol to one side.

"Excuse me," Cheryl mumbled, pushing brusquely past Magda and the knot of gawkers. "Excuse me."

She walked up behind Will and said in a barely muted tone, "You should wait until you're back at the hotel to whack off."

Will jumped, splashing a small wave of alcohol onto his exposed penis.

"Oh, Jesus, Oh, Jesus. Now you've done it," he croaked, clutching at his suddenly flaming member and waving it in the air for relief.

All eyes in the coach turned to face Will, who had, until this moment, kept his nakedness and his cleaning pretty much to himself. Deeds looked embarrassed while Engelure chuckled. Only Magda Gertz said anything.

"Isn't is a little too late in the day for trolling?"

Will turned and buried himself back behind Cheryl in the rear of the bus.

"God, I'm sorry," Cheryl whispered, "if I had known you were going to react like that I would have rung a bell before I came in."

"That's okay. That's okay," he muttered, trying, unsuccessfully, to take his focus off the chemical burn between his legs. Will quickly pulled off his riding shorts and replaced them with a pair of team-issue khakis.

"Rather bold, isn't it?" Cheryl asked with a crooked smile. "You dressing while your friend, the Nordic Princess, and her buddies are on hand?"

"I've dressed and undressed in the middle of a press conference at the end of a race. This is nothing new for anybody."

"Well, it's certainly nothing new for me ... but ... it may be something new for the Fraulein."

"Oh, Jesus, would you just lighten up with that? I didn't invite her here."

"No, you were just the floor show."

"Give it a rest. Look, you've seen it. They don't care. And I'll bet a dollar to donuts that she's seen things a lot more impressive than Major Tom here. Fourth, and probably most important, I can't imagine her being interested. Wait, fifth and most important, it was itching like crazy down there and I had to get the damned things off. At that point, I don't care who is watching."

Cheryl felt a wave of jealousy pass like a warm breeze. "As long as you weren't 'trolling.'"

"Never." He leaned over and kissed her on the forehead, catching just a sense of a long, hot day running last-minute errands for Deeds in the team van. "Besides, I don't have the bait."

"And you run your motor too fast."

"Oh, my. We are particularly chilly today, aren't we? Problems with the soigneurs?"

"Screw you," Cheryl said sharply. "I'm a pro rider who's been reduced to lugging bags across the French countryside and solving all mein commandant's problems." She cast her thumb over her shoulder toward Deeds. "I don't need any of your sarcasm."

Will smiled sympathetically. "Ahhh, trouble in paradise. But just remember: you're still in showbiz."

She slapped his hand away and he laughed quietly. She smiled back and calmly gave him the finger.

"The guy behind the elephant is in showbiz, too," she opened the refrigerator, snagged a bottle of water, and collapsed on the bench seat across from Will, "and as of this moment, I think he's a step higher on the food chain."

"Are you up for dinner tonight?"

"Depends," she muttered between gulps, "depends on Deeds and that damned 'to do' list of his. The thing grows at an alarming rate each and every hour. It's like a fungus."

"Say no."

"Can't. I'm my momma's daughter."

"You say no to me all the time."

"That's different. You're a mealy puke I push around to satisfy my feminist tendencies."

"Thank you, Germaine," he laughed, giving his scrotum one last swipe with the alcohol through the zipper of his pants.

"You know, that's a disgusting image. It's like you're practicing for a pocket pool tournament."

"Wanna break?"

Cheryl barked a laugh and belched.

"My, what a charming tableau."

Magda Gertz had broken away from her crowd of admirers and moved to the back of the bus, stepping between Will and Cheryl as they laughed. Her sudden presence chilled them both.

Cheryl was taken aback. "Sorry. Didn't mean to startle you."

"Oh, you didn't startle me, my dear," Magda Gertz said sweetly, "I just didn't expect a sound like that from a source so dainty."

Will smiled, out of politeness more than anything else. Cheryl Crane was many things, but dainty was not among them. He glanced her way and realized that the expression on her face had not changed, but had merely grown a shade cooler, the flush of the day leaving her cheeks as the unexpected emotional frost chilled her outward temperature.

"I learned it from my brothers," was all Cheryl could think to say. Her only hope was that it might satisfy this woman and make her turn away.

"They must be so proud." Magda Gertz smiled and turned with a snap of the head, sending her hair in a cascade around her shoulders. Cheryl sighed and dropped her head back against the window with a "thunk."

"Will, could you join me for dinner?"

"I'm sorry?"

Magda ignored his mental fog and smiled. "Would you join me for dinner?"

Will shook his head and realized, suddenly, what was being asked. "No,

I'm sorry. I can't."

"Prior commitments?" She smiled without acknowledging Cheryl behind her and leaned, casually, against a wall.

"Yes. Team commitments."

"Well, I'm sure Carl will let you out of them." She called out, "Carl, you will, won't you?"

"Of course, anything for you, Magda," Deeds replied absentmindedly.

"Then it's set."

Will was silent for a moment and Magda Gertz began to stand up. Just before she turned, Will's brain finally clicked into gear. "No, wait. Yes. Yes, I'm busy tonight and no, I can't have dinner with you." The words fell out like silverware dropping to the floor, in a sing-song, irregular pattern. "I can't. I'm sorry."

Magda Gertz looked back at him, her back still conspicuously full to Cheryl.

"So am I," she whispered. She leaned forward. "Some other time then."

Will blushed. When Magda Gertz stood and turned toward the front of the Haven team bus, Will looked directly into the eyes of Cheryl Crane. They were filled with an angry hurt.

He raised his hands in a plaintive gesture and mouthed the word, "What?"

Magda turned at the top of the steps and, waving gaily back into the bus, said, "*Ciao*, everyone. *Ciao*."

The men collected at the front of the bus stopped their chatter and waved, running toward the front of the bus like the Munchkins waving goodbye to Glinda the Good Witch. Will waved absentmindedly. Cheryl waved her right fist with one finger extended.

"That's not very nice."

"Well, excuse me all to hell, Will," Cheryl said sharply. "While you were busy climbing her chest, she was trying to make me guess the date of the dime in her back pocket. I'm sorry. I don't react well to having somebody's ass shoved in my face."

"Calm down. I'm not going to dinner with her."

"That's not the problem, pal," she said, standing up and stepping toward the front of the bus. "The problem is: you wanted to."

Will opened his mouth to protest. But nothing came out. His brain had disconnected again.

CHAPTER TEN:

INTO THE LION'S DEN

McReynolds wasn't going to make it.

Winston McReynolds had been hoping, praying, for a chance to wear yellow through England and through his hometown of Goudhurst on Wednesday. The first Englishman in years to earn the yellow jersey was working hard toward wearing it home, even if only for those few hours in *Angleterre*. It was a big dream, perhaps a bit too big for the time, the place and the man.

McReynolds had continued strong in the first two stages, but his phenomenal time through the prologue course was slowly being chipped away by competitors, the sprinters with the long haul energy and burst of speed at the end, as well his own miscues and those of the team. Cippolini was closing in. As was DuChateau. As was Bresson.

Team ComNet, he had to realize, wasn't strong enough to hold off a serious challenge to the jersey. By the time he hit the Eurotunnel entrance at the end of the 60-kilometer team time trial, somebody else would likely be in yellow.

McReynolds stared at his socks, lost in thought.

Will stood off to one side, watching him watch his socks and felt for him.

Everybody in the world wanted to wear the yellow jersey. In nearly a century, precious few had ever won the chance, and far fewer had worn it in the city where it really mattered, in Paris, at the end of the race.

Unless you could wear it there, unless you felt it on your back it in Paris, the City of Light, it was not an airy Lycra, jersey, but pure chain mail, weighing the bearer down with responsibility and history and a target on his back. You became the hunted. You became dinner. Each and every day, the rest of the pack walked to their bikes, their eyes and minds were on you and no one else.

McReynolds was the hunted and felt every bit of it this morning.

"Good luck, man." Will said quietly beside him, almost in a whisper, but it still startled the man, jerking McReynolds back to this moment in time at the starting line in Calais with a *bang*, and forcing him to realize again where he was and what he was about to do. The Englishman looked at Will for a moment without sight, nodded without thought, then turned back toward his own private hell and stared again at his socks, unraveling a single thread with his eyes.

The yellow jersey was on the line.

CARL DEEDS WAS IN RARE FORM THIS MORNING. THROUGH NO FAULT OF HIS own, he had a rider challenging for *le maillot jaune*. Not, necessarily, the rider he wanted to be challenging for the yellow jersey, but a rider, nonetheless. Henri Bresson stood only two steps down from the throne and everyone was suddenly taking notice, especially after a magnificent ride in the second stage.

Midway between Roubaix and Boulogne-sur-Mer, Bresson had tangled in the pack on the descent of a Category 4 hill, the Mont des Cats, 50 kilometers into the 200-kilometer stage. It was listed in the race bible as one of the day's two danger spots: '*descente sinueuse et étroite*.' A neo-pro lost control on the 'winding, narrow descent,' floated over to the side and touched wheels with Bresson.

Bresson hit the tarmac hard, skittering along on his back, then rolled up and over into the gravel. Blood streamed from his scalp and his ear, while his jersey, and his skin, were in tatters across the middle of his back. His bike was wrecked, the front rim twisted into a rough approximation of the Normandy coastline. The pack watched and rolled by, as the Haven team car, alerted by Will, raced up to give aid and to patch up their highest-placed rider.

Shaking off the pain in his head and the ringing in his ears before starting to shout, insanely, for another bike, Bresson picked up his mangled and twisted ride, throwing it down a short incline into the shrubs and bushes just below. After the team car pulled up, grinding to a stop in the gravel, Bresson ran to it, blood everywhere, as the mechanic pulled a replacement bike down from the roof of the Fiat wagon.

Louis Engelure jumped from the back seat and, with antiseptic wipes, tried to clean some of the blood from the rider's back. As Bresson gritted his teeth through the pain, Engelure whispered to him and Bresson nodded.

The bike was down.

"Are you ready?" Deeds yelled across the hood.

Bresson didn't answer, but threw his leg over the new bike already fitted to him. He paused.

"*Allez. Allez!*" Deeds yelled, waving his hand in a frantic effort to send Bresson back into the fray. The rider ignored the directeur sportif and stared down the road, watching the race vehicles pass in a blur of exhaust fumes, screeching brakes and and gunned engines. Engelure rose again out of the car and tapped the metal and glass syringe with the tip of his finger. He was about to pull up a corner of Bresson's shorts to expose the gluteus when he realized that a patch of the shorts was already torn away. He wiped the blood and dirt away with an alcohol pad, hearing a sharp intake of breath from Bresson, then drove the needle home, hard, hitting the plunger at the same time. He pulled it free, gave the small, clean area one last swipe with the pad, then slapped Bresson on the back again, in the middle of his road rash.

"Go!"

Bresson had risen off his saddle in pain, turned to Engelure with a look of momentary hatred, then returned his focus to the task at hand and disappeared up the road. Deeds called ahead to Will, asking that Cardinal or Cardone sit back and help pull Bresson close the 45-second gap to the back of the pack. Cardone had refused and struck off on his own, but Cardinal had slowed his pace, waiting for Bresson to catch up.

It wasn't necessary.

Despite the blood still running down his face from the tear in his scalp and the pain from the road rash, Bresson rocketed back to the peloton, then picked his way through to the front on the Category 3 climb at Cassel. He used the next, flat, 80 kilometers to his advantage, made himself known at the front, and burst away with the sprinters for the grand finale, taking the stage and moving himself up to third, only 15 seconds behind McReynolds in yellow.

For the first time and only time in his life, Henri Bresson had become the talk of the world.

Listening to the finish commentary in the team car, 45 seconds behind the leaders, Carl Deeds had turned to Engelure and wondered aloud, "What the hell did you give him?"

"Antibiotics for the rash."

"And nothing else?"

"A little something of my own design."

"You didn't juice him? He's got testing as the stage winner."

"No. No. A vitamin package. It works, I tell you, Carl. The vitamins work."

"Apparently so."

"Haven will make millions."

"Oh, good," Deeds said, without the slightest trace of enthusiasm.

*

WILL HAD LEFT DINNER THAT NIGHT AS DEEDS BEGAN TO TEAR INTO CARDONE for the third time, Carl's voice rising in a call for teamwork and setting aside your individual needs in order to help those who *can win* do so, and if Cardone wanted to *remain* on the team he had better get his *act in gear* and do his job.

Will rose and scanned the dining room quickly for Magda Gertz. She was nowhere to be seen. Oh well. It was a dangerous game he was playing here, a moth-to-the-flame kind of thing, especially with Cheryl around, but he couldn't deny that he was aroused. As Will turned the corner into the hall that night, he heard Deeds double Cardone's fine, again, for ignoring his orders. It now stood at 1000 francs.

Will stopped in the lobby.

Earlier, he had tried to talk with Henri in their room, but Bresson was lost in his own world, both of pain, from the accident, which adrenaline had seemed to mask during the race itself, and of thought, as he stood on the threshold of a long-held dream. Could he win it? Could he wear it? And would *le maillot jaune* still be anointing his back in the ride through downtown Paris?

Will understood and left the room for dinner. Bresson would eat there.

Will looked at his watch and wondered if Henri was asleep yet. Maybe.

Maybe not. Rather than go back to the room, he turned to the front door of the hotel and stepped out into the cool of the Calais night, turning toward the sea front six blocks away.

A nagging doubt was fiddling in the back of his head; something dark, something he didn't want to face, for as much because of what it said about him as what it said about Bresson. Will had suddenly felt small for his thought. He should feel happy for Henri and everything that he had accomplished this day.

And yet.

Will stepped out onto the seafront and looked over the gray water in the gathering dusk.

A breeze had kicked up in Calais. Something was blowing in off the Channel. Something was coming in from the sea.

FORTY KILOMETERS INTO THE 60 OF THE TEAM TIME TRIAL AND WILL FELT electrified. He had ridden team time trials before, everywhere from backwoods Michigan to the streets of Moscow, but this, this was something new. In the past, his teams had been little more than patchwork quilts of talent, some strong, some embarrassingly weak, including himself, but this, this was a team riding on the top line, without, at least today, a weak link to pull it off the mark.

Here was a team with two riders sitting in the top 10, Bresson and team leader Bourgoin. They were both in a position to wear the yellow, if not now, then soon. Bresson was within a mere 15 seconds of his moment of glory.

It hadn't been easy.

The course was nothing but rolling hills, climbs that confronted alone wouldn't have caused much problem, but coming in a pack of nine chewed at a team's energy and peeled off the weaker riders by the end. Losing too many riders across the ride could cut into a team's performance and time, as the clock didn't stop until rider No. 5 crossed the line.

That didn't appear to be a problem today for Haven. Deeds's team training was paying off as Haven shot along the coast from Wissant to Sangatte like a machine on rails, shifting, pounding, turning, everything in unison, everything at full power, with both Bourgoin and Bresson leading the way.

Haven was the third team from the end, with ComNet and McReynolds bringing up the rear 10 minutes behind Haven at the start. There was no way, Will thought, that McReynolds's team could keep up this kind of pace. When Le Tour stepped onto the train for the Chunnel transfer to England, someone else would be in yellow, and Will had a vague notion that he'd be rooming with him.

Will shifted his focus once more and took his pull at the front.

Haven flew.

And, as they passed through the finish area before a last five-kilometer loop, the home crowd roared for the French team.

The colors of the day exploded in fluorescent rainbow around them as the team turned into the final straight and began a full sprint toward the line, nine riders in unison, crossing the line together, arms up in a victory salute, looking like a red-black-and-gold representation of the Alps, nine jagged peaks in salute as the crowd screamed in joy.

Minutes later, the ComNet team turned the corner, four finishers with a fifth almost 90 meters behind. The team had been decimated. The four, led by McReynolds crossed. The fifth struggled toward the line as the clock ticked. And ticked. And ticked away. Before the fifth ComNet rider had cleared the white letters of 'FIAT' painted on the finish line, Winston McReynolds was in tears. The crowd was ecstatic.

Today, France would wear its jersey.

Tonight, France would be in yellow.

THE TRAIN ROARED THROUGH THE CHUNNEL, THE TRAIN LINE BETWEEN FRANCE and England carved out of the soft chalk rock beneath the English Channel. Will kept stealing glances toward the walls, fully expecting to see a drip, a drop, if not a jet of water filling the passage and sealing their fate. That could prove to be interesting. The entire Tour was on board this convoy of trains. A little accident like that would bring the race to a stop real fast....

Will turned back to the race bible sitting in his lap. He had been over it innumerable times and knew the next day's Dover-Brighton run like he knew the back of his hand. He stole a quick glance at the back of his hand. That's right, he thought, just like I know that. Where did that little spot come from?

He turned to face Henri Bresson, radiating a glow of happiness beside him on the train, lost in his own thoughts, still wearing the yellow jersey, as if to take it off meant he would have to give it up.

"How does it feel?" Will rolled the bottle of Haven Power Juice in his hand and watched the tiny bubbles foam and break up along the sides. The wretched-tasting orange electrolyte solution was supposed to aid in recovery. It was only aiding at the moment in his growing wish to strain dinner through his nose.

"How does it feel?" Bresson smiled. "It feels … it feels …" he rubbed his arm along the side of the yellow jersey, down the words 'Credit Lyonnais' in black along the top of his left breast, "it feels golden."

Bresson raised the bottle of purple swill the kids down at Haven R&D called "Grape" and downed it in a swallow. He cracked open another bottle and took a sip, filled his hand with vitamins from the box that Engelure had dropped at the seat only moments before and ladled them into his mouth, then swallowed hard, washing the caplets down with the replacement fluid. Strange, Will thought. Monsieur Engelure had not left a little box for him.

Watching Bresson work the vitamins down, Will was thankful not to have them. He cringed at the thought of the rough and rugged little bullets sticking halfway down his throat and setting up a lovely gag reflex here, hundreds of feet under the English Channel. No, the drink was bad enough. Engelure's hard-assed, professional-strength vitamins tasted like crap, as well. Together, Will could only imagine what was going on in Bresson's gutworks.

"I never thought, Will, I never thought that I would be here and do this and feel this — this good. This strong. But, I've done it. You should listen to Monsieur Engelure. So should Bourgoin."

"Richard is," Will countered. "Maybe not as much as you, but certainly more than me. He's taking his I.V.s and swallowing pills by the boatload and getting his rest."

"And you?"

"I hate needles. But, I'm trying. I'm doing my I.V.s. I'm trying to be a good boy."

The short train ride was over. Will and Bresson grabbed their shoulder bags and joined the other riders, walking to a line of buses waiting to take them to their hotels. A handful of fans was there to greet them.

"Eh … *félicitations*!" The young couple smiled and waved, an obvious pride in seeing the yellow jersey on a fellow Frenchman. Bresson waved back, strong, sure, confident. The girl blushed, then, in a burst of inspiration, ran forward to grab Henri around the neck and kiss him deeply, full on the lips.

Bresson kissed her back.

The boyfriend smiled with pride. "We have come to *Angleterre* to cheer for you." Bresson waved. The girl ran back to her beau, smiling and laughing.

Henri smiled, too, and turned to Will.

"Now, wouldn't you like to have something like that happen?"

"With my luck, the only people who would chase me down to kiss me would be little old ladies and people with green teeth."

"*Quelle tragedie*."

"Such is the life of a true stud muffin."

"Eh?"

"*L'homme manifique*."

"Your French is atrocious."

"You ought to hear my Italian."

"No thank you."

"I know how to say 'The frog is in the house' and 'It was not I who made your daughter pregnant.'"

"That is good." Bresson laughed, as they sat down together in the first bus. Then he grew quiet again, the weight of the jersey he wore making itself known through the happiness of the moment.

"Wearing, isn't it?"

"Eh? Oh, yes. Before today I didn't worry about tomorrow. Now, I do. I worry about tomorrow. And Friday. Sunday. The next two weeks. I wonder how long I can keep it. How many stages before I collapse and watch every other rider, worthy or not, ride over my bones. I wonder. I worry."

"There is no reason in the world why you shouldn't wear it right into Paris, man."

"Ah. Do you think Bourgoin will let that happen? Or Deeds? Think I'll get the support? I don't think so."

"Bourgoin will be cool about it. And Deeds wants what's best for the team, which is, in other words, what's best for Deeds. Just ride your best. The team will back you up." He realized that he was beginning to sound like his father.

"Team or not," Bresson whispered, as if to himself, "I will ride my heart out." He gulped down with one swallow the last of the fizzy, purple drink he still had in his hand.

You know, thought Will, I just bet you will. I just bet you will.

❂

BRESSON SNORED PEACEFULLY IN THE NEXT BED. THE ROOM, FOR THE FIRST time in the Tour to date, was cool, the air off the Channel crisp and clean.

Will couldn't sleep.

He had gotten used to the heat and humidity, the sounds and smells of two men, both athletes, sharing a small room with no cross ventilation. He had wished for a room and a night and a breeze like this for the past week. Now he had it, and it was keeping him awake.

That, and the nagging thought that continued to creep into the back of his brain pan. Could he? Would he?

Did he?

Or, was Henri Bresson, in what appeared three weeks ago to be his last season, truly burning as a supernova and taking his one last shot at the brass ring?

Will felt guilty.

Jealousy?

Perhaps.

Envy?

Most certainly.

He rose up and sat on the edge of the bed, leaning his head into his hands and deeply rubbing his eyes with the fat of his thumbs.

God, he thought, give Bresson a break. Even if he is shooting up somehow, he seems to know what he's doing. Other people do it. It exists. Let him live it out.

But, somehow, out of concern, or ego or self righteousness, Will wasn't buying his own argument. Not now. Not tonight. The past-midnight darkness gathered around him and he grew cold.

❋

THE FIRE HAD BURNED ITSELF LOW IN THE FIREPLACE OF THE ENGLISH HOTEL'S carpeted lobby. Will stepped around the wing-back chair to reach the small wood pile and jumped when, out the corner of his eye, he spotted Prudencio Delgado, sitting silently in the shadows.

"Oh, man — you scared the hell out of me."

Delgado said nothing, but continued to stare into the glowing embers of the fire.

Will continued his conversation, out of embarrassment, true enough, but also a desire to reach this one teammate, this one person, this one rider, this younger brother of the man who had been Will's best friend, over time and lousy teams and bad rides and a dying career.

"So...." there was no answer, no acknowledgment. "You're doing well." Again, no reaction. "You did well in the time trial today. Deeds was very happy with you. So am I. Tomas would be proud."

Without a word, Prudencio Delgado slowly turned his head and stared at Will Ross, the fire reflected in his eyes burning into Will. The first flush of embarrassment, of walking on eggshells, was suddenly replaced with a cold, hard anger. Will had played too many games here with Delgado, had taken too much, had allowed it to go on too long. Perhaps they wouldn't be friends, but the days of wearing sackcloth and ashes had reached their end.

Will shifted a bit, foot to foot, then, asked, quietly, "Mind?"

He pointed to the other armchair. Delgado turned his head slowly to look at it for a moment, then turned back to Will.

"Yes, in fact, I do mind."

"Tough."

Will sat down hard in the ancient chair, the cushions sending a cloud of light brown dust toward the ceiling. "So," Will said without any further preamble, "what's your problem?"

"You are my problem."

"Me? How so?"

"You know how so."

"S'plain it to me, Lucy."

Prudencio shot him a glance, then settled back into the corner of his chair, crossing his arms defensively before him.

"You killed my brother."

"I didn't kill your brother."

"Oh, yes," he said, flatly. "You killed him. It was your bike. Your ride. Your ex-wife."

"My ex-wife who was trying to kill me. Your brother walked into the middle of it. He was an innocent bystander."

"Bystander?" His voice began to rise. The small and balding man behind the desk began to stir out of a fitful sleep. "He was a victim. A victim of the games *you*," he pointed hard at Will, "were playing."

"I was just as innocent. I didn't know why I was hired by the team. I didn't know why they wanted me here. I didn't know what was going on." Will felt a sweat break. "I … I was just as much the patsy as your brother. I was being played for a clown, and it was the death of your brother that made me decide not to play that any longer."

"Fine. You should be dead."

"That's right, Prudencio. I should be dead. I should be dead instead of Tomas. But you know what? I'm not. The damned bullet missed me for some reason…."

"It was a bomb."

"... the damned bomb missed me for some reason and my best friend died. No shit. My best friend. And now I've got to tiptoe around his little brother every day like I'm some kind of pariah. Well, I'm not, kid. Have been. Been there. Done that. No more. You're on Haven. I'm one of the leaders of Haven. You want to play ball … get a little civil. You want to place well at Le Tour so you can jump to another team — without any brother-killers on board? Then do well. Somebody will pick you up. But remember something. You can't do well without me. That's right. It takes the entire team to make somebody stand out in this damned race. We've all got to be working together. And you aren't. You're sitting back in the G.C. looking like some kind of goddamned roster fodder. You want that? Fine. That's all yours. But then don't come and blame *me* when you can't get anybody to take a second glance at you."

"I don't want any favors."

"I'm not offering any, kid. I'm not offering any. I'm not offering friendship, a truce or therapy. I'm offering you jack shit, frankly, unless you wise up and start to show that you know what it takes to be a rider in Le Tour de France. Nothing more. You don't have to be my friend, my buddy or my pal. You just be bad-assed Prudencio and ride like hell. Then — yes, then — I'll be happy."

"My brother is still dead" Prudencio said with an empty sadness.

"Yes," Will felt his anger deflate like a cheap balloon. "Yes, your brother is dead. My friend is dead." He took a long breath. "He would be alive — maybe — if it wasn't for me, if it wasn't for my ex-wife, if it wasn't for her boss, if it wasn't for Milan-San Remo, if it wasn't for a lot of things." They both stared at the fire for a long, hard moment. "But, all those things collided. And they collided right over Tomas." Will felt, suddenly, bone-jarringly tired. He hadn't accomplished anything tonight, except to anger Prudencio further.

He rose out of the chair, a cloud of dust that had been angered during the argument rising up with him, past his head and toward the chandelier hanging lopsidedly from the ceiling.

"This doesn't change anything," the brother said quietly.

"Didn't expect it to. Get some sleep," he patted Prudencio's shoulder. "We've got 200 kilometers tomorrow, with quite a few climbs."

Will padded out the door and toward the hall leading to his room. Behind him, he heard Delgado stir, then walk off toward his room in the other wing. Maybe, thought Will, maybe, we've touched base. Even if for a moment. Do it once, you can do it again. Maybe.

He reached for the doorknob and turned it. Locked. Locked. Key. Damn. No key. Locked out of his room, at 2:30 in the morning, with another stage looming up like grim death before him, Will suddenly, like a ton of bricks, felt like he was going to fall asleep right there, curled in a ball on the mat before the door.

He rattled the doorknob, quietly.

"Henri!" he hissed, shaking the knob again.

He heard the click of a door behind him and sensed, rather than smelled, the perfume.

"Are you sure you want to do that? Wake the leader of the Tour at, what, 2:30 in the morning?"

"I'm locked out, Magda."

"I can see that."

"I'm tired."

"I can see that, too."

"I, uhh, left my key."

"Stands to reason."

"I've got to get some sleep."

"Surely."

"So, well … I'll just go to the lobby here," he mumbled, pointing over his shoulder. "Get a key."

"Oh, why wake the doorman? He seemed so happy. Come on." She turned on her heel, the long, white, men's dress shirt she was wearing, billowing slightly in the air around her, the very happy air around her. She stopped at the door, paused for a moment, then, looked back over her shoulder.

"Coming?"

Will seemed frozen in time and space. He stood, staring, after her, then, slowly, dumbly, nodded and shuffled toward her door. She smiled.

Men.

✷

"I HEARD WHAT YOU SAID TO YOUNG DELGADO," SHE CALLED SOFTLY FROM THE bathroom. "That was an ugly business in Milan, the bomb and all. That was an awful early season for you and Haven … but … you were right not to blame yourself. You were a target — that's all — and the brother, Tomas, simply got in the way." She ran her hands along her chin, then touched the bottom of her lips. "It was not your fault, Will. Not your fault at all. The young one must realize that at some point."

The top two buttons of the shirt were already undone. She undid a third and spread the gap just a bit more. She reached to the small, French perfume bottle and touched the stopper to the gap between her breasts. "But it was good of you to talk to him. It was good of you to tell him the reality. Even if he doesn't like you." She smiled. "Though there are some of us who do, Will. Who do like you...."

She stepped out of the bathroom, leaving the light on in a calculated maneuver to accentuate her figure through the thin linen of the shirt. It was almost a presentation.

"Ah, finished."

She strained a bit through the darkness when there wasn't any reaction from the bed. She stepped out of the light to see better, despite the fact that it broke the scene. As her eyes adjusted, she realized that Will wasn't in the bed at all. She quickly scanned the room and found him, asleep, dead to the world, gently snoring, curled into a ball on a half couch in the corner. She considered waking him, working him back toward the bed, then, simply slid between the sheets alone.

You are, she thought, a different one. You'll need some time. And time I've got.

Will concentrated on the couch to keep his breathing regular. When he saw her stretch out in the bed, alone, he began to relax. This love seat was damned uncomfortable, but it was nothing like climbing into bed with Magda Gertz would have been. He took another glance over at the bed, the figure of Magda Gertz clearly visible through the thin sheet.

"Oh, Cheryl," he thought, as he crossed the invisible line, "you wouldn't have forgotten the key."

And he was gone.

WILL STIRRED UNCOMFORTABLY ON THE LOVE SEAT IN MAGDA GERTZ'S ROOM. Disoriented for a moment, he sat up suddenly, then, realizing where he was, shook his head to break down the cobwebs already forming there. He glanced at his new watch. 7:30 a.m. Breakfast. Glancing over at the bed, he noticed that Magda wasn't there. She was in the bathroom. He thought about saying something, thanks, goodbye, something, but decided instead to quietly steal out the door and make as little fuss about the night as possible. He slipped on his shoes, then crept, quietly, to the door, trying, without success, to keep the creaking to a minimum. He turned the knob. When it refused to give, he released the locks, slowly, quietly, acting as if the process of breathing added to the sound. The door pulled free, silently, in his hand and he stepped into the hall.

Thank God that's over.

Will ran his hands through his hair and strode toward the dining room.

Let's see, he reasoned, I got five hours of sleep, if I eat right and stuff myself full of Monsieur Engelure's magic pills, I just might make it to the end of the stage.

Alive.

He caught a glance of himself in a lobby mirror. The scars on his face from the accident with the Peugeot this spring had filled themselves with tufts of whiskers. Given the pale look of a man who got perhaps half the sleep he needed, plus the facial hair, Will Ross looked like a hirsute map of downtown Kalamazoo.

No wonder I scare little kids.

He walked quickly across the lobby to the dining room door and stepped through. The entire team turned, as a man, to face him. No one said a word.

For an uncomfortable moment, it was a stand-off of sorts, until Tony Cacciavillani broke into a wide smile and began to applaud. The rest of the team picked it up, filling the room with noise and laughter.

Will stood silently, his face contorted with embarrassment. Shit, he thought. Now what?

Magda Gertz stepped up beside him. "Don't worry," she whispered. "You're a hero now."

She turned and smiled enigmatically at the Haven team table, before raising her right arm in a fist and slapping her left hand down on the elbow. It could be taken as an insult, or, a boast of size.

The table roared, then, just as suddenly as the noise began, silence returned.

Will followed the others' eyes to the door, where Cheryl Crane stood, bedecked in a Haven team jumpsuit made of a wrinkled and billowed parachute fabric, her neck surrounded by a forest of Tour passes.

She looked at the crowd of riders at the tables, then swung her gaze to Magda Gertz, then on to Will.

Will felt each and every scar in his face sing a tune in a bright red hue.

Cheryl quietly turned and walked back into the lobby.

Swell. He thought. Just plain swell.

LUC GODOT STUMBLED INTO HIS OFFICE AS THE DAY MOVED ON TOWARD 11 A.M. Even to his dedicated mind it had become ridiculous to keep coming in at 7 to an empty building with a management team busy elsewhere. He picked at his mail again, moving closer to the bottom of the pile. Junk mail, mostly. Even those who normally sent him letters had given up in the face of Le Tour and were merely sending him meaningless press releases and slick ads for security equipment that no one other than a techno-amateur could ever want.

The pile had been growing for days, as he had been chasing Isabelle naked through the rooms of their flat. How fascinating, he thought, that in less than a year he had seen one life end and another begin, and had found again the key to life.

Isabelle.

He sighed contentedly. If only she would let him smoke in the apartment. Now that, that, would make life perfect.

He reached for another envelope on the top of the teetering pile and caught the corner of a letter with his ring. As he moved to pull it out, the pile shifted to one side, then back, then cascaded to the floor of his office.

"*Merde*," he muttered under his breath.

He reached down from his chair and picked at a few pieces of mail, then finally gave up the fight and got down on his hands and knees, gathering the collection like a farm girl gathering freshly threshed wheat.

Ads, fliers, a magazine or two, piled up around his knees. Finally, he reached the manila envelope hidden on the bottom. He carelessly tossed it on the top of the pile, then left the pile on the floor.

He pulled himself up and sat down heavily in his chair, the years he had lived and the sex he had enjoyed over the past few days taking their toll on his reserves of energy.

He unwrapped a Cohiba and cut the tip, rolling the cigar with delight in his fingers. He reached for a large wooden match. His hand stopped in midair as the thought crowded into a brain that wasn't particularly crowded at the moment. He paused, sat back slowly as if not to disturb what he was trying to think, and turned his head toward the manila envelope now perched second from the top of the pile of mail, just below a colorful plea from an animal rights group trying to save the Norwegian Blue Parrot.

He brushed the parrot flier aside and scanned the plain envelope below it carefully, trying to catch what had brought him to such a sudden and deliberate stop. It was addressed to him at this address, but without the Haven Pharmaceutical name. The envelope bore the stamp of the Eindhoven police district and the initials P.V.B. in the corner. Godot reached for it slowly and broke the seal.

The four copied sheets, addressed by hand to police inspector Luc Godot, were designed and produced to clear up the confusion surrounding the cause of death of one Henrik Koons, racing cyclist.

Godot scanned the pages quickly, trying to remember his initial interest in this case, other than simple curiosity. He was about to toss the report aside, when within the legalese, one word stood out in bold letters.

What had been a minor mystery to him before now saw the light of a Paris morning. Godot took a deep breath and crushed out the unlit Cohiba in the ashtray.

Hidden in a pyramid puzzle of meaningless words, Godot saw a problem, an 800-pound gorilla sitting in the middle of his office, promising to make a mess of the coming months if it were ever released or acknowledged.

A mouse ran quickly along the edge of the far wall, beneath the couch, then stopped in the corner and rose up to sniff the air of the office, heavy with dread and stale cigar smoke.

Godot did not react to the intruder. His eyes never left a single, boldfaced line in the Dutch police report: 'Cytabutasone/HP.'

CHAPTER ELEVEN:

DIGGING

Godot bit down on the end of the Cohiba and reached to turn the paper toward him. Cytabutasone/HP. He read through the report, the condensed version suitable for those other than research chemists, and shuddered at the description: rejuvenation, recovery, power increase, followed by increasing dosages, liver damage, uncontrollable hallucinations, dementia and death.

Sounds like a fun ride, he thought.

His eyes jumped back quickly to the crime scene photo, pulled from the pile at the end of his sofa which he laughingly called a file system, and noted that just a part of Henrik Koons's corpse was exposed to the world. Fun ride for a while, anyway.

He glanced back to the chemical analysis. Cytabutasone/HP.

I wonder what, he thought, I wonder what that HP stands for? Some medical thing. He puffed the cigar deeply and let his mind wander, then, felt his stomach knot, almost unconsciously. He blew out the smoke as a very slight wave of nausea crept over him.

HP. He knew it, even if he refused to admit it.

Some medical thing.

Or a company stamp.

I hope I'm just guessing, he thought.

I hope I'm not right.

WILL HAD BEEN TIMING HIS MOVE ALL DAY. HE HAD STAYED IN TIGHT, TUCKED behind a batch of hot young riders who would keep him toward the front during the stage. He wasn't looking for positioning to set himself up for the final sprint. He was looking for positioning to set himself up for Cheryl. Because of her experience and position with Haven, she had been asked to drive the team's No. 2 vehicle for the day. What wasn't being said was that a bout of late-night binging had left the usual driver, an assistant to the directeur sportif, nursing an incredible case of what the team was dubbing the "flu."

All Will wanted was a chance to talk with her, if even for a moment.

The team's No. 1 car remained behind the main pack with Bourgoin, the race leader, so when Will slid into a breakaway group and they took a minute's lead, Deeds summoned up car No. 2 to drive ahead to the break. The break probably wouldn't last long, but for the moment, this was as close as he would get to her, and Will knew it.

He eased to the back of the group, then slid in next to the driver's window of the Haven car.

Without looking, he said, "I wish you'd hear me out."

Cheryl replied, without looking, "I wish you'd get the hell out of my life."

Will glanced over to her and saw her jaw set and her eyes straight ahead.

He reached for the door handle, only to steady himself, but there was an immediate shout from the UCI commissaire sitting in the passenger's seat.

"Hands off!"

He waved Will off and turned his attention back to the race.

"I didn't sleep with her!" Will said with sharp desperation. His tone caused the race commissaire to glance across at Cheryl for her reaction.

She never turned away from the wheel.

"Screw you," was all she said, suddenly swerving the car to the left and sending Will spinning away toward an ancient stone fence on the side of the road. He fought for control of his bike and caught it, just as a chase group began to pass him.

He fell into their rhythm and continued the stage, with them, but apart from them.

Two thoughts were on his mind at that moment: first, how he had so thoroughly screwed up with Cheryl; and, second, how his old bike, "The Beast," would have never let him come anywhere near kissing that stone wall.

GODOT HAD BEEN BUSY.

He hated this part of the business, this part that kept him strapped down to an office chair for days at a time while he dug through papers and records and reams of computer printouts. He was in the foxhole, doing the dirty work, checking ream after ream of internal reports pulled from the system in hard copy to save space.

As if this would somehow save space. The room was filled with boxes of paper carried up from the company basement. It looked like a beige mountain range painted by Picasso.

Godot scanned another page of computer sheet and realized his eyes had skittered across the page without ever really seeing anything. He sat back, frustrated, and rubbed his eyes, hard.

This, he thought, was no damned fun, losing your eyesight, so early in the day. He sat back and looked over the room, his eyes stopping at the wall clock. 4 p.m. It wasn't early in the day after all. He rang Isabelle.

"Yes?"

"Is Bergalis back in town?"

"As far as I know."

"Contact him. I need to talk."

"Anything special?"

"Just what you're working on. Wouldn't you like to be done with it all?"

"I'll get him right away."

There was a hard, telephonic click in his ear and he replaced the receiver. He sneered at it. It was one of those classic French phones with the curved handle and mouthpiece. Despite his love of his native country, he wanted one of those hard and heavy black American phones from the 1940s. The great detectives had them. Spade. Marlowe. Columbo.

This was something Catherine Deneuve might use.

Insane.

Godot scanned the room again and realized that the cigar and cigarette smoke had begun to take on a life of its own in the office, almost hanging in clumps along the walls and in the corners, next to the couches. Whereas the rest of the building seemed bright and alive, this small island of smoke had taken on a grayish brown aura.

It turned his stomach.

He reached up over his head and turned the exhaust fan to full, then, walking to the window, pulled the curtains open, wide, and threw open the heavy, wood-framed window. The first breath of air, heavy with humidity, struck him full in the face. He could pick out the scent of auto exhaust, but after the atmosphere of the room, it was almost sweet.

Perhaps, he thought, we should smoke outside from now on.

He walked across the office to the west window and pulled the drapes aside. The room suddenly filled with direct sunlight. Godot turned and almost half expected to see smoke gnomes racing for cover, as if they'd be hiding, crawling and breathing their last in the sunlight.

He struggled with the century-old wooden window. This one was going to fight him. He tugged. He pulled. He strained. The window refused to budge. Godot picked up a large book and threw it through the antique blue-green glass. The shattered bits of window fell silently into the grass two floors below, while he drank in the first true cross-ventilation the room had felt in years.

Behind him, he heard the click of the door and a creak as it opened.

"Luc?"

"Henri, I'm over here, fighting with this damned window."

"I think you have won. Isabelle told me you were in the midst of an investigation."

Godot took another deep breath. "Yes. The Eindhoven police autopsy on that rider, Koons, mentioned a drug."

"So?"

Godot took one last deep breath of fresh air and turned to face his boss, the head of a multinational, multi-billion-dollar concern. "They identified it with an HP."

"Hmm. That's not good. That would be a Haven Pharmaceutical brand."

"That's what I thought."

"What drug was it?"

"Something called Cytabutasone."

Henri Bergalis stared at him, blindly. Godot watched, fascinated, as all the color drained out of the man's face, leaving him the color of a four-day floater.

CHAPTER TWELVE:

LAB RAT

His eyelids felt like two deadweight curtain sashes, their increasing bulk no longer held up by a collection of wheels and cords and pulleys. He took another deep breath to clear his brain and shook his head furiously.

No good.

Paul van Bruggen had reached the end of another 13-hour day, and the day had won. He stood up and walked away from the computer, determined to finish up his personal overtime work on the mysterious Cytabutasone, but knew that he'd have to start fresh again tomorrow.

He turned toward the door for no particular reason and tried to look beyond the partially frosted glass into the darkened hallway. Had he heard something, or was he just stretching his ears? No matter. He'd be out of here in moments, joining the other employees of the police research division in some seedy Eindhoven bar for beer and a bite. If, of course, he could stay awake that long.

He reached over to the computer and began the download, transferring the information to disk so he could start afresh at the same point tomorrow morning without the wasted time of searching for a start point.

The computer went about its work silently, a blinking light on the drive and an icon on the monitor his only indications that what he wanted to happen was actually happening.

He walked over to the lab desk, covered in a chopped-and-cut black rubber, and bent himself backward over it, his back cracking deliciously, delightfully, with each inch he grew closer to the table top.

His head touched and van Bruggen dozed.

❂

HE AWOKE, SUDDENLY, IN DARKNESS. VAN BRUGGEN WAS STILL IN HIS AWKWARD position, bent backward over a grimy lab table, but his nearly drugged sleep state of before was gone. He was instantly alert to — something, he wasn't quite sure what.

Slowly, the lab technician slid down off the counter, rolling his back like the hood of a rolltop desk, until he sat on the floor, his back flush up against the drawers of the lab table.

He took a deep breath and tried to remember where he was and what he was doing. He glanced over to the side and saw the computer monitor. It was blank, except for a small icon that flashed at him: "Document Erased."

"Document Erased."

"Document Erased."

Van Bruggen wiped his hand down his face, from his forehead to his chin in a slow, deliberate move. What, he thought, was going on here? He realized, as he pulled his hand away from his chin, that his hand was covered in a cold sweat.

He took a breath and began to crawl over to the computer, his brain still not sure what was going on, or where he was, or how he had come to be here. He didn't trust himself to stand up. He blinked hard as he crawled, trying to change the message that called back to him from the screen.

"Document erased."

He pulled himself up on the chair and stared at the computer screen.

"No," he said to no one in particular, "no — I copied you." He punched a key. "I downloaded you." He punched a flurry of keys. "I saved you," he cried, in a loud, almost desperate voice, punching keys maniacally, trying to get something, anything to respond on the monitor. He stopped and simply stared at the cyclopean eye that stared back at him.

"I saved you, goddamn it. I saved you," he mumbled.

He stared at the computer screen, then, slowly, began to let his eyes drop lower, toward the base of the monitor, and lower, still, to the CD-ROM drive. The access door was open. The disk he had placed inside for memory was gone.

"*Mein Gott*," he thought, "I've been robbed."

He sensed the movement behind him before he heard it.

He stood, turned and cried out to an empty hallway on an empty floor of an empty building in an empty section of the city of Eindhoven.

Empty, except, for himself and the one other who now stood before him.

The last thing he saw, consciously, was the hole in the pipe, fatter than the barrel of a gun, he thought, and the puff that came out of it. The last thing he heard was the hollow "thup" that greeted the puff as it left the hole in the end of the pipe. The last thing he felt was a slap on his forehead, just above the bridge of his glasses, that joined the "thup" that greeted the puff as it left the hole at the end of the pipe.

The slap knocked him backward slightly and bent him over the computer monitor in the same awkward position in which he had been sleeping only moments before.

He had a sense of his sinuses draining and clearing themselves for the first time in any number of years and then the pictures and feelings and sounds all smeared together in a flash of color and cool blue and black…darkness.

A hand reached over and rolled the body of Paul van Bruggen to the floor, then touched three keys on the computer.

An icon appeared asking the question: "Are you sure?"

The hand touched the "y" key. The computer did as it was told.

The hand detached the silencer from the end of the gun and put it in a pocket of the light summer jacket. The weight of the piece pulled the jacket slightly sideways. The handgun, a 9mm member of the Glock family, was tucked under the jacket in a hidden pocket. The hand reached over and touched a pocket on the other side, feeling the disk case and confirming that it was safely in place.

The hand reached for the door and turned the knob, but not before eyes attached to the body attached to the arms attached to the hand turned back toward the computer to see a message blinking for a moment: "Hard Drive Erased."

"Hard Drive Erased."

"Hard Drive Erased."

The message blinked for a moment, then disappeared, replaced by a lonely cursor blinking in the middle of a sea of blue.

The hand pulled the door closed behind it.

The door, locked on the inside, shut with a loud "Click."

The cursor continued to blink.

CHAPTER THIRTEEN:

REACH OUT AND TAG SOMEBODY

Today, hell begins, he thought, for today we find the mountains.

Will pulled his thin-as-gossamer Haven team jacket tightly around him as he sat in the civic courtyard of Cahors, in southwest France. He was waiting, watching and wondering about the day before him.

He was also three hours early for the start of this year's second-longest stage.

By all rights he should just be climbing out of bed now, but Will had slept in snatches all night while keeping an eye on his roommate, half out of concern, half out of jealousy, half out of wonder.

Will shook his head. Wait a minute. That made three halves.

Damn it to hell, too, but Henri Bresson had slept well in yellow. He had won it some six stages earlier and still wore it to the amazement of the world, the team and the man who slept in the same room. Bresson had become a giant of the road, while Will had stepped forward early for that opportunity, only to slip back into the world of the domestique, the water boy, despite his title of team lieutenant, despite his spot on the roster.

Last night had been particularly ugly.

Miguel Cardone, watching and riding tight to Bourgoin, had pulled himself up in the G.C., the general classification, the standings, until he stood poised to pull himself into the top 30. Bourgoin had slipped down to 11th in a strong field, but the times were still so tight that he remained within sight of the final podium. Still, he faced a Tour without a strong lieutenant to marshal his forces for him and a team shifting its focus to Bresson.

And Will did have to admit that the team lieutenant had been on an express elevator to the basement, if not the sub-basement, missing breaks, falling behind, and making a general mess of everything.

Cardone had brought it up.

"I think there should be some order on the team."

Deeds cocked his head to the side. "Order — like what?"

"Order in that the team lieutenant should be riding in a strong position to help the leader. Our team lieutenant is not. Has he been anywhere near a finish lately? How does this help Richard?"

Every eye at the table turned toward Bourgoin. Deeds knew there was a problem, that Will was falling off the pace, but the call would have to come from Bourgoin. He was the team leader. He made the call on the course.

Bourgoin said nothing.

Will felt the scars on his cheeks begin to burn, brightly, out of embarrassment. This was no show of support.

"Well," Deeds pushed, "if there is a problem here, I want it solved now, before we hit the hills."

"No problem," Richard said slowly.

"You sure?"

"Yes. I'm sure"

Bourgoin never looked up from his plate.

Will felt his skin tighten.

"Then," Cardone sparked, throwing his napkin hard against the table, "none of you knows what a problem is."

He turned to Will.

"This man. This man is a problem. He is a team problem. He has been advanced beyond his abilities and is not performing his duties as team lieutenant. He has not brought Bourgoin into the top 10. He has not brought Bourgoin near the podium."

"We have a long way to go. This race is often won in the mountains," Bourgoin said quietly, without anger or enthusiasm.

"Yes. In the mountains. But not by men like him." Cardone's voice had risen to a high, hard pitch as he turned and pointed sharply at Will.

Everyone paused, waiting for a reaction.

"You'd be amazed," Will said quietly, pointedly pronouncing each word as he rose from the table, "what a man like me can do."

Will scanned the faces at the table. Each face he passed turned away from him, almost out of embarrassment. Even Bourgoin averted his eyes. Only Cardone and two others held Will in their gaze.

Cheryl's eyes looked at him with a bitter edge, her anger since the incident of "the other woman's bedroom" forming a wall between them that only she could bring down, when and where she pleased. Meanwhile, Prudencio Delgado watched him carefully, almost as a man staring at a bothersome squirrel in his yard that he hoped would have a heart attack at a very great height.

Will turned to Deeds.

"Do what you will, skip," he said quietly. "Let me know tomorrow at the start."

As he walked heavily toward the door, Magda Gertz appeared before him. The team table went immediately silent.

"Will, is everything all right?" She reached out to touch his arm.

He raised his head and looked into her icy blue eyes for only a moment before pulling her hand away from his arm, dropping it brusquely and saying, with a good deal of conviction, "Excuse me, I don't mean to be rude, but haven't you done enough? Just leave me the hell alone."

He turned back to the hallway and walked away from the room.

Magda Gertz stood in shock, then looked over at the Haven team table as the sound slowly began to rise, catching the eye of Cheryl Crane. The two stared at each other silently for a moment, before Magda turned and walked toward the door that led to the street.

Cheryl watched her go.

A smile played across her lips.

WILL SHOOK HIS HEAD AND RUBBED HIS EYES, HARD. THE MORNING CHILL OF THE town square had yet to burn off, despite it being mid-July in the south of France.

They were throwing their concern in the wrong direction, Will thought. Lieutenants and team leaders, stars and water carriers blow up in this race every day. Look at Helfiger. Last year, he was on the second step of the podium. Yesterday, he tangled on a narrow stretch and broke his collarbone and fell out of the race. There is nothing, nothing, new about it. But a rider, an older rider, coming out of a four-year fade and burning like a supernova in the biggest race in the world, that, that, was a concern, and, yet, no one was asking the obvious question: how?

"AAAAAuuuuggggh!"

Will didn't realize he had shouted out his own frustration, nor that the entire city square, filled with pre-race functionaries, had stopped its activity for a moment to stare at this strange man sitting on a curbstone, barking at the morning mist.

Maybe there was no concern. Bresson had passed every drug test with flying colors, then dutifully stepped back to his room for a shower and an I.V. filled with Monsieur Engelure's magic vitamins and restoratives. The rest of the team had followed suit, including Bourgoin, as hateful of needles as he was, and Will, who had quickly come to the realization that he needed every bit of help in existence.

And yet, Will couldn't help but wonder. Each day, every day, stage after stage, Henri Bresson gained strength on the road and won as his reward a forest of replenishment I.V.s. Will failed miserably, but still received his forest of liquid vitamins. He tapped his foot on the edge of the curb.

He received his vitamins, too.

Or, did he?

Why did Bresson's bags have a slight yellowish tint to them while his seemed a vague and pale blue? The numbers were the same. Will had checked. And the ingredients read the same. But the colors were different.

Or was it a trick of the light as Engelure had said?

Could they be getting different feeds? There was the tint, there was the reaction on the road and there was that edge.

There was an edge to Henri Bresson. There was an almost mechanical sense to his riding, Will thought, coupled with an emotional sharpness that hadn't been there before.

He kicked at a stone and watched it roll onto the top of an ant hill. A furious collection of minuscule residents suddenly emerged to move the obstruction.

It could be written off to the physical peak of the yellow jersey, the desire to hang on to it, the emotional burden and release on the road that the jersey engendered, but, somehow, Will sensed there was something more, something false, something unreal about it all that was going to rise up and bite Henri Bresson and the entire Haven team in the ass.

And, then again, it could be, simply, nothing more than jealousy. According to the medical control for Le Société du Tour de France, Bresson was clean of all banned substances, "stimulants, steroids, pain pills, heart reactants" and showed no indication of blood doping. Will was clear of all chances to ride near the front of the race and showed no indication of doing anything different. In fact, given his diminishing status, he'd be lucky to be on the bike in Paris at all.

Was he simply jealous of a man who had been a lesser rider a mere month ago and now stood at the pinnacle, the top of the pyramid, in yellow, as a god?

Yes. Will knew the little green monster was there and, in fact, wasn't so little.

And no. Something stunk here and it wasn't the wagon load of road apples on its way out of town to fertilize the fields of Aulery.

Will squinted to work the last bit of sleep out of his eyes and peered through the light gray curtain that covered the town. There was some fog surrounding the square at the moment. It was predicted to burn off and fill the day with brilliant sunshine. Just what you need on a long, hard climb up the Hautacam: 1130 meters of climbing in a little over 13 kilometers. *Hors categorie.* Out of category. A mountain that simply could not be rated as a climb. Swell. Just the kind of ride he needed today: 263.5 kilometers and the climb from hell at the finish, with the sun burning a hole in the top of his head all along the way.

At least tomorrow was a rest day, in Lourdes, of all places. Perhaps he could bathe in the fountain, if they would let him, though given his level of sin, he'd probably dissolve in the water. Will snorted at his early-morning humor and shifted his focus to the unfolding drama across the courtyard.

The race organizers were arranging the drivers of the promotional caravan into their positions for the day, with the biggest sponsors — Fiat, Coca-Cola, Crédit Lyonnais — getting the prime positions at the front of the caravan. This meant they would pass the crowds as their interest peaked, before the boredom of chasing advertising doodads and knickknacks set in and the fans began that annoying whistling for the race to arrive.

The caravan, as always, was a hot ticket item this year, the chance to roll through the crowds gathered on the Tour course, perhaps an hour ahead of the race, to promote your team, your product, your industry. It was a major promotional push for a number of companies and had grown in stature, featuring a number of multinational race sponsors. And yet, today, Will noticed, for the first time, among the cola and film company vans, two battered light blue Mercedes trucks. One carried a huge fly on top, while the other sported a gigantic orange fly-swatter. Both were emblazoned with the name, Les Insectes Guys, which Will was sure somebody thought was cute but probably made the majority of the French citizenry grind their teeth with the raw Americanization of their language. The two drivers, a man and a woman, were fighting. The woman, it seemed, drove the swatter van. She was jealously protecting the truck door. She turned sharply and marched off toward Will.

Oh, no, he thought. Don't bring it over here.

The man was directly behind her, head down, staring at his feet as they stomped across the erratic cobblestones of the square, as if driving each one down to level with each step. His concern was playing out in a growing panorama on his face, while the woman approached Will over the last few steps with a look of embarrassment mixed with anger at the man close behind.

"*Pardon, monsieur.*"

"*Oui?*"

"You are American?"

"*Oui.*"

"Do you speak French?"

"A little."

"Please, if you would. Settle an argument."

"I…uhh…will…damn…do what I can."

"Jacob — my husband —"

"*Bonjour.*"

"*Bonjour.*"

"— believes that he knows how to sell an audience on our services."

"Your services?"

"Yes. We are —" she paused dramatically for emphasis, "— The Insect Guys."

"I am pleased about your acquaintance."

"We are part of the caravan."

"I see."

"We promote our services by driving in the caravan before the race and throwing the crowd promotional items for our company."

"Good. Such?"

"We throw them dead flies, monsieur, what do you think?"

The man snorted derisively at Will, shaking his head with the sheer stupidity of it all.

"No, no," she said quickly, "we throw fly swatters and such to them. All with the Insect Guys name and phone number printed — ah — prominently on the side. Do you understand?"

"Yes. So why not understand?"

"Americans. You are American. We recognize you from *L'Èquipe*. Americans don't understand French."

This guy, Will thought, was really on a roll.

"Perhaps I don't French understand always. But — I do understand bugs and selling bugs. Killing."

Jacob threw up his hands in frustration. He was dealing with an idiot child here. What his wife thought to accomplish was beyond him.

Marie spoke slowly and distinctly to the American. Americans knew how to sell. This American would see her point.

"My husband thinks that the fly should follow the swatter. He feels that it would be a good joke and get us noticed. I think the swatter should follow the fly — otherwise, we look foolish. What do you think?"

The American stared at her for a long moment, leading Marie to believe one of a number of things: that he didn't understand; that he was obviously the idiot that Jacob said he was; that he was thinking; or, finally, that he was dead and simply staring off into space before falling over.

"Uhm — monsieur."

"I think that the fly should follow — but not every day." Will said haltingly, in atrocious French. "Twice a week, perhaps — many stages apart — because it will get attention, but every day will make it look like you can't kill flies that chase you."

Jacob leapt into the air.

"Ah-hah! *Bravo, monsieur*!!"

He jumped over and kissed Will lightly on the top of the head. Will cringed, almost expecting to be punched. Marie crinkled up her face, obviously at a loss over her loss, and smiled tightly.

"*Merci, monsieur.*"

"*C'est rien.*"

"Your French sucks, monsieur."

"Eh?"

"*Rien.*"

The couple walked back across the town square toward their trucks, bickering all the way. The trucks carrying the swatter and the fly both sat nose to nose in some kind of automotive standoff, looking much the worse for wear, as if Le Tour were as tough or tougher on them than on the riders.

It must be difficult, Will thought, to drive a van with a 50-pound fly on the roof. Aerodynamics must be hell. He twisted his head to the side for a different perspective. Big damned thing. Must be a horse fly.

"Bug problem?"

"Hmm?"

Will turned his face up and back to find Cheryl standing behind him. He visibly started, surprised that she would talk to him at all, let alone in a pleasant voice, especially after the frosty reception of the past few days.

"Bug problems are what I'm concerned with at the moment," she said, lowering her voice to a mutter, "I mean — big damned blonde Nordic bugs."

"She's Dutch, but who's counting?"

"May I sit?"

Will smiled and moved sideways on the wide and empty curb, making the pretense of offering a seat.

"So, there I was, minding my own business," she said, "preparing for another day of hauling the Haven team underwear over hell's half-acre, when I look over and see these Haven team colors poking out from the middle of an insect argument. Do you always consult with two exterminators just before a stage?"

"I have a few pests to take care of, but I wasn't consulting with them. They were consulting with me."

"Ahhhh. Bug expert now?"

"I know how to kill the good ones while protecting the ones that sting, bite and do major crop damage."

"Really. That is a talent."

"I'm a talented guy in such things." He paused, then said, quietly, "Haven't seen you lately."

"Miss me?" She slid close.

"Yes," he said, nodding in exaggerated earnestness. "Yes, I have. Horribly. And I've gotten no damned reaction from you."

"Well, what do you expect?"

"I expect some friendship. Maybe a bit of sympathy."

"Oh, yeah. And you wandering out of that dame's room one morning while she pulls the 'baby's arm with an apple in its fist' routine, then you run away and hide with no explanation —"

"I didn't hide," Will interrupted.

"— so that I get to deal with the anger and frustration and the insults from all the guys who want to rub my nose in the idea that you were boinking their Barbie Dream Date."

"I didn't."

"What?"

"I didn't boink."

"Who?"

"Her. I didn't boink her."

"Who her?"

"Magda. Gertz. Magda Gertz."

"I know."

Will stared at her in complete, total and utter surprise.

"What?"

"I know. I know you didn't turn her into a woman." Cheryl produced a very fat and satisfied grin.

"Then — what — the," he sputtered a mangled oath, "the — Jesus — oh ... damn."

"And you're trying to say?" She waved her arms in a sarcastic tone of questioning.

"Well, if you knew I didn't then why have you been treating me like yesterday's meat loaf for the last week?"

"Because I didn't."

"You didn't what?"

"I didn't know."

"You didn't know what?"

"I didn't know you didn't sleep with her."

"But you just said—."

"I said I knew, but I didn't know until last night."

"What about last night?"

"Look," she turned and held his hands, staring at him hard as if she wanted to make sure he understood something she wasn't sure he'd understand. "I didn't know until you and Ilsa, She Wolf of the SS, locked horns at the dining room door last night. You don't treat anybody you sleep with like that."

"How do you know how I treat women I sleep with? Except, for you, of course."

"You even treated your ex-wife nice. Remember? I was the one who had to shoot her."

"You didn't shoot her."

"I shot at her. According to my uncle, it's the same thing. Anyway, I know how you treat women and you didn't treat her like a former bed partner. You always act as if they've given you a very special gift. You treated her like she had screwed you, if only figuratively."

"You could tell all that from one, quick, doorway conversation?"

"No problem."

"Jesus. Dick Damn Tracy."

"Actually, I could tell more from the way she looked at me after she lost you at the door. It wasn't a look of sorrow, it was a look of somebody who just got caught in checkmate, as if she had been denied something she wanted very badly."

"And what would that be?"

"I'd say a torchlight parade with you lighting the way."

"Really?" Will smiled.

"What's with the grin?"

"I mean — why? Why would she want me?"

"Look, I realize you're no prize, but why don't we think it's just to piss me off? Women do these things at times."

"No, I'm serious," Will grinned. "Why, with all the talent that she could choose from, why would she choose me?"

"Maybe because she thought you didn't want to be chosen?"

"Huh?"

"You were a challenge."

"Well, I'll tell you. That's just damned odd." He paused for a moment and smiled, wickedly. "You think she still wants me?"

"I'm sure she does, but she won't after I cut Mr. Marvelous off with pruning shears and throw him in the freezer."

"Any particular reason why?"

"I, my dear, now claim proprietary rights."

Will smiled and put his arm around her, drawing Cheryl close and kissing her lightly.

"And you are welcome to them, my dear. You are welcome to them."

The fog continued to clear over the town center of Cahors. Will and Cheryl watched it move quickly to the roof tops, the steeple tops and then into some ethereal mist without saying a word. It was going to be a strikingly clear day.

It was going to be hot. Very hot.

NOW HE WAS CONFUSED.

Two-hundred-fifty kilometers in, through Lourdes, where he realized that no one, absolutely no one was swearing, through Ayros and now onto the base of the Hautacam, facing 1100 meters of vertical rise, straight up, and Will was no where near the race, at least mentally.

Deeds had stopped shouting in his ear kilometers before, after Will set the sprint, which launched Tony Cacciavillani another step on his way toward the green jersey. It was easy work. No matter how people might look at Tony

C. as a person, setting him up for a sprint was no more difficult than lighting a rocket and standing back.

A bang, a whoosh and he was hauling the mail.

The sprinters and their attendants were beginning to fall back now at the base of the climb. As much as they might struggle, this was not their territory. Will fell back with them.

Cardone was sitting in tight with Bourgoin. He'd haul Richard's butt up the mountain if it became necessary. That was fine. Bourgoin wanted to get there any way necessary and if Will wasn't up to the task, for any reason, he had to look elsewhere. It hadn't been a burden on their friendship, at least, that's what it seemed, but it was simply a reality of the game, the life on the bike.

And Bresson? Bresson was on a tear. Charging, feinting, swearing, sprinting and now climbing, hard, up the Hautacam, the man in yellow was determined to remain the man in yellow. Will had tucked in close behind Bresson earlier and began to match Henri's pace, stroke for stroke, soon realizing that despite frantic manipulation of the gears, Will's legs were about to explode from the effort. He had never felt a fire in his thighs like this, but it wasn't fazing Bresson in the least.

How the hell was he doing it?

"Henri, Henri," Will panted, like the fat kid on the ride asking everybody else to wait up, "cut me some slack here."

"Will, come on, Will, we've got them today," Bresson replied.

"I don't think so, pal. I don't think I've got it."

"Get in tight, Will, I'll pull you up the mountain." Bresson laughed high and hard, and dug down into what seemed to be an endless reserve of power. His bike very nearly lifted off the ground in a burst of speed and Henri Bresson blew away from Will Ross like a sports car flying past a Model T. Will watched in amazement, for Bresson was breaking away on a climb, in the midst of the rise, as if he were on a flat road on a Sunday afternoon ride.

Will watched Henri disappear in the distance, a crowd of riders in desperate pursuit, and returned to his own problems, trying to concentrate on the chainring. Tuck and around. Circle. Make a circle. Tuck and around.

He focused to the point that his mind began to blur. Tuck and around. Tuck and around. The repetition hypnotized him and floated him off on a sea of faces. Cheryl. Richard. Henri.

Gertz. Magda Gertz. What was her game? Jesus. Tuck and around. What was she up to? Why the hell did she pick him? He was flattered. No doubt about that. It wasn't every day that breasts like that wanted to talk to you.

Will took a breath and it caught in his chest, forcing him to gag and hawk a huge snot ball toward the crowd lining the mountain road.

Around. Tuck and around.

Klaus Schwabe of the German BelJanus team fell back like a feather caught in a wave. He had fought the flu valiantly for the past few days, but it had finally caught up with him, as his pace was off, his pedaling was erratic, and worst of all, a sudden and uncontrollable diarrhea poured down his leg. Determined to finish, the final straight would not be a pretty sight for Schwabe or any one standing too close to the barricades.

Don't lose the pedals, Will thought, gagging for a moment on the cloud of smell he rode through in passing Schwabe. Watch the pedals, focus on the pedals. Tuck and around. Tuck and around.

His mind floated in the midst of repetition. Tuck and around. Tuck and around.

Tuck and around.

Perfect circles.

LUC GODOT PACED HIS OFFICE LIKE A CAT WITH HIVES. HE WAS AT THE WALL, he was at the window, he was sitting at his desk, then, he was up and around and back in the trail he had worn through the carpet.

He wanted a cigar in the worst way, but he had promised himself he would get through Le Tour de France without one. The life he had won with Isabelle had made the difference, the way she loved him, the way he wanted to love her for years to come.

But, oh, he missed the other love, as well. What did the American say?

"A woman is a woman, but," what? What was the line?

"A woman is a woman, but a cigar is a smoke." Yes, indeed, he thought, a cigar is a smoke. He paced the room again, his mind seemingly blank, as if his nervous jogging was nothing more than a nicotine craving, and, yet, Godot knew there was something else bothering him, something eating at his thoughts, intruding in the dead of night, almost with a sense of guilt, as if a small corner of his subconscious was working overtime to make him face his own ignorance.

He stopped and stared out the window.

This was his new life: an office, a paycheck, a woman named Isabelle and loyalty to all.

Still, a portion of his past was determined to make itself known in his mind, for no matter how hard he tried, after 30 years on the force, he simply couldn't stop being a cop. No matter how he tried to hide it. No matter how he tried to make it go away. No matter how he tried to ignore the questions that arose.

As he stared out the window at the panorama of Paris that spread out before him, he knew the question he should have asked, but had not, out of fear and friendship and his own ignorance of who he was and what he believed.

"Why, Henri?" he asked aloud to the city, "why do you want me to leave this alone?"

He tapped the newly replaced glass in the window with his fingers and pondered his own question, which led to a flurry of questions racing through his mind.

"Why? Why do you want me to leave it alone? Why does Cytabutasone frighten you so much? Why did you parry every time I asked you how Haven was involved? What is making you so afraid? What is making you sweat, my friend?"

He realized he had been chewing hard on the end of his pen. Godot pulled it out of his mouth and absentmindedly dropped it to the floor, crushing it into the carpet with his foot.

He looked out the window, took a deep breath of fully conditioned air, and exhaled slowly.

"Let's find some answers, shall we?" he said to no one in particular.

TUCK AND AROUND.

Tuck and around. The climb was outrageous. It was the first out-of-category climb of the Tour, the first climb so steep and crazed and high that they didn't even know how to describe it. Straight up for another three kilometers, wave to the crowd at the top, then drive back down to Lourdes, wheezing and gasping and puking all along the way.

This is such a delicate sport.

The road was easing out and Will felt the crowd starting to push in toward the center line. It was going to be a hallway ride, with a lane, perhaps two or three feet wide, through a crowd of people eight deep, all pushing, all slapping, all throwing water on their heroes and whoever else might wander by.

Tuck and around. Watch the line.

Will couldn't breathe. It was as if the crowd was sucking oxygen from the lane, making it a vacuum of bad smells and thin air. It was harder to ride here than on the peak of K2.

Tuck and around.

One rider ahead, Prudencio Delgado fought his way through the crowd, the young rider slapping away pushes and cheers and bottles of water thrown in his face. His anger and his exhaustion played themselves out in a battle with the crowd, a battle to the line.

Tuck and around.

Will put his head down and watched the lane. Follow the path through the crowd, man, follow the path. Tuck and around. Perfect circles.

He looked up and was blinded for a moment by something thrown in his face, something hot and burning, he blinked his eyes and sat up on the bike to wipe his face and blinked again. The damned stuff was hot. He was on the edge of panic before he caught the scent of coffee. Someone had thrown coffee in his face.

Son of a bitch.

Ignore it. Back to work. Tuck and around. Tuck and around.

Each breath was becoming an effort. Tuck and around. He began to wrestle the bike forward. Tuck and around. He was passing exhaustion and falling into a new mental plane. Tuck and around. Circle. Perfect circles.

Come on. Tuck and around. He was panting, furiously. He was distanced from himself, his vision stretched, his hearing nothing but a far-off buzz. There was no oxygen in this crowd. Tuck and around. Forward. Go forward.

Ahead, he saw Prudencio fall off the line and into the crowd on his right. As one, they lifted him back to level and pushed him forward, a hundred hands carrying him toward the line in a human wave.

Tuck and around.

The screaming from the crowd, the shouts of encouragement were distant echoes in Will's mind. The road itself began to take on a new shape, an otherworldly aspect, like a candied ribbon bent and twisted by a demonic child. Tuck and around. Tuck and around. He was riding on instinct, adrenaline and nerves, like a grasshopper after somebody stepped on it.

Tuck and around.

He had been riding in this crowd for years — tuck and around — getting nowhere. It was an endless path. Leading. Where?

Tuck and around.

Suddenly, they all fell away, as if his solitary canoe had drifted out of a stream and back onto the Mississippi. Tuck and around. There was nothing but room on all sides and the riders, breaking into the open after an endless procession through the crowd, blinked as if this were something completely beyond their comprehension.

The breeze hit Will like a shot of cold water and it filled his lungs with a new found energy. He stood up on the pedals and instinctively began to drive toward the finish, his mind clearing and finding a new focus 300 meters away on a line that read FIAT. Two-hundred-fifty meters. Delgado sat just ahead and to his right, while the Banesto rider who had separated them in the line through the crowd carried the center line.

Me, thought Will. This one is mine.

It was an exercise in futility and a part of his mind told him that. Winning a sprint here was wasted effort, but it was his effort and it would be his sprint win. It meant nothing, except to him. It was merely one more stage finish, one more spot in the G.C., one more kilometer toward Paris, with no meaning for anyone except him.

Except Will.

Tuck and around. He rose out of the saddle and began to pour on the coal, the new bike, not yet "The Beast," responding as it should, smoothly, cleanly, with a sure feel that drew him closer to the finish.

Still, he realized that this bike wasn't talking to him. Not yet.

The Banesto rider picked up on the obvious sprint from Will, as did Prudencio, sensing it and determined to make it a race.

Two-hundred meters.

Prudencio pulled in tight on the right, not giving an inch, edging Will over to the left side of the road, holding the middle for himself, elbows out in a hard pump. The Banesto rider dropped in close behind Prudencio.

They bumped. One-hundred-fifty meters.

They bumped again, hard.

One-hundred-twenty-five. The pace was up.

One hundred meters. A thought flashed through Will's mind. The face of Tomas Delgado. His friend. The brother. In that second, Prudencio bumped hard from the right, pushing Will toward the Coca-Cola barrier close in on the left. Thirty meters along the barrier, Will saw a gendarme, holding a huge orange, step back through, sensing that he didn't want to become a part of this, part of the unavoidable accident heading his way.

Will froze on his dream image for a second and made the call: "Bless you, Tomas."

In that moment, there was a spark, a kernel that rose out of his gut and burned hot and hard and gritted his teeth and pushed him and the bike to the right in a bump, a bash, a shove that sent Prudencio Delgado skittering across the pitted tarmac and off his pace. The Banesto rider behind rode straight into Delgado's bike and suddenly found himself airborne.

Will shot across the line, alone and a winner. A winner in 83rd place.

He braked almost immediately to avoid the crowds that had filled the finish area — the press and TV crews, team support personnel, riders and hangers on — all milling around to congratulate, console and grab whatever freebies might be left unattended.

Will sat up on the bike and felt the flush of exhaustion in his legs. A long, hard day had come to an end. He needed water and a rubdown and a shower and a dinner and a bed. Alone.

The thought of Cheryl flashed across his mind.

Oh, yeah. Alone. Drat the luck.

He took a deep breath and stepped off the bike, snapping his right pedal to free himself from his nearly eight-and-a-half-hour day in the salt mine. Now, his legs felt like water, forcing him to reach over and steady himself on a photographer. The man shook him off, then turned, looked beyond Will, stepped back, focused and snapped off five shots on the motor drive. Will turned to see what was in the field of view and saw Prudencio step across the line carrying his bike, the front wheel twisted, blood running down his leg. In the distance, on the road, the Banesto rider was down, his face covered in blood, his clothing torn to shreds.

This was one hell of a tangle, Will thought. He grinned and turned and walked toward the Haven bus. A tangle I won.

He whistled a formless tune from a forgotten musical and went to find a bottle of water.

ISABELLE MARCHANT PICKED UP THE PHONE, MOVED THE SAUCE OFF THE burner, turned off the gas, and cradled the phone between her shoulder and ear in one fluid, easy move.

"Don't tell me. For god's sake don't tell me you will be late," she said, knowing who had called without asking.

"I will be late," he said quietly, with a trace of boyish guilt in his voice.

"Oh, Luc, for heaven's sake. What could possibly be keeping you at an empty office tonight?"

"A question."

"But there are no answers tonight because there is no one there to give you an answer. They are all in Lourdes, from Henri Bergalis to François the janitor."

"François the janitor? He's been invited to Le Tour?"

"No, he has family there. Why are you late?"

"I have to know something."

"What? Perhaps it is something I can answer."

"I need to know something about my computer."

"The little black button on the side turns it on."

"I am doing a search ."

"*You*? *You* are doing a search? A computer search?"

She laughed in a way that made Godot blush like a schoolboy caught in cooking class.

"Oh, my," she chuckled, "this is the millennium, isn't it? Isn't this the final sign before the Second Coming?"

"Please. I need your help."

She looked quickly at the sauce and pushed it aside. It was already beginning to congeal. Dinner was a lost cause, but he had amused her so that her anger was already a thing of the past.

"What," she asked with amusement, "what can I do for you?"

"I am doing a search."

"Yes."

"For a substance. A chemical."

"What file are you searching?"

"Well, I'm not sure. I've been through administration, memos and something else."

"It wouldn't be there."

"Where would it be?"

"That depends."

He paused, waiting for her to continue. "Yes — on what?"

"That depends on what it is. Is it an industrial chemical or a fertilizer? Is it a vitamin or a drug? Is it standard or experimental? Has it been approved? Is it a cleaning agent or a plastic?"

"Yes, yes, all right. I understand. It is a chemical, no, a drug. It's a drug. A performance-enhancing drug."

"Is it on the market?"

"No."

"That would put it in R&D, Research and Development."

"Can I access them?"

"They have a file, but it is restricted access."

"So how do I access it?"

"Use the password."

"I don't have the password."

"In the top drawer of my desk, there is a blue book with a red border. Go get it."

Godot did as he was told.

"I have it."

"Open to the middle section. The section marked in yellow along the border."

"All right. I have it."

"The password for Research should be the third or fourth one down."

"There is something that says R/Francour."

"R for Research, Francour is the password."

"Thank you," Godot said, peck-typing the word in and watching the screen change as he entered a deeper, secret world of Haven Pharmaceuticals. "Hmm. I'm in. If I may be so bold," he said, somewhat distantly, "could you please tell the Chief of Security how you got the password for a restricted area inside the company?"

"Oh, love, you should know. I got it from Helene in sales, who got it from Claudine in administration, who got it from Marta in shipping."

"It is a regular network you have."

"Of course. Secretaries, as you know, are really the power behind the throne."

"I am beginning to believe that." He looked at the computer screen. "Now what?"

"Now access your search, type in your chemical and see what happens."

Godot pulled up the search field and typed in the word Cytabutasone. He hit enter, then sat back and watched the tiny clock appear and disappear, appear and disappear.

"What's happening?" she asked, moving the saucepan to the sink and rinsing it out, already plotting where she would make him take her for dinner.

"I am watching a clock."

"It is searching." Over the phone, she heard the unmistakable beep, the tone that told her the search was completed.

"What is it telling you?"

"Well," he said, turning his head to the side as if to see the screen from a new and more understandable angle, "I haven't the slightest idea."

"Well, tell me."

"All there is in my search field is ..." he squinted at the screen, "an 89 surrounded by two arrows."

"Which way are the arrows pointing?"

"To the — left. They are pointing to the left."

"You are off the computer."

"No, I'm still on the computer."

"No, my dear, you are off the computer. Haven didn't computerize until 1989. You are off the computer and into hard records."

"Hard records?"

"Paper. The records. You have to find the paper trail."

"Where is that?"

"I'm not sure. It could be in the basement. It could be in one of the books at the company archives. That's near the Gare du Nord. It could be destroyed. Beyond that, I don't know."

He was silent for a moment.

"Where are you taking me to dinner?"

"I'm not sure yet."

"About where?"

"About dinner. I have a stop to make. Thank you, my love. Don't wait up. I don't know when I will be home."

Isabelle Marchant sighed with frustration. Without saying good-bye, she hung up the phone. She looked at the wall of the kitchen and threw the pot at it with all her strength.

"*Merde*!" she shouted at the empty apartment. "*Merde*! If I had wanted to fall in love with a policeman I would have fallen in love with a policeman!"

She stopped suddenly and then burst into laughter.

That, in fact, she thought, was exactly what she had done.

WILL WAS ON HIS SECOND BOTTLE OF WATER WHEN THE FIRST STORM BROKE.

Henri Bresson calmly picked up a metal folding chair and drove it through the windshield of a poorly parked Lexor Computer team car.

"That — is what I think of your question, *salaud*."

Then, Bresson calmly picked up a second chair and pounded out a tattoo on the side of the brand new, mint condition Haven team bus, much to the chagrin of Monsieur Engelure, who stepped forward to calm the rage that broke over his charge and caught a chair leg between the eyes for his efforts. Engelure dropped hard to the ground, blood seeping out of his forehead. No one stepped forward to help him. No one stepped forward to stop Bresson.

And the beat went on.

Will stepped over to the reporter, the technical editor for America's *VeloNews*.

"For God's sake, what did you ask him?"

"I dunno what set him off. All I said was, 'Can you stay in yellow to Paris' and he got this weird look and starts rearranging the furniture."

Bresson stopped, glanced at Engelure, threw a second chair over the heads of the crowd and marched to the door of the Haven team bus. Every eye in the area was on him, but it was as if he had no concept of the crowd. He slammed his hand against the safety glass of the window, popping the seal, and stomped onto the bus. Louis Engelure slowly got up, ignored both the crowd and his bleeding forehead and quietly followed Bresson.

The silence slowly mutated into mumbling, then a full-throated chatter as the world of the post race returned to normal.

"How about you," the reporter asked. "Can you make it to Paris?"

"In yellow, or, just make it?"

"What are the chances of being in yellow?"

"None and noner. But I'll be in Paris."

"What about Cardone? He's pretty much become the team lieutenant, hasn't he? He brought in Bourgoin today."

"The team does what the team does. That's why it's called a team, man. One person falls off, another steps in."

"Kind of a come down, though, isn't it?"

"How so?"

"Winner of Paris-Roubaix, distant finish at the Tour?"

"I dunno. I guess it's just my turn in hell's half-acre."

Will had meant it as a joke, but the reporter missed the reference. A shout went up from another quarter and the reporter turned away, looking for another story and an easy quote or two.

Downing the second bottle of water at a gulp, Will began to think of recovery. He turned to find a third bottle of water and some kind, just about any kind, of food, when Deeds slammed a hand down on his shoulder and spun him around.

"What the hell do you think you're up to?"

"What do you mean, Carl?"

"What the hell do you think you're doing, taking out Delgado and Melzi? This isn't some goddamned bumper-car race! We need Delgado! Jesus, Will — what the hell got into you?"

"Carl," Will put out his hands as if to calm Deeds, knowing full well that with this head of steam, Deeds would likely rip them off, "I was the bumpee, not the bumper. I was being pushed into the barricade by that little son of a bitch Delgado and I reacted as I should have reacted. I'm not going to lose my goddamned Tour because that little bastard wants to teach me a lesson."

"That's not what Delgado is saying. That's not what the crowd is saying and that's not what Banesto is saying."

"Well, Delgado is lying, Banesto is wrong and the crowd is an ass."

"Goddamn it, Will — your Tour is over, pal. The UCI doesn't like what it sees on that videotape and they'll boot your ass out of here so quick that you'll think it happened last week. God in heaven, Will, what were you thinking?"

Now it was Will's turn to get angry. He felt the blood rush to his face and charge the nerve endings along the road map of scar tissue on his cheeks.

"Look, Carl, what I was thinking was survival. Survival. If Prudencio wants to take me out — he can sure as hell try, but I'm going to fight the little son of a bitch every step of the way. Even if that means taking him out along the way."

"Jesus, Will — *Think. Think.*" Deeds knocked his head, setting off a hollow ring. "Let him take the damned sprint. It's not worth it! What the hell were you thinking? Goddamn it. I think your brain is all mush from that comedy you're playing with Gertz."

"*What*? What the hell is that supposed to mean?"

"You know exactly what that's supposed to mean."

"What the — oh, my god — you're jealous."

"Fuck you, Will — keep to the point."

"That — seems to be the operative word here, now doesn't it Carl?"

The crowd had hushed again to hear the very public screaming match between Deeds and Will. Now, it parted as Prudencio Delgado, pale, shaking and covered with sticking plasters, pushed his way to the Haven team bus. He broke into the clearing surrounding Will and Deeds and turned to face Will with an undisguised hatred in his eyes.

"Thank you, Mr. Ross. You damned near killed me."

"Calm down, Prudencio. You were bumping and grinding and you got bumped back."

"What — you can't take a little competition without trying to kill it?"

"What?"

"Kill it. You know the term. You know the concept. Kill it."

The crowd hushed. Instinctively, the photographers in the crowd poised their cameras, the auto drives engaged.

"You know — kill? What's the matter, my brother wasn't enough for you?"

Without thinking, Will's right hand shot out. He slapped Delgado hard across the face, then, snapped the hand back and forward and back and forward again, the sounds from the slap and Prudencio Delgado's startled mouth merging to form a "smek, smek, smek, smek" that reverberated through the crowd, joining with the sounds of the motor drives racing at high speed, "jzet, jzet, jzet, jzet."

In a corner of his mind, Will could sense that every eye in the world was on him at that moment. An alarm bell rang wildly in the back of his head, but the die was already cast and he was running on pure emotion, pure adrenaline.

The crowd paused.

Will slapped Delgado one more time.

"Snap out of it," was all he said, before turning back toward the bus.

The crowd stood in stunned silence.

The only sound was that of the cameras, the motor drives in over drive.

Jzet. Jzet. Jzet. Jzet.

THE LIGHT DRIZZLE SEEMED TO FIT THE MOOD OF THE STREET. THE ARCHIVES for Haven Pharmaceuticals were squirreled away on a street just off the Rue de Chartres, within sight of the Gare du Nord train station.

Godot sat in the car for a moment staring at the single bulb illuminating a heavy metal door, watching the mist curl and fall around it. Bad place, he thought, bad time of day, but now he was in the hunt and beyond that, nothing really mattered.

He stepped out of the Haven company Renault and dug in his pockets as he stepped toward the door. A large, black, electronic lock stood to one side. He pulled his master key-card from his wallet and swiped it through the lock.

Nothing.

He tried again. Nothing.

Interesting, he thought, that the Chief of Security for Haven Pharmaceuticals wouldn't have access to the company archives.

He swiped the card a third time, trying to allay his natural inclination toward suspicion, a talent developed over 30 years of police work.

Nothing.

He put the card back in his pocket and began to walk around the edge of the long, single-story building, pushing through a heavy growth of weeds on his way toward the rear of the structure. On the back, about seven feet off the ground, he found what he was looking for, a window just big enough for a puffy, out-of-shape former police inspector to wiggle through.

He then began searching the ground around him for a suitable key.

CHAPTER FOURTEEN:

REST DAY

Will was busy being a pariah today.

The rest day in Lourdes was meant for recovery and restoration, a chance to hang back for a day and figure out where you were in the great grand scheme of Le Tour de France. For most teams, including Haven, that's exactly what it was: a day of sleep and food and team meetings and endless, mind numbingly boring discussions on team positioning.

With the exception of Bresson, who seemed full of fire and fury that night, Will had met little support on the team after playing bumper bikes at the Hautacam finish with Delgado. The press, the fans, the other riders were standing with Prudencio and against Will. The UCI had split on the incident and was still reviewing tapes. It would make its decision today. To Bresson, it was a no-brainer.

"He bumped you, Will — you bump him back. You kill him if you need to."

"Gosh, Hank, I wouldn't go that far—."

"Hank. I like Hank. I would kill him anyway."

Then, Bresson pulled on the yellow jersey and went for a two-hour training ride, which on the day off was either a sign of true dedication or a sickening madness.

Will didn't have it, to be sure. His legs felt like warmed-over mush, and he couldn't seem to clear his head. The fog that had rolled in days before still sat there, a deepening exhaustion that simply leeched the energy and enthusiasm right out of him and into the floorboards. He simply wasn't recovering. Perhaps, he thought, he should talk to Engelure and boost his vitamin intake in the I.V.s. Something. Whatever he was doing now simply wasn't working.

He had fallen that night into a deep sleep, the sleep of the dead, the sleep of the dead checkered with dreams of the dead.

Tomas sat before him. Silent. Unsmiling. The face of his dead friend glowered with a look that spelled only distaste for what had happened at the finish line. The orange lay squashed on the floor of heaven, or wherever dreams come from.

Damn, he thought the next morning, feeling guilty and depressed as well as exhausted, even my dreams are against me.

Will showered and dressed and stepped into the hallway where Deeds caught him on the way to breakfast.

"You might want to pass this one up."

"What do you mean? I'm hungry. And I've got to talk to Engelure. I'm dying out there, man."

"Well, Engelure isn't in a mood to help you right now. Prudencio is one of his favorites. Big in the vitamin game. Thanks to Cardone, most of the team isn't backing you, either. And neither, really, is much of anyone else. The sprint and then that slapping business is big news around the world and just about everybody wants you out."

"Any word from the UCI yet?"

"No. They said they'd have an announcement at 11. Here." He dug into his pocket and came up with 500 francs. "Get lost today. Go sightseeing. Eat hearty. Do it on me. We'll see what happens.

"What do you think happened, Carl?"

"Frankly, Will, I wanted to kill you last night. Then I watched the video tape. I'm not happy with how you handled it, but, honestly, I can see your point."

"How will the UCI see it?"

"Who knows? Remember Bauer and Criquielion at the World Championships? How did you see that? How did they see it? Everybody saw it differently. They made their decision and then it took — hell — how many years to die down?"

Will paused.

"What about Richard?"

"He's waiting. He's in your corner. He wants you back and in form. He can't stand Cardone. But until you start riding again, pal, he's stuck."

"Understood."

"Clear out. Take the back door. Keep to yourself. The UCI will make itself known this morning and we can get on with our lives and this damned race."

"Thanks."

"By the way — what was the deal with the slapping?"

"Long story."

"I want to hear it. Sometime. Until then, if you're going to slap somebody, slap Cardone."

"Don't tempt me."

WILL TOOK HIS TIME THAT MORNING, EATING A LONG, LEISURELY BREAKFAST and filling up on coffee, magazines and newspapers. His picture was prominent. Two or three different shots. The one he liked the best was Delgado and the Italian sprawled out in the background while he stood smiling up front, just a cold and calculating jerk of a human being.

It was too nice a day to worry about it. The morning breeze in the south of France was warm and inviting, carrying a sweet smell despite the morning traffic that buzzed and honked around the café in Lourdes.

Perhaps, he thought, he should drop by the shrine, as it would make his mother immeasurably happy, bordering on ecstatic, but time was against him at the moment. The UCI announcement was only an hour away and it would take most of that time just to wander back to the hotel on foot, meandering, shopping, looking, chatting, living.

The thought crossed his mind that he was suddenly no longer a part of the team, from the team meetings to the camaraderie to the internal support. If so, then so be it. He had been a lone wolf before and had survived. He could do it again.

Passing a *pharmacie*, a sign caught his eye for BioLode vitamins, an American sports medicine firm that was trying to break into the European market and carve out a chunk of Haven's turf. Nothing in particular caught his eye in the advertising, it was more of a sense, a guess, that perhaps he needed a change. Perhaps, just perhaps, he had maxed out on the Haven brand name and was simply spinning his wheels in some weird sort of vitamin vacuum. Maybe BioLode would jump start him.

Who knew?

It couldn't hurt, especially since Monsieur Engelure wasn't about to bend over backwards to help him. He checked the cash that remained from the clutch of bills Deeds had given him: 325 francs. Good enough for a start. He stepped into the pharmacy and bought every BioLode product in sight and a bottle of Perrier to wash two handfuls of the things down.

THE REAR DOOR OF THE HOTEL WAS LOCKED. SHINEOLA, WILL THOUGHT, WHY the hell am I skulking around here, anyway? No reason in the world why I can't just walk in the front door, go right through the lobby and act like a real man.

He paused for a second, then knocked quietly.

Nothing.

Will walked around the hotel and stepped into the lobby. Bresson sat in a corner chair, reading a day-old copy of *L'Èquipe*, the French sports journal. The page one picture was of a Henri Bresson who looked far better in print than he did at this moment in person.

"Are you all right?" Will asked, with more than just a little concern creeping into his voice.

"No. Frankly, I have no problem telling you that I am not all right." Bresson looked almost yellow in this light, his face drawn, the wrinkles, what there were of them, sinking deeply into his face and aging the rider quickly.

"What is it? Do you want me to get Deeds or Engelure to check you out?"

Will started to step away when Bresson grabbed him by the arm.

"*Non*. No. I'll be fine. I'll be fine. I've just been pushing it —"

"That's an understatement."

"... and it's catching up with me. I think it's catching up with me."

"Something happen on your training ride this morning?"

"No. Yes. Well, yes — I hit the wall. I was riding. Spinning. I felt great.

And then, I couldn't do anything. I couldn't pedal. I couldn't see. Will. I was blind. I had to find a ride back into the city."

"You've got to see the doc."

"No. Just let me rest."

"Anything I can do?"

"Just let me rest."

"You've got the day, man. Take it."

Bresson picked himself up, painfully, and pushed himself upright out of the chair. "I need today. Yes. I need today."

Will stood, stupidly, in the middle of the lobby, not knowing what to do or how to do it. He placed his hand on Bresson's shoulder and patted him twice, then watched the man in yellow shuffle off toward his room. If anybody deserved to be wrung out, it was Henri Bresson. Will only hoped he could recover by tomorrow and its two climbs, both *hors categorie*.

"Ross? You Ross?"

"Huh? What, me? Yeah. *Oui*."

"There is a woman looking for you."

"Merci."

The desk clerk pointed to a dark room next to the lobby desk hidden by a partially opened, heavy oak door. Will nodded. He stepped in and pulled the door closed behind him as he eyes adjusted to the semi-darkness.

"Hello?"

"My, oh, my, but you are the talk of ESPN today."

"Cheryl?"

"Hi, Will. *Ça va*?"

"Look, will you speak English to me? All this French talk is making my brain mushy."

"Appears that way. First you knock some poor Spanish kid into some poor Italian kid, then you start slapping everybody up."

"I don't know why I did that."

"Sure you do. You were pissed."

"Thank you for your insight."

"You're just upset because this kid is some relation to Tomas."

"Brother."

"Oh, brother."

"Yeah, brother. Why are you surprised?"

"I'm not surprised. I'm using 'brother' like you use 'oh, shit.'"

"Oh. So, how are you?"

"No, the question now is, 'How are you?' I've been looking for you all day. Deeds told me he sent you packing. Back in time for the decision?"

"Can't wait. Just hope they don't burn criminals at the stake anymore.

"What's the old Three Stooges line — I'd rather have a hot stake than a cold chop any day?" She looked at her watch. "So — when's your chop?"

"It's still about 10 minutes off."

"Do you want some company?"

"I dunno. Won't it hurt your image with the team?"

"I have no image with the team, remember? I've been reduced to being a bell hop." She looked at him for a long and quiet moment. "How are things with you?"

"I'm doing crappy, thank you," Will said. "I'm blowing my top with punk kids and I can't seem to recover from even walking across the street. It's almost like I developed a tolerance for Haven Pharmaceuticals, the Vitamins of Kings. So I switched over to something new."

"What?"

"BioLode. I picked up a bunch of the stuff this morning."

"Good brand. They're hot in the States. I didn't know you could build up a tolerance to vitamins."

"Me either. Who knows? The stuff I'm taking sure isn't working."

"You might be right. Different formulation might help you out."

"Hmm."

"Uh-huh. Uh, look — this UCI thing is coming up in a few minutes and I've got to find a seat. Unless, of course, you want me to go with you."

He squeezed her hand and smiled into her eyes. "No, that's okay. You go ahead, I'll be right along."

"Okay. Hang in there."

"Okay."

"I love you, Will."

The silence that followed the three words crashed around Will's ears.

He felt the skin on his neck contract, his eyes sting, his palms sweat to the point of sogginess. He was finding the small, dark smoking room stifling. He was taking deep breaths and not getting any oxygen. This was silly, he thought, nothing more than emotional hyperventilation.

Cheryl shook her head and patted his hand. "Don't get into a state, Will. I'm here no matter what happens."

She smiled with understanding and stepped through the door into the sunlit lobby. Will watched her go, then slapped his forehead as the heavy oak door swung back and forth, back and forth until finally quiet.

"Asshole. That's what you are. Asshole." He kicked at the door in reaction to his own accusation and caught it hard with his heel. It swung open and slammed with a *bang* into the side of the hotel desk.

"Hey, watch it!"

Will leaned forward to see Magda Gertz against the desk. The swinging door had missed her by inches.

"Oh. Sorry."

"What are you going to do? Slap me, too?"

"Stop it."

"Though I suppose I wouldn't mind if it was in the right context." She smiled and raised an eyebrow.

"Please."

"I'm sorry. What? Bad news from home? Or just 'news from home?' I find that I'm always depressed by it whether it's bad news or not."

Will smiled.

"Where are you off to?" he asked, as politely as he could muster.

"I thought I'd watch the UCI announcement of your fate. France 2 is carrying it live. Part of their 'Rest day' coverage. I told Henri that I would let him know what happened."

"Some rest day," Will muttered. "You've seen Bresson?"

"Hmm? Yes, I just saw him before I came down here. He'll be better tomorrow."

"Really," Will cocked his head as he looked at her, as if to ask, 'how would you know,' and shook it off. Well, I hope so, he continued, he's waited too long and worked too hard to get here. It would be quite a letdown to run out of gas halfway through the fun and games.

"He deserves to wear it in Paris."

"Yeah, well, don't tell that to the rest of the boys."

"They've set up a television set in the dining room," she said, "care to join me to learn your fate?"

"Yeah," he said, his senses suddenly alert, "I'll wander down there with you. I've been bound for the gallows all day. They might as well spring the trap."

She offered him her arm in a exaggerated, theatrical way. Will smiled, but ignored the proffered arm, brushed past her in the narrow doorway, and began to walk across the lobby. He stopped, turned and looked at her.

"You coming?"

Magda Gertz stood, frozen as a statue, in the doorway of the small smoking lounge, her arm still hooked in mid-air, offered to him, accepted by no one. She dropped it slowly and walked over to Will.

"You're rude."

Will slowly dropped his sunglasses to cover his eyes.

"Yes, you're right. I am."

He snapped her a smile and turned toward the dining room.

THE MOUSE WASN'T USED TO COMPANY.

This was his territory, his, and that of his rapidly growing family. He wasn't used to company, human or otherwise. He examined the hand carefully for signs of danger, signs of life.

Nothing. He stepped on it, with trepidation, and skittered quickly to the middle of the palm, nerves and muscles taut, in anticipation of a threatening move.

He flexed his toes once in the soft skin at the base of the thumb and felt a twitch in reaction. He paused, for only a moment, to gauge the response.

It cost him his life.

Without conscious thought, Luc Godot slapped his hand sideways, flinging whatever it was off and toward the concrete block wall at the rear of the archive building. As he forced himself awake, he heard a small "slap" and a quickly strangled "squeak."

He looked blindly, frantically, at his hands, trying to wake up, trying to figure out what, if anything, had been there. He took a deep breath, then a second, blinking and stretching his eyelids.

First things first. Where was he?

He turned in a full circle around him, not recognizing the place, the bare walls filled with metal bookshelves and reams of paper, a few sticks of cheap furniture and what seemed to be a single light bulb in the center of everything.

He took another breath and tried to calm himself. Slowly, he began to remember the night before, from breaking the window to finding the light switch to marching by finger through sheet after sheet of incomprehensible laboratory nonsense about every product known to Haven, except, of course, the one he was looking for, what was its name? He took another breath and focused on the problem at hand.

Cyta ... Cyta ... Cyta ... something.

Damn.

The last thing he could remember was looking at his watch, which read 4:12 a.m. Now it read nearly 11 and he had reached a dead end.

Either he'd have to find someone who knew their way around these files and what might be in here, or, he'd actually have to face down Henri Bergalis, who had shown absolutely no interest in talking about this four days ago. Or was it five now?

God, he thought, he had never seen Bergalis go so cold, so fast. The color had drained out of the man's face like coffee from a broken cup.

Godot began to wipe his face with his hand, then realized that whatever had woken him up had done it with that particular hand. He shifted to the other and rubbed his eyes.

He sat back on the hard office chair he had found in a corner of the archive building the night before and plotted his next move.

Breakfast. Breakfast might be nice.

And a call to Isabelle, with apologies.

And perhaps a call to Eindhoven and the lab rat who was filing the reports on that Dutch rider.

He placed his hands on his knees and pushed himself up, feeling every moment of the night in a hard-back chair ripple through his spine. He straightened up, put both thumbs on either side of his back and pushed, hard, feeling a satisfying crack ride up the vertebrae.

He sighed with relief.

That's when he saw the door.

THE DINING ROOM WAS FILLED. THE HOTEL WAS HOSTING LEXOR AND ROL, THE insurance conglomerate team, as well as Haven, causing a cordwood effect when everyone hit the lobby at the same time. A 16-inch TV set at the end of the room sparked and rolled, showing, at the moment, another video replay from the middle of Will's bumping incident. The UCI officials would likely be next. As intent on the TV as everyone had been up until this moment, all heads turned as one when Will and Magda stepped into the room. She reached through and grabbed his arm, tightly, pulling him close into her breast. Will tugged hard and then felt her nails dig into his bicep.

"Jesus."

She turned and flashed a dazzling smile. "Relax, Will, and enjoy the moment."

Cheryl had stood, then gave Will a hard stare. He waved his free arm, and she sat with obvious anger.

"Yah. Yah." Cardone chirped, jumping and pointing at the television with an indescribable ecstasy, "This is it. This is it!"

The sports anchor in Paris tossed to the live feed from the UCI officials in Lourdes. As the image was brought up on the screen, the picture fuzzed, then froze, then became clear again. Satellite troubles. The official began speaking in French.

"We have taken the past 24 hours to thoroughly examine the videotape and photos of the incident that occurred at the finish line of Stage 12 at Hautacam yesterday. We have also spoken to many witnesses on the scene and officials who were nearby. It is the conclusion of the UCI that the rider in question, William Ross of Haven Pharmaceuticals —"

"Here it comes! Good-bye, dear Ross!"

"... was within his rights to react as he did rather than be forced into the barricade. It is our belief that a serious accident might have occurred with riders just behind Monsieur Ross and rider Prudencio Delgado, if Monsieur Ross had ridden into the barricade. Prudencio Delgado of the Haven team will be assessed a time penalty for interference. It is our ruling that no further action shall be taken in this situation and that Monsieur Ross may remain as a rider on the Haven team in this, the current edition of Le Tour de France."

The room was silent. On the TV set, the live feed from Lourdes disappeared and was replaced by the French anchorman who seemed to match the shock on every face in the dining room with the exception of the face of Magda Gertz.

"Yyeess!" she shouted in a heavy Dutch accent that gave the phrase the tone of a German drill sergeant shouting at American POWs. She turned to Will, took his face in both hands and pulled him to her, deeply kissing him full on the lips.

The surprise of the announcement and the kiss, the rich fullness of it, the softness of her lips and the rich scent of her perfume, caught Will off guard.

He kissed her back.

She broke from him smiling, triumphant, flushed with victory.

He broke from her erect, embarrassed and desperate to run from the room.

She laughed and turned to the assembled teams, the riders, mechanics, coaches and drivers, soigneurs and managers in the room.

"I suggest you all get over this." She smiled directly at Cheryl. "The gods have spoken. The sin is cast out."

She laughed and turned to leave, pulling Will with her. As Will's head spun around, he saw Cheryl Crane trying to fight her way across the room and to him.

He should have stopped.

But he was being pulled along in the vortex of a powerful force.

GODOT EXAMINED THE DOOR CAREFULLY. THE ELECTRONIC LOCKS GUARDING the building didn't extend to this room, as it was secured by a series of three dead bolts.

Godot pondered the problem for a moment, the dilemma of either searching for the keys back at the corporate offices, waiting for Henri Bergalis to let him in on the secret or just doing it himself.

The third lock yielded to his picks as he continued to ponder what he should do, and he pushed the heavy metal door open, revealing six large metal file cabinets with heavy combination locks.

The labels on the first two indicated 40 years of financial dealings. The third was labeled 'RETIRED FORMULATIONS.' That was a possibility, Godot thought. The fourth was 'PERSONNEL.' The fifth marked 'SALES.' The sixth, was unmarked. He shoved the last file cabinet to see if it was empty. It wouldn't budge.

"And so," Godot said, "I will start with you."

He took his jacket off and carefully laid it across the dusty top of the first two cabinets. He looked at the heavy steel case and the security lock with care before leaving the archive building to go to his car for the combination to open it.

He returned with a hammer and crowbar and set to work.

CHAPTER FIFTEEN:

LIQUID COURAGE

The rainbow moved languidly across the surface of the brown liquid, caught in the grip of some small but determined current. It traveled to one side of the glass, hit the wall and spread out in a thin line in both directions, slowly curving around the vessel until it reached the beginning, where the surface tension of the air bubble pushed it back toward the middle again. Watching the drama unfold for the third time, a single thought entered Will's mind.

"This is one dirty damned glass."

It didn't stop him from drinking the whiskey, however.

It wasn't, probably, the wisest thing he had ever done, given the situation he was in, but Will didn't consider himself particularly wise at the moment. He considered himself far more lucky than wise.

He had survived the "inquisition" by the UCI, cycling's governing body, despite the fact that just about everyone in the world from his teammates to his friends, from the press to very likely his father's dog, had screamed for his head on a platter. They didn't get it. Now, he was sitting in a dirty little bar in Lourdes, an odd city in which to be drinking, that's for sure, while the assembled masses were elsewhere, either recovering from their shock or expressing their disappointment in loud and angry tones.

It was like his very own version of the Simpson verdict on a sub-atomic scale.

Will stared at the double Jameson and slowly raised it to his lips. The smell began to hit him and caused him to smile. It had been a very long time. As the first drops hit his lips, he felt a hand run up his back and over his shoulder. The shock of the move and the move itself, a kind of loving push, caused him to slop the drink up and over the forward edge of the glass away from his mouth. It washed back and ran down his chin.

"Ooooh, sorry, Will," cooed Magda Gertz, her breasts entering his peripheral vision before she did.

"That's okay," he muttered, wiping his hand across his chin and then across the thigh of his jeans, "I like to take a bit of each day for an Abbott and Costello routine."

"Excuse me?"

"Sorry. Dated reference. Lost on foreign women."

"I don't know what you're talking about."

"It's nothing," he said. "What can I do for you, Magda?"

"I joined you to celebrate."

"Oh, my miraculous resurrection. That's what I was trying to celebrate as well." He raised the glass in a showy, jerky motion and another wave of the whiskey spilled over the edge of the glass.

"Been at it long?"

He looked at the growing puddle of whiskey on the Formica bar before him and shook his head.

"Hardly at all. Hardly at all." He very nearly cried at the sight. "Some celebration, huh?"

"Oh, I just like being with you, Will," she whispered, "you should know that by now."

Will lowered his head and scratched his forehead with his fingernails, trying to find the one spot that wasn't barking back at him from today's layer of sunburn.

"I suppose I do, Magda," he drawled, "but I don't know why. Honestly. For the life of me, I can't figure out what you want with me or why you want it or how you intend to get it. No offense, but that's just the way I am. I can't take a hint unless it's on a billboard 40 feet high and even then you can't be sure I'll catch on."

"I want you. Isn't that enough?"

"No, frankly. It should be," he shook his head, thinking back to a world of missed opportunities because of something his mother had probably jammed deep into his programming, "it really should be, but it's not. I can't tell you what or why or how, I can only tell you that, well, that's me."

He raised the heavy glass of Irish whiskey to his lips, but she stopped it just short of his mouth by putting her hand on his wrist. They were locked in a gentle battle of wills for a moment, he, wanting to take a sip, she wanting him to look her in the eyes.

As the battle progressed, Will watched in sadness as another swallow slopped over the edge of the glass and onto the bar. There appeared to be equal amounts now on the bar and in the glass.

He let out a sigh, put the glass down and turned to face her.

He looked deep into her arresting blue eyes.

"I want you, Will. I want to hold you and love you and be with you. I want to help you in this race. After the race, I want to be with you more, unlike any man I've been with before. You have time off, don't you? I have a place at Cap d'Antibes. You and I could spend it there, alone. Together. In the sun. In the village. In bed."

He stared at her for a moment, his eyes seemingly lost in hers. She smiled seductively.

"How do you want to help me in the race?" he asked, brushing aside nearly everything she had said in a single sentence.

"Uhh," Magda Gertz took a sharp breath, unsure of what direction to suddenly follow. She had never been countered in a seduction. Was this man so incredibly dense that he didn't understand or realize a proposition?

"I, uhh—"

"No, tell me, please. How would you help me in Le Tour? I truly appreciate the other stuff, I'm very flattered, but at the moment, I'm concerned about a race through the middle of France that appears to be killing me. So I'm fascinated with your offer. That one most of all."

"Well, I'm, uhh, I'm—" she pulled her hand away from his arm and took a moment to compose herself. "I'm a medical researcher."

"An assistant or officially a medical researcher?" he asked.

"I'm not an assistant," she replied, with a trace of bitterness. "I am a scientist. I am a doctor. I have degrees."

"Sorry. Sexist, I know, but a guy's gotta have his standards."

"I," she said, regaining her confidence, "am a researcher with a major medical supply company. We have a line of vitamins and supplements that far exceeds Haven Pharmaceuticals in terms of recovery and replacement."

"Really? Lock and load, huh?"

She didn't respond to what she didn't understand.

"So, what's the chemical makeup? What is this stuff? Heavy-duty multi-vites or some other chemical combination? Steroids or uppers or something along those lines?"

"Nothing illegal," she said, somewhat offended, "but a vitamin-and-chemical mix that aids in recovery, while boosting performance."

"Ah, super pill," he nodded. "I take it that Henri Bresson is on board?"

She smiled. "Perhaps. A girl has got to have her secrets."

He smiled back. "And I suppose that he got the invitation to Cap d'Antibes as well?"

Her hand shot out and slapped his face, hard, causing another sip of the whiskey to crash up and over the lip of the glass and down to the Formica before it joined the lake of liquor that grew before him.

"Those are not the words of a gentleman."

Will laughed, "I've never been accused—."

"That is the second time you've acted so small with me today."

"You'd better get used to it, for I am a small and shallow guy." He paused for a moment. "What was the other time?"

"Well, it's not very gentlemanly," she murmured, "you celebrating your victory announcement with me and then disappearing from the lobby when I stop in my room."

"I didn't celebrate with you. I was merely standing next to you when the UCI read their decision."

"Still, you kissed me."

"You kissed me."

"You kissed back."

"Force of habit."

"And then, you simply disappeared."

"It's just the way we Ross men are, Magda. We're ephemeral."

"I'm sorry?"

"We float on the wind. We're like spirits."

"Yes, indeed," a voice said, just behind them, "they're real will of the wisps, each and every one of them."

Cheryl Crane sat down on Will's left and bumped his arm, sending another cascade over the edge of his glass. "Vodka, rocks," she called to the bartender. "In fact, I'd almost say, Magda, that this boy comes from a long line of wood nymphs."

Magda Gertz didn't bother to hide her disappointment at the appearance of Cheryl Crane. Cheryl Crane didn't bother to hide her joy at being able to cause Magda Gertz disappointment.

Will dipped his finger in the pond of Jameson that sat on the table top before him and tasted it. Ohhh, he thought, very smooth. Before he could taste it again, the barkeep brought Cheryl her drink and wiped the whiskey off the bar with a filthy rag.

Will sighed.

"And how are you kids tonight?"

Magda Gertz didn't answer Cheryl, but Will looked over jealously as she took the first sip of her drink.

"Make sure you skim the fusel oil off the top."

"Naw," Cheryl answered. "Gives it flavor."

"Excuse me," Magda interrupted. "But, we were having a private conversation here."

"Oh, I'm sorry. I just thought, 'Here I am, a lonely girl in Lourdes, looking for a drink and a good time and there are two of my best friends, maybe I can join them for a bump.' And so I sat."

Will smiled. "Happy to have you."

THE DOOR OF THE APARTMENT SWUNG OPEN WITH A KICK AND LUC GODOT stepped into a very angry situation.

Isabelle Marchant stood before him, fire in her eyes, and lips curled in anticipation of a fight. Her fists were clenched and even her dress seemed tied in little knots of anger.

"Hello," she said without a trace of emotion.

"Yes, I know."

"What? You know what?" she asked, the anger growing in her voice.

"I know I'm late."

"Late? Late? Ha!" she cackled. "Late is one hour. Two maybe. Three with a phone call. That is late."

"So what am I?" Godot asked.

"You are dead. You are legally dead." The dam burst and the words poured from Isabelle Marchant.

"You don't call. You don't write. You don't let me know anything. You simply drop off the face of the world for," she looked up at the clock, "27 hours and you don't tell me *anything*!'

"I should have called."

"Yes, you should have, but you didn't. I didn't know if you were alive or dead or in a hospital or simply out on the town having a good time while I sat here waiting — waiting — patiently — patiently — for you. I even — I even went to work today hoping — hoping — to find you there, but I didn't. I didn't. I didn't find you there. In fact, I didn't find anyone there, because no one except you is stupid enough to work at Haven Pharmaceuticals during Le Tour de France."

"Are you done?"

"Oh, oh — *oh*, am I done! Yes, perhaps I am. Perhaps I am done. Perhaps I will walk out that door right now and you can cook for yourself and clean for yourself and go back to that wonderful life you had before me in that one room walk-up flat in the seediest part of the city."

She took a deep, rumbling breath and felt her anger rise over the top and start heading back toward calm. "Damn," she thought, "why can't I ever stay angry at *anyone*?"

"Now are you done?" he asked.

"You are," she cried, "*un salaud*." She paused. "Yes, I'm done."

"Good." Now that he didn't need them for protection, Godot put the two boxes of records on the floor. "You have every right —" he raised a finger as she started to speak. She stopped and he continued, "— every right to be furious with me. I didn't call. I should have told you where I was or what I was doing. For that, I am sorry."

"You should be."

"I am. Truly," he said sincerely, even though he wasn't sure if he believed what he was saying or was just saying it to defuse the situation.

"But — I was on a case."

"You're not an inspector anymore. How can you be on a case? And a case of what?"

Godot ignored the image and continued, "Something, as you know, has been bothering me for a few weeks now about a dead cyclist."

"Someone on Le Tour?"

"No. That Dutch cyclist. Henrik Koons."

"That was weeks ago and far away. I have never understood—."

"I know. Perhaps it has simply been 'old habits never dying,' but the case intrigued me nonetheless. I wanted to know and I wanted to know everything."

"And so you decided to go to the Netherlands, without me, to investigate a death that no one cares about so that you could be a hero to — who?"

Godot held his temper in check. "I did not go to Holland. I was here, only blocks away, really, digging through records."

"For 24 hours?"

"Yes. I slept in a chair. I peed in a corner. I broke locks and windows and my watch," he said, pulling the dead soldier out of his pocket and holding it in the air by the strap for her to see, "so that I could find what I was looking for."

"And did you?"

"I," he said, the anger and power going out of his voice, "don't know. I just don't know."

He slumped in a chair.

Isabelle watched him for a moment, put aside the hurt and frustration that had built into a mighty edifice over the course of the previous night and stepped over to his side.

"Give me your coat. It needs to be cleaned. Strip down and take a shower. You smell vaguely of dead leaves. Pile up everything outside the door and I will have it washed. Take your time and I will make you dinner. Then, when you are ready, *we* will go through whatever it is you have brought home to find whatever it is you're looking for."

He reached up and took her hand, pulled it to him and kissed it.

❂

"WHEN DID SHE GET HERE?"

"She was here right from the start, boss. She was in Lille for the prologue."

Carl Deeds felt himself sinking into the huge leather chair at the end of the executive board room conference table, a heavy mahogany block big enough for a half-court basketball game. Deeds wiped a drop of sweat off his chin. Despite an air conditioner that was working overtime, the Haven directeur sportif continued to sweat profusely. He ran his hands back and forth across the table and felt small ridges in what appeared to be a smoothly polished surface, but while his fingers questioned them, his face and mind were focused elsewhere.

At the other end of the table, walking from a spear of light coming through the window from a setting sun to a pit of darkness on the other side of the room and back again, Henri Bergalis paced anxiously.

"You're sure you noticed her at the prologue?"

"Yeah, I mean, it's tough not to notice Magda, if you know what I mean."

"Yes," he answered coolly. "Why didn't you tell me?"

"Well, I didn't think there was anything to it. I mean, she's been around in the past, few years ago, anyway, and nobody bothered. I didn't think there was anything to it until you called me here tonight. She's been hanging around most of the stages, staying at our hotels, showing up with Bresson, or Ross, or Cardone. That Delgado kid."

"She's, what does Will say, 'playing the field'?"

"Yeah, that's it."

"And she's been with Will. Anything there, you think?"

"I dunno. I dunno with any of them. Will and Cheryl, though, seem pretty tight, even though I thought she was going to deck him a few days ago."

"Really? Why?"

Bergalis's sudden interest in the relationship of Will and Cheryl set off a warning bell in the back of Deeds's brain pan, but then again, he thought, Bergalis had been chasing Cheryl earlier this season himself. Maybe that hadn't quite cooled off.

"I dunno. It was a fight of some sort. She was pissed, I dunno, maybe about Magda. somebody said they saw Will coming out of her room one morning looking somewhat the worse for wear."

"Ah, interesting. As for Magda, you can always rely on certain people to act in certain ways."

"I suppose."

"Carl," Bergalis said, quietly, stepping back into the darkness in the corner of the room, "what do you think she's up to?"

"Cheryl?"

"Magda."

"Sorry, boss. You keep changing the subject." Deeds thought for a moment while he unconsciously rubbed his hands back and forth across the polished table top.

"I can't guess. Who's she working for now?"

"BioSyn."

"What are they big into?"

"Stealing everyone else's ideas."

Deeds sat quietly for a moment, then brightened upon finding a possible answer and pleasing his boss. "Hell, just to hazard a guess, I'd have to say she's after whatever Louis is cooking up."

"Engelure?"

"Yeah, that's all I can figure."

"Hmm. Interesting. Have she and Engelure talked at all?"

"I dunno. I haven't seen anything, but, Jesus, I don't really pay any attention to Engelure. He does his thing and I do mine. He doesn't get in my way and I—"

Bergalis held up a hand, stopping Deeds in mid-sentence.

"Understood, Carl. Understood."

"Sorry."

"Where is she now?"

"Magda? I dunno. Uhh, the last place I saw her was leaving the dining room with Will in tow after the announcement, then I saw her looking around the lobby and hustling out the door a few minutes later."

"With Will?"

"No. She was alone, but, she seemed to be looking for somebody."

"Will?"

Deeds raised his hands. "I dunno. I'm sorry."

"Cheryl?"

Again, Deeds raised his hands, shrugging his shoulders at the same time.

"Well, keep an eye on her."

"Who, Cheryl?"

"No. Magda Gertz. Keep a close eye on her. I want to know everything she does, everyone she talks with, every time she gets close to Monsieur Engelure."

"How can I do that? I've got a team to run."

"If you don't, perhaps you won't. There is a rat in the rice, here, Carl. Stay close to her any way you can. Sleep with her if you must."

"What? Me?"

"Don't worry, Carl," Henri Bergalis said softly, a trace of hard honesty laced with edged sarcasm filling his voice, "she'll sleep with anyone."

Deeds suddenly realized that the back of his shirt was wet, but not as wet as his neck, which was not as wet as his face, which was not as wet as his hands, smearing a trail of water across the top of the dark wooden table.

"I should know, Carl," Bergalis said distantly, "I should know."

WILL PEERED INTO THE BOTTOM OF THE DOUBLE-SIZED, HEAVY-GAUGE SHOT GLASS, carefully examining the remaining whiskey, which had shrunk down through spillage to a drop barely large enough to wet a Q-Tip. He put the glass carefully on the bar and tilted it slightly to the right, pooling the liquor in one corner. Gently snaking out a finger, he reached into the glass to mop up the dregs, misjudged the false bottom of the shot and dropped it flat on bar top. The last of the golden liquid ran past his finger and out onto the mottled Formica.

Will sighed heavily.

"Drinking problem?" Cheryl asked.

"The worst kind," he answered, licking his finger with relish, "the kind where you can't drink."

"I don't know how wise it is anyway. You're in training."

"Thank you, Angelo Dundee."

They both looked over to Magda Gertz, who sat watching the pair of them with an ill-disguised contempt. She continued to smile at Will, but it was a smile that had lost a spin off its seductiveness, as if she were growing tired of the game.

Meanwhile, it was easy to see that she had been tired of Cheryl since the first days of Le Tour, as she never did appreciate competition in such things.

The conversation had grown sullen and silent. Will looked up at the clock sitting beside what passed for a cash register. Twenty after. Perfect. Conversation always stops at 20 of and 20 after the hour.

Couldn't remember where he heard that, but it seemed to hold true.

HIS DUTIES FINALLY DONE FOR THE DAY, LOUIS ENGELURE STEPPED OUT OF THE hotel lobby and into the cool dusk of the evening. Turning up the collar of his jacket, he looked left, then right, then behind, as if to make sure, one last time, that no one saw him stepping away for the evening, perhaps for the night.

He'd pay for this tomorrow, he knew, when the race went on and he fought to keep his eyes open, but for now, he was thrilled to be out from under, for however long he could make it, the overwhelming and oppressive thumb of Haven.

He turned one last time to make sure he had preserved some modicum of secrecy and hurried off in search of life.

"TELL ME AGAIN, WHAT ARE WE LOOKING FOR?"

"Anything to do with a chemical called 'Cytabutasone.'"

"Yes, all right," Isabelle Marchant answered. She stared sadly at the piles of papers that were now littering the floor of her freshly cleaned living room. She yawned and returned to scanning sheet after sheet of research data for her elusive word.

She realized after a very short time that she could only do one or two pages at a time, as the words and formulas began to smear and run together if she didn't take regular and consistent breaks. She rubbed her eyes and blinked twice, before returning again. The sheets were endless and her living room was a mess and they had hardly cracked even the first box of records.

"We're going to be at this forever," Isabelle muttered.

"Yes," Godot said, dropping a sheet and rubbing his eyes. "Yes, we are."

"Is there any way to sharpen the search? Give it some focus?"

"Well, this is the true joy of police work," he said lovingly, "it's not chasing bad guys and shooting them with a smile, it is digging through records and hoping upon hope that you're not too tired to recognize the clues when you pass them in print."

"But there has to be some way to tighten this up. A date. A test. Something that would tell us where to go. After all — it is all dated. These boxes are chronological."

Godot thought for a minute and then smiled. She was helping him in something that, for all intents and purposes, she should be ignoring. It was drudge work. It was a pain. He should be able to tighten the search.

Godot leaned back against the sofa and stretched his back, feeling a delicious stretch in two of his upper vertebrae. He stared at a corner of the room, just beyond a small, rusty water stain in the shape of Provence, and pondered the possibilities of who might be able to date stamp this search for him, help him trim it down to a manageable size.

He suddenly brightened for a moment, then receded. There was a man, the fellow who had led the charge all along the way, but, as he stole a glance at the clock, it would probably be too late to call tonight. They'd either have to continue searching or give it up until morning.

"What are you thinking?"

Godot turned to Isabelle and smiled. "I'm thinking 'long shot,' but it might work." He struggled off the floor and stretched, feeling another two bones in his back adjust themselves like cannon shots.

"Oh, God, I heard that."

"You should have heard it from my side." He waddled toward the phone in the entryway, trying to stretch the ligaments in his hips, which had shortened in the time on the floor to the length of elbow macaroni. He picked up an envelope on his way to the phone, opened it, checked the number, cracked his fingers and dialed.

WILL WATCHED IN ENVY AS MAGDA GERTZ FINISHED HER THIRD GLASS OF WINE. He knew he should just ignore what had happened with his drink and order another, but somehow he didn't have it in him. He had promised himself one, and one was what he had had. No matter that it had wound up in every corner of the bar except him. He had had his one drink.

Will rubbed his forehead.

"Tired?" Magda asked, ignoring Cheryl, "perhaps I should take you back to the hotel."

Will felt a sudden and barely controllable need to duck.

"No. I'm fine."

Cheryl didn't react. A wave of relief passed over him. Over the past hour, he had felt the thunderhead building.

"Well," Magda said, "I must be getting back to the hotel. It is a big day tomorrow. Many people to see. Many people to do."

"I don't doubt that."

"Excuse me?" Magda Gertz shot a hard look down at Cheryl.

"Nothing," Cheryl replied with a slightly evil smile.

Magda Gertz was not about to let it go. "If I may ask, politely, what is your problem with me?"

Cheryl never looked up from her glass. "You really want to know?"

"Yes, I would."

"No, Magda, I mean," she said, turning, and looking around Will to face the voluptuous blonde who had become a personal, internalized nemesis, "do you *really* want to know?"

"Yes, as a matter of fact, I do."

Will's head was locked in a position staring at the back of the bar, but his eyes were darting side to side in a desperate attempt to find a hiding place.

The Ross family was known for its ability to skirt confrontation in a variety of creative ways, and true to his central program, Will looked quickly for a safe and silent exit.

"Sorry you're in the middle of this," Cheryl stage whispered.

"Just don't throw things," Will said, sounding, much to his surprise, far more calm than he felt.

"Magda," Cheryl said, slowly, winding up carefully for the pitch that was to come, "my problem with you is that I don't like you."

"I don't like you, either," she replied.

"I figured that. But, frankly, it really goes beyond like and dislike, because I can't stand people getting in my way. I can't stand the idea of working my ass off to get somewhere in the world, in the company of men, and then having somebody blow in and wiggle her ass and suck up, almost literally, and muck it all up for me."

A hint of triumph crossed the face of Magda Gertz. "Jealous?"

"Oh, yeah. No doubt. Can't help it, though, when I you see you waltz in and begin massaging the crotch of every man in the room."

"That's not fair. Do you know how many degrees in research chemistry I have?"

"Doesn't matter," Cheryl said, her voice rising in sarcasm, "because you *don't use them, do you*?"

As the tension grew into a smothering blanket around him, Will felt his legs begin to dissolve and his butt scoot forward to the edge of the stool, prior to his collapsing in a puddle on the floor.

"What are you saying?"

"Oh, for god's sake, Gertz. You know and I know. You might be Alberta Einstein but you're acting like Suzy Creamcheese. I don't care how smart you are, because you don't care how smart you are. You don't use your brains. You're a manipulator. You get what you want by shoving your," she searched for a word, "'assets' into everybody's face."

Another smile crossed the face of Magda Gertz. "Assets you wish you had."

"Yes," Cheryl said with quiet exasperated tone, "sure. Doesn't everybody? But — the point is, my problem with you is that you don't care about anybody but you. You don't care about Will or this team or this race. You don't care about anybody but yourself and whatever it is you're doing here. That's fine. But don't act like you're concerned and don't act like you care. Because you don't. You care about yourself and whatever it is sitting on your game plan."

"I have no plan."

Cheryl chuckled evilly, "Oh, sister, yes you do. I don't know what it is, nor does our little friend here," she poked Will, who grinned in a haphazard way before returning to his shell, "but you have a plan. And it has something to do with this team and I'm going to find out what it is and there will be hell to pay."

"There is no plan."

"Then, Magda, you are wasting a lot of prime ass-wiggling."

"I wonder why Will finds you attractive, when you spend so much time being bitter and angry toward others."

"I'm intelligent, I'm goal oriented *and* I'm great in the sack."

"Really? So am I — but those are talents I don't parade in French bars." Magda turned to Will, who remained frozen in his position at the bar, hands clutching an empty shot glass, eyes staring straight ahead, ran her hand along his shoulder and said, softly, "Coming? No," she pulled her hand away, letting it drape across his back, "no, of course you're not." She turned to Cheryl, "Not tonight."

As Magda Gertz rose, she picked up her bag and ran her hand deliberately across the surface of the leather, just behind the handle. For some reason, Will noticed the move and immediately wondered what she was so worried about. Swinging her hand up into an exaggerated gesture of goodbye, Magda Gertz turned and walked confidently toward the door, waving, "Ciao, everyone. Ciao."

Cheryl watched her leave and turned to Will, who had watched the exit in the mirror over the bar, a position that had provided a unique view and had proven many of the theories that Cheryl had been expounding on only moments before.

"Well," Will said, quietly, "*that* went well."

"I blew it, didn't I?"

"You were busy arguing against the harsh reality of the world."

"And what might that be?'

"Sex sells. You can have the most reliable car in the world, but everybody wants the hot and sexy Italian job that can't go 50 feet without a week in the shop."

"Are you saying that I'm a Ford Escort?"

"No, I'm saying that you're a Mustang. Fiery, determined and gutsy, with great lines and a proven reliability."

"Nice comeback."

"Thank you. I was working on snappy allegories all the while you two were fighting."

"It wasn't a fight."

"Well, then, all through your chat. Your 'heated' chat."

They were silent for a moment before Cheryl said, quietly, "You were a big damned help."

Will stared straight ahead, a sense of calm finally returning to his insides.

"My daddy always told me," he croaked, "never step between two fighters."

"And his reasoning?"

"Because it's the peacemaker who always gets killed."

ISABELLE MARCHANT CAREFULLY PLACED HER THIRD REAM OF RESEARCH reports on top of the other two. The tower of paper remained steady for the few moments she watched them — and then promptly toppled to the floor the moment she turned away. She sighed, heavily, and thought about cleaning them up, but then waved her hand at them in a vague and disinterested way. It will all clean tomorrow, she thought, somewhat amazed by her change in heart from when they had begun this process only four hours ago.

She picked up another ream of paper, tied lightly with large, industrial-strength rubber bands, and peeled them away. She blinked her eyes, hard, twice, to clear and refocus them, and dove back into the sea of words she didn't understand.

"Cytabutasone," she muttered, reminding herself what she was looking for, "Cytabutasone, Cytabutasone, Cytabutasone…."

The creaking of the floor, muffled by her mother's rug, made her look up and toward the arch that led into the entryway. Godot stood there, the look on his face a cross between shock, frustration and concern.

"What, Luc?"

He didn't say anything, his mouth moving, but no words coming out.

"What? Did you find your man? Did you get what you needed? Or, do you have to call back tomorrow?"

He turned to face her and answered without emotion, "Yes and no and no."

"What do you mean?"

"Yes, I found my contact. No, I did not get what I needed. And no, I do not have to call back tomorrow."

"Because ..." she asked, expectantly.

"Because Paul van Bruggen is dead, his records are gone and it would be a waste of time to call him back tomorrow because his funeral was today."

"Oh, my. How did he die?"

"He was shot. Between the eyes."

Despite years in a police station, typing up the most grisly reports, Isabelle Marchant could not stop herself from raising her hand to her mouth and exclaiming, "Oh, my."

"Yes," he said, quietly, "I agree."

Godot ran his hand over the top of his head and stretched again before stepping over to the second box of records and lifting the lid. "I hope you are ready for a very long night and a very long tomorrow," he said quietly to Isabelle, "for somewhere, in here, is our answer."

Isabelle nodded.

"You hope."

Godot stared at the packed piles of reports in the box.

"Yes. I hope."

CHAPTER SIXTEEN:

ONE-HUNDRED-SIXTY-FIRST MAN ON THE MOUNTAIN

It was quickly turning out to be a vicious day.

It had started hard in Lourdes with a false start and nine kilometers of neutralized racing, followed by the early climbs. They were nothing much, really, little more than bumps on a long and winding road to hell in the Pyrenees, but they were climbs nonetheless. Will had wrestled the bike to the top of the first, a sharply angled category-three jump, with the bike fighting him each and every step of the way. This was no "Beast," he thought, at one point, actually considering climbing off and carrying the thing up to the summit.

At least, he had the energy to think such thoughts today.

WILL HAD DUTIFULLY TAKEN HIS I.V., AS PRESCRIBED BY MONSIEUR ENGELURE, right alongside Henri Bresson, hoping, upon hope, that Henri wouldn't notice the sly glances he was throwing his way in an effort to keep an eye on Engelure and whatever it was he was giving Bresson. No doubt, he thought, looking at the landscape that shimmered through the yellowish liquid dripping into Henri's arm and the blue into his, these are two very different concoctions.

Very cool, Will thought, very slick.

"I look like a weasel trying to convince an egg I'm not interested in eating it," he had said earlier to Cheryl.

"Well," she replied, "you've certainly got the weasel part right."

When he was finished, Engelure pulled the I.V. and patted Will on the shoulder. "Don't worry. I've got him now."

"Got who now?" asked Bresson, looking hale and healthy and recovered from his dead-man's gray of the day before.

Will looked at Engelure, whose lips were flapping without any sound coming out.

"Monsieur Engelure," Will said, "is singing to you. He's singing the famous Sonny and Cher tune, 'I've Got You, Babe.' Any connection between that and his closely held personal feelings for you is purely coincidental." Will turned and walked quickly to the bathroom, as Engelure knelt beside Bresson to remove the I.V. Henri slapped him, hard, on the side of the head.

Will smiled. "If he's on some drug, *that* is a good side effect."

Will stepped into the bathroom, opened his shaving kit and unloaded the packets of BioLode vitamins he would need for the day. It took him two or three minutes to collect all the pills he was going to take, and three handfuls, each with a large glass of water, to get them down.

Who needs food, he thought, when you can eat chemicals?

He cleaned up his mess and stepped back out into the room. Engelure was gone and Bresson sat alone.

"You don't think I can do it, do you, Will?"

"I didn't, Henri. I'm beginning to change my mind."

"You think I'm on the needle?"

Will paused. Bresson had been honest with him, all along the way, and a friend, even in the harsh times just prior to the race. He deserved an honest answer, which Will couldn't provide.

"No."

"Well, I'm not."

"Didn't think you were."

"Yes, you did, Will. Everyone did. Everyone does." Bresson paused and looked at Will with an icy stare, a stare that cut right through Will to his deepest, darkest place within. "Who are you, Will? What do you believe?"

"What?"

"Who are you, Will?"

"Are you just being wacky or is this Philosophy 101?"

"I need to know, Will."

"Know what?"

"Who are you, Will? What do you believe?"

"I am Will Ross and I believe I need breakfast."

"You have no idea, do you, my friend?"

"I have a fairly good idea. And that idea is hungry." He stepped quickly out of the room and pulled the door closed behind him, wiping his face with a cold hand that came back hot and sweaty.

Man, that cut it, Will thought. Bresson *is* on the needle. In college, everybody doing dope always asked those same damned questions.

"Who are you, man, no really? Don't you feel the earth breathing, man? Didja ever think there could be a whole universe in a piece of dandruff, man? That's why I never wash my hair."

Will shook his head and started down the hall toward the lobby of the hotel. "Breakfast?" he asked himself. It was a question he could answer.

"Good idea."

WILL KICKED THE BIKE HARD UP AND OVER THE SECOND CLIMB, A FOURTH category, easier than the first, less steep, but with the bike fighting him all the way. It was like riding up a flight of stairs in a wooden wheelchair. Approaching the summit, Will dropped off the pace and raised his hand, sliding to the side as the Haven team car pulled up.

"What?" Luis was already out of the car as Will was pulling off the front wheel.

"It's fighting me like a turkey that doesn't want to be dinner. I think I'm losing a bearing up front."

Luis already had a wheel down from the top of the car, took the stem from Will's hand and slammed the wheel home, locking it in with one, smooth motion.

"There. Set. Go."

Will was back on and climbing toward the summit. The entire exchange had taken less than 20 seconds. On the third climb, the Mauvezin, the bike fought him once again. This, he knew, was no bearing. This, he knew, was a battle of wills.

It had become the bike or him. Anybody else could ride this machine and find a magnificent bike, but for him, today, this race, he was on two wheels that carried an attitude. He slammed his hand down on the handlebars, next to the race computer, and felt the impact shudder through the frame.

That's no way to treat it, he thought, but his frustrations were getting the better of him.

There was a false summit at 500 meters on the Mauvezin, followed by another 50 meters of stiff climbing to the true top of the ridge. Will remained in the pack, but it was tough going.

God, he thought. It's like I'm dragging a yacht.

The pace picked up considerably on the back side of the Mauvezin, the quick descent dropping out to 50 kilometers of flats before the four major climbs of the day, two category 1 climbs, followed by the Col du Tourmalet at 2100 meters and Luz-Ardiden at 1700, one right after the other, 1200 meters of vertical rise followed immediately by another 1000 meters of vertical rise, followed by Will launching breakfast into the crowd and hoping that it hit somebody he didn't like.

The bike continued to fight him.

"I'll trade you in on a damned moped," he barked. Will shot right through the peloton, raising jeers of "Hey," "Watch it," "Goddamned amateur!" He fought the bike back onto the line and stared straight ahead.

"Aha," he whispered, leaning forward to the bike computer, "so you are alive."

WALKING THROUGH THE HALL TOWARD BREAKFAST, MAGDA GERTZ HAD SLID beside Will and wrapped her arm in his, scaring the hell out of him.

"Where did you come from?"

"I'm glad I have such a soothing effect on you. Where were you last night after our little conversation? It was a rest day. I thought we could rest."

"You don't give up, do you?"

She shrugged. "Never. You're always welcome, you know that."

"I'm sorry. I have multiple-personality syndrome. Even when I sleep alone it's a crowd, and you wouldn't want that."

Despite her scent and her warmth, and the smoothness of her skin next to his, Will couldn't help but feel his skin crawl, especially given her battle with Cheryl the night before.

He was skittish. He was full of vitamins. He was hungry.

They stepped into the dining room together and Will began to turn toward the Haven table. Magda Gertz had frozen in place. Will felt like his arm was wrapped up in a cast iron lawn jockey.

"I can't stay," she whispered quickly in his ear. "Things to do." She released him quickly and turned, walking briskly, just short of a jog, back toward the hall leading to her room.

Will turned and looked at the team table. Cheryl stepped through the entrance and joined him.

"I just saw your little friend making book in the other direction. Did she suddenly learn that you chew your toe nails and toss them behind the sofa?"

"No, it was something disgusting."

"Ah, the sweet breath of romance. It dies so quickly."

The soap opera that had played itself out between Will, Cheryl and Magda had already lost its appeal to the majority of the riders, with the exception of Tony C., who was interested in anything that had to do with sex. None of the riders stirred from their muesli and yogurt.

Only Bergalis was staring, staring hard at Will and the spot in the universe that Magda Gertz had occupied only seconds before. Cheryl didn't notice, but Will suddenly felt like a naked man on display, with a booger hanging out of his nose.

"Will. Cheryl. Join me." Henri Bergalis waved them down to the seats beside him.

"The muesli is very good."

"Cheryl — here," Bergalis said, patting the pad of the seat next to him. Cheryl stepped over and sat down, not realizing that that was the only seat left at the table. Henri Bergalis immediately occupied Cheryl in conversation, while Will gathered his breakfast and looked for a chair. The only spot he found was at a small table, not even set for dining, in a corner just behind Cheryl and Bergalis.

Will ate, even though the majority of the food tasted like a cross between library paste and old shoes.

That hardly mattered. What bugged him was the notion that once again his aunt and uncle had put him at the kid's table for Thanksgiving dinner.

THEY WERE APPROACHING THE DAY'S ONLY TWO POINTS SPRINTS. TONY Cacciavillani had taken off like a shot toward the line, the remaining sprinters of Le Tour jumping out with him, all sensing, all knowing, that this was the last moment of the day, perhaps of the race itself, when any of them would be noticed at all. Within a few kilometers, it would be a whole new event, the race for the King of the Mountains jersey, a whole new race for yellow.

Few believed that Henri Bresson would continue in yellow, even Will. Only Henri Bresson believed.

Bresson did not charge with the sprinters, something he might have done earlier in his wearing of the jersey to ensure that he would be wearing it tonight. He held back in the peloton now, more confident in his talents and his position, but also more aware of the very real fact that he was a marked man, marked by every other rider in the bunch. If he so much as twitched, the rest of the field reacted. He sat back and waited for them, waiting for him, waiting for them.

He stood up on the pedals.

The peloton tensed.

He stretched his neck to look up the road.

The peloton mimicked the action.

He talked into his wrist, as if wearing a radio.

The peloton leaned forward to hear.

And then, like a shot, he was gone, flying up the road in a rage. Will was shocked by the move and even more shocked to be on Bresson's tail, tight behind, actually riding with the leader of the race in something that appeared as natural as a belch in a chili house.

Twelve other riders immediately followed suit, tight in the mix, while the rest of the peloton strung out behind, trying to stay up with the frantic pace, not wanting to be left behind by the leader at the base of the first of four major climbs less than 30 kilometers ahead.

The pace was frantic, the pace was mad, given what they faced so soon, but there was also a method in the madness, the method of casting out and letting the crowd reel you back in on the climb, but not completely, then, casting yourself out again on the descent, fast, tight, out of control at 65 miles an hour, then, allowing them to chase, and draw close again on the next climb, and the next, and the next, and somehow hold on, somehow time the jump and their exhaustion to send you across the line safe again in yellow.

On the other hand, this was not a worry for Will Ross. He was as safe as a child in his mother's arms. No one was concerned at all about him. He could be two hours ahead of the peloton and no one would be concerned. Will was a cipher lost toward the rear of the standings. One afternoon at the front of the race would not be a small loss, it would be no loss at all.

Bresson was another case altogether. The entire peloton now reacted to any move by Henri Bresson. Some reacted with fiery moves of their own, others with resignation. Some faced directeurs sportifs screaming into radios that Bresson would either leave them all in the dust or explode on the Col de Peyresourde.

Let him go, ride your race, watch the others.

Catch him, catch him now or your day is done.

In the midst of it all, Bresson charged.

Will held tight to his wheel, calling ahead for Bresson to let him take a pull at the front. Bresson did not react, or slip aside, or seem to hear. He charged toward the first mountain, the first category one mountain of the race, like a man possessed by demons. Demons wearing yellow.

"OH, MY GOD, LUC. DON'T TELL ME YOU WERE AT IT ALL NIGHT."

Luc Godot rubbed his eyes and blinked twice, pulling himself up by the edge of the sofa until he could drop back into it with a crash.

"Uhhh, yes," he said, turning to face Isabelle, who stood, tying her robe, in the doorway to their bedroom, "yes, I suppose I was."

"You promised. You promised only 10 minutes. Only 10 more minutes."

"Well, it became something like 10 more hours."

"You're not going to work today. I refuse to let that place kill you. You realize that, don't you?"

"Yes, I realize that."

"So. I will make you breakfast and then send you to bed. You're no good to anybody in this condition."

"No, I suppose not."

He stared out from his perch on the sofa, his tired, aching eyes scanning the sea of research reports that covered the floor of the living room. Isabelle's rug, her mother's rug, had disappeared in a spray of white and gray and black.

He bugged his eyes and yawned.

"Did you find anything?"

"What?"

Isabelle stuck her head out of the serving window in the kitchen and repeated, "Did-you-find-anything?"

"What? Oh, no. No, I didn't. All I found out was that Haven Pharmaceuticals has spent years and millions developing hundreds of formulas that went absolutely nowhere."

"Well, where else could it be?"

"I don't know. It depends on how important it is — to someone."

"Then maybe whoever it is wouldn't want it in the archives where somebody like you could get at it. Where anyone could get at it. Those records could be anywhere: in an office, in a safe, in a home or nowhere, destroyed."

"These were behind a double-locked door, and locked in a heavy security cabinet."

"So, how'd you get the keys?" she asked, stepping over another mound of papers and handing him a large cup of black coffee.

"I made them," he said with pleasure. "I am a very handy fellow."

"That, I know."

They sat on the sofa, silently, for a number of minutes staring at papers and boxes and heaps of rubber bands, until his eyes fell on a thin leather case locked with a small, but solid, brass latch.

"Is that yours?" he asked.

"What?"

"That."

☼

THE VILLAGES OF BERTREN AND ESTENOS FLASHED BY, THE SITE OF THE TWO sprints. The crowds still in place, watched for the leaders, their heroes. Will and Bresson flew past, the pace hot, stepping in just below a sprint, and the crowd applauded politely. The 12 riders who had jumped onto the breakaway were applauded, too, if only with measured enthusiasm.

Then, as they reached the outskirts of Estenos, Will heard it, vaguely behind him, the eruption of applause, the frantic cheering, the explosion of the village.

It gave Will pause.

Zarrabeitia.

Antonio Zarrabeitia was up in the pedals and beginning his ride toward yellow. This was his territory. These were his people. The villages were giving way from French- to Spanish-sounding names. The mountain people of the border rose on their own to embrace Zarrabeitia as one of their own. They were cheering for him now, no more than 45 seconds back.

This was not a breakaway, Will suddenly realized. This was desperation. He fumbled for his radio to get team information and a time check. He lost his pace for a moment, but pulled back to Bresson's wheel. He didn't have a radio. His had been pulled and given to Cardone who was supposed to stay with Bresson, while Will stayed with Richard, while Richard stayed with the leaders with his eye on the final prize.

Man, oh, man, this was turning into one screwed-up day.

Will unconsciously shifted gears again.

A flash of color, moving backward, brought him out of his focus on the rear tire of Henri Bresson. They were passing through the group of sprinters, quickly enough that some actually appeared to be pedaling backward.

Luchon passed in a blur of faces and shouts.

Bresson was keeping the pace high on the steep wall of the Col de Peyresourde. Will hadn't even realized they were climbing. That was nice. He wondered if he could find that alpha state again and not come out of it until he crossed the line at L'Alpe d'Huez a few days from now.

No such luck. Within moments, he felt the first tingles of the climb racing along the top of his thighs. He wasn't locked into a series of mindless, locomotive exertions yet, but this, again, was merely the first of four. He'd have plenty of time to scream later.

Will shot a glance over his shoulder. The 12 riders who had caught the break were now seven. He looked beyond them quickly to the main pack, the peloton, chasing close behind. The 45-second gap remained, if only just, but there simply didn't seem to be a frantic need to catch up, despite the man in yellow ahead.

At least, not yet.

The pack swam as a shark with the leaders, the favorites of Le Tour, aboard, slowly circling, quickly striking, only when they were damned good and ready to strike.

And obviously, Will thought, they were not damned good and ready.

Still, he couldn't help feeling like a grouper.

Will turned his head to the front, to see Bresson continue his charge up the first of four climbs. This guy had to have a break, Will thought, or he's going to explode when he least expects it and can't afford it.

"Henri," Will shouted, "give me the pull."

Bresson did not hear.

"Henri, goddamn it! Give me the pull! Let's do this together!"

Bresson did not react.

The charge continued, with Will tucked in tight on the rear wheel of Henri Bresson, when the realization struck him. His bike wasn't fighting him anymore. Perhaps there was no symbiosis, no electrical tie that brought the two together, but there was no more fighting, no more battling for each and every pedal stroke, no more attitude. Will hadn't broken the bike to his will as much as both sides had simply given up and called a truce. They were neutral, now, with both watching each other warily for the next insult, the next infraction, the next bending of the rules of physics, the road, or Emily Post.

The charge continued.

"OH, GOD," ISABELLE MOANED, "IF THAT IS WHAT WE HAVE BEEN LOOKING FOR, I am going to commit suicide."

"And why, my love?" Godot asked, carefully examining the lock on the leather case.

"Because that was on top of the first box of reports last night and I picked it up and put it aside before I began work."

"And the first shall be last and the last shall be first," he said, quietly.

He looked carefully at the lock, a heavy gauge brass number in a very small package, determining what tools he would need to defeat it. He stepped into the kitchen and came back with a thin wood chisel and a small hammer.

"Hold it," he told her, "No, this way, on its side."

He carefully placed the edge of the chisel at the base of the lock hook and tapped the other end with the hammer.

"Delicate work?" she asked.

"Yes," he replied, bringing the hammer down on the chisel head with all his strength. The ensuing boom rattled everything in the room, including Isabelle Marchant.

"What are you doing?" she shouted in surprise.

He didn't look at her, but remained focused on the job at hand, prying what remained of the latch away from the clasp on the bag. "Delicate work," he whispered.

"Delicate work."

THEY CRESTED THE SUMMIT OF THE COL DE PEYRESOURDE AT 1569 METERS, shooting down the backside with the bit in their teeth. This, Will thought, was the fun part of the day. The fun wasn't in the ceremony, the pack in motion, the climb, no, not the climb, the fun was in the descent, the big-ring, pedal-your-life-out-descent, when you dropped 2500 feet in a little over 10 kilometers, while your tires sang a tune and you shot down a strip of asphalt on the rough and ragged edge, knowing, way back in the dark recesses of your mind, that a stone, a pebble, a tear in a tire, a break in the asphalt, a pothole no bigger than a silver dollar, a fan, a photographer, a moto, a van, a car parked wrong, a bird, a dog, a piece of litter, could throw you off the track, off your line and into the guardrail, the trees, the ether, bound for heaven, hell or the hospital.

What did the guy at the Indianapolis 500 always say? "This, then, is sheer racing excitement."

You don't know the half of it, Jack.

They approached Bordères-Louron without slacking their pace. Will shouted up to Bresson, but, again, got no reaction at all. Will kept the pace and tucked his head, glancing under his right arm. No one to be seen. Somehow, they had broken off from the remaining riders of the breakaway and were leading the race alone.

Will sat up as they approached the feed zone, expecting to slow, but Bresson would have none of it. He continued in the big ring and rode as a man possessed, blowing through the zone without a look to either side. The Haven soigneur looked shocked, then amazed, then folded a second musette bag down to his hand from his shoulder and held them both for Will, who grabbed them, at speed, nearly tearing his right arm out of the socket.

Will flung the bags over his shoulder and picked up his pace to reconnect with Bresson.

Still on the descent, Will unloaded the musettes, quickly, into the pockets of his jersey, the energy drinks, the fruit, the sandwich, the water. He tossed his empty musette to the side of the road, then, shouting ahead to Bresson and receiving no answer again, pulled beside and began to shout directly at this man who was so in focus, so on the line, that he couldn't take the time to eat. Bresson would have to take that time or he would collapse in a heap on the slopes of the Tourmalet, no doubt about it. Nobody, no body, could take this kind of punishment, this kind of exertion and not be fed, be stoked, be refueled.

Bresson continued to ignore him.

They reached the base of another climb, and Will immediately felt the pitch of the new ascent, the Col d'Aspin.

Aspin?

Aspen?

Like to go there, hang with Ivana. Better than hanging here. He finished a bottle of water and threw it ahead and to the side, toward a bike standing by the roadside. Souvenir. The kid ducked and the Coca-Cola-emblazoned bottle shot past.

Hmm. Not a big enough star, Will thought. Make it Jalabert or Riis or Kruse, and the kid would have leapt upon it and clutched it to his bosom like a map to King Solomon's mines.

The energy drink, a thick, green mass of carbohydrate-enriched goo, sat in the back of his throat like November phlegm, cold, unmoving and unyielding. He washed it down with a gulp of water and immediately felt some relief in his upper thighs, the lactic acid flushed, if only for a moment, by the carbos.

He shouted ahead, again, to Bresson, still in the pipeline, still on focus, still on pace.

Somehow, until now, given the pace and the curlicue nature of the road, they had often been alone, away from the stare of the helos and motos and commissaires, but early on the slopes of the Col d'Aspin, they picked up a lot of company.

As the last of the early breakaways fell back, the race chief commissaire's car fell back as well, picking up the two Haven riders stepping into the lead. The moto for France 2, the television service providing live and taped coverage for the majority of the world, roared up from behind, shooting miles of video of the two riders who were breaking with the conventional wisdom of the stage and riding hard at the front.

Overhead, the live coverage helicopter of France 2 roared and shot its microwaves back to wherever, the images then relayed around the world for an ever-dwindling audience.

And, still, despite the noise and confusion and company, Henri Bresson did not break stride, did not allow Will to take the pull, did not allow his focus to drift.

He was on the mountain.

The mountain was his.

"WHERE ARE THEY? WHERE THE HELL ARE THEY?" DEEDS SHOUTED TO NO ONE in particular.

Mechanic Luis Bourbon replied from the rear seat of the Haven team car that Radio Tour had them approaching the summit of the Col d'Aspin, 25 seconds ahead of the chase group, 50 ahead of the peloton.

"Son of a bitch," Deeds shouted, pounding the wheel, "Son of a *bitch*!" He slammed his hands down, hard. "*I wish someone on this damned team would listen to me*!!"

Bourbon nodded. He had heard this all before, many times before.

"Well, let's get some kind of support up to them. They're gonna need it."

Bourbon nodded again and spoke quickly and quietly into a radio.

Up front, in the passenger's seat, Louis Engelure stared out the window and pondered the imponderable. How in hell could Will Ross be keeping up with Bresson? He had been so sure.

Ross should have collapsed by now.

"IS IT WHAT YOU WERE LOOKING FOR, LUC? HAVE YOU FOUND IT?"

Isabelle Marchant was desperate to see what Godot had found in the leather bag, the one she had put aside so many hours before only to rediscover it now.

"Is it what we hoped, Luc?"

Godot didn't answer. He was lost in his own thoughts, a growing sense of horror at what he was holding and what it all meant to him and anyone who got in the way of this chemical, this medicine, this demon.

He continued to scan the pages and report logs, knowing that what he held was a corporate time bomb if ever there was such a thing.

"Luc," Isabelle said quietly, "is — it — what — you — were — looking — for? Have you found it?"

He stared at the pages, riffling them back and forth, one after the other, scanning the names that crossed the pages in signature and reference and copies sent to boxes.

"Luc," she said with exasperation. "What have you found?"

"Hell. A whole new level of hell."

❁

THE CROWDS LINED THE SUMMIT OF THE COL D'ASPIN. THESE WERE THE PEOPLE who were turned back from the slopes of the Tourmalet and Luz-Ardiden and kept working their way along the course in last night's darkness, looking for a place to park, to sleep, to eat, to drink, to cheer.

French flags, Spanish flags and Basque flags waved in the afternoon sun. The colors fascinated Will, if only for the fleeting moment in which they crested, before he brought himself back to the thin black line of Bresson's rear tire.

"Jesus, Henri — please, let me take a pull so you can *eat*!"

The crowd cheered and spritzed water and Coke and wine at the pair as they shot past.

"Henri, please — for God's sake."

Will realized he had taken on a tone of pleading, begging Bresson to pull up, if even for a second, but the lead rider, the man in yellow, the leader of Le Tour de France had no intention of breaking his stride, despite the fact that he was, in effect, giving Will Ross a free ride.

They crested the summit of the Col d'Aspin at 1489 meters and shifted to the big rings for a power descent of the mountain. Using the descent, Will pulled himself alongside Bresson and shouted at him. Still there was no answer, no indication that Henri even knew that Will was there.

Suddenly, Bresson sat up, upright on the bike, hands off the handlebars at 50 miles an hour on a mountain descent, pulled off his sunglasses, and wiped his forehead, slapping his glasses back on and going back into a deep tuck for the remainder of the drop.

In that split second, the hair on Will's neck rose and he felt a cold hand run along his spine.

Bresson's eyes had been blood red. Not bloodshot, not the pink of conjunctivitis, but the deep, rich, red of a hemorrhage: a bad ass, in your face, popping rivets inside your brain hemorrhage.

Will reached for the radio again.

Goddamn Cardone!

A moto drew up from the back, this one carrying a press photographer.

Will crossed the line and drew up alongside. The driver slowed and Will shouted above the roar of the wind and the engine to the photog, "Get Deeds! Get Carl Deeds up here! *Now.*"

The photographer shook his head.

"I can't help you — I can't even talk to you!"

"Goddamn it! Just get him! I'll take the rap!"

Will slugged the photographer on the shoulder and slid back to the line, pulling up tightly on Bresson. The France 2 helicopter had captured it all, and, up ahead, in the distance, Will could see the UCI commissaire's car, bristling with officials, all taking notes.

"Great. Just damned great."

Ste. Marie-de-Campan shot past and they were suddenly climbing again. Will shifted twice, trying to find the right gear to stay with the madman just ahead. He stepped up on the pedals and the bike shifted a third time, by itself. Christ, he hated when it did that. His fingers reached for the Campagnolo Ergo lever and, then, drew back. It was a better gear.

"Oh, yes," Will thought, "better gearing by accident."

The crowds were growing now. The roadside of the Col du Tourmalet was filled with picnickers and bicyclists and family cars and fans, many in the most unlikely spots, perched on rocks, between trees, on a carved pass.

The climb was getting steeper. Despite the feed zone, despite riding shotgun the entire day, despite the focus he had been able to keep, Will was feeling the climbs, deep in his legs, his chest, his lungs, his heart. He realized that if he felt this as the caboose, what must Bresson be feeling up front?

A fan ran alongside waving the French tricolor and threw a cup of water at Bresson, who ignored him completely. Strange, Will thought, the usual reaction to these twits was to brush them off with the back of your hand, but Bresson never broke focus, never turned away from the road.

The eyes, the focus, the obsession. Damn. This was getting scary. Where the hell was Deeds?

Almost in answer, the Haven team car pulled up beside the pair. Will slid over to the side of the car. The moto was up ahead, the UCI car nowhere to be seen, so Will grabbed the window frame and cadged a ride.

"What is going on — why don't you pace him, Will?"

"God, Carl, I'd love to, but he won't let me. Every time I've tried to take the front he's ignored me. It's nuts."

"Oop. UCI car. Let go."

Will started pedaling and let go of the car. The UCI officials slid around another corner up ahead and Will grabbed the car again.

"Something's wrong here, Carl. He's been obsessed today."

"He's in yellow. It does that."

"This is different — you've got to see his eyes."

"His eyes?"

"Yeah. His eyes. It's like every blood vessel in the world has blown — they look like two red ping-pong balls stuck in his face. Scary as hell, Carl."

Deeds looked straight forward for a moment, down the road toward his own future. He mumbled, "Oh, shit," and then nodded to Will.

"Stay with him."

Will broke from the car and slid back behind Bresson, still charging up the mountainside like a high-powered locomotive on a cog railroad. Deeds shouted, "You've still got 30 seconds on the chase and 40 on the pack. Henri — hey, Henri — *Bresson*!!"

There was no reaction.

"*Bressooonnnnnnn*!"

Nothing.

Will shrugged as if to say, "See?" then recaught Henri's pace and followed him toward the peak of the Tourmalet.

"WE'VE GOT A PROBLEM," DEEDS SAID STIFFLY INTO THE CELL PHONE.

Henri Bergalis set the glass of wine to one side and turned his back on the rest of the crowd filling the Haven hospitality area at the top of Luz-Ardiden.

"What?"

"We've got the problem!"

"What problem?"

"The rat in the rice."

"Carl, for god's sake—."

Deeds paused for a moment, trying desperately to simplify the code and still keep it a code.

"The HP. Remember the HP? I think we're seeing it today."

"What," Bergalis paused. The light went on in his head. "Oh, God."

"No shit."

"Where?"

"In the lead."

"How do you know?"

"Behavior for one. But his eyes. You mentioned eyes didn't you? Ross says the eyes are bright red."

"*Mon dieu*. We have to pull him."

"How, where, now? We can't. There's no way."

"He's hemorrhaging, Carl. We must pull him."

"He's got to ride or we're going to be in the middle of an even bigger scandal."

"What if he collapses?"

"They're crossing the Tourmalet now. One more climb and they've got it hacked."

"Hacked?"

"Finished. Done. We'll deal with it then."

"What about medical?"

"It hasn't turned up yet, it shouldn't turn up now." There was a long pause. "Should it?"

"I don't know."

"Great. Just damn great." Deeds slapped the cell phone shut, took his elbows out of the spokes of the steering wheel and continued driving, fast, toward the finish.

THEY HAD COVERED THE CREST OF THE TOURMALET, LOSING A FEW SECONDS, yet still remained well ahead of both the chase group and the peloton. Despite the ease of riding behind Bresson all day, Will realized that he was quickly approaching the divine state of crash and burn, when your only thought is to keep your pedals going around and around and around just long enough to cross the damn line and collapse in the team bus.

They were entering the sharpest descent of the day, 1400 meters over a mere 18 kilometers distance, filled with turns, cliffs, rock faces and nasty crosswinds. Will threw his focus forward, past Bresson, in an attempt to read the next obstacle.

Sharp right.

The pair dropped into the turn, tight to the wall, then rose out into a sharp descent. Will felt the cool air warm, as they lunged toward the valley, the humidity growing with every meter. Sharp left, the pair shot through as if on rails. They passed the first sign for Luz-St. Sauveur, the village, still far ahead, that marked the end of the descent, and the start of the final climb of the day.

Sharp right, hairpin turn, hard left. Their speed continued to grow. There was no point, Will knew, in talking to Bresson at all. His mind, his entire focus, was on the road itself. Perhaps it was all chemically induced, but it was there, nonetheless. Man had become machine and Will was merely trailing in the wake.

Long straight.

The computer beside the stem read out 55 mph. Will kept switching it back and forth between miles and kilometers. Then 57 — 59 — 60. Hard right ahead. Bresson sailed through the turn without even touching the brakes, centrifugal force pushing him to the far left side. Will followed, the sweat breaking out on his forehead despite the 60 mile-an-hour-manufactured gale surrounding him — 61 — Will could feel the front wheel begin to shimmy, just a bit, in his hands — 61. He tightened his grip and leaned forward to put more weight over the front tire. He looked up.

Hard left.

He was late.

Bresson didn't see it at all.

Will panicked, grabbing the brake levers and pulling for all he was worth. He heard the scrape and a thin, high-pitched squeal of rubber on warm asphalt, then felt the rear end of the bike slide out and away from him. He was going down. He threw his weight up and right and waited for the first kiss of the road as it ripped its way through the spandex covering his hip and began to chew at his skin and the muscle that lay directly beneath.

Despite the sudden alarms of pain rocketing through his side, in the moment that he fell, Will watched, with fascination, as Henri Bresson, wearing a golden yellow shirt, rode, without pause, through a small gap in the guardrails, then off the edge of the cliff and high into the air, pedaling, his rhythm steady, in the big gears, making perfect circles, while the sun, having crossed the meridian, created a shocking gold-and-blue background. Bresson rode, rather than flew, through the air and sailed out and down, out of Will's view, as Will hit the pavement, and bounced and rolled, not feeling the tear and the rip on his skin, but thinking, as he tumbled head over heels, how beautiful it had looked, if even for that moment, to actually see Henri Bresson fly.

When he hit the stanchions of the guardrail, Will Ross stopped.

Suddenly.

And the pain began.

THE UCI CAR HAD STOPPED DOWN THE ROAD AND RADIOED BACK FOR HELP.

The photographer's moto behind had slowed on the last two turns and caught up just as Will hit the railing. Bresson had already disappeared over the cliff. The moto driver radioed for help and then began to wave riders around the accident.

The helicopter of France 2 captured the last shudders of the barricade as Will rocked back and forth against it and then rolled across the ground toward his bike. The camera then trailed off over the edge of the road in search of Henri Bresson. The pilot frantically radioed for help.

The chase group roared past, sitting up, only for a moment, to take a look at what had happened to the pair they had been chasing all day.

A string of riders — including Bourgoin, Cardone and the other leaders of the race — passed in a knifelike line down the mountain. They had broken from the peloton and were chasing the chasers. Will stood, on shaky legs, and waved, dully, at the rainbow of jerseys passing him on the turn.

The man stood beside Will dressed in a style Will recognized only from antique photos of his great-grandfather. The thin man wearing the turn-of-the-century brown plaid suit with the high gloss, pointy-toed, patent leather shoes, placed an icy hand on Will's shoulder.

"You go ahead," said the fellow, distantly, "I've got him."

Will nodded dully. Where did you come from? No matter. There was a race to ride and finish and that was all that mattered. He reached for his bike and threw up as soon as he bent over. The retching racked him until his head felt like it would explode. The tall man with the aquiline face and oddly ancient suit smiled. "You must go now."

"What about me?"

"You'll live."

"Thank you."

HANGING FROM THE DOOR OF THE HELICOPTER, ERNESTO DEGAS PEERED through his video eyepiece at the drama that was playing out before him. He was live on France 2, but he couldn't help himself.

Zooming in on Will, the image buffeted by the turbulence of the chopper caught in a crosswind hover, Degas asked aloud the question that millions of international cycling fans were asking themselves at that very moment: "Who the hell is he talking to?"

WILL THREW HIS LEG OVER THE SADDLE AND PUT HIS RIGHT FOOT IN THE PEDAL.

The main peloton roared past in a whir of gears and chains and wheels and pedals, while cars and support vehicles followed closely behind.

He pushed the bike off the shoulder and back onto the road, clumsily finding his footing on the left pedal.

The thin, distinguished man in the brown plaid suit watched Will wobble down the road, heading in the general direction of the base of the mountain.

"You'll live. For now, anyway," he whispered under his breath, as Will fell off to the side and then scrambled back into the center of the road.

Will was out of gear. He shifted and felt the familiar drag on the pedals and on his thighs. He shook his head and wiped his nose. Blood.

Cars began to arrive en masse at the scene. He could hear the confusion behind him as he rode down the mountainside toward Luz-St. Sauveur. Sirens. Horns. Voices. Suddenly distant. All distant.

He couldn't find the line on the road, the line down the mountain, so he tucked himself into a ball and flew down the hill: 35, the computer said — 35 — 37 — 40.

Forty is good — 40 is good.

He could feel the pain in his head, as if someone had taken a cheese grater to his ear, but, he could live with it. The pain was far away. Long ago and far away. And his elbow. His left elbow. His entire left arm was shaking. It seemed to radiate from his elbow. And his hip, his left hip. There was a cold and burning sensation along his left hip.

Fifty — 50 is good.

He looked up and could see the rear of the peloton up ahead, as if through a shattered piece of stained glass. Hah. They hadn't left him behind. Not him. Not. Uh. Not Will Ross. He reached up and touched the side of his face. The sunglasses fell away in pieces and the shock of the sunlight made him squint and sit up on the bike.

Fifty-five — 54.

He was pedaling in the big gear now and approaching the rear of the peloton. The stragglers. You haven't left me behind, he thought. You haven't left me behind.

Luz-St. Sauveur. Seventeen kilometers to go. He looked to the side. Villagers and cars lined the streets. There was a strange quiet, as if he were riding through a glass tunnel set in a main street being watched by a crowd of disapproving Amish farmers.

He waved. A child pointed. Forty-five.

Forty-five is good.

He looked at his hand and realized it was covered with dried blood. He drunkenly wiped it on his jersey and kept pedaling. Where was Bresson? Hadn't he been following Bresson all day?

Forty-five.

A short climb out of Luz-St. Sauveur. Thirty-five — 30. Keep pedaling — 25 — keep pedaling. Descent. Short descent. Thirty-five.

Thirty-five is good. Keep pedaling.

He was alone again, in a gap between Le Tour and the accident he had left behind.

Luz-Ardiden. What category? No category. The climb grew steep. No category. Keep pedaling. He was picking his way through the peloton. What category? Thirty. No category. He looked to his sides. The peloton had disappeared in the distance. Keep pedaling. Find a rider. Find a wheel. Out of category. Out of the peloton. Twenty-five — 20 —.

Twenty is good. Keep pedaling.

His cotton cycling cap felt odd. He ran his left hand through his hair. The cap pulled away and burned as it did. The dried blood had been wiped away by fresh, while his cap, black and red and gold, was now predominantly red and wet with something sticky and covered with hair. Will tried to throw it to the side, but it stuck. It stuck to his hand. He threw it hard, snapping his arm as he did and felt a shock run through his elbow, taking his breath away. The hat fell away from his fingers in slow motion. He shifted. He couldn't keep turning the pedals.

Kick it around.

Tuck and around — 17.

Seventeen is good, he thought.

Tuck and around.

Fifteen.

A moto pulled up beside him. Outside his mind, Will could hear something, a buzz, like a bug shouting at him, close to his ear. Shouting. Bzzzzzz. Bzzzzzz. Buzzzzz. He brushed it away with his hand and swayed. He grabbed the handlebars tight and focused on his front wheel. A white spot came around, a mark on the tire. And around again. And around again. And around again.

Will tried to bring it around faster, but it wouldn't work. Around. The white spot. The great white spot.

Will looked at the cycling computer. Ten.

Ten is good.

He felt a dull ache in his ear that began to spread to his jaw and then his teeth, but only the teeth on the left side of his mouth. The lower teeth. It stopped right at the center of his mouth. Damn, that's strange.

Keep pedaling. Keep pedaling. He shifted again. He couldn't make the white spot come around. There it was. Come on. White spot. Come on. *White spot.* He slowly began to realize that he was changing colors. His left arm, clutching the left handlebar, just to the left of the white spot on the tire, was red. Bright red. Except for one patch, about the size of a kiwi fruit below his elbow, it was red, bright red. And his right arm was brown, a rich, tanned brown, except for where his shirt had pulled up to reveal a fish belly white bicep. He looked back and forth between the two. He liked the red the best. He liked the red. Tan was nice. White was nowhere.

He heard the buzzing again and looked off to his left. There was a moto, trying to come in close, waving, frantically, to get him to — what? Get him to what? Get away from me, I'm riding. I'm riding Le Tour de France, man. You touch me and the little UCI bums will disqualify me, quicker than you can say, what? Say what? Say 'mein lederhosen iz gerpinchen mein naughty-bitzen.' He snorted and could feel the snot run out of his nose. He wiped it away with the back of his right hand. Ha! That was turning red now, too.

Seven — 7 is good.

Wwwwwhite spot. I like that wwwwhite spot. Still there.

He looked to the side. The moto fell away. Suddenly, there were people. People on every side. Some shouting. Some pointing. Some crying. Some pushing. This is good. Pushing is good. To hell with the UCI. Let them push.

Seven — 7 is good.

He had stopped pedaling. The pushing was bringing the white spot back. Again and again. He felt something cold splash on his face and for a second, he couldn't see and began to fall to his right. Hands, thousands of hands, picked him up and pushed him along a path he couldn't see. He blinked his eyes clear and found the strip of pavement through the crowd.

Five — 5 is not good. He began to pedal again. Six. Six is better.

Now the pushes began to feel like slaps. Slaps on his back. Each one shot down his spine and through his hip and into his knee where the pain, just from turning the crank, around and around and around, began to feel like a knife thrust each time. He looked toward his foot, and each time the knee came around there was blood on the knee and a flap of something, like he had left the access door to his kneecap open. Suddenly, he was out of the crowd and riding on a street a wide street with barricades on the sides. The moto reappeared and pulled in close as if to touch his knee. Will stood up in the pedals and forced himself away. In the corner of his eye he could see the man on the rear of the motorbike wave in frustration at Will.

Eight — 8 is good.

Will saw that the barricade was swinging up on his right, swinging toward him. He turned the front wheel and leaned, then suddenly realized that the left barricade was swinging up toward him. Shit. Find the line. Find the line. He couldn't feel his shoulder anymore. He couldn't feel his left shoulder. Ten. Keep pedaling.

Ten is good.

He could see the crowd behind the barricades. No one waving flags. No one cheering. Where was he? Where was the line? Where was the finish?

Nine — 9 is good.

White spot. See the white spot? It's right there. On a black tire. On a field of white and blue. On a black tire on asphalt. On a black tire on a field of blue with a big white "F" on it. A white spot on a black tire on a white line.

Then, suddenly, people were grabbing at him and his bike again. This time, grabbing hard, pulling him off the bike, pulling the bike away, and he fought, with whatever fight he had left, the pedals still turning, even though his feet were no longer attached to them. Someone pulled him up and away from the bike by his left arm and what hadn't had feeling only moments before exploded in a carnival of pain. He felt his stomach rise and fight to find its way up his throat and strain breakfast through his nostrils. The hands brought him up to a full standing position and he could feel them let go and allow him to stand on his own, coltish, legs. As he wobbled for a moment and looked around him, his head bobbing uncontrollably like a plastic dog in the back window of a car, he saw Richard Bourgoin running toward him and Cheryl Crane, with tears streaming down her face, and Carl Deeds and Henri Bergalis.

Slowly, without any notion of haste, he leaned forward to say hello and then toppled over like a telephone pole cut at the base, Mother Earth mercifully stopping the fall by placing herself in the path of his face.

CHAPTER SEVENTEEN:

THE ROUGH AND RAGGED EDGE

The stitch tugged at the deadened skin.

"This is bad."

"Hmmm."

"You were stupid to attempt a descent that fast on that road."

"Hmph."

"Your friend has truly paid for it."

The flap of skin around Will's left knee had been almost an afterthought. It had been hidden under a gauze for the past three hours and had been lost in the loose shuffle and utter madness of a late-summer emergency room afternoon.

Part of his hair had been shaved away to sew up his scalp. Will now had a Frankenstein version of his grandfather's haircut.

Four nurses had spent 40 minutes picking rocks out of his hip and scrubbing away the dirt with disinfectant and a plastic brush, while a plastic-and-cloth brace now surrounded his elbow, making his hand tingle with sleep. As a second finale, they had butterflied his lip to close the tear that kissing the pavement just beyond the finish line had given him as his 'thanks for finishing the race' prize.

"I'll need more sutures."

This was the third time the doctor had called for more needle and gut.

"These are dissolving stitches. The others hurt when you pull them out. These hurt when they dissolve."

He laughed at his own joke, then tried to swallow his laughter when he realized that Will wasn't following suit. In fact, Will still wasn't following much of anything yet, as his consciousness still climbed to reach the surface of his own reality, a slow, hard process after a long, ugly day.

It had all seemed like a dream then, and it retained a unique unreality now, from the breakaway and his part in it, to the descent, the crash, the flight of Henri Bresson, and those eyes, those bright red, staring eyes that haunted him from the moment he first saw them to this particular moment in time.

Will turned away from the patchwork quilt being made of his knee and glanced across the cold terrazzo room, under pale green fluorescent lights, at an oxygen tank covered with so much rust that the gas, he realized, must be held inside by surface tension alone.

He felt the tug, tug, tug at his knee grow sharper. Either the local was wearing off, or his seamstress was coming 'round the mountain and entering the sphere of influence of the next nerve bundle.

"You are a mess."

"Hmm."

"You must be in severe pain."

"Hmmm."

If he was, Will wasn't feeling much yet. It should make sleeping real interesting tonight. Sleeping. Alone in the room. Bresson is gone, remember?

Everyone, it seemed, had gone out of their way to avoid talking about Henri Bresson. Cheryl merely wept and clutched Will's hand, kneading it like a small meat loaf, not realizing that every squeeze sent a shock wave up and through his eyeballs. Deeds twisted his little cap into a variety of cartoon animals. Henri Bergalis? The head of Haven had simply disappeared.

No one needed to talk about Henri Bresson. Will knew the second he saw that mindless, drug-induced and yet, somehow, magnificent flight into the ether that Henri had bought the farm and the little tractor that went with it.

He snorted. Blood and snot shot out his nose.

"Stop moving."

"Hmm."

The doctor threw the last of the sutures into a metal pan on the gurney beside Will with a hollow 'clang' and wiped the knee with a reddish-brown fluid that burned like three shades of blue hell. Will sucked in his breath, feeling the tug along his lip from the stitches there.

"Sorry."

"Hmm."

The doctor turned for a dressing and Will loosened the Velcro straps on the elbow brace, immediately feeling the blood flow to his fingers and ease the tingling sensation along the ridges of his fingerprints.

"Uhh-uh-eh. That should remain tight — that's quite a pull there. I still think it's a fracture, but I have been overruled." He reached to tighten the straps again and Will silently brushed his hand away.

"Fine. Fine. Yes, you are a giant of the road, correct? A king? What does a humble doctor of Lourdes know, correct? You come in here, broken into pieces, I put you back together — I — put you back together and you never say a word and now, you are taking apart your repairs. Lovely. I expect you will want to retie your sutures next, eh?"

"My apologies, doctor."

"He talks! Call the press! The hero talks."

Will stared with dulled eyes as the doctor sarcastically strutted around the small observation room cackling, sticking his head out the door and braying the news, waving his arms and fingers in some overwrought and bizarre approximation of a man in the full-force throes of ecstasy.

The doctor stopped, turned and looked hard at Will.

"I am sorry. I've had a bad day." He reached over and took hold of the Velcro straps that appeared to be holding Will's left arm together and pulled them tight, tighter than they had been before. Will immediately felt the blood flow disappear from his hand.

"Leave that alone. You won't, but do."

"Hmm."

"And learn how to speak again. That crack on your head has not affected your ability to speak."

"Hmm."

"I'm going to give you something for the pain. When the local wears off, you are going to hurt in places in which you didn't even know you had places." He chuckled again at his own joke.

The doctor opened another sealed plastic pan and pulled out a syringe. He attached the needle and twisted off the blue plastic tip, tossing it, blindly, into a corner of the room. He picked up a clear bottle of a clear fluid, and speared the rubber stopper with the needle, filling the syringe half, no, three-quarters of the way full. Will watched the doctor discard the bottle and reach for an alcohol wipe.

He was still foggy, in a way, still rising up out of the damp, but he did realize that if he was injected with that solution, no matter what that solution might be, his Tour was finished. It was certainly on the UCI banned list. They might make an exception. He might not get called to medical control. Sure as hell, though, he would get called and would light up the testing units like the Christmas tree in Rockefeller Plaza.

Horns-of-a-dilemma time.

The doctor cleaned an area on Will's right leg. He posed the needle over the one antiseptic area of Will's body and started to thrust down, Will catching his wrist just as the needle brushed his skin.

"This won't hurt. It will make it stop hurting."

"It's not hurting I'm worried about."

"Then, what?"

"I can't ride on drugs. It's illegal."

Dr. Paul Flacon chuckled. "You don't seem to understand, young man. Your race, your Tour, is quite finished."

He moved to drive the needle home and Will pushed his hand away.

"It's not. I'm riding tomorrow, no matter what you or Carl or anyone else says."

"Who is Carl?"

"Look — I need something for infection. Some major-league antibiotic for infection."

"You have already had that — the shot should be good for 21 days."

"I don't want anything for the pain."

"You have already had something for the pain."

"Locals don't count. I can explain them away. Nothing more."

"You will not ride."

"I will ride."

"How? How will you make the climbs you did today?"

"Tomorrow is a day of flats. Sprinters day. The climbs on Sunday are all at the head, when I'm fresh. Then, it's another flat day — until Ventoux at the end. That's three rest days with a bitch of a finish."

"You will never make it."

"Bets?"

Dr. Flacon held up the syringe and let the flat light of the room play off the crystal fluid within. "By midnight tonight, you will pray for this."

"You may be right. But the chances also are that by midnight tonight, I'll be so far gone that only my dreams will feel the pain."

"Then here, take these — you'll want these." He tossed Will a yellow tin. "Aspirin. Even the UCI allows aspirin in certain doses. By midnight, you'll be licking the bottom of the box."

"Your concern is underwhelming."

"Eh, I do what I can."

Will slid off the edge of the gurney and stepped into something wet on the floor. His own blood. Just the change from sitting to standing made his scalp and elbow dully throb. Oh, yes, this was going to be fun. Doctor Flacon smiled in a smug, superior way as Will hopped toward the door. Will turned back to the doctor.

"Am I done?"

"Oh, yes, you are done. But you don't believe me, yet."

"Doctor, I believe you. Even though I cannot listen to your advice. Thank you, doctor." He turned back to the door and for a split second, the world beyond the door smeared. He broke into a cold sweat and leaned to the side for support. Dr. Flacon did not move.

"Oh, yes. I would take your time in moving around. You have lost a lot of blood and fluids. You may experience some disi ... diz ... *vertige* ... for the next few days."

Will pulled himself up, slowly, along the door jamb and hobbled into the hall.

"Good luck with your race. I will be watching. It should be quite exciting."

"All the more reason to do it," Will muttered, "just to shove it back in your face, you over-paid quack."

He pushed himself along the hall, working the right side of his body.

He couldn't hear out of his left ear and it was tweaking his balance. He hobbled along the wall, hop, step, lean, hop, step, lean. He was coming to the waiting room, where he would run out of wall. Hop, step, lean. There was an umbrella stand full of canes just inside an open office door. Will leaned against the door jamb and looked them over, plucking one with a brass eagle on the handle out of the middle of the bunch.

That helped. Now, he could hop, step and lean on his own, no walls necessary. A flush of pride and freedom washed over him, along with a wave of nausea and another cold sweat.

Cheryl and Luis Bourbon, the team's lead mechanic, sat in the waiting room.

"Hey, Luis. Are you my taxi?"

"Well, I uhh — don't know. They told me you would be in the hospital overnight. I was just supposed to get your condition and call."

"My condition is released. Tell them to send the bill to accounting and let's get the hell out of here."

"Jesus, Will, Jesus, Mary, Joseph." Cheryl raced to him and grabbed him out of love and relief, the move throwing Will to the side and making his eye explode with pain. He thought, for just a moment, that his right eye was going to leap out of his head.

"Oh, God — I'm sorry. I'm sorry, Will."

"It's okay, Cheryl. It's okay." He looked at her tear-stained face and grinned crookedly, the tear in his lip pulling his smile oddly to the right.

"I've got to get out of here. Just get me out of here."

Will lurched toward the door in an uncontrolled rush and fell on the glass, using his weight to swing it open. The movement gave him a brain rush, followed by another desire to throw up. Cheryl stepped between him and the door and let him lean on her as they walked outside. The cool night air revived him.

Luis Bourbon came through the door behind him and took his left arm for support. The pain literally lifted him up off his feet. "No no no no uh uh uh," he slowly lowered himself back onto Cheryl's shoulder. "I'm sorry, Luis. Sorry."

"Never touch a man there." He laughed, drunkenly.

Using the cane, for a very nearly useless support on the left, Will and

Cheryl waddled across the tiny parking lot toward the one car decorated like the lead wagon of a psychiatric circus.

INSIDE, DR. PAUL FLACON SCRIBBLED ILLEGIBLE NOTES ON THE FILE OF WILLIAM Edward Ross, occupation: cyclist, and clicked his golden pen closed. Cyclist. Hmmph. No more. Not with those injuries. He stepped out of the observation room and strode down the hall, first toward the nurses' station and, then, toward his office. Passing a nurse, he threw the file, with a sideways toss, toward her. She flinched, then, slapped her hands on it as the file hit her breasts. Flacon laughed. She did not react. She had been through this far too many times to find amusement.

Flacon stepped into his office and sat down in his leather chair, leaning back and snatching his pocket recorder off the desk before gravity and inertia threw him back into a fully reclined position. He made a quick note, a personal note, into the recorder and glanced at the activity that passed in the hall.

He should be in Paris, he thought. Chief of Emergency Services in Paris. He continued to make notes as his eyes wandered around the door, the hall, the umbrella stand, where they stopped.

Slowly, Dr. Flacon leaned forward. He stared at the stand for a long moment, then shouted out to the nurse in the hall, who was still rubbing the side of her breast where the point of the medical folder had caught her only moments before.

"Where is it?"

"Where is what?'

"The cane."

"What cane?"

"The Eagle's cane."

"What cane is that?"

"de Gaulle's cane."

"Hmh. Would that be Charles de Gaulle?"

"The cane with the eagle's head on it."

"I don't know. Is it missing?"

Dr. Flacon began madly pulling his office apart. Emergency room nurse Aimee Panoncillo watched him for a moment until the sputtering of a car, a car painted like an advertising display, roared past the emergency room entrance and into the gathering dusk of Lourdes, pulling her attention away from the comedy within the ER.

She smiled.

Enjoy your cane, she thought.

"Him," Flacon shouted. "That son of a bitch stole my cane!"

The doctor ran to the door and threw it open, racing out into the parking lot in a futile attempt to chase the car down.

After a few hundred meters, he stopped, grabbed his side and gasped for breath.

"I'll catch up with you, you son of a bitch. I will get my cane."

"WHERE'D YOU GET THAT?" CHERYL ASKED, POINTING AT THE ORNATE CANE that Will feebly clutched in his left hand.

He looked down at the brass eagle's head and the intricate scrollwork along the sides that led down to a smooth tip and a brass point.

Will turned toward Cheryl and said, in a dull, hollow tone.

"It followed me home, ma. Can I keep it?"

At which point, he passed out.

FOR ONE FINAL NIGHT, THE HOTEL IN LOURDES WAS HOME TO THE HAVEN PHARmaceutical Cycling team, as the next day's start, in Bagnères-de-Bigorre, was only 40 kilometers away. It hardly seemed worth the effort to move, especially tonight. The team, down two, sat silently in the hotel dining room, picking at the food presented by the hotel chef and the team nutritionist. Only Cardone ate heartily.

Deeds stepped down into the room, his battered leg rattling the wooden floor with a hollow 'thunk' as he swung it down to each new level. When he thought about it, when he worked at it, he could move silently, like a man who had not been crippled by a shot to the knee, but he wasn't thinking about that tonight, he was thinking about Henri Bresson. He was acting like a man who had lost an employee, a teammate, a friend.

"What is the word, Carl?"

Deeds walked heavily to the table and collapsed in a chair next to Bourgoin.

"The start is at 10:30 tomorrow morning from Bagnères-de-Bigorre. We will be in front, for the first seven kilometers. It is a salute to Bresson."

The table grew silent. Even Cardone stopped chewing.

Finally, Bourgoin, as team leader, spoke again, quietly, as if afraid to hear the answer. "Carl, what happened?"

"We don't know yet. At the bottom of that cliff, his body was so broken up that it will take some time to truly discover what happened."

"What do you think?"

Deeds didn't have to think. He knew the answer, but he said nothing.

Bourgoin nodded. No one else at the table reacted. Only Cardone ate.

"What about Will?" Bourgoin asked, then froze, looking at the door as if in answer to his own question.

"Yef. What abou' Will?" Will realized suddenly, as the drugs were wearing off, that it was becoming all the more difficult to speak. His lip felt about the size of a boxing glove and his elbow as beginning to hurt like hell. He chewed on two aspirin and wondered if skipping the shot of painkiller an hour ago was the wisest thing in the world.

"Jesus God, Will, what the hell are you doing here?" Deeds jumped out of his seat and raced across the room with an erratic gate. He grabbed Will's left arm and Will squeaked in pain.

"Sorry. Sorry." Deeds took Will's right arm and walked him, gingerly, over to the team table. Will sat down carefully on the padded chair, his weight all on his right butt-cheek.

"You're supposed be in the hospital overnight, Will. You're supposed to be under observation."

"You're supposed to be dead."

The table grew silent and all eyes turned toward Miguel Cardone, his mouth dripping with overcooked pasta. "Well — after that crash, what do you expect?"

"I expect you to have some manners."

"Manners are for the weak, Carl. It is too bad, Will. A great rider dies and you survive. It just proves there is no justice in the world."

Will smiled. The exploding lip gave him a lopsided look. "No, there is no justice, Mig. You will get a chanz at the top of da team."

Let it go, Will thought. Let it go. You aren't in any shape to duke it out with this son of a bitch.

"It's about time, too." Cardone ignored the looks of the team around him and returned his attention to the soggy pasta filling the plate before him.

"You aren't supposed to be here, Will. You're supposed to be in the hospital. Jesus, man, you're all torn up."

"You look horrible, Will," Richard Bourgoin said, quietly.

"I feel it, Richard," Will replied, "but there was no way I could stay in da hospito," he took a deep breath, "and let da Toua go."

"What?" Deeds was incredulous. "What are you thinking? You're not riding the Tour. I'm pulling you. You've got more stitches in you right now than a custom shirt from a big and tall shop. You're not riding tomorrow."

Will turned his head slowly toward Deeds and stared at him, hard.

"How is ma bike?"

"Your bike is fine. It didn't have a scratch on it. Your bike — is smarter than you are — it — knew how to fall."

"Fahn. Hab it on the line tomorro at 10." Will picked two bananas off the table and two pieces of bread. "Goodnigh, teammaze." He smiled drunkenly at the other members of the team and pushed hard on the brass eagle's head of the cane to push himself upright.

"What — you're riding?" Cardone barked a laugh, sending pieces of half-chewed pasta across the table. "That, I must see."

Will turned slowly. "You will. You will."

Cardone smirked. "Will you kill someone else tomorrow? That should be exciting. Who shall it be? Who shall it be?"

"Let it go, Miguel." Deeds voice was sharp and commanding.

"Why? Why should I? He kills Henri Bresson — the man wearing the yellow jersey in Le Tour de France and he doesn't say a damned word about it — not even 'hey, fellows — sorry?'"

Will turned toward the entrance to the dining room and took one shuffling step toward it.

"How did you kill Henri, by the way? Was it cutting him off, bad handling, or maybe just you were just out of control and sent him over the edge?"

Will stopped.

"You did kill him. You know that don't you? He's dead. And you're alive. God is a practical joker. Quite a joker."

It had seemed so safe, so easy, until that moment, the bully picking on the kid in the wheelchair, but, suddenly, without warning, the cane shot up in Will's right hand, spun in a weaving arc, and crashed into the middle of Miguel Cardone's dinner plate, shattering the ceramic and sending bits of pasta and broken dinnerware in hundreds of unrelated directions. Startled, Cardone fell back in his chair, held at a high angle by the close-in wall, and, before he could fall forward, felt himself pinned by a brass eagle's head against the base of his Adam's apple, choking him, kicking the gag reflex into high gear.

"Joke dis, asshoe." Will gave the cane a jerk with his right hand, pinching the beak of the brass eagle a bit deeper into Cardone's neck. "Say wha you will about me, you son of bitch," the voice threatened, "excep onc thin — I didn' kill Henri Bressnn — you know? Henri killed hiself. He was in front and he was in charge. He rode off da cliff — no me. If you wan to discuss this futher — then you make room in your schedule tomorro."

The head of the cane pulled away from Cardone's neck and he gasped, finally able to raise his head. He looked at the face of Will Ross, the scars on Will's face glowing bright red. When combined with the fat lip and the sutures that dotted his features, he looked like Sonny Corleone after the dance at the toll booth.

With difficulty, Will turned back away from the edge of the table, placed the tip of the cane back on the floor and slowly shuffled to the door, through the lobby, and down the hall to the room that lay beyond.

The dining room was silent.

Bourgoin turned toward Cardone and gave him a look that said nothing, yet said everything.

Cardone rubbed his throat.

"Don't give me that, Bourgoin. He can't ride. You know that. Look at him. He's fallen so far back he was within 30 seconds of today's time limit. He's in 151st position. Ten more and he is dead last. He can't help the team. He can't help you. And I'll be damned if he will get in my way like he did Bresson's."

"You don't know that."

"I know what I know. And I know he can't ride."

Bourgoin was silent for a long moment, then turned to Deeds and smiled.

Deeds saw the smile and thought for a moment then returned the grin. He turned to Cardone.

"Miguel, for being such an incredible know-it-all, you certainly are an asshole."

"What?"

"You heard me. Pure and simple."

"Yes, pure and simple," Bourgoin added, "Solid gold."

WILL REALIZED THAT HE DIDN'T HAVE HIS KEY, BUT THE DESK CLERK HAD followed the crippled rider to his room and opened the door.

"How did you know?" Will asked.

"You didn't have a pocket to put a key in," the clerk replied.

Will wanted to laugh, but simply couldn't manage it. He realized that he was still wandering around in loose hospital scrubs and they were beginning to stick and stink. He stepped into the darkened room and closed the door behind him, tossing the food and the cane on his bed, the bed nearest the door. He shuffled to the bathroom, and, for the first time, leaning hard against the lavatory on his right side, examined the mess that remained of his face. From the top of his head to his left ear, there was a patch where they had unceremoniously chopped his hair back to make a path for the stitches. They had continued their sewing on his earlobe. The dark red antiseptic wash covered the side of his neck down to his shoulder. He filled a glass with water and drank it down. Then, two more, each with as many vitamins as his quickly shrinking mouth could hold comfortably. Recovery. Think of recovery. Busy day tomorrow. He opened the tin and ate three more aspirin. God, they were bitter. Another glass of water. One more vitamin. The pain. The pain was incredible. He was dying on his feet. Will turned and hopped on his right leg back into the darkness. He took a bite of the food and felt his cheek explode. Damn. He put the rest of the bread on the nightstand and the cane on the floor. Carefully, he peeled a banana and gingerly took a bite. The consistency was perfect. It mushed up in his mouth and actually seemed to dissolve as it slid down his throat. He ate the second banana and drank one last glass of water before carefully arranging himself on his right side, his back to the window, his back to Henri Bresson's personal effects, and drifted off into a deep and dream-filled sleep. The dreams of Bresson and Tomas and some guy in a brown, plaid, turn-of-the-century suit, were interrupted only by an occasional spasm of pain and a voice, a distant voice, calling "Will? Will? Will?" very softly, very carefully.

Magda Gertz.

I wonder, he thought, as he stepped over the line, whatever happened to her?

"WILL?"

Magda Gertz waited quietly until the breathing became deep and regular. She remained hidden in the dark and had watched him in the mirror as he struggled to take vitamins and drink water. Poor fool. What a mess.

It was quiet now.

She reopened the suitcase of the late Henri Bresson and resumed her search.

CHAPTER EIGHTEEN:

I DID IT MY WAY

Some old poop with a rule book and a bad attitude had tried to stop him. Will had argued for nearly half an hour over the wisdom of his decision to ride today, to continue in Le Tour, until finally he pushed the official aside with the brass head of the cane and half hobbled, half hopped to the table and signed in at the huge sheet on the starter's table.

The official, a low-ranking civic nobody with an overblown sense of power and nothing to do with the race, grabbed Will by his left elbow, his bad elbow, and received a severe rap on the knuckles for his efforts. No one else tried to stop him.

No matter what anybody said, no matter what anybody did, Will Ross was a part of today's stage, a mere 10 days away from Paris.

By now, his lip had already shrunk down to just beyond its normal boundaries; his scalp throbbed, but that would just sit under a cloth hat all day; his hand was a cold, bright purple, which presented him with 30 minutes of needle-and-pin agony after he loosened the brace and felt blood flow freely again; his left buttock was already scabbing over; and the knee looked angry.

He had enough antibiotics inside him to cure an elephant of syphilis, but the flap of skin on the left side of his left knee gave him the biggest worry. His head didn't ride, nor his arm, he could work with that, his ass merely depended on how he arranged himself on the bike, but the knee would have to work. The entire day would be lopsided, that was for sure. He could throw a lot of the work to his right, his strong side to begin with, despite the continuing pinch in his right calf, but he knew he'd eventually reach a point where the left would have to do something to balance out the equation.

Christ.

How did he get himself into situations like this?

He drank another bottle of the new electrolyte solution, Haven CrocJuice. He had tried to explain to Henri Bergalis that GatorAde was developed for the Florida Gators football team, thus the name, but Bergalis was having none of it. CrocJuice was a big hit with junior high kids in France and that was the market Bergalis wanted. The name was the game, that, and a cool Croc logo hanging out on the label while smoking a Gauloise. Joe Camel meets Jack LaLanne. An interesting mix of images. Add the fact that the stuff tasted something like Mountie piss the morning after a two-case bender and you had a real world beater.

Will turned his face toward the morning sun and glanced at the clock: 10:30 a.m. As if on cue, the city fathers, who had paid a hefty sum to be the hosts of today's starting festivities, began their speeches. Will weaved his way to the Haven team area and tossed Carl Deeds his cane.

"Here pal, all yours until Albi."

"Are you sure you want to do this?"

"Think about it. What would you do, Carl?"

The light morning breeze picked up the sides of what was left of Carl Deeds's hair and blew it into a ring around the top of his head.

"Follow your bliss, Will."

Will stared at the sight for a second and smiled.

"Thank you, Augie Ben Doggie."

"Just know something, Will," Carl whispered, "I'll do whatever I can for you today, but you'll get nothing special from the team. If you're left behind, you're left behind. We can't wait for you. You're alone. The team has no part of it. I can't believe I'm letting you do this."

"Relax. And rest assured in the very real fact that you're a brick," Will smiled in reply.

"A what?"

"A brick. It's a prick with a better consonant."

Will grabbed one last bottle of CrocJuice from the cooler at the van and took the bike from Luis Bourbon. He twisted himself into a vague sort of stretch and moaned with the pain.

"Jesus," Deeds winced with exasperation. "I'll see you in 20 kilometers when you collapse by the side of the road."

Will slid his sunglasses down and smiled. "Nope, Carl. I'm a centerline man all the way."

Deeds turned and marched off, his shoulders lower, his gait more unsteady than even the day before. The death of Henri Bresson had been a crushing blow to the man and, in many ways, to the spirit of the team. Carl had wanted to pull out, but Haven corporate made the call in the form of Henri Bergalis and, now, Deeds was stuck. No matter how much of any desire to be here, to lead a team to victory, had been leached from him over the past 24 hours, he still had to make a show of it all.

"How can you drink that stuff?"

Will panned his gaze from the receding back of Deeds to the face of Cheryl Crane, her neck covered with a blizzard of passes and I.D. cards.

"French eighth graders think it's hot."

"French eighth graders think John Tesh is hot."

"He is."

Cheryl stared at him for a moment.

"Oh, well — yes — that stuff," she said, changing the subject, "I've thrown up stuff that tastes better. What flavor is that — grape? God. That's the worst."

"Cheryl," Will said, draining another half-liter bottle, "no grape ever got within a mile of this bottle except in transport, and so it does not taste like grape, but like purple. There is a difference. No, my love, this is a chemically infused joy ride of goodness that is going to make me pee like Secretariat in about 30 minutes."

The coldness of the last bottle was making Will just a bit shaky. Maybe he had overdone it. The loss of his recovery time last night, with no big meal to cap the day, was potentially more dangerous to him than the injuries. He was trying to rush recovery, give himself every edge he could, from an early breakfast, double that of his teammates, to a constant flow of vitamins and energy drinks, even down to one of Engelure's I.V.s before scrubbing himself down with rubbing alcohol and suiting up for the day's pleasure.

Engelure, he recalled, was not pleased, though that was nothing new between Will and the Vitamin King.

"You should not be riding."

"You're right."

"You are going to make a fool out of yourself and your team."

"You're right."

"Haven does not deserve this."

"You're right."

"Henri Bresson does not deserve this — his memory deserves something other than 'you're right.'"

"You're absolutely right."

Engelure sighed.

"You're hopeless."

"You're most certainly right."

Will shook the memory off as he gingerly lifted his left leg over the bike, lowered it and gently put pressure on his knee. He felt the sandpapered skin on his butt begin to crinkle and sing.

"There is no disgrace in giving it up, Will," Cheryl said.

"No," he replied, quietly, "I realize that. I know it. By the end of today, I may be screaming it from the back of the bike, but, for now, I'm in. Pretty much dead last, but still in."

"Where doesn't it hurt?"

He thought for a second and pointed at a spot just below his right eye. She kissed him there, lightly.

"God, you smell good."

"You smell like a hospital."

"Thank you. You're lucky I didn't wind up in an abattoir, yesterday."

"No, but it was close." She took her thumb and gently wiped a smear of lip gloss from his face as she said, quietly, "I'll see you at the finish."

"You bet. Drinks on Henri Bergalis." Will paused for a moment, looking at the ground. "You know," he said, "he still has the hots for you."

"Yes, I know," she replied, "but I don't have the hots for him. I have the hots for a skinny bicycle rider who comes in pieces, ready for assembly."

Will felt a flush of warmth on the right side of his head, almost as if a major blood vessel had let go, sending the thoughts in his brain racing uncontrollably.

Say it. Don't convince yourself, just say it. Say it. Say it.

The drunken ramblings of Henri Bresson came back to haunt him. Who are you, Will? What do you believe. What do you believe?

"I believe ..."

"Huh?" Cheryl shook her head with worry as Will stared at the ground, muttering to himself.

"I believe."

"Will, you can't ride this — you're punch drunk."

"No. I believe."

"What?"

"I believe that I love you."

She stared at him for a moment, then burst out laughing, the sound drawing looks from the assembled masses in the square, including Deeds, who had been searching for her for the past few minutes. He began working his way toward the small knot of riders where Cheryl continued talking to Will.

"Your sense of timing is absolutely amazing."

Will now flushed red with embarrassment while Cheryl flushed red for different reasons all together.

"I do. I do love you."

"In other words, in future, to get an honest emotion out of you, I should throw you off a bike at 60 miles an hour?"

She immediately regretted the joke. There was too much pain and too many memories to make light of the day before.

"Look," she said, reaching for the one spot on his arm that appeared unbruised, "I wish you weren't riding today —"

"Crane! Goddamn it, Crane!" Deeds shouted from the crowd.

"— but, in a strange way, I love you all the more for doing it —"

"Let's go, Crane! We gotta go! Leave Mr. Potato Head and let's go!"

"— do you understand that?"

"You know, I'm sure I'll understand a lot more when I'm done with this and don't hurt so much. But, I thank you for the thought. And I love you Cheryl. I love you. And I'm sorry it took me so damned long to realize it."

"You acted it. That was enough for a while. But, I've got to admit, I'm glad you finally said it."

Deeds popped to the side of the crowd and stopped.

"Crane. Come on. We've got to finish instructions and hit the road. You're riding with me today."

Cheryl turned away from Will without taking her eyes off his face.

"How did I win such a lovely prize, today, Monty?"

"Cheryl, please," Deeds whined, "may we leave sometime today?" He remained six feet away from Cheryl and Will.

"He'd come and get you," Will said, "but he's afraid I'm catching."

"Screw you, Ross. I wipe my hands of you today."

"Thank you, Mr. Pilate."

Cheryl leaned forward and looked deeply into Will's eyes. "Ride safe today, love. Wherever you wind up, I'll be waiting there."

"Check the garbage heap." Will smiled crookedly and kissed her hand. Cheryl turned to Deeds and followed him into the crowd. Will watched her head move through a sea of faces and helmets and racing caps until it was swallowed up by a Coca-Cola sign.

Will duck-walked the bike, a clumsy and painful act, to the edge of the peloton, a tattered bunch of riders already humbled by the greatest race in the world, most just trying to hold on for another week, and now just waiting for the last of the incredibly boring civic speeches to end.

Two weeks on the road had taken their toll. More than 20 riders had dropped out, but of those remaining, at least 20, perhaps as many as 40, were sitting on the rough and ragged edge with Will, trusting as much to luck and pride, rather than talent or reserves, to get them over the mountains and into Paris. You could double the number of riders already gone by the time the pack dropped out of the Alps in seven stages' time. Seven stages. Jesus. A whole world of riding left.

Will sat in the bunch, waiting for the start of the neutralized riding, looking around at the faces surrounding him. Twenty-three riders had dropped out. He wondered if he'd be No. 24. He was musing on that thought when it hit him. Twenty-two riders had dropped out. Most of them had been hanging on by their toenails in the back of the pack.

One rider had died.

One rider in yellow.

Will leaned carefully onto his left leg and snapped his right shoe into the pedal.

He had denied it for the past 18 hours.

Completely.

He had not only watched a man die, he had watched a friend die. Then he had gotten back on the bike and ridden away.

He had ridden away as a man who had shown him friendship sailed off a cliff and fell to his doom.

A heavy curtain of guilt draped itself over Will's shoulders and neck and sagged him down onto the bike. He had ridden away from a friend in trouble.

A dead friend.

The flood of thoughts was suddenly crowding out all sensation in his body or from the crowd around him, for he realized that Henri Bresson, his friend, had been dead as a mackerel on the bike itself. Will had been riding with a dead man for a leader.

He glanced over to one side of the street, then the other and back again, as if searching for an answer that wouldn't present itself in his mind.

He had been riding with a dead man. Like a stomped grasshopper, Henri Bresson had simply been going through the motions until he missed that turn and the Grim Reaper called in his chips. Will had watched, fascinated, then ridden away, leaving Henri Bresson with some dude in an antique plaid suit.

The guilt picked at him, but was slowly being pushed aside by something new that Will began to feel, a furnace catching fire and burning inside him, a small, peach pit of anger beginning to flare and burn.

Henri Bresson had killed himself, Will knew, but he sure as shit had help.

Henri had pulled the trigger, but someone had bought the gun and aimed it at his head for him.

The peloton began to shift around him, like a breeze around a dead tree, in anticipation of the start. Will skipped on his left leg, the pain shooting up his side.

Use the pain, he thought, to keep your focus.

Use the anger, he thought, to figure this out.

The figuring, he thought, kept coming back to one person.

MAGDA GERTZ QUIETLY PULLED THE DOOR OPEN AND PEERED DOWN THE HALL. It was empty, which was good. She had sat awake in her room since nearly 5 a.m., listening to the growing madness as Haven packed and moved out after a three-night stay in Lourdes. She was now registered under her mother's maiden name and staying as far away from the Haven team as possible. The sight of Henri Bergalis had made her blood run cold.

She looked at her watch again: 10:35. The stage was starting. Haven functionaries had wandered through the halls nearly an hour before, picking up bags and suitcases and equipment for the jump to the next hotel, in Albi.

All was quiet.

She had paid up with the night clerk. She told him she was checking out early and would simply leave the key in the room. At the rate she was paying, it made no difference to him.

She waited.

The silence was so profound that she could hear a strange buzzing in her ears, as if her mind were desperately searching for some sound, any sound, to fill the void.

She waited.

11 a.m.

Today, she would make the jump to Castres, the start of tomorrow's stage. She had things to do and people to see.

She picked up her bags and swung her head to throw the hair away from her face. She put on her sunglasses and stepped quietly to the door. She listened for a moment, then turned the dead bolt, pushed the handle down, and pulled the door open toward her.

She gasped.

Henri Bergalis stood before her, framed by the dark wooden outline of the door.

"Hello, Miss Gertz. Mind if I come in?"

She recovered quickly.

"Yes, in fact, I do mind. I have a schedule to keep —" She tried to push past him.

He grabbed her arm, just above the elbow, in a viselike grip.

"It will keep. It will keep."

"What do you want?"

"Just a moment of your time, *s'il vous plait.*"

He walked her back into the room and pushed her, unceremoniously, onto the edge of the unmade bed, before stepping aside and turning toward the door.

"I can sue the hell out of you for this."

"But you won't, Magda. Your fingerprints are all over this one."

"Henri —" she said, breathlessly, as if someone had just punched her in the stomach.

"Going somewhere?"

"Yes. I have a business meeting."

"I know you do — that restaurant in Castres?"

"Yes."

Bergalis nodded. "Good. Good. I'm glad you intend to keep it."

Magda Gertz lowered her eyes and gazed at the floor, her eyes shooting back and forth in a pointless attempt to see a way out of the room. Henri Bergalis reached down and took her chin, gently, in his left hand and lifted it, her eyes rising up to gaze again on his face.

"It's nice to see you again, Magda."

"And you, Henri."

"I'm sure."

There was a silence in the room.

"May I leave, now?"

Henri Bergalis walked quietly to the entrance of the room and closed the door. The room grew dark, and, unlike before, ominous.

"No. Not quite yet."

"When? I have a schedule to keep, as you well know." She tried to keep her voice level, but fear crept into it, uncontrollably.

"Yes, yes — busy. Magda is always busy." Bergalis paused, looked away, and then back again.

"Tell me, Magda, who is your meeting with today?"

"You know who." She brushed her arms through the air with a sense of insignificance.

"Ah. Friends and business. And what will your friend think of how you have handled this little situation?"

"He won't be happy."

"No, Mr. Fortuna won't be happy, will he?"

She sighed. "For heaven's sake, Henri."

"Mr. Biejo Fortuna will not be happy at all."

She was beginning to find her courage again. "Oh ... no. No," she barked sarcastically, "not Mr. Fortuna."

She realized she was still sweating. Her attitude was merely a front as her skin tingled from fear. For a moment, she considered screaming.

"Just getting together for lunch, is it? Lunch. Lunch would be nice," he smiled, showing sharp teeth. "Yes. I would like lunch. So," he added, with ill-disguised venom, "would Bresson. You remember Bresson, don't you? Henri Bresson? He would like lunch as well. Maybe we should get a table for three today, eh?"

Magda Gertz could feel the blood pounding in her neck. It was becoming difficult to breathe.

"You know Henri Bresson — don't you? Aren't you intimate in your knowledge of Henri Bresson? If you weren't, I would be surprised." Bergalis reached his hand back silently into his pocket and pulled out a silvered object, bringing it forward and covering it with his other hand.

"Now, let us see. Last night, you were looking for something in Bresson's room. Will Ross entered — did you talk to Will at all? Working on him, too, are you, as requested? No matter. It seems that you were looking for something in Henri Bresson's luggage. Something personal? A remembrance? No. You're not the remembrance type."

She stared at his hands and what they still concealed.

"No. You are not sentimental — at all, are you, dear?" Bergalis gave her a hard, cold smile.

"So, you were looking for something else. Something you had given Bresson? Something that spoke of you in a loud and clear voice to anyone who knows you? Something that spoke of you and Biejo Fortuna and your little business?" His voice began to rise and grow sharp, a tone that made

Magda Gertz lean back and away. "Something that only you would give a man in this day and age in a gesture of your love and friendship?"

Magda Gertz shook her head blindly, tears streaming down her face.

"Something like this, Magda?"

He pulled his hands apart and held up a plastic bag. Clearly visible within was the classic design of the glass and silver syringe. Visible on the inside was a dried droplet of a pale yellow fluid.

"Most people use plastic, disposable syringes in this day and age. You should think about it. It doesn't leave quite the trail."

Magda Gertz looked up at the face of Henri Bergalis, her eyes red and puffy, the tears streaming uncontrollably down her face, ruining her makeup.

"Before you killed him, Magda —"

"I didn't. I didn't."

"I hope you fucked him."

"I didn't. I didn't."

"He should have at least gotten that out of you for all his trouble."

"I didn't. I didn't."

"You made a mistakc, Magda."

"I didn't. I didn't."

"You did. You will pay."

"I didn't. I didn't."

The rage poured out of Henri Bergalis in a single blast of fury, so quickly that Magda Gertz had no time to react. Bergalis braced himself and threw his open hand, hard, against her left cheek, the full weight of his body behind the blow. It drove her along the edge of the bed and threw her over the foot-board. Magda Gertz fell heavily to the floor, weeping.

"Keep that in mind the next time you push the dosage, bitch."

The slap still resonated in the small, dark room. It faded until only the quiet sounds of her weeping could be heard. Bergalis turned toward the door, opened it and stepped through without breaking stride. As he pulled the door closed, he could hear the quiet sobbing in the room and a distant voice saying, over and over again, 'I didn't. I didn't."

"I didn't."

THE SPEECHES ENDED.

The flag of France was up, catching the breeze in long, languid waves, then, snapped down toward the ground, held by the short, round and sweating mayor, looking not unlike a refugee from Munchkinland.

Will pushed off with his left foot and felt the burn in his thigh. His right took the majority of the load, forcing the pace while his left did what it could to snap the pedal around and bring it back up in some semblance of a circle.

His ankling technique, he realized at once, was shot to hell. Since he was favoring his left, he was cocked slightly right on the bike, throwing the weight to the side. This could prove to be a problem over the next few hours, building a whole new world of saddle sores on tender territory not primed for the rigors of the ride.

Turning right, slightly, also brought his stiffly bandaged left arm up toward the Campy Ergo levers. The majority of the shifting would come from his right hand, to be sure, but there was enough going on to make life exciting for his left.

He built up to speed, about 30 kph, playing with his weight, shifting it here and there over the saddle and the center of gravity, until he found a spot, an infinitesimal corner of the universe where all the parts came together in balance and rhythm, a spot where he knew, if he didn't lose his focus or his center, he'd be able to ride for the next six hours.

Six hours.

Hell, he thought. I don't even do things I like for six hours.

Yet, he was in it now. He could have stepped away and ridden in the back of the team car or the Haven bus for the next 10 days, even disappeared into the back streets of Paris on an expense account, but, instead, he chose this day in the sun. There was a way to do this, he knew that for sure, as all sorts of riders did it daily. Long haul? No problem. One leg? One arm? Adds to the challenge. Out of my way.

The concentration and the desire to find the sweet spot on the bike had taken his focus for the neutralized zone out of town. He didn't notice they had passed the start until he heard the klaxon of the race director's car, saw the flash of a small flag, and watched the car spin away. Will glanced to either side and waited as the peloton began to pass, their tribute to Henri Bresson gone in a rush, a roar and a quick good-bye.

He could hear the whir, the mechanical roar of 160-odd bikes just behind him, then beside, then ahead and already fading in the distance.

He tried to glance up, but felt his balance shift just a noodge and wondered if it was worth it. Don't worry about them, he thought. The pack is there ahead. The pack will remain there ahead. The pack, he thought, will finish today what you will likely finish tomorrow.

The pain in his left thigh began to subside, as the natural stretch on the bike began to do its work. His elbow throbbed, but that was to be expected, as was the steady drum, drum, drum that coursed through his scalp. Those he could handle, those he could live with. He needed that left leg to keep going, to keep moving, to keep rolling, one kilometer down the road, just one more kilometer at a time.

He concentrated on his rhythm and pacing, watching the cracked plastic cover of the cycling computer tell him he was passing through 47 kilometers per hour. His speed was slowly beginning to build. His conditioning had brought him this far. Without any help, however, he didn't know how long he could keep it up.

He slowly inched himself back toward center on the bike. The pain rumbled through his left leg and up his side, stopping at different points along the way, to remind him that hurting like hell was a current and long-term state of being. One last shift, one last burst of a white-hot poker in his side, and he realized he was centered again on the bike.

This can be done, he thought. This can be done.

The right leg continued to produce the majority of the power. The pinch in his right calf that had bothered him before the race had either worked itself out or disappeared in the magnitude of what had happened to the other side of his body.

Will still couldn't turn the left pedal with the precision and strength he had earlier, but it was turning. There was a circle here, in a vague and loopy kind of way. He realized, as he crested a short rise above a field of long summer grasses and stared out over a sea of sunflowers, high and bright yellow and reaching toward the sun, the road nothing but a ribbon of gray running through the center, that he was here, in France, in the middle of summer, riding in the greatest race in the world, somewhere behind 170 of the greatest endurance athletes in the world and he was in love, with life, with the wind in his face, the sun on his back and a woman, unknown kilometers away, covered with tags and labels and angry comments from Carl Deeds, who did nothing more than love him in return and believe in him, even when he was a creep.

The thought had struck him like a ton of week-old bagels, and despite the constant pain, brought a smile to his face. His pace was growing now. He slid, almost unconsciously, into a runner's high, an alpha state, that put the pain of the road and the pull on his right calf on a new plane, up and away from his state of being. He could hear the thump of the France 2 helicopter in the distance overhead, yet it was only part of the window dressing of the moment. It had no impact on his world.

He rode.

❋

HER FACE STILL STUNG.

As she pushed the Porsche along the main highway toward Castres, to the south of the race route, she gingerly touched her fingertips to her cheek. A bit puffy, not bad. Possible black eye. She hoped not, but it was always a possibility, even though she had been moving with the punch before he threw it.

Henri has changed, she thought.

He's found some backbone.

She touched the cheek again.

Bastard.

❋

THE CLIMBS OF THE DAY PASSED EARLY AND QUICKLY.

Will dropped out of the foothills, fading over the distance until the broom wagon, the final vehicle of the race, marking the end of Le Tour de France, sat just behind him, a safety net in a way, closing the road while offering a final respite, and, yet, hovering not unlike a vulture waiting on a branch until the fight had finally gone out of dinner. Two sharp, quick beeps and a lagging moto passed Will on the left, racing forward to catch up with the race and whatever riders were dying just ahead.

Will sat up for a second, feeling the strain along his back for the first time.

"I'll finish, you son of a bitch!"

It took a lot just to scream. Will fell back onto the saddle in a lump. Until the end of the race, another four hours down the road, the road was as flat as an ironed newspaper, with the exception of two bumps masquerading as climbs.

Will knew climbs. These were no climbs.

On he rode, toward a finish that would mean nothing to anyone.

Except himself.

THE OPEN AIR CAFÉ IN CASTRES WAS LOVELY, SET IN WHAT APPEARED TO BE A medieval flower garden. Heavy-headed roses hung from the trellis along one wall, while pots of flowers and flower boxes ringed the dining area in ancient, chipped terra-cotta.

Magda Gertz ran her finger around the surface of her face, just below the left eye. The soreness was beginning to fade. She readjusted the Audrey Hepburn, larger-than-life sunglasses and finished her glass of wine. Snapping her fingers at the waiter and pointing at the glass, she ordered another.

There was a surge of voices in the darkness of the restaurant that moved toward the door before bursting out into the sunlight, led by Biejo Fortuna.

"Magda! Oh, my Magda. *Ça va?*"

"Warm, wise and wonderful, Biejo," she said, a sickening lump rising in her throat. "And you?"

"Fine. Marvelous. Beautiful. Couldn't be better."

"I'll bet."

"Why the sunglasses, my dear?"

"Flat light makes me sneeze."

"Ahhh, what's that?" He said, pointing at a space just below her left eye.

"Ran into your cupboard."

"You should be more careful."

"Yes, I suppose I should, shouldn't I?" she said with barely disguised anger.

"What? You are looking at me — strangely. For what? Why?"

"How can you tell?"

"I don't need to see your eyes."

"You haven't looked at my eyes since I walked in."

He laughed, caught, again, in her net.

"I looked once. It's been so long since I've seen everything else."

"Stop staring."

"Touché. Would you like to order lunch?" he asked, holding the tattered menu toward her.

"No, thank-you. I'm not very hungry this afternoon. Just another glass of wine."

"Do you have something else on your mind?" he said suggestively, with a touch of hope, if not pleading, just behind the words.

"Yes," she said, smiling. "There's a little something I'd like to know about the game we are playing."

He smiled and flushed, pulling a 100-franc bill from his pocket and quickly tossing it on the table. He stood up and thrust his hand toward her. She didn't move for a second, then quietly took his hand and stood up beside him.

"Anything," he whispered, darkly, in her ear. "Anything, my dear, for you are the one who has played the game so very, very well and will continue to do so," he said, a trace of threat filling his tone.

Together, they walked out of the beauty of the courtyard and back into the humid darkness of the restaurant itself.

WILL HAD BEEN SURPRISED BY THE FEED ZONE. HE HAD BEEN SO LOST IN thought that he came around the turn and was shocked to see a small forest of team assistants milling about, each looking like a tree stripped of its musette bags. He spied François, Haven's man with the meal, three-quarters of the way down the human hedgerow. Will swooped in and cleanly snagged a bag from the dangling arm, then snagged an extra one, clutched by a Lexor flunky who had been milling about without paying attention.

Will sat up on the seat and slung both bags over his shoulders. Just the act of raising his left arm off the hoods made his shoulder explode in a plasma ball of pain. Sitting up, keeping his rhythm, he slowly transferred the contents of the musette bags to the back pockets of his jersey and the frame of his bike. When the Haven bag was empty, he started digging through the Lexor musette, looking for treats and surprises. He smiled. Obviously put together by an older soigneur, there was something other than scientifically processed meals on board. There was actually a sandwich, with a slice of ham and heavy cream cheese wrapped in cellophane. Real food for real men. There were also boxes of electrolyte solution, a different brand than the Haven stock, but still just as tasteless, as well as fruit and Le Surge Bars and bits and pieces of engineered goo that would keep him going and make a turd if they ever got that far.

He ate and drank while sitting up on the bike. The food and the stretch of the ride were making him feel a bit more human. His speed picked up.

He glanced back. Will was alone on the road with the exception of the ever-present broom wagon. Even those fans who had been waiting all morning to claim their territory in the middle of nowhere had left, discarding little pieces of their lives along the road to mark their passage.

Will pedaled on.

Up ahead, at the bottom of a slight descent, he realized that the road crossed a railroad track, upon which was the first third of what appeared to be a long, slow freight train. Through the frustration, the pain and fatigue, he began to laugh. The sound rolled out of him in deep, uncontrollable waves, as if determined to beat back the fates and what they continued to hold in store for him.

Will pulled up to the crossing and tapped a stopwatch button along the silvered edge of his new watch as he stopped.

He settled in, waiting patiently for the lanterne rouge, the scarlet lamp that signaled the end of the passage.

"WHAT ARE YOU DOING?"

"I'm working with you, dear."

Biejo Fortuna fiddled with his glass and stared at the white tablecloth.

"I know you're working with me," Magda said, coldly. "I want to know why we continue to play this game."

"What game?"

"This game of hide-and-seek. Of mouse-and-cat. The game of 'who is the rat?'"

"It's necessary."

"I'll let you know," she said, stabbing his arm with a well-manicured nail, "I won't take the blame for this. I won't be the falling guy."

"I think the Americans say 'fall guy,' but I understand your point."

"I won't do it," she whispered angrily, "I'll go to the police or the press first."

"You will?" he asked, with a cold smile.

"I won't play these games anymore."

"I don't know what you mean, my love." He showed her a cold and worthless grin in a mouth filled with gold-filled teeth.

"I will not take the blame."

"That's fine," he said, quietly. "Then you can join your friend, what was his name, van Bruggen?"

Magda Gertz felt an ice-cold blast down her spine. "Was that really necessary? Killing Paul?"

"Yes, in fact, it was. Don't tell me you were beginning to feel for him."

He smiled lewdly.

"Not so much," she said, her hands shaking slightly. She stared at them almost in an effort to will them to stop. "But he was not a threat."

"Oh, but he was. He was hot on our trail, the trail of Cytabutasone. He was on the trail of its history. He was passing the information on to Haven Security. He was a threat. And you were right, Magda, to kill him."

She felt a nauseating cramp in her stomach, the illuminating moment when she realized, suddenly, that she had to play out the string, that she had to play out the cards that fortune had dealt her.

But in that moment, she also realized that she didn't have to play the game by the rules of a man who couldn't accept that he was living two separate and distinct lives, building a company and tearing it down, both at the same time.

He watched her eyes move as she considered the position she was in, then leaned toward her and whispered, "Are you ready to play with Biejo?"

"Oh, for Christ's sake! Drop the Biejo Fortuna bull shit. We are in this together my dear and believe me — if I go down, you go down."

Biejo Fortuna sat back and smiled, coldly, but, behind his mask, he suddenly saw a game gone awry and an immediate future that was filled with time bombs.

As she stared at him, Magda Gertz quietly reached to her side and ran her finger along the side of her bag, feeling the outline of one of those time bombs, a computer disc stolen from a dead lover in the midst of a murder scene, a computer disk that she had been steadily adding to for days.

*

FOR THE PAST UNTOLD HOURS, WITH A SIX-MINUTE STOP FOR A TRAIN, WILL HAD been on the bike and, yet, nowhere near the thing. The bike knew the way back to the ranch, he merely supplied the pedal strokes, one, after another, after another, after another. The rhythm of the ride opened a door to another world for him, a world where he could think clearly, without the distractions of his own, cluttered life.

Henri Bresson was dead. Will had watched a dead man ride a bike into oblivion.

Magda Gertz was beautiful and smart, but cold as a snake.

Louis Engelure was a creep who was feeding him placebo I.V.s.

Miguel Cardone was an asshole.

Prudencio Delgado was bitter.

Henri Bergalis was confusing.

Cheryl Crane was wasting her life and talents here.

Carl Deeds was out of control.

Richard Bourgoin wanted to win, to the point of ignoring a friendship.

And Will Ross was back on the bike. Feeling like something a sick horse might leave on the road, he was back on the bike nonetheless, and, unless something had happened while he was unconscious, either desperately trailing Stage 13 or dramatically leading Stage 14 of Le Tour de France.

Despite the pull and the pain on his left side, he glanced back and was shocked to see that crowds had remained, how long after the field had passed? Amazing. He turned forward and saw a bright red sign announcing five kilometers to the finish line.

Long past due.

Will struggled on, once again having to work to find the sweet spot on the bike. It was more centered than he had originally figured it would be. He picked up the pace a bit, slowly building it from the saddle, trying not to give anything away.

Four kilometers.

He was in a position to finish one last stage of Le Tour and no one was making a move to stop him.

He was right on the line as far as the time limit was concerned. Too far outside the time of the stage winner and he'd be automatically eliminated, but, what the hell, he was already outside the race. He was dead as far as the officials were concerned, dead as far as his team was concerned. There was no support, other than possibly François wandering around the feed zone with an extra musette.

He had ridden as a tourist with a number on his back.

He was as dead to them as Henri Bresson. Perhaps more so. They thought fondly of Bresson.

Then it hit him.

Two kilometers.

It was a show. The crowds were getting deeper and cheering now. No one had left the finish.

It was a show, but not for him.

He could ride and he could cross the line and everyone could cheer, but the show was for someone who had died the day before, a show dedicated to the memory of a journeyman rider who had died at the peak of his powers.

No one said a word about the possibility of drugs.

And they wouldn't.

Le Tour didn't want that sort of publicity, nor did the riders, the teams, Haven in particular, the families, the friends, the sponsors or the cycling press. It would always be a rumor, but it would never be brought into the harsh light of public scrutiny.

They might have a right to know, but it really didn't matter, now, did it?

Five-hundred meters.

Will realized, finally, what it was all about. The lack of support. The patient vigil of the broom wagon. They were setting up a drama. If he had faded and died on the course, they would have simply wrapped things up, but with him struggling into Albi, the race directors had unconsciously created their very own melodrama that would pay off in international promotion for the race on every newscast the world had to offer. Best of all, the drama featured an American. Even the American TV newscast, with its three minutes to give you the world of sports, would push the local baseball team aside for 30 seconds to tell this story.

They were looking for a moment, a gesture, and in that second, Will understood what they needed to see, what he needed to do, what both he and the crowd needed to feel.

He centered himself on the street and dropped back a bit, off his own, rather meager pace. He sat straight on the bike and pulled his jersey down, preening, making himself presentable for the finish. The crowd grew and roared around him, the streets of Albi packed with fans and flags and festival.

The cheers of the crowd rose up as a gigantic wave, crashing over Will as he moved toward the line. The fans knew what was happening and they realized that they were being allowed to join in a piece of cycling history. For the next 50 years, they would say, "I was there," and the numbers who said that would grow, like Woodstock, until the crowd was five or six times the reality of the moment.

Will approached the line.

He sat up on the bike, which held the line perfectly, dead center down the middle of the street, despite the angle at which he was draped across the frame. The bike seemed to be compensating on its own.

Will looked up to the heavens, his head back, as if basking in the summer sun. He raised his arms as if in supplication to the sky above. Just before he crossed the line he opened his eyes and pushed one finger toward the sky as if to say, "You!"

The crowd looked skyward in the salute to Henri Bresson, the wearer of the *maillot jaune* now riding in heaven, and exploded around Ross in a deafening roar. One woman, staring into the sun for a few moments screamed, "I see him! I see him!" She pointed frantically toward the sky. "I see him!" She then passed out in a fit of religious rapture. The man beside her bent over, put her jacket under her head for support and stole her purse.

Will kept the smile on his face and his arm pointed skyward across the line, and, then, rather than coast into the crowd of reporters waiting to strangle what words they could out of him, broke hard to the right and made a beeline for the Haven motor home and the face he saw before it.

Luc Godot stood silently by the side of the Haven team van. Will stopped directly in front of him. Godot didn't say a word. Will snapped his right foot out of the pedal and winced as it touched solid ground for the first time in hours. Godot remained silent.

"You and I have to talk."

Godot stared silently at Will.

"You think you might want to end this thing before more people die?"

Godot didn't twitch.

"You think you might want to stop being a security knob for a minute or two and start being a cop again?"

Slowly, a smile formed around the face that once again began to look one heck of a lot like that of the TV detective Columbo.

CHAPTER NINETEEN:

GIVEN AN OUT

The wind came out of the north, sharp and colder than expected for mid-July in the south of France, creating the coldest evening on record and sending the assembled journalists scrambling to change their lead from a new face in yellow and the champion straggler so far outside the time limit that he was almost in next year's race to Mother Nature throwing a meteorological curve. The wind snaked through the medieval streets of the town of Castres to the dead end of the closed window of the hotel, battered itself against the creaking pane, then shot off in a million directions at once, carrying the smells, the dust and the scraps of another day.

The blue-green window was chilled on one side, frosted on the other from the humidity of the ancient shower that had just stopped running. The heated water gave the room the sense of a steam bath, but after the cold of the late afternoon, neither man inside the room seemed to mind it.

"I have a job," said the one.

"I know. I'm not saying don't do your job."

"You're saying that some woman name Magda Gertz is behind this. I don't think so."

Will Ross stumbled over the edge of a tear in the carpet and swore quietly under his breath. His left knee had taken a battering earlier today and throbbed dully. He turned to face Luc Godot.

"Then who do you think is behind it? She had opportunity. She saw Bresson the day before he died on the road. She was the one who said, 'He'll be fine,' and by God, he was. What more do you need?"

"You've given me opportunity. You need motive, you need weapon, you need hard evidence of a crime. I don't have any hard evidence of a crime. Preliminary autopsy reports don't show any drugs in Henri Bresson's system."

"I don't care what you say, I don't care what the autopsy says, he was on the ball. You should have seen his eyes, Godot. They were bright red. He was dying inside and he couldn't stop. He couldn't stop pedaling."

Will realized that he was trembling. He leaned over the bed, felt the pull of his knee, and spread his hands wide. "Henri Bresson — hell — he could have had the stuff since Lille. Been playing shooting gallery like it was pinball. Hell, I dunno. But what I do know is that he was on it. He was on the ball and he couldn't get off."

The two stared at each other for a moment as a small steam cloud floated through the air between them.

Godot watched it pass, then turned back to Ross, his face a battleground of arguments and concerns, victories and defeats.

"You may be right, Will. There may be something in what you say, but I see it differently. You and I want to find the same answers, we are simply using a different path to reach them."

"So, how do you see it?"

Godot held up his hands as if to push the question away. "Right now, I cannot say, but, you will know soon enough."

"Before how many more riders die?"

"That depends on the riders. That depends on you. That depends on this Magda Gertz person. That depends on me and how fast I can move in my rapidly approaching old age."

Will stared at him for a moment and then said, quietly, "That's all well and good, Inspector Godot, but keep in mind that despite your age, you're going to have to look in the mirror every morning and see yourself and live every day with the decisions you made and memories of the bad guys who slipped through your fingers and the victims you didn't save."

Godot didn't say a word.

"Gotcha, didn't I? First and foremost — you're still a cop."

"No, I'm not a cop."

"I don't give a rat's ass what's on your goddamned check, Godot!" Will swept his arm across the top of the cheap Formica dresser, scattering hotel knickknacks and a picture of Cheryl Crane. It wasn't intended, but it had a hell of an effect on the Chief of Security for Haven Pharmaceuticals.

"That's like a rider — a real rider — sitting back on his ass in his new big money job as a network announcing flunky and not sweating each time there's a damned breakaway and *he's not in it!* But he is — you see — he is. In his mind — he's thinking — screaming — there — *there* — there's your hole — *punch it!* He can't let go — *you* can't let go."

"I cannot tell you what I know."

"I didn't ask you to — I asked you to open that fourth wall of your thick skull. Think outside the box and do what you were trained to do: investigate all the possibilities. Hell, who are you protecting?"

"I'm not protecting anyone."

"Sure as hell sounds like it."

"I —"

"Look, Luc. People are dying. Bresson. That kid from Lexor who did the Mexican Hat Dance in the middle of his apartment? Remember him? And who knows how many other people are on the hook? Is your check worth that?"

"You think you know — don't you? You think it's somebody with Haven, don't you? You still hate this company, don't you, Ross? Despite what they've done for you. All because of Martin Bergalis and what he did to you last spring."

"What the hell are you talking about? I didn't say shit about Haven. I don't carry hatred for anybody — except maybe that little bastard who pantsed me in the hall in eighth grade."

Godot looked at him quizzically.

"I carry a grudge."

Godot shrugged.

"Look. The deal is this. People are dying. People are going to die. The stuff is in the peloton somewhere and its up to somebody to put their foot down. And, in the words of Dean Vernon Wormer, 'That foot is me.'"

"Are you speaking English?"

"A rough form of it, yes. What I want is your help. Can you overcome your love of Haven and your paycheck and whatever else might be holy and help?"

"I need —" Godot was thinking.

"Yes?"

"I need — more."

Will sighed heavily.

"Will — nothing has been found in regards to Bresson's death. There was nothing in his bloodstream. He was clean."

"What about the final autopsy?"

"That's tomorrow in Paris."

"Will you believe it then?"

"Believe what, Will? That Haven is behind this? Some groupie chasing the peloton? Some drug czar is pushing drug deaths? You tell me to be a cop. I am being a cop. I'm being Sherlock-shit-fellow-Holmes here —"

Will smiled at Godot's attempt at colorful cursing.

"— but — *but* — there is nothing here. *Nothing*."

"Yet."

"Yet. Yes. Yet. That doesn't mean I'm sitting on my derriere waiting for more people to die. And I rather resent you saying that I am, just because I'm on the Haven payroll. I am a cop. Deep inside I am a cop and I will always be one. Whenever I read of a crime in the paper — including this one — I'm wondering what evidence was found on scene — what was the lab report — what did the witnesses see — where is the big or small or infinitesimal bit of evidence leading to the perpetrator going to be — if there is one at all. Yes, Will — I am still a cop, but as much as I love American TV police shows, I cannot solve this crime in 50 minutes. Things are not sitting on top of the ground for me to pick up and examine and point at the killer — if there is a killer. Being an investigator means just that, Will. You investigate. You sit in stuffy rooms and look over dusty pictures and boring records and you run computer searches until the data sheets are running out of your — your — your butt."

Will smiled at the image.

"But you don't just jump and accuse and arrest. It doesn't happen that way. At the moment — in my mind — Henri Bergalis is not a suspect. You are as much a suspect as Henri Bergalis. If not more — you were Bresson's roommate. You knew him. Watched him. Slept in the same room. How could you *not* know of his drug problem — if there was one?"

Will's face puckered into a look of concern.

"I never said anything about Henri Bergalis."

"Ah, see how easy it is to become a suspect? I am concerned. I am 'on the job.' I am doing my Columbo routine, as you call it. I don't want to see people die. Even you."

"Thank you so much."

"But I am going to handle this as a police investigation should be handled. I will gather facts. Do the research and the leg work."

"Round up the usual suspects."

"Yes. And I will do it without your help."

"Well — we'll always have Paris."

"What?"

"Never mind."

There was a knock at the door.

"But still, Will, even now, I need more. Two deaths and only one autopsy are not enough."

Will turned toward the door. "I don't know what else I can give you unless I crap out on the pavement — full of junk."

"More likely full of junk food, but I would prosecute your case to the fullest extent of the law."

The knocking became more insistent.

"Yeah? *Une minute.*" Will smiled at Godot. "I'm sure you would. And I would sail off to that great Ghisallo in the sky happy in that knowledge."

He opened the door with his right hand twisted behind him and turned to face a stone-faced Carl Deeds.

"Hey, Carl."

"We need your number, Will. You're done."

"Yeah, right, Carl."

"You were outside the time limit, Will."

"Says who?"

"Tour rules, Will. Come on. You know the deal — a percentage beyond the finishing time and you're finished. Hell, the broom wagon nearly passed you by. It nearly passed you by, Will."

Will felt the flush in his face, the scars from his crash in the spring singing like a musical tour of Venice. Deeds was right, of course, those were the rules. He had been at least four-and-a-half minutes outside the time limit. Not even close enough to spit. The last item on today's tour had been him. Will Ross. Haven.

Standing just behind Deeds were two men, both ancient, both important looking, even if it was mainly in their own eyes. One wore the tags and passes of a UCI commissaire, while the other, according to his shirt, anyway, was representing the race itself.

It didn't look good for Will or the team. Best, probably, to simply say that he was felled by a virus and have him disappear like Jimmy Hoffa, holding up a goalpost in the Meadowlands until the final stage was safely finished in Paris.

"No."

"Give me your number, Will."

"You can appeal to the *Société du Tour de France* if you want, Carl, but I'm hanging on. No foolin'. I'm hanging on unless they come and hold a gun to my head and take it."

"Rules is rules."

"Yeah, and they've changed the rules before, they've made allowances."

"Not this time."

"This time, you bet. What about that train? Six minutes at that train? Why didn't they take it at the race today? Why didn't they come over and pull it in that hour I was talking to the press and getting saddle sores like nobody's business? Because if they make an allowance for that six-minute train, I'm still 90 seconds inside today's time limit. I'm still in, Carl. I'm still in.

"And how about this: I get them more American coverage by crashing, busting my ass to flinders, then struggling across the line, never give up, never give up and you're telling me that they're going to say, hey, thanks for the effort — you're gone — American TV can watch the Italians for the next week? Right. Most Americans get their spaghetti sauce out of a damned *jar*, Carl! They don't care about the Italians or the French or the English. Do you understand? They're more parochial than the damned Russians, Carl! Unless there's an American making news, first or last, locomotive or caboose, it doesn't matter, Carl. It just doesn't matter."

The man in a Tour de France polo shirt in the hall spoke up, quietly. "We don't do this to please American TV."

"Don't you? Are you sure?"

"Please, Will. This was embarrassing today. It is embarrassing now."

"And it could be embarrassing tomorrow, Carl, but it is real. And it is drama. And it is the story that ESPN will be looking for when they rip off the British TV coverage tomorrow and revoice it and hand it off to American viewers. 'Hey, where's the guy who struggled up to the finish yesterday, the American who wouldn't give up?'"

He looked beyond Deeds into the hall.

"You gentlemen would like that, wouldn't you? Le Tour de France, brought to you by Coca-Cola, a proud American company, featuring the broken and bleeding American rider who never gave up and then was interviewed by the world for an hour today for coming in last. Dead last. The guy who was just in front of the grill of the broom wagon and 10 minutes in front of the Ride the Tour vacation folks? The rider who was interviewed by the world press for an hour after his little stunt? The rider that America is talking about tonight and will be watching for the day after tomorrow on 'the killer climb' of Ventoux? How's that gonna play? And how will it play if you don't let him ride? Not well. Not well at all."

"This isn't a game, Will."

"Bullshit, Carl. It's all a game. And the name of the game is to finish and get as much damned press as you can, because press means attention, attention means endorsements, and endorsements mean money."

"Will —."

"What's the line? No bucks, no Buck Rogers? How's this: No francs, no Tour de France. Simple as that." He glanced out into the hall. "Gentlemen, your answer?"

The two men behind were silent for a moment, before the Tour official spoke up.

"If we make allowance for the train, and the driver of the broom wagon acknowledges the time, we can overlook the time limit and allow you to start tomorrow."

Deeds exploded. "What? Goddamn it, we had an agreement. You came to me — you, we, wanted him out. Damn, you, aw, screw you all!" He turned and shuffled quickly down the hall, his right leg in a lock step, dashing ker-plunk away from the people, the situation, the argument. His anger hovered behind in the air like a swarm of annoying lake gnats.

The two officials stood there for a moment, watching Deeds disappear down the narrow, darkened hall.

The UCI official said, "You do realize, that you are being afforded a great favor, not that your director seems to see it as such."

"You are being allowed to start," said the Tour functionary. "There will be no more favors. You will be listed as last, the final rider, *la lanterne rouge,* tomorrow. It is no honor. You are simply being allowed to start. If you do not finish within time tomorrow, you are finished in Le Tour. Understood?"

"Crystal, gentlemen," Will said, sliding back into his room. "Anything else?"

The two stood in the hall, silently.

"Then, may I wish you a jolly and joyous goodnight. May you have sweet dreams and find some mud for your turtle. Excuse me. I need my rest and recovery time." He closed the door quietly and turned to face Godot. He suddenly and quite deliberately began to shake and sweat.

"That," the security chief said, "was a brilliant performance and one of the biggest loads of *merde* I have ever seen."

"Thank you. It is an honor to perform in front of such a sophisticated audience."

"And it was shit, was it not?"

"Maybe. But who do you remember: the '62 Yankees or the '62 Mets?"

"Who?"

"Never mind. Americans love the locomotive. Americans love a winner. But, they also love the caboose. Because the caboose, the guy who wanders in dead last against all odds, usually makes the best story and is, somehow, more interesting than the squeaky-clean champion with the straight teeth and Wheaties contract."

"I don't understand a word you're saying."

"Consider Le Tour. Until recently, riders having a bad Tour used to fight to be dead last, the red lantern, you actually won an award for it. Why? No. 5 doesn't matter. Six or eight or sixteen. But then, No. 121 when there is no No. 122, well, that's an achievement. You get noticed."

"The caboose."

"Exactly."

"What's a caboose?"

Will stared at Godot for a long, cold moment, then smiled. American reference, he thought, lost on European railroads.

"Will you help me?"

"In your race or your quest to throw everybody connected to Henri Bresson into prison?"

"Remember Henrik Koons."

"Will, the death of a junkie rider is simply not enough. I'll keep my eyes open, but believe me, I need more."

"You'll get more. I just hope that more doesn't mean that you'll have another dead body at your feet before you'll take this seriously."

THE NIGHT WAS COLD. THE NIGHT WAS LONELY. EVEN WITH THE BLANKETS from the other bed piled on, Godot couldn't shake the chill he felt. He wished Isabelle were here. They could talk. They could love. They could warm each other. She could help him find the way.

As he lay in the darkness, he couldn't help but see before him a medical report from the Netherlands, the report of a lab technician in Eindhoven, the lab report that had labeled a synthetic steroid suspected in the death of Henrik Koons, secondary rider for a secondary team, with the manufacturer's code.

HP. A code that he had found again, deep inside the archives of Haven Pharmaceuticals attached to a list of names that included one Magda Gertz.

And others. Godot hoped sincerely that Ross could keep his mouth shut about all this. He smiled. Highly unlikely.

And yet, Ross, for all his bluster, had been right. Godot would have to look himself in the eye every morning and remember that he had pulled his punches when his paycheck was at stake.

The thoughts hung in the air before his eyes like a lighted sign, keeping him awake through the night.

THE LUMP OF BIOLODE VITAMINS FERMENTED IN HIS STOMACH TO THE POINT that the taste rising into the back of this throat woke him up. Will sat up on the edge of the bed and hawked twice, then took a long drink from the bottle of water on his nightstand in the hopes of washing the burning Bs and As and Cs and god knew what else back into his guts. He sat lost within the silence of the room, within the quiet cool of the late night/early morning of the village, thinking past tomorrow, when he faced a sprinter's day and could hide himself within the group, sucking off their wheels for power and support, and thinking on into Monday, where beyond tomorrow's pause, he faced a challenge of his own creation, a gauntlet that he had thrown down to Deeds and Le Tour, the UCI and, in a way, Godot.

Ventoux.

"God in heaven, Cheryl," he said aloud to the dust bunnies and dirty socks, "what the hell was I thinking?"

She ran her hand along the cool of his back and up to his shoulder, pulling him back to his pillow.

CHAPTER TWENTY:

UNDER THE VOLCANO

Montpellier sits on the hills 10 kilometers from the Mediterranean and the Golfe de Lion, east of Toulouse, southwest of Avignon — the seat of the breakaway Vatican of the 14th century — and directly west from Marseille, across the long and sloping Lion bay.

Will was thrilled to be here. After days of sweating and freezing it out inland, feeling and smelling like a hospital wastebasket in the heat and the rain, Will was grateful for the onshore breeze that was freshening the starting area and rejuvenating his newfound resolve.

He kicked at a chunk of curbing that had finally broken free after years of stopping poorly parked Renaults, and let his eyes wander across the crowds of fans and teams gathered for the start.

He took a deep breath and walked toward the Haven team area, where Luis Bourbon held his bike.

YESTERDAY HAD BEEN A MARVEL TO HIM, A DAY ON THE BIKE YOU SIMPLY couldn't buy. Everyone had been shocked, including Will. It hadn't been a question of survival, nor a question of power, it was a question of tactics. Will, offered a bike and a box lunch in Herepian, and, beyond that, no help from Haven, had set his focus on being a leech. He didn't initiate. He didn't support. He'd find a mark, someone who didn't look to be either too gun shy or too much a gunslinger and he sucked their wheel. Luckily, he had chosen wisely.

After the Pyrenees, the two sprint days changed the focus of the field dramatically, with the riders who had shone in the first days of Le Tour taking their final turns at the head of the peloton. For the most part, the rest of the pack simply let them go, as there were too many days of climbing yet to come to waste their energy flying out of Bedarieux.

And so, he leeched. He sucked. He centered himself on the bike as best he could, his left side still singing a symphony of ache to him, and hung tight to the wheel of riders from any number of teams until they shook him off with a curse and a tightly balled fist. Near the finish, just outside of Aniane, on the start of the climb of the fourth category Puechabon, hardly more than a bump in the road after climbing mountains, Will fell into a clot of Haven riders and pulled up behind Miguel Cardone.

"Hey, off you. Off!"

Cardone brushed his hand backward as if swatting at a fly.

Will smiled and *bzzz'd* at him, only serving to make Cardone angrier.

Cardone spat an angry oath and broke away, sprinting up the road. Will watched him go and slid over beside Richard Bourgoin.

"*Bonjour, Richard.*"

"Oh, yes, *bonjour*, Will."

"How are you, my friend?" Will asked out of genuine concern. Bourgoin, with the team's help, had risen to fourth in the G.C., but looked, as always, as the race progressed, as if someone had tried to strangle him with dirty socks. His face was an ashen gray, one step above deathly white, while snot ran perpetually out his nose.

"I have missed you, Will."

"Well, I've missed you, too."

"You have missed the race."

Will laughed. "Richard, I dunno what I've missed up here, but believe me, I haven't missed the race."

"Will —" Richard paused, whether from the effort of the climb or the emotion, Will wasn't sure.

"— Will," he said quietly, "I'm sorry."

"Sorry for what?"

"Sorry for ignoring you. Sorry for turning my back on you. Sorry for not standing up for you in the team meetings. I am *un traitre*."

"A traitor? To what? To me? Jesus, Richard, I understand. I wouldn't have supported me, either. I collapsed in a heap. How could you help me? You couldn't. I had to help myself. And I don't know if I did or not."

"You're still here."

"Well, that's what I mean. Is this good or bad, right or wrong? I'm just here. That's the reality."

"You have shown heart. *Courage.*"

"No. I've shown stubbornness and stupidity. But, sometimes, that's a lot more important than talent."

Bourgoin laughed and shook his head. "You see? That's it. That's what I miss. Everyone else is just so damned serious about this race. Each stage. Each breakaway. But you — you actually make the race fun."

"I know. I didn't get you anywhere close to the podium, but by God, you laughed your ass off in the four corners of France."

"Sometimes, I think, that is more important."

"You want to hear a laugh," Will whispered conspiratorially, "you tell that to Carl."

Bourgoin laughed again and smiled at his friend. Despite how he had treated Will, here the man was, riding at his side, lifting his spirits. Bourgoin shifted his hands on the drops and smiled sadly.

"I'm sorry."

Cardone dropped back quickly and picked up Bourgoin, all the while talking frantically into his radio.

"*Allez,* Richard," Cardone barked. "Deeds wants us moving up and into position for the climb."

"Climb, Christ," Will cursed aloud, "I've seen bigger butts on hamsters."

"Screw you, Ross," Cardone said stiffly, "this is not your team anymore. *Allez! Allez!*"

"Will —" Bourgoin said as he watched Cardone marshal the forces.

"Hey," Will replied before Bourgoin could get a start on a new guilt trip, "ride well. That's what all this is about, Richard. Riding well. Riding strong. Finishing high. I expect to see you on the podium in Paris."

"And where will you be, my friend?"

"I'll be riding in three days later."

Bourgoin laughed out loud, causing Cardone to shoot another angry glance back at Will. Before he had a chance to command again, Bourgoin was up on the pedals and sprinting ahead to join his teammates.

Prudencio Delgado, who had sat six feet behind Bourgoin during Will's conversation, began to pass.

"Ride well, Prudencio," Will offered.

"To hell with you," Delgado answered.

"No doubt," Will replied, "but the words remain: ride well."

Delgado, looking stronger than he had in the previous two weeks of Le Tour, rose out of the seat and charged ahead to rejoin the team.

"Ride well, my friends," Will whispered as the black, red and gold of the Haven team jerseys disappeared into the distance ahead.

"Ride well."

He plowed along, alone, for a few moments, until another group began to pass him. Will slid over to the side and firmly attached himself to the back wheel of another rider, ignoring the curses and taunts that flew back his way along with an occasional water bottle.

And so, yesterday he entered Montpellier, tired, aching and into the wind, but deep within the absolute middle of the pack.

TODAY, WILL PUSHED THROUGH THE TIGHTENING CROWD IN A WEIRD CROSS between a waddle and a lock step. He still couldn't put his full weight on his left side yet and used the cane extensively. On his right side, his calf tightened up again, despite 20 minutes of stretching exercises. Will pointed his right toe at the sky and walked on his heel in order to give the calf one last chance to stretch itself out. Fans in the crowd moved aside for a man, scarred, torn and weaving, who obviously was not in his right mind.

"That looks stylish."

Will turned to see who had spoken and found himself looking into the eyes of Magda Gertz.

"Are you trying to pick me up?"

"I just said hello."

"Well, if you're going to pick me up, you've got to carry me," he pointed, "over there."

"I don't understand."

Will looked at Magda Gertz and sighed. It was a weak joke, he knew, but he also knew that she understood. He got the feeling, just by looking at her, that she was always on some kind of make, on the prowl for the next piece of action, whatever that action might be. Not a whole lot got past her. He had known a lot of guys like this, but few women. Hell, she even made his ex-wife Kim, now playing second harp in some heavenly choir, look like a Girl Scout.

"I hear they tried to force you out."

"Yeah. Maybe. Not so much," Will offered, "Le Tour wanted me out. The UCI wanted me out. The team wanted me out. I appealed to the somewhat coarser market realities of everyone and they let me stay. But now the team feels backstabbed, the UCI feels ignored and Le Tour hopes I crash and burn. Frankly, I can hardly blame them, and I was pretty much on my own yesterday. No support, no help. If I died, I died and somebody other than Haven would have swept up my naughty bits off the side of the road."

He realized that he was nervously babbling.

"Your 'naughty bits?' I don't understand."

He looked at her and smiled. "I bet a little girl like you would understand just about anything."

She cocked her head in a questioning way.

"Anyway. I'm here, they're pissed and life goes on. Amazing how that happens, isn't it?"

"Yes, I suppose it is." She looked down at the Place de la Comédie, what she could see of Montpellier's main square in a sea of sneakered feet, and murmured, "I'm sorry you don't like me, Will."

A sudden wave of embarrassment crossed his face. "I don't — *not* — like you, Magda." He felt trapped in his own distrust of her, it had shown in his face and in his actions with her and with Cheryl. He didn't trust her; he knew she was tied to the death of Bresson, but he was strangely drawn to her as well, and had been since that first day in Lille, a mere two weeks ago. He was drawn, even though he knew it was like a moth to a butane torch.

"I — I —."

"I understand, Will. Sometimes relationships will not allow such things to happen. I know." She smiled. "Friends?"

Warning bells were ringing in his head like it was V-J day, but his natural inclination to avoid a fight and make the peace pushed him to offer his hand in return and reply, "Sure, friends."

Their hands touched for just a moment and he could feel the electricity running through her skin. She smiled, snapped him forward and kissed him lightly.

"I have *very* close friends." She smiled and turned, disappearing quickly into the crowd.

Once again, Will didn't know what to make of this woman. Her presence created a flood of conflicting emotions within him. He searched the crowd again, as he resumed his trek toward his bike, looking for a glimpse of Magda Gertz. She was dangerous, he reminded himself. She was suspect, he reminded himself. She was drop-dead exotic, he had no need to remind himself.

Danger, danger, Will Robinson.

He cast his eyes wider, finally coming to rest on the head of Magda Gertz, deep in conversation with Prudencio Delgado. Will watched and walked as they talked, their heads pressed very close together.

She leaned forward and kissed Prudencio full on the lips, a deep, lasting, longing kiss. Will felt a twinge of something — jealousy, envy or threat — spark deep inside him.

He rocked his way on toward the Haven team van.

"WHY AREN'T YOU IN PARIS?" THE QUESTION HAD A MOCKING TONE, AS IF AN employee had been caught deep within a faked sick day, but it also had an edge, the edge that an angry employer might take with someone who had shown up at an inappropriate place at an inappropriate time.

Henri Bergalis leaned back in the chair of the one private area of the Haven VIP and hospitality area and looked across the tent of white plastic chairs to Luc Godot, his chief of security, standing in a festival tent, in the south of France, in mid-July, dressed in a rumpled suit and tie and threadbare trench coat.

"We really should give you a clothing allowance, don't you think?"

"Perhaps."

"You should take the perks while you can, Luc. There comes a day when the money train stops and you won't be in line for them anymore."

"Yes, well, such is life."

"Yes, it is. So," he said sharply, directly changing the subject, "what can I do for you?"

Godot scratched his forehead for a moment, his skin beginning to sweat from both the humidity of the tent and the tension of the moment. He didn't quite know how to begin.

"Look, Luc," Bergalis said, quietly, "if it is a personnel problem in Paris, we'll handle it next week. If it is a security problem, that is your area and I give you full control. I trust your judgment. If it is anything else, we simply won't bother with it now. It can wait. Understood?"

Bergalis began to turn as if the moment had passed and the audience was over. He was already reaching for a sheaf of papers that held sales contracts negotiated by Haven over the past two weeks of Le Tour. It had been a profitable race. A little hospitality, a few drinks, a photo with the riding stars and bag of Haven knickknacks and you could sell just about anybody just about anything. They wouldn't even feel buyers' remorse until sometime next month when the shipment arrived with the bill close behind.

Henri Bergalis smiled. Now he realized why his father had been so deeply entrenched in this sport and this race.

Bergalis turned back and shook his head in shock. Godot still stood before him, despite, what Henri felt, had been a rather definite dismissal. Godot continued to wait, staring and uncomfortable in the sticky air of the tent.

"Yes, Luc? Is there something else I can help you with?"

"Yes, Henri."

"And that would be?" he asked, drawing out the question sarcastically.

Godot took a deep breath. "That would be," he paused, "Cytabutasone."

Bergalis's hand stopped in mid-air, his fingers frozen for a moment, before slowly closing in tension. Henri caught himself quickly, and mentally forced his hand to relax.

"I thought we dealt with that weeks ago."

"We did."

"This is about that Dutch rider, correct?"

"Him," Godot said, "and others. Possibly Henri Bresson."

"Bresson? You must be joking. The autopsy has not even started. How can you make such a conclusion?"

"It is a guess. Merely a guess."

"Quite a guess."

"Sometimes they are, sometimes they aren't."

Henri Bergalis sighed, "What else do I have to tell you, Luc? What else do you need to know? Yes, Haven developed Cytabutasone as a synthetic steroid-replacement therapy. It had unexpected benefits and unexpected side effects. My brother chose to produce it, while I chose to go to my father and shut down research. It caused a rift between myself and Martin that was never healed. But I had to do it, Luc. There were too many questions." His voice drifted off into a field of memory. "There were too many problems."

"Yes, I know," Godot said, quietly, "I have been in Toulouse."

Henri Bergalis felt his mouth go dry.

FOR THE FIRST TIME IN DAYS, WILL WAS PROPERLY SEATED ON THE BIKE. IT was a strange, and oddly painful position, following two stages in a riding attitude that was a cross between sidesaddle and the letter Q. The flap of skin along the outer edge of his left knee had scarred over nicely and had stopped seeping blood and pus the day before, encouraging Will to leave off the dressing today, as his father said, "to give it some air." In addition, his elbow felt looser than it had and his sandpapered scalp was slowly losing the pins-and-needles sensation that had annoyed him since the crash.

The crash. Three days before, only three days, and it already seemed like a lifetime, while Henri Bresson was already being relegated to a place deep inside the collective memory of the press, only to be recalled and hauled out in highlight shows and Le Tour documentaries.

Will pulled up behind a Lexor Computer rider and hung onto his wheel for dear life for the sprint through Dions. The rider cursed and gestured, Will having destroyed his line through the sprint zone. As they passed the eastern boundaries of the small town, Will pulled away, looking for another shark to carry his lamprey. The Lexor rider made a hard gesture of contempt, in answer to which, Will smiled and waved, which only made the rider angrier, pleasing Will no end.

"Yes, Oprah, I have always seemed to have had this strange and magical effect on people," he chuckled.

Coming out of Dions, Will started to climb the first of three bumps that stood in the way before the base of Mont Ventoux.

Ventoux.

He felt his forehead grow warm and moist.

He should have listened to the doctor.

"SO, GODOT, TELL ME," HENRI BERGALIS SAID, QUIETLY, "WHAT DO YOU KNOW of Toulouse?"

"I have seen the records. The notes."

"Where did you find them?"

"The archives."

"Ah, the little lost building in the middle of nowhere. I have always thought we should move that to a new facility."

"It could use some face-lifting."

"Yes. How did you get in? I have the only access."

Godot was silent for a moment, then, proceeded honestly, "I broke in."

"Ah. A creative solution to the problem of curiosity. That explains it. I got a report from the Paris police the other morning of a break-in at the facility." He paused. "Did you find what you were looking for?"

"Yes, I did. And no. No, I did not."

"No? Why? Did answers simply give you more questions?"

"Yes. Yes, they did."

"It is often the way," Bergalis nodded. "And so, my dear Luc, what did you find?"

"I found records. Signed by you. I found reports copied to you. I found stories of convicts, the criminally insane, used as guinea pigs in experiments on a steroid you couldn't control."

"Ah, but we could control it, Luc. At first. We could control it. As for the convicts, well, thanks to Bardot, we can't use animals, now, can we?"

Godot ignored the joke and the quiet hardness that was easing into the voice of Henri Bergalis.

"I found experiments on human beings that were authorized by you and carried out by your team of researchers."

"Yes, such things happen," he said, sadly.

"A team of researchers," Godot continued, "led by a woman named Magda Gertz."

❂

THE CLIMB BEGAN AT 168 KILOMETERS AND WOULD CONTINUE, PRETTY MUCH, straight up for the next 22 kliks. It was only the third time in 25 years that Le Tour had returned to the slopes of Ventoux, only the third time since Tom Simpson, an English rider, challenging for the yellow jersey, had died just before reaching the summit of the extinct volcano, from what many said later was a combination of drive, desire, heat exhaustion and amphetamines.

Will planted himself behind a Banesto rider on a tear and drafted up to the village that marked the real start of the climb, ahead of the peloton, before being brushed away. Will pulled off and directly into a patch of Haven riders: John Cardinal, Tony Cacciavillani and Prudencio Delgado. The three essentially ignored Will, though Tony C. winked and smiled quickly, before returning to the desperate situation he faced. This was not a sprinter's day and Tony C. was dying. This would be about the time he said good-bye to Le Tour, but he was too close in the hunt for the green sprinter's jersey he was determined to wear in Paris.

Both Cardinal and Cacciavillani were falling hard off the pace, so Will, filled to just below his larynx with vitamins and sports drinks, pulled up behind Delgado.

The young rider glanced back quickly, made a face, waved him off once and then returned to the road, eventually paying no heed to the leech that rode just behind.

Will smiled and tucked himself in for the ride. "Nothing like folks being happy to see you," he muttered.

He adjusted himself on the seat, tuned his ankling technique and focused on the climb.

"YOU SEE, LUC," BERGALIS EXPLAINED, "THIS WAS MY OWN LITTLE WORLD. THIS section of Haven R&D was mine, given to me by my father with express instructions to Martin to keep his damned hands off." Henri paused to let his flash of anger subside. "With that in mind, I was able to choose my own team. And on my own team, I placed, in high authority, a highly recommended researcher with excellent credentials."

"Magda Gertz."

"Exactly."

"I've seen her credentials."

Bergalis laughed. "You can hardly miss them."

Godot let the laughter die. "Her résumé was in the file."

"Yes," Bergalis chuckled, "indeed. Ahh — um — from there, we did research, and, as you can see from the records, research on volunteers only. We told them of the dangers. We told them of the risk. They were offered time off and conjugal visits if they participated. Many did."

"Magda Gertz led the research. What did you do?"

"I ran the project in my division. Everything, at least that was the plan, was supposed to go through me."

"And did it?"

"I thought so. Obviously not, if Cytabutasone is now a part of the peloton."

"Who else was on the project?"

"About 10. Three or four have died, after all, it's been 10 years. Others have left the company for other research. A few have stayed."

"Like who?"

"Well, Louis Engelure, for one."

Will ignored the pain that grew along the side of his left knee. The spinning of yesterday and the first five hours of today's stage hadn't put too terrible a strain on the wound. But now, about 1000 meters into a 2000-meter climb, Will was beginning to feel the pressure along the scarred stitch ridge, as well as a growing tightening in his right calf.

And yet, he held the focus on the rear of Delgado's wheel as they passed a clot of angry men standing next to idling trucks and continued to climb the mountain, Delgado providing the power like an engine on rails.

"WHAT WAS ENGELURE'S PART IN ALL THIS?" GODOT ASKED.

"He was an assistant. Worked with Magda a lot. When the project fell apart, he was one of the few enthusiastic about keeping it alive, saying that one failure was not a reason to ignore such promise."

"One failure."

"Yes. All the test subjects died."

WILL GLANCED AHEAD TO DELGADO. DESPITE THE TENSION THAT HAD FESTERED and grown between them over the past few days, Will still felt a touch of concern for the brother of his best friend, his late best friend. At the very least, Will thought, he should offer to take a pull, no matter how crappy he felt. He had not felt this need or compulsion with any other rider or team, but now, he knew, he at least had to make an offer.

"Prudencio," he yelled, "slide over and let me take a pull."

Delgado snorted and shook his head like an angry, wet bull, a sea of sweat and snot sailing off him in 360 different directions. He hunched his shoulders and powered ahead, Will close on his tail.

"Pardon me," Will said, then let his gaze drift back to the rear wheel of Delgado. An errant thought began to wander through his head.

"I've seen this before," Will muttered. "I've seen this before."

He pondered the thought, while staring at a thin black tire working its way, surely, steadily, up a mountainside.

"Oh, my God."

"YOU HAD A PROBLEM WITH THAT, I SHOULD HOPE," GODOT SAID, THINKING back to a pile of dead convicts who had volunteered to be guinea pigs.

"Well, I did," Bergalis said. "I did have a problem with it. I was sickened by it all. The problem is, or was, that my brother didn't. Did you see his memo? It should have been near the top of the file. He wanted it to continue. Engelure did as well. Engelure said it was a crime that this was not being tested and produced by Haven or someone else."

"And Magda?"

"At the time, she listened to me."

"At that time?"

"Yes. At that time, she was my wife."

Godot stood in shock, while Henri Bergalis casually looked toward the monitor at his side. On the screen, he saw a great mass of riders blocked at the Chalet Reynard turnoff of Mont Ventoux by a barricade of trucks.

"Hmm," Bergalis noted. "It seems we have a situation here."

AT 1600 METERS, WILL GLANCED AROUND AND DISCOVERED THAT HE AND DELGADO had found the gap, that almost mystical place in a race, or on a highway, where traffic is either in front of you or behind you, but nowhere near you. They were also in a small gap as far as the crowds were concerned, as it seemed that police had kept the fans back at Chalet Reynard, while few had ventured across from the other side to spend a day along the hot, bleak and exposed upper slopes of Ventoux.

God, Will thought, but I hate it here. Although, he thought, in 400 meters, I'll cross the summit, scoot down into Carpentras and know, know, that Ventoux has been conquered by me. He laughed out loud. By little old me.

He glanced back again. The France 2 chopper was hovering in the distance, capturing something on video tape, he wasn't sure what. Whatever it was that had held up the peloton was now out of sight. Despite the height they had attained, he couldn't see them anymore. Will shifted himself on the bike to give himself a new angle and still couldn't see anyone coming up behind. Oh, he thought, that must have been a merry muck-up.

He turned forward again and pulled back on Delgado's wheel. Ahead, he could see the marble memorial looming at the spot where Tom Simpson had collapsed and died in 1967.

Suddenly, as they continued their charge toward the summit, Will noticed an erratic shudder entering the pace, high and low, high and low, one, two, three — then one, three, two — one, one, one. Delgado's tempo threw him off and Will felt a spike in his left knee. "God, no. Not now," he railed, "not so close to the damned summit!"

Delgado shook his head. Once. Twice. The snot and sweat sprayed across the expanse of the road.

And suddenly, along with the spray, there was a shower of blood.

CHAPTER TWENTY-ONE:

DEATH WEARS A BOWLER

Will watched with fascination as the spray of blood and sweat circled the head of Prudencio Delgado, not unlike the slow-motion movie of a Labrador retriever stepping out of a pond with a duck in its mouth.

The deep red drops caught the harsh, unfiltered light of an afternoon on Mont Ventoux and looked like rubies caught in the grip of a shower of diamonds.

Suddenly, Delgado stopped pedaling and began to slide across the empty road, losing speed, losing momentum, in an unguided crawl toward a shallow ditch filled with sharp rocks.

"Prudencio!" Will shouted, still moving in slow motion. "Prudencio!"

His scream broke the hold of the molasses clock, and with it, Delgado's fork twisted to the right, dropping him, hard, to the road. Ignoring the pain that shot through both legs, Will leapt off his bike and pushed it forward toward the ditch, the bike, as if alive, turning at the last moment away from the danger and falling backward onto the road.

His cleats scraping madly across the asphalt, Will knelt beside his collapsed teammate, the stones of the road digging into his knees with a sun-baked intensity.

"Goddamn. Prudencio. Don't leave me, man, don't leave me," he shouted, unzipping the fallen rider's jersey. Will quickly turned Delgado over and pulled off his own jersey, wadding it up to form a pillow behind the young rider's head.

"Come on, man, come on," he pleaded, watching Delgado's eyes roll maniacally back and forth in his head, as if he were watching and riding a road that existed only in his mind.

Will stood and turned a complete circle, looking for someone, anyone, to help him. The road ahead, stretching up toward Simpson's memorial and the summit that lay just beyond, was empty. Turning in the opposite direction, he could still see the France 2 helicopter hovering in the distance.

"Yo! Yo! Goddamn it! *Yo!!!*" He screamed, waving frantically to the chopper. No luck. Their focus was elsewhere. He was wasting his time.

He turned back to Delgado and stopped in shock where he stood. Beside Prudencio knelt a man in what appeared to be an antique, turn-of-the-century style, brown plaid suit. He wore a high celluloid collar, slightly yellowed from use, and a tightly knotted brown-and-blue silk tie. Will could see, just before the edge of the pushed-back bowler, a few strands of a thinning hairline above a sharply etched face.

"Jesus in a jumpsuit! Who the hell are you?"

"I'm here to help."

"Yeah, maybe, but who the hell are you and where the hell did you come from?"

"I saw you had problems so I stopped by."

"Yeah, but from where?"

"It doesn't matter. Your friend matters. Don't worry. I'm here to help him. I'll ease his pain. You go on. I've got him."

Will stood panting in both fear and exhaustion for a moment, then began to unconsciously take a step toward his bike.

Something, an unrealized, half-remembered thought, stopped him.

"Wait a minute," he said with a growing disbelief. "Wait a goddamned minute."

"You use that word to much."

"Too goddamned bad, Jasper. I know you. I know you," Will said, his voice rising as he turned back to face the pair.

The man nodded with an obvious sense of shyness.

"I met you once before on the Tourmalet," Will said in a panic. "I met you there with Henri Bresson and you said the same thing to me. You told me to leave — don't worry — take off — you'd help now. You'd help. And then he was dead."

"And then he was dead."

Will slowly stepped toward the figure, frightened half out of his mind, but determined to step between him and Delgado.

"He was dead, yes, indeed," Will rambled. "He was dead, and who are you?"

"I know you. I know your family."

"Oh, Jesus," Will said with a frightening realization, "I bet you do." Despite his fear, he continued to edge forward.

"I know your dog — Hartley, wasn't it? I know your grandparents and your uncles and a few of your aunts. I know Tomas. And Kim. And Martin Bergalis. And Henrik Koons. Paul van Bruggen. Well, I know him. You don't, but I do. Henri Bresson. Didn't I almost get to know your father once?"

The levee holding back the flood of fear and emotion broke in Will and he charged forward, planting his hands on the chest of the stranger and shoving him back and away from Prudencio Delgado, who suddenly struggled for breath on the hot tarmac of Ventoux.

"Yes. Yes. I know you real well, you son of a bitch."

Will crouched beside Prudencio and began to gather him up in his arms. "But guess what — you're not getting him."

The stranger stared, showing no emotion. "I'm not worried, Will. I'll get him. Today. Tomorrow. 50 years from now." He smiled, coldly. "There is no hurry."

"Yeah, well, not today. Not today. Not today." Will picked up Prudencio behind the shoulders and under the knees. He bounced once and lifted from his back, feeling the muscles pull and tear. He shifted the pressure of the lift to his left and felt the sickening rip of the stitches as they tore away from the side of his knee and the blood begin to seep out and down his leg.

"You can't save him, Will. Why don't you save yourself?"

Will turned frantically to look down the side of the volcano, and realized that, still, there was no one in sight.

What the hell is going on, he wondered.

"Protest," the stranger answered to the unasked question. "Protest. Truckers are protesting a new government program to trim their benefits and pay. So, they've blocked Ventoux during Le Tour. They've played it well, not giving anyone a bit of warning. Should get a lot of national, if not international, coverage of their demands."

Will had taken two steps down the mountain, then turned to face the summit. It was closer. It was far closer than the protest and barricade could ever be and he had no idea what hassles he'd face at the barricade.

He began to walk toward the summit, Prudencio Delgado collapsed in his arms, his muscles already beginning to scream from the unaccustomed weight. His cleats began to slip and skid on the superheated surface of the road. He kicked off his shoes and began his struggle toward the peak, feeling the tarmac burn through his socks with each step.

The stranger walked in comfort beside him.

"Let him go, Will. Let him go," he whispered. "Save yourself. You'll die on Ventoux along with him. Most certainly, your career will die. Your Tour will be over. *Fini.* Get on the bike now and you can be one of the top finishers today. There are only a few ahead of you. Truly. Fourteenth? Wouldn't fourteenth be worth it, Will? More worthy than this, that's for sure, isn't it? Delgado hates you, Will. He has hated you ever since the moment his brother died. Why sacrifice your career for him? He's laughed at you every step of the way, Will. Every step of Le Tour. He's torn you down, he's laughed. He's played you for the fool."

"I'm ... usually ... pretty good ... at ... doin' that ... myself," Will panted.

Will kept walking but his pace had slowed. He stared straight ahead and focused on the memorial to Simpson, now only steps away. In the distance, at the summit, a few people who had been looking down before, watching the drama unfold with Will and Prudencio, were pointing and running aimlessly about in a panic, desperate to find the right person to talk to, the proper thing to do.

The stranger continued to whisper, "Let him go, Will. Save yourself and your race. Save your career."

Delgado lurched in his arms in a spasm of coughing. He gagged on something and began to vomit a milky white fluid. On the second spasm, Will felt an explosion in the calf of his right leg and dropped Prudencio's legs as they both fell to the ground.

"Oh, Will. Too bad. You've just gone and torn your soleus. Your calf muscle. Your Tour really is done, now. No argument can talk your way out of this one. By the way, I enjoyed your point about Coca-Cola the other night.

That was good."

Will ignored the stranger, swallowed his nausea, focused on the summit and struggled to rise, pulling Delgado with him by the arm and putting all the pressure on his left leg. The flap of skin that had been held together with scar tissue and stitches had now pulled completely free and hung down at the bloody side of his leg.

He draped Prudencio's arm over his shoulder and took a step forward. His right leg started to collapse with the pain and Will vomited down his bare chest.

"You see, Will? He's nearly gone. And what do you owe to him, Will? What do you owe to him? Give him to me, Will. Give him to me. The pain will be gone and you can just lay here until help arrives, Will. Give him to me, Will. Give him to me."

The words rang in Will's ears, but were suddenly pushed aside by another sound, the memory of an explosion behind a cheap hotel in Milan and the friend whose pieces had been scattered for the birds over a block-wide area because of a bomb aimed for him.

Prudencio had been right all along. Will had killed Tomas Delgado. Will and a few ounces of C4 *plastique*. Will had killed him. Will had killed his best friend.

"Let him go, Will. He hates you for that and all the other reasons in the world. Give him to me," he whispered.

Will roared with pain and swung his arm back toward the stranger, knocking the black bowler hat off the top of his head and throwing himself off balance.

He screamed like a man possessed. "Get the hell away from me! Goddamn it! You hear me? Get the *hell* away! You can't have him." Will felt the anger and frustration and pain roar in his ears and pour out of his eyes. "You can't *have him*!" he wailed, turning back toward the summit and pulling Prudencio's arm over his shoulders.

"You can't have him, you son of a bitch."

He took a hobbling step.

"You can't have him."

He took another step.

"You can't have him."

And another. And another. The cry became a mantra, not unlike the relentless beat of an engine as it struggled up a hill.

"You … can't … have … him. You … can't … have … him."

Delgado coughed and gagged.

Will shot him an angry glance. "Don't you die. Don't you die on me, you piece of shit. Don't you dare do it."

He struggled past the memorial to Tom Simpson and plodded on, one step at a time, toward the summit, his socks in tatters, his feet blistered and bleeding from the roadway. Ahead, he could see a car racing down the road toward them, toward the two walkers who, only minutes before, had been racers. Behind, he heard, turning his head slightly, a growing sound, as if the barricade had been broken and the flood of Le Tour was racing toward them once again.

He stepped. And stepped again. One foot after another. He stepped, his right leg collapsing in pain. He stepped again, his left leg throbbing, his right a mass of torn muscle and cartilage, his throat suddenly dry and constricted on the desert that was Ventoux.

He stepped and stepped again, using his right leg only for balance before dragging it ahead again.

"You can't have him," Will whispered, his anger fading with the last of his strength.

"You can't have him."

Will felt a blast of wind. Another trick, he thought. Another trick.

"You can't have him."

Suddenly, there were cars and people around him as he took a step, another step toward the summit, which was now only a few hundred meters away. He took another step. And another step.

The video cameras whirred and the still cameras snapped and Will felt the heat of a fill-flash just before his eyes.

Why would you need a fill-flash on such a beautiful day, he wondered?

He struggled ahead and felt arms pulling at Prudencio, trying to take him away.

"*You can't have him*," he screamed at everyone, at no one, at the stranger no longer there.

Another flash caught him off guard again and, suddenly, there was a face before him, the face of the woman he loved, the face that was Cheryl Crane.

He began to cry helplessly, crying for nothing, crying for everything.

"Save me," he whispered through the tears. "Save me, Cheryl."

She took him in her arms and pulled him close, supporting them both until the paramedics slipped under Will's arm and pulled Prudencio Delgado away.

"Save me," Will whispered, his legs collapsing under him.

"Save me."

She arched her back just a bit to support his weight and stroked his hair. "You're safe, now, Will. You're safe."

As she held him, the riders of Le Tour de France who had been held up for nearly 10 minutes by a large group of protesting truckers, groaned past the assembled cars and emergency personnel on their way toward the summit of Ventoux, knowing that, once again, for the third time in two weeks, Will Ross, a mediocre or worse rider on the Haven squad, had once again stolen their thunder with the international media.

The gears whirred and the tires sang and the heat of Ventoux rose into the sky.

CHAPTER TWENTY-TWO:

THE HIGH PRICE OF VISIONS

By the time Will had been half dragged, half carried to the summit of Mont Ventoux, Prudencio Delgado was already gone, whisked away by medical helicopter to Avignon, the nearest city of consequence. Will would remain, at least for the time being, as there was no other medical transport, the ambulance drivers having joined the truckers protest back down the mountain.

Two motorcycle paramedics worked frantically on Will, wrapping his left knee to stop the bleeding, and massaging the frightfully torn muscle of his right leg in the hopes of relaxing it past the spasms.

Will leaned back on a vague sort of lawn chair and drank everything in sight, from two bottles of water to four of Haven CrocJuice, right down to something red that a man in the crowd had handed him, with tears in his eyes, that Will found to be absolutely delightful.

In the clutch of humanity that surrounded him, Will could hear the whir of the video cameras and the snap of the stills, his world lit by a steady barrage of flashes.

The truckers would be annoyed by this, for sure, as they had been pushed to a secondary position in coverage, even in France, along with the rest of the riders of Le Tour. The image of the day became the injured American hobbling up Ventoux, carrying the unconscious Spanish rider cradled in his arms.

It was drama, it was sacrifice, it was pure, unadulterated Hollywood. This would be the drama of Le Tour like nothing since LeMond in '89, overcoming every other image of the day, perhaps of the race itself.

Even at that moment, in Carpentras, some 30 kilometers down the road, the stage winner and the race leader were being awarded their long-awaited prizes at a near-empty finish line, the media occupied elsewhere, the fans surrounding their TV sets for continual coverage of the drama atop Ventoux.

Will had taken center stage again. Not a win to his name in this edition of Le Tour. He was, in fact, the lanterne rouge. But for the third time, he had captured the imagination and the focus of the world's cycling press.

The stage winner, Winston McReynolds, once the rider in yellow, threw his roses to the ground in disgust as the ceremony came to an end.

In an empty town square, the roses made no sound.

At the top of Ventoux, a support van had finally been commandeered and blankets spread across its ridged metal floor. Two burly paramedics pulled Will out of the lawn chair by his arms and saddle-carried him to the rear of the van. He was recovered enough to crawl in slowly and collapse atop the padding.

Cheryl Crane and Carl Deeds crawled in behind him before the doors were closed, shutting off all the light except for what came through two, tiny round windows along each side of the van.

The engine started with a rattle and began a weaving ride down the mountainside.

"Where are we going?" Will whispered.

"I would suspect Carpentras," Cheryl answered, massaging his hand. "There are pretty good medical facilities there, and the team docs will poke you a bit. Maybe sew you up."

Deeds sat quietly in a corner, his face mostly in shadow.

"Dark in here," Will muttered. "Like living in a black-and-white movie."

"Yes," she answered, stroking his forehead.

"Will," Deeds asked, in a barely concealed anger, "what …"

Cheryl froze him in mid-sentence with a sharp look. "Not now."

"What?" Will said, slowly rising up on his right elbow. "No, go ahead, Carl. What do you need to know?"

Cheryl sat back in frustration against the van wall. A sharp turn threw her to the side, and Deeds off his balance in the back. The driver banged the wall of the van and shouted a muffled "*excuscz-moi.*"

"Nothing happened, Carl," Will said, quietly.

"What do you mean?"

"I mean that the 'nothing' that happened to Henri Bresson just happened again, this time to Prudencio Delgado."

"What are you talking about? Bresson was clean. They found nothing."

Will nodded. "And that's the nothing I'm talking about. Whatever nothing that drove Henri to ride off the side of the Tourmalet, caused Prudencio to flame out on the side of Ventoux, with me just behind."

"Will, you're leaping to a conclusion that nobody can support."

"Jesus Christ, Carl," Will spit, "what the hell do you need?" He started checking the bullet items off in mid-air, the invisible chart fluctuating wildly with the increasing rock and roll of the van. "Power, but erratic. Refusal to acknowledge anyone around him. Hemorrhaging. Collapse. God, what do you want? A neon sign saying Rx, prescriptions filled here?" He fell back heavily on the blankets just as the van hit a bump. Will's head rose into the air for a second, then slammed back down with a hard and hollow 'thunk.'

"Shit."

"You're convinced?"

"Yeah, I'm convinced," Will said angrily, staring at the top of the van.

Cheryl leaned forward and tried to calm Will. Deeds began to talk again, and Cheryl raised her hand.

"Look, Carl. I dunno what or why you won't believe, but Will has seen them both and if he says there is something in the pack, then, by God, I'm going to believe him, even if you won't. And if you don't do something about it, then I will."

She uttered her last sentence as a challenge, with enough conviction and force to make both Will and Deeds realize that she would have no problem, whatsoever, with marching into the UCI medical office and saying there was a drug in the race, a drug that was decimating Haven.

Deeds leaned forward into a shaft of sunlight entering the van and pointed an angry finger at Cheryl. "Look you," he barked, stabbing at the air around her with his fingernail, "I run a clean team."

The concern and fear for Will that had built within her over the past hour, brick by brick, suddenly fused into a white-hot core of anger. Cheryl slapped his finger away and barked, "Carl, it's not a clean team just because you think it's a clean team! It's not clean if you refuse to acknowledge that you might have a problem! You're living in a fool's paradise! You're so damned determined to win this race, to get somebody, anybody on the podium, that you're willing to look away from a very obvious problem. Hell — if Will can see there' s a problem, it's gotta be carved in Mount Rushmore."

"Thank you, so much," Will said sarcastically.

Without thinking, she kicked at his elbow. The pain of the earlier injury lifted him a full foot off the floor of the van.

"Oh, geeze, sorry," she said.

Deeds hadn't reacted to Cheryl's last tirade. He sat back in his corner of the van to face the reality of the situation before him. Deflated, he fell in on himself until, in the shadows, he looked like a pumpkin that stayed outside too long.

"There is."

"There is what?" Cheryl asked.

"There is something, I don't know what, in the peloton."

"You mean a drug."

"Yes," Deeds said quietly, "I mean a drug."

"Then, why didn't you say something?"

"Because, because I didn't know. I had suspicions like everybody else, but yes, I turned away from them. I wanted to win. I was sure that Bresson was on the needle, but I couldn't prove anything. He couldn't ride like that without help. No one could. Not with that strength, not that consistently. But yes, I wanted to be on the podium. After 25 years in this sport, I wanted to finally be there. And so, when the autopsy reports on Bresson were inconclusive, I looked away. I shouldn't have. But I did."

"Oh, Carl," Cheryl said, her anger floating away, "don't kill yourself over this. We all could see it. It was there for all of us to see. But who saw? Who acted? We're all to blame. I saw the same things you did. I could have said something, but I didn't think it was my place."

"Bergalis thought it was an isolated incident."

"What? Bergalis knew?"

"Suspected," Carl said distantly. "Henri thought that Bresson was an isolated incident, but he said that he knew who was behind it. He said he could handle it."

"Famous last words," Will muttered.

"So I let him handle it."

"Who is it? Who did Bergalis suspect?"

"What?"

"If Henri Bergalis suspected someone, who did he suspect?"

"Christ, Cheryl," Deeds said with surprise, "what planet have you been on?"

"What do you mean?"

"It's Magda Gertz."

"No foolin'," Cheryl said with a smile as the van ground to a halt in Carpentras and the doors burst open to reveal an assembled media horde.

HENRI BERGALIS DOWNSHIFTED THE FERRARI AND TOOK THE TURN AT 55 KILOmeters per hour, smoothly accelerating back up to speed in his race toward the hospital in Avignon. Luc Godot pried his fingers out of the side of his seat and settled back into the deep, rich leather.

Both men, for much the same reasons, wanted to see and talk with Prudencio Delgado.

One, wanted to save his company. The other, wanted to save his company and solve a crime.

"You think it is, Luc," Bergalis said, picking up the line of conversation that had been lost in the turn, "you think it is the same thing as Bresson?"

"From the reports, I'd say yes. All the aspects there, right down to the milky white vomit. Koons had that up in Eindhoven, Bresson had that at the base of the cliff, reports are that Delgado had it all over his shirt." Godot stared ahead and planted his fingers in anticipation of the next turn. Bergalis took it without slowing down.

"Where do you think it will take us? Back to the Toulouse project?"

"More than likely. We'll have to see who on the staff is still in the business," Godot said, "then determine who had access, opportunity and motive, not only for the murders, and they are murders…."

"In this case," Bergalis said quietly, "I hope it is only attempted murder."

"… but for the theft of the formulas and research data."

"That should be simple. There are still two people active in the business, Gertz and Engelure. We should start there. Industrial espionage, you think?"

"What, Gertz and BioSyn? Could be. But there is also revenge. Extortion...."

"We haven't had any demands," Bergalis said.

"Might not until after the race. 'You've seen what we can do to you. Now, pay up or see worse.' That sort of thing."

"I see."

"So, we work quickly, but carefully, and ignore no step."

"Including Mr. Delgado. Tell me, why are you in such a rush to talk to him?" Bergalis asked.

"I talked with Deeds. He said that Delgado was in very bad shape, which, if he dies, would leave us short one more witness, one more participant."

"And we're back to the start."

"Yes."

Henri Bergalis passed the outskirts of Avignon in a blur, the black Ferrari slicing through the late-afternoon humidity. In the near distance, he could see the outline of the hospital rising up above an open field.

"Luc," he said, slowly, "I don't want to muddy your investigation. That is your job. That is your talent. That is why I hired you. But, I want you to think of a connection here. A connection between Magda Gertz and Louis Engelure. They were awfully close then, they may be awfully close now."

Godot turned and studied the face of Henri Bergalis carefully. Whatever he was suggesting here was causing great internal turmoil, a distaste, as if he were turning his back on two longtime acquaintances, employees, even friends, to get to the heart of the question at hand.

"No, I'm serious, Luc. Magda will sleep with anyone to get what she wants. Now, she could be in league with Engelure. She could be sleeping with him."

A look of surprise lifted Godot's right eyebrow and kept him frozen upright in his seat as Bergalis took the last hard turn, at speed, into the parking lot of the Avignon regional medical center.

THE DOCTOR IN CARPENTRAS CURSED THE DAMAGE ON WILL'S LEFT KNEE, THE flap of skin, the size of a mayonnaise jar lid, chewed and torn along its edges from the separation of body and stitch.

"You should not have been riding," he said to Will, punching out every word.

"I know," Will answered in the same, singsong rhythm.

"But you did and here you are now," the doctor said with disgust. "I don't know what you expect me to do with this."

"I expect you to clean it up, dress it up and stitch it up as best you can, holding to the tenets of the Hippocritic oath."

"Hippocratic."

"I like mine better."

Cheryl smiled in the corner of the medical tent.

Will was filled with enough painkillers for the moment to put him in an expansive mood. He returned her smile and said, "You know, when I was racing in Colorado once, I was at a hospital where they had just brought in some guy who had carbon monoxide poisoning. TV news showed up and this reporter was standing in front of me doing a live report and said, 'They've just now put him in the hyperbolic chamber.' I couldn't help myself and I screamed, 'Oh no! He'll come out as a gross exaggeration of himself!' On live TV. True story."

Cheryl burst into laughter and even the doctor smiled.

The laughter made Will feel better.

Though he had to admit, the drugs didn't hurt.

GODOT STEPPED CAREFULLY AROUND THE FOREST OF MONITORS AND I.V. POLES, making his way by a roundabout route to the bedside of Prudencio Delgado. Henri Bergalis took the more direct approach, ignoring the nurses and moving the equipment aside.

Godot turned to a nurse standing at the end of the bed who was glaring at Bergalis for having intruded on her territory and rearranging the furniture.

"Any condition yet?"

"Not officially. He's guarded."

"What does that mean?" Bergalis demanded.

"Yes," Godot said, quietly, "what does that mean?"

"It means that we have stabilized his blood pressure and his heartbeat," she said, never taking her eyes off Henri Bergalis, "but we don't know of internal damage yet and we aren't sure where he will be tomorrow."

"Prudencio," Bergalis called. "Prudencio?"

Godot watched in fascination as Bergalis tried to get a response from the rider.

"Prudencio!" he said sharply, shaking his arm.

"You can talk and shake and prod and poke and beat him all you want," the nurse said, "but you're not going to get anything out of him other than the babble he's been spouting since he came in."

"Oh," Bergalis said, his gaze snapping up to meet hers. "And what would that be?"

"Yes," Godot said, quietly, "what has he said?"

"He simply has called out a name. Once or twice …"

"Magda," Godot said.

"Magda!" Bergalis shouted.

"Yes," the nurse mumbled, with surprise, "Magda."

"Magda," whispered Prudencio Delgado.

But no one heard him.

WILL WALKED UNCOMFORTABLY OUT OF THE MEDICAL TENT, HIS RIGHT LEG IN a cast with the toes pointing up, to stretch the torn muscle during healing, his left knee sutured like a darned sock, a ridge of black thread forming a wall around the edge of the wound. Beyond that, it was wrapped tightly and encased in a locked-out brace to keep the skin of the tear in position and unbendable.

Will supported his right side with his cane and swung the left like a battering ram through the crowd. Most of the reporters and teams had moved on, but a few members of the American cycling press held on for a last word, a final picture.

"You out?"

"You bet," Will smiled, looking at his watch. "Right now I'm, let's see, two hours and 45 minutes outside the time limit. Even Perry Mason couldn't argue his way out of that."

"No, I suppose not."

"What's next?"

"Home and a hot bath, I suppose." Will looked down at his legs. "With my head underwater and both legs up against the wall."

"You gonna miss Paris?"

"You mean the end, the podium?" Will thought about it for a second, what he had seen, heard, felt over the past two weeks and wondered if any of it had been worth it. He smiled. "Of course. Of course I'm going to miss Paris."

It was true, despite it all, despite Henri and Prudencio and everyone and everything else, that this was the race of champions, this was the race to finish. In a strange and perverse way, nothing else mattered.

The reporter thanked Will for his time, offered them a ride to Valreas, start of the next stage, or Marseille or wherever. Cheryl and Will thanked him and watched as the reporter squeezed his six-foot frame into a coffee can with wheels.

The car belched a cloud of blue and disappeared in the gathering dusk of the city streets.

The hairs on the back of Will's neck rose suddenly, in anticipation of the touch. The hand moved along his shoulder and smoothly down his arm. Before he turned, he knew and said the name quietly.

"Magda."

Cheryl, without the foreboding, turned, saw Magda Gertz standing behind her and jumped.

"*Jesus!* Don't you ever knock?"

Magda Gertz ignored Cheryl Crane and looked deeply into Will's face, caressing his scarred and dirty cheeks with her hands.

"And you are?"

"I'm Will Ross."

"No. I'm asking you how are you?"

"I'm fine, Magda."

"Yes, he's fine, Magda," Cheryl said, wanting desperately to pull Magda's hands away from Will's face and beat her to death with the bloody stumps of her arms.

Magda ignored Cheryl again, concentrating all her focus on Will Ross.

"Thank you, Will. Thank you for what you have done for Prudencio."

"I thought you'd be thrilled."

"He's only a boy, Will. Only a boy. There's nothing between us, Will. Nothing."

"Nothing," he repeated, trying to keep the sarcasm out of his voice.

"Nothing," said Cheryl, not bothering.

"Thank you for his life. You are a hero."

"Yes. I'm a regular Johnny Weissmuller."

"I'm sorry?" she asked, missing the reference.

"I'm sorry, too, Magda," he answered, offering no explanation, "but I really do have to go. My ass is killing me. I've been in these shorts for hours. I can't walk and I need a drink. A drink I can drink without anybody checking my urine for it tomorrow."

Cheryl brightened. "Oh, are you buying?"

"Actually, Carl Deeds is," Will said, triumphantly. "Since I knew we wouldn't catch up with our luggage tonight, I figured I'd just lift his wallet and live off that."

"You are bad."

"Yes, I am."

"May I join you?"

Magda Gertz looked hopeful and yet, not, as Cheryl and Will stared back at her.

"No, I don't think so. Not tonight," Cheryl said politely.

Will watched Magda Gertz as she looked at Cheryl and watched her hands drop toward the large leather bag she carried constantly at her side. Her right hand ran along the upper section, feeling the leather as if to assure herself that something important remained inside. On a hunch, a self-made dare, Will shifted his weight slightly and fell toward her. Instinctively, Magda Gertz reacted, throwing up her arms to catch Will. She did, but it was her chest that stopped his face and carried his weight as, off balance, he began to slide toward the ground.

As Magda Gertz lowered him, Cheryl stepped up to the side and supported his arm.

"You all right?" she asked.

"Yeah, I'm sorry. I'm sorry, Magda," he mumbled. "Lost my balance."

"That's fine, Will. That's fine."

Will fumbled on the ground for a moment, until the two women would lift him, one under each arm, into a standing position.

"I'm sorry. Very sorry."

"That happens, Will," Magda Gertz said soothingly, "I must say … I enjoyed it."

She shot a triumphant glance toward Cheryl, who reacted with a frozen smile and, behind her back, flipped Magda Gertz the bird.

"Well," Magda said, "I suppose I must be going. Need a lift anywhere, you … two?"

"No," Will said, "I think we're fine."

"All right. Have a nice evening."

Magda turned with a flair, arching her head to swing her hair, in a circle around and behind her. The rays of the late-evening sun caught it and set it ablaze for a moment as she walked away to great effect.

"Well, that was cute."

"What was cute?"

"Your little stumble. Couldn't resist copping a last feel?"

"If I'm going to cop a feel, I'm going to do it with my hands."

"I don't know. While all that was going on, I couldn't see your hands. Where were they?"

"They were working," Will replied.

"I'll bet," Cheryl answered with a bitter smirk.

Will turned his back and reached into his riding shorts, now beyond festering and well into the petri dish stage.

"Oh, God, what are you going to pull out of there?"

Will turned and held up a golden computer disk in a clear plastic case.

"What's that?"

"Who knows? But I've been watching her guard that bag like a mother hen for the last few days. And I just decided to see what might be in there of interest. And this was what I found."

"How did you learn to do this?" she asked, taking his arm and turning his back toward the center of town.

"Who, me? I'm into all kinds of sports."

"I'll bet," she smiled.

"By the way," he said, glancing around the now deserted town square. "How are we going to get out of here?"

GODOT SAT BACK INTO THE DEEP LEATHER CHAIR WITH HIS EYES CLOSED, HIS mind empty. He swirled the heavy liquor around in the base of the glass and brought it to his lips for the umpteenth time of the evening. He was getting drunk, pleasantly, completely drunk. It dulled the questions that ran incessantly through his mind.

He took a deep breath and opened his eyes, the hotel room beginning to move around him in a gently swirling motion. Bergalis had dropped him off here, paid for the room and shaken his hand.

"Keep things working at the office," he said, before driving off, madly, in the Ferrari. "By the way, Luc," Bergalis added, "good job on this. I'll remember it when I return."

Godot nodded. The office would be working after he returned to Paris tomorrow by train.

He took a deep breath to steady his vision and then finished off this third double bourbon. He covered his eyes for a moment, pulled his hand hard across his face and threw the heavy glass with as much force and accuracy as he could muster against the wall on the opposite side of the room.

He settled back into the chair.

"*Merde.*"

CHAPTER TWENTY-THREE:

NIGHT TRAIN TO PARIS

Somehow, he knew, the scenery of France was passing by in a blur, a stream of forests and villages, country roads and highways, hidden by the dark of night, illuminated only sporadically by the flash of a passing lamp.

He stared out the window, reaching with his eyes into the darkness, trying to catch some indication, any, of where they might be in relationship to where they began and where the TGV would end.

The high-speed train cutting through the night kept lulling Will into his own form of highway hypnosis, a drifting sense of sleep that led to a light doze that felt sweeter than sex, before — *pow!* — another light shot past, this time close to the train, shaking him awake and making him feel far worse than before. Both of his legs ached, the left from the tear on the knee, freshly sewn, that the painkiller had lately departed, the right from the tear along his calf that would mar the symmetry of the leg until the day he died, giving him something new to worry about each and every day.

"That will happen again, you know," the doctor in Avignon had said late yesterday after examining Will's injuries and redoing the cast. "It's going to happen again."

"When?"

"Sometime. Anytime."

"Well, won't it strengthen somewhere along the line?"

"Yes, just like a torn pair of pants. Leave them in the closet for a while and the ends of the tear heal themselves. Anything else?"

"Some major league painkillers would be nice."

"I've got Haven 22/15s," he said, offering a small, sample box.

"No, I think I'll pass."

The train continued to roar through the night, while Cheryl Crane slept quietly in the seat directly across from Will.

She looked pale, worn, tired and, from Will's incredibly biased perspective, simply beautiful.

He smiled, worked himself into a wobbly standing position and wiggled himself carefully past her and into the aisle. For as fast as this train was going, Will thought, it was incredibly smooth. He'd ridden Amtrak trains going 20 miles per hour that had tossed people around like salad fixings.

Using his cane, the solid walnut cane with the brass eagle's head on the grip, and the seats for balance, he worked himself back to what he hoped would be a lounge, a bar, a club car of some sort.

The doors between cars opened with a nearly silent hiss and Will stepped through. Late as it was, or early, depending on your perspective, the bartender continued to keep watch over his diminishing flock. Two people slept it off at a table, while a man in a worn and weather-beaten trench coat held up a corner of the train wall. He was awake, but not by much.

And he was familiar.

Will quietly walked up to him. "Hello? Inspector?"

Godot's eyes fluttered full open from half-mast and he looked at Will with a mixture of shock and surprise as he tried to find his place in the universe. Godot shook his head and pushed himself up, away from the wall, using the bar and then Will for support.

"I know you."

"Yes, you do."

"Don't tell me."

"Okay, I won't."

Godot took a deep breath and waited for a second, the last bubbles of the previous night's drunk finally popping themselves out of existence and his bloodstream.

"Ahh. Ahhh, buuuurg." He belched. "Will. Will Ross."

"Thank God, I thought you were simply belching my name."

"Uh? No. No," Godot said, waving the idea away along with whatever fumes had risen from the pit of hell.

"You okay?"

"Who, me? Yes, yes, I'm fine," Godot answered, defensively. He looked down the length of Will's frame to the brace encasing his left knee and the cast running up to his right. "Although, I might say, things are not fine with you?"

"It aches."

"Which?"

"All. But, I'll live."

"Nice cane."

"Thank you."

"Looks like something de Gaulle would have used. Hmm. Strange."

"Just good taste."

"I seem to recall a newspaper article out of Lourdes — something about a doctor who claimed a racer had stolen his cane. An antique. Brass eagle on the crown. Used to belong to Charles de Gaulle."

"Really?"

"Really. By the way, police are investigating."

"Fascinating story. I'll keep it in mind."

"You'd be wise to do so."

The TGV roared through the night, the two men turning to the task at hand, one drinking himself to sleep, the other drinking away the hangover from the day before.

"This is my second train today."

"Really?"

Godot nodded. "I missed the first one due to problems on the platform."

"Luggage?"

"No. Vomit. I was throwing up into a waste can when the train pulled out."

"Oh," Will said, trying to ignore the image that presented itself, "well, it took us all of last night and most of today just to get away from Carpentras to the Haven team trucks to find our luggage, then back to Avignon to check on Prudencio Delgado and to have the doctor check out my various wounds and then to hustle across town to the station. We caught the train with about five minutes to spare."

Godot stared at the wall for a moment, catching the shimmer of reflecting light flashing past the train. "Delgado," he said distantly, "wasn't he the one on Ventoux? The one you carried? Or was he the one in Milan, the one who was vaporized by a bomb?"

Will sighed. "Both. Tomas was the," he paused, "bomb victim. His brother Prudencio was the one on Ventoux."

"Well," Godot said, missing Will's emotion, "you've made points with heaven, that's for sure. Losing one and saving the other."

"Perhaps. Perhaps."

"How's he doing?"

"Prudencio?" Will straightened and tried to change his sudden burst of gloom. "He's on the line. They're flushing him out. Hoping for the best. Don't know yet."

Godot tipped his head to the side, indicating Will's legs.

"Bad?"

"Bad enough. I'm pretty much done."

"No more Tour?"

"No more anything, pretty much. It looks like I'm done cycling."

"Will you return to America?"

"I don't know. I like it here, I just know that I can't ride."

"What will you do if you can't ride?"

"Honestly, I haven't thought about it. Try and get on as coach, I suppose, somewhere over here. I honestly hadn't thought about it. I've spent so many years trying to push away the finish," he laughed, knocking his brace, "the inevitable finish, that I really couldn't conceive of the end. I mean, Jesus, Godot, this is what I do. This is what I've done for 20 years. I don't have any other skills. I rode in high school. I rode rollers during high school phys. ed. when everybody else was doing calisthenics and climbing ropes. I rode during football practice and basketball practice. I rode when I was supposed to be in college. I rode over there, I rode over here. And whenever my father complained, I told him I was getting a continental education that money couldn't buy."

He sighed.

"And now, here I am with a flayed knee and a torn calf and enough metal and plaster on me to build a gas station, and I'm at the starting line again. I'm at the starting line, Luc, and the road is not bright and vivid, but shades of gray. I'm riding into a fog of my own making and I haven't the slightest idea what waits for me at the finish, or…"

Godot finished the sentence, "or … if a finish waits at all."

Will turned his head and stared with mild surprise at the former police inspector for a moment. "Yes," he said sadly, "that's it exactly."

"I know this, Will. I know this well, this feeling," Godot said quietly. "I spent nearly 30 years grubbing around with the police department for a pension and a thank-you and a 'good-bye, we have other people who know your job better.' I took a job at the end of my career that promised me more money in two years than the police paid me in 10. I now have respect and money and a beautiful woman at my side, and, yet, the one thing the department gave me, a sense of what is right and what is wrong, no matter what is in the path, is now determined to rise up and destroy everything I have. And for me, Will, the path is gray. What only a few days ago had been so clear and easy, is now shades of gray."

"And of course," Will said, waving his arms with expectation of the next sentence.

"I can't talk about it."

"Of course." Will nodded with understanding. "But, can you live with it? That's the question."

"Can you?"

"I can. I can now," Will said. "I've paid my debts. All but one. And that one I expect to take care of when we reach Paris."

"And that is…?" Godot asked.

"I can't say. Not yet. It's a personal thing. Bit of vendetta."

"Vendettas can be dangerous."

"Yes, but what I've learned," Will said, "is that life itself can be dangerous as well."

"Deadly," Godot said with a deep and abiding sadness.

"Yes," Will said distantly, "deadly."

The train sped through the night, the blackness of the sky slowly giving over to a weird pitch of gray. At first, Will could see perhaps two, then three feet from the train. With each minute, the distance increased exponentially, so within 10 minutes, he could see well off into the distance of central France in early morning.

"Well," Will said, putting the glass down with far more force than he intended, "now that the sun is up, I am ready to sleep."

"Yes," Godot replied, wiping his gray stubble, "yes. I could use a few moments."

"A couple of winks."

"Winks?"

"You should know it, Godot. It would make a great Columbo line, "I'm gonna grab me a coupla winks."

"Coupla winks."

"Exactly. And remember to grab them," Will said, wrestling himself upright and in the right direction.

"Whatever happens, Will, best of luck. I hope you make the right choices in your 'vendetta.'"

"And you. I hope that when you make your choice, you are happy."

"Yes. Thank you."

The two nodded at each other. They had seen a lot of each other over the past seven months and very little of it had been pleasant. Now, it was, and both wished, if only for a moment, that he could have talked about what was on his mind, with somebody who faced something as immense and pointed as both of them did at this mark in time.

As Will worked his way back to Cheryl, he wondered if he should have shown the disc to Godot, perhaps asking his advice.

As Godot sank into the lounge seat and shut his eyes, he wondered if he should have shown the file to Will Ross, perhaps asking his advice.

Both men shook their heads as the train raced across the boundary of night and into a July morning in France.

MAGDA GERTZ HAD BEEN THROUGH EVERYTHING AT LEAST TWICE, POSSIBLY three times. Her leather bag lay torn and dismembered beside the bed.

She discovered the disk was missing late on Thursday, when, standing near the finish of the stage to L'Alpe d'Huez, she had obsessively patted the side of her bag again, for the 20th time that day, and realized, suddenly and with horror, that the edge of the disk she had been so confidently touching was the edge of her makeup mirror.

She had knelt on the ground in the crowd and pulled the bag apart, her panic growing with every moment, the sweat beginning to push through her makeup and ruin the image she had so carefully developed through the day.

Despite responsibilities to two riders who continued to look to her for "inspiration," she raced back to her hotel room and tore the place apart, ignoring the check-out time, ignoring the passing of Le Tour to its next stage start, ignoring everyone and everything in the pursuit of her disk, her destiny, her fate.

She had finally collapsed in despair, earlier in the evening, convinced that it was Fortuna who had the disk and who now had her. When she awoke, she took an hour to convince herself that it couldn't have been him. Despite Fortuna's reach, he had no opportunity along the stage to Ventoux, when she had obviously lost the disk. She remembered seeing it at noon in a corner of the case while digging through her bag. After Ventoux, there was no opportunity, for the bag had never left her side.

She reviewed the day on Ventoux, from riding in the Lexor team van, the bag on the floor between her feet, one strap wrapped around her ankle, to the delay at the barricade, when she slipped into the peloton to stroke the hand and wink at Nathan Sandeloz, one of 'her boys.'

No. There was no chance. There was the accident and the scene at the top of Ventoux, the bag never leaving her side. Then Will Ross and that woman in Carpentras. Then back to the hotel, alone, the bag beside her on the front seat of the car.

And bed. Alone.

Nothing. Except. She thought back, her hand unconsciously running up and across her breasts, where Will had accidentally planted his face. Where Will, accidentally....

She remembered the fall. And his chin caressing her chest and how, off balance he had slid down her front toward the ground, pulling her right arm up to his side, leaving his hands free to search and strip and steal.

Magda Gertz smiled. What a dirty, damned trick, she thought, what a foul trick. She looked at her watch: 6:15 p.m. With any luck, they didn't know what they had and were taking their time in finding out. That might give her the time she'd need, the time she'd need to find out from Deeds or Engelure where they went, the time she'd need to find them and learn what they knew.

Then, she'd kill them.

Just like Paul. Just like Bresson. Just like Koons. She snapped the hastily packed bag shut. And maybe Biejo Fortuna, once and for all.

She laughed and the sound of a thousand angels filled an empty room.

CHAPTER TWENTY-FOUR:

HOME AGAIN, HOME AGAIN...

Paris welcomed the weary trio home with a heat wave that slapped them as they left the train with the sense like they had stepped into a giant's maw.

Within moments, Will started to whine about the cast on his right leg.

"It's already sweating in there. God, this is driving me nuts. I can feel the little drops running down my leg inside the damned thing."

"Look, I'll muster up some sympathy for you," Cheryl said, "if you'll at least grab one of these bags."

"I'm crippled."

"You've still got a hand free, even with your cane. Grab it." She tossed him the lightest one and he caught it with his left hand. He could do this, he thought. It might even balance him out.

They began their procession to the station concourse, with Godot, silently, following by their side.

"I thought you were going to muster up some sympathy for my predicament."

"I'm sorry," Cheryl said, batting her eyes in a dramatic flutter, "I wish there was something I could do for you."

"That's not sympathy," he pouted, "that's sarcasm."

She laughed. "Yes, I guess it was. Sorry, best I could do at the moment."

"You could at least carry me up the stairs."

"Dream on, Gumby. I believe in self-fulfilling therapy. You see it. You want it. You do it."

"God, I hate you progressives."

Godot pointed over to the side. "There's an elevator."

Cheryl shook her head. "He needs the exercise."

Godot shrugged.

"I think," Will said, his voice filled with relief, "that our dear friend here has a marvelous idea." He patted Godot on the shoulder and began to pull him toward the elevator with them.

Cheryl silently agreed as one of the bags was now digging into her shoulder and would leave a horrible mark, with or without the stairs. Putting the bag down, even for a moment, would help immensely.

Will pushed the button and the elevator doors slid open. As soon as they were in and the doors slid shut, they all grew silent, three people trapped in a small, moving room, refusing to look at or talk to each other.

As soon as the door opened, the conversation began anew.

"What are you doing tonight, Inspector?" Cheryl asked.

"It's not 'Inspector,' anymore," Godot answered quietly.

"I'm sorry. I just don't want to call you 'Chief.'"

"Call me Luc. Or Godot."

"Well, can we call you for dinner? I'd rather stay in air-conditioned Paris today than head back to a stuffy flat in Senlis. We can put that off until tomorrow. What do you say, Will?"

"Sounds good to me. We're flush," he said, patting his wallet.

"Luc? Join us for dinner?"

Godot thought for a moment, as if weighing his options, when, in fact, his only concern had been how to separate himself from these two and get back to Isabelle.

"Uh, no. No. I have plans tonight. I have things to do."

"Well," Cheryl said, quietly, sensing his discomfort, "another time then."

"Yes."

They stood before the doors to Paris and Godot reached out his hand to Will. "Best of luck, in whatever you do, monsieur Ross. You have made life interesting."

"Thank you, monsieur Godot. I take that as a compliment. Good luck with your decision, whatever it may be."

"My thanks. I may need it. Take care with your problem. Don't let it double back on you."

"I appreciate that."

They shook hands, unsure as to whether they'd ever see each other again.

Cheryl leaned forward and kissed Godot on the cheek.

"My best to you and Isabelle."

"Thank you." Godot pointed back at Will. "Take care of him. He's accident prone."

"Yes, I will. Trouble does follow him, now, doesn't it?" She laughed a bit, to cover the growing tears in her eyes.

"Good-bye. *Bonne chance.*"

Godot smiled and turned, walking slowly, with slumped shoulders, toward the sun and heat of a Parisian day.

"You know, in a way," Cheryl said, wiping away a tear, "I'm going to miss him."

"Yes, so am I," Will said, picking up the bag and heading toward the exit on the opposite side of the station concourse. "I'm going to miss how he tried to charge me with murder. I'm going to miss how he tried to shake me down. I'm going to miss how he blew up my apartment."

"Philippe blew up your apartment."

"Yes, but Godot told my landlady to open the door."

"He survived."

"Yes, but I could never get the last of the landlady out of my socks."

"Oh, gross," she cried, punching him in the shoulder and making him nearly faint with pain. "I don't understand — for a second — why I hang out with you."

"Because I keep your life on the cutting edge."

They walked through the sliding glass doors and were enveloped by the heat of the city. As the automatic doors closed behind them, Will turned to Cheryl and said, "Oh, yeah, by the way, I need to find a computer...."

❁

FINDING LOUIS ENGELURE HAD BEEN EASY. HE WAS HUNKERED DOWN IN THE back of his medical van, diligently working on his reports. Getting him to talk had been easier still.

"Louis, please. I need to find Will Ross."

"Why? Why would anyone need to find Will Ross?"

"I would tell you he owes me money, but ..." she said with a laugh.

"He owes Deeds a credit card. Carl Deeds is convinced that Ross stole his credit card."

"Why is he so convinced?" she asked, gently leading him on, though given his volubility, without need.

"He's a thief. A pickpocket. He stole Deeds' credit cards earlier this year … went on a bender with them. Whenever Ross needs money, Deeds locks up his wallet."

"But this time ..."

"Not quick enough, *cheri*." Engelure shook his head. "Carl was simply not quick enough. I suggested he put the police on the matter and arrest the thieving bastard, but Deeds almost looked like he enjoyed it."

"Enjoyed it?"

"Yes," Engelure stopped logging the remaining doses of vitamins and turned to her, "yes. It's almost like a game to him. He knows he'll get it back sometime. It's almost a game." He shook his head and returned to the job at hand.

"Any idea of where Ross is now?"

"No. One of the mechanics said he and Cheryl Crane picked up their luggage and left yesterday morning, early, for Avignon, to see Delgado. Then, they were going to catch a train back to Paris."

"Paris. Is that where they live, Paris?"

"No. They don't have enough style for Paris," he sniffed. "They have an apartment in Senlis."

"Together?"

"Oh, yes, they are inseparable …"

Very good, Magda thought. Two birds. One stone.

"… and I don't mind telling you that the managers around here are very upset with little Miss Crane. It seems she up and left them without a word and now they're scrambling to fill her niche."

"Maybe I can pick up the job in a few days," she said, barely disguising her sarcasm.

"Oh, fine," Engelure snorted, "you — doing grunt work. Haven't seen that in years."

"My thanks, Louis." She rose, leaned forward and kissed him on the cheek. He blandly smiled his good-bye and went back, immediately, to what he was doing before.

"Incidentally," she said, stopping at the door, "you told me when Le Tour began that you were going to have a control group. Was Will in that control group?"

He put his pencil down with an attitude that very nearly bordered on exasperation and looked up at the woman who, 10 years ago, had stood alone with him when the Toulouse project had collapsed around him and very nearly destroyed his career.

"Yes. You, I will tell," he said, lifting his half-glasses to his forehead from the bridge of his nose. "There were two groups. Groupe Jaune and Groupe Bleu. Bleu was placebo, sugar water. Jaune was the vitamin cocktail."

"Who was in your control group?"

"Will. Will Ross."

"And...."

"And no one. He was all I needed. You see, it's not nice to insult the man in charge of your recovery."

"Then how do you explain his riding later in the race, with Bresson and Delgado and the others?"

"Who knows?" he asked. "Ha! Maybe it was our Toulouse Tonic, eh?"

"Why would you say that?"

"Why not? A miracle that hasn't existed in 10 years can't be mentioned?"

"Speaking of mentioned, did you ever tell anyone that all you were giving Will was water?"

"It was a glucose solution. It gave some recovery. Who needed to know?" He tossed his hand in an expression of indifference, and returned to his work.

In return, she smiled and gave a flip of her hand, part good-bye, part dismissal.

He's still a gutless worm, she thought as she left.

She still wears too much makeup, he thought, as if in reply.

Two hours later, she was on a flight bound for Paris.

❦

"YOU KNOW, DON'T YOU, THAT YOUR CAREER WITH HAVEN IS OVER?"

"Look who's talking," he replied, drying his hair with the heavy white towels of the Hotel George V. "You walked away from your job in the middle of a race. I'm sure that Deeds is going to love that."

"I was leaving in four days, anyway," she said, in a poor attempt to disguise the guilt in her voice. "Maybe they can treat it like a sick day."

"More like a sick week. More like a bail out."

"Thanks, I really needed that support."

"Oh, for Christ's sake, Cheryl, they'll survive," he said, sitting beside her on the couch and putting his arm around her shoulders. "Haven has the largest support team of anyone in Le Tour. They've got people on top of people."

"What?"

"In the nicest way, of course," he laughed. "But you had — how many assistants? Each and every one of them is now thrilled that you're gone, because they've moved another step up the ladder of responsibility. You are missed. I'm sure there were a few hours of chaos yesterday, but now, I wouldn't worry about it."

"But I do."

"Okay. So, before you fly off to the States to ride a mountain bike, you say 'I'm sorry' to Carl Deeds and Henri Bergalis. They're big boys. They'll understand."

"Perhaps." She stopped and looked at the floor for a moment. "But what will I say to you?"

"What?" The question caught him off-guard.

"What will I say to you, Will? Will I say good-bye, or, will I say," she smiled, "want the window seat?"

"I don't know," he said, pulling his hand away from her shoulder. He pushed himself upright and began to hobble around the room, away from her. "That, I just don't know. I haven't been to the States in nearly 10 years. I don't know if I want to go back."

"What's here?"

"Without you, there was still Haven," he said, seeing, perhaps for the first time, the hopelessness of the position that now presented itself, "but now, there's not that, either."

"Unless, of course," she said, as an option, "you can convince Deeds he needs a new assistant next season. You could help him run the team."

"How many European teams want two Americans calling the shots? Carl has French and Italian backup. He won't need me."

"That's a good attitude. Shoot yourself down before you even take off. What about the States?"

"What's there?"

"A lot more McDonald's than when you left, that's for sure."

"Great. I can learn a new sentence: 'You want fries with that?' Great."

"I dunno, Will. Hang out. Hang with me. Cut my mother's lawn. You could live with her into the next century before you'd have to work. But, you will have to make a decision."

"Why?"

"Because I'm leaving on Monday."

He had worked his way to the other side of the room from her. With that bit of news still ringing in his ears, he paused, for only a moment, then began to cross back, across the fine oriental carpeting, to the couch where she sat. As he moved, he reached out his hand and stretched it toward her. She stood, took it and pulled him closely into her. Despite the ache in his legs and his arms and his face, the ache in his heart overwhelmed them all.

The kiss went on for some minutes.

ISABELLE MARCHANT WAS SHOCKED WHEN SHE OPENED THE DOOR INTO HER apartment. An open bag had spewed its contents, a variety of worn and wrinkled clothes, across the carpet. The last of them led to a bottle cap, which led to a foot, which led to a pair of faded gray trousers, a heavily wrinkled beige trench coat and, finally, the pale face of Luc Godot, who, at the moment, was finishing the half-liter bottle of bourbon in his favorite chair.

"Good God, Luc — I nearly had a stroke. When did you return?"

"I returned this morning."

"And I see you've been busy ever since."

"I have."

"Really?"

"Yes. I've been busy — thinking."

"Oh, yes, always hard work," she said sarcastically, bending to pick up his clothing and pile it back into the torn and tattered overnight case.

"It is. This is."

"What is, dear?" she asked, tired of the trauma, tired of the games he brought home each and every day.

"This is hard work."

"Yes, dear."

"It is. *It is!*" he shouted, pushing himself out of the chair and reeling in a wide, looping circle as he stood before her. "*It is hard work!*" he yelled, before falling back into the chair.

Isabelle was frightened now, frightened of him and whatever demons possessed him.

"What dear," she asked, calmly, "what is hard?"

"I have to charge my boss with murder. The man who saved my life. I have to charge him with murder," he cried, his voice straining to get out the words.

"*How about that*, eh? *Eh?* How about that? Is that hard, do you think? Eh?"

He closed his eyes and dropped his head, his breathing immediately taking on a shattered, but regular, rhythm. Isabelle Marchant wanted to say something. Her mouth moved, but no words came out.

AS MAGDA GERTZ STRODE DOWN THE AIRPORT CONCOURSE AT PARIS-ORLY, SHE looked at her watch, blocking out her timetable for the rest of the day: rent a car, no, no rental, it leaves a record, hire a cab, take a train to Senlis, find the apartment, kill them both, recover the disk, catch the next train back, cab to the airport and return to Moutiers to make an appearance at Le Tour tonight or tomorrow morning and allay suspicions.

Very good. It had, after all, worked before with Paul. It would work again now.

She picked up a small bag at the carousel and stepped out into the late-afternoon sun. She raised her hand and a cab dropped in quickly and quietly to the curb.

"Gare du Nord," she said.

With barely a pause, the cab slipped back into traffic.

CHAPTER TWENTY-FIVE:

THE TIMELY VISITOR

The sun streamed through the half-opened curtain of the Hotel George V — "Five Stars in the Heart of Paris" — slowly moving across the exquisite carpeting of the spacious room until it touched and warmed Will's foot and his leg and his knee.

She finished packing about the moment it began to move above the brace and toward his fish-belly-white thigh.

"Worried about tan lines?" Cheryl asked.

"I'm sometimes amazed by my definition here," Will said, running his finger along the top of the tan like a runway model.

"Very sexy. You should be more worried about skin cancer."

"Yes, I should. Thank you Walter Cronkite for that little dose of fear in my life."

"Ah, Cronkite has been gone for years, now it would be, let's see, Geraldo or Barbara."

"Streisand?"

"Walters."

"Really?"

"How do you feel?" Cheryl asked, swinging the black leather carryall up and over her shoulder.

"Well, for a guy who has draped his legs outside his bathtub for the past two days while he soaked his ass in tepid water, I'm okay, I suppose."

"Hmm. Guess the record moves on now, huh?"

"What record?" Will asked, wrapping the sling of the Haven duffel over the head of his cane.

"The fastest-stripper record. Takes you forever now, which in Will-years, puts you at about the same pace as everybody else."

"Thank-you. I do appreciate your concern, even though that was a seventh-grade record."

"And there are those who say you peaked in junior high." She shook her head, laughed and shouldered the bag for the trip to the lobby.

"You know," he said, opening the door on wobbly legs, "there are people who carry this stuff for a living."

MAGDA GERTZ STRUGGLED TO STAY AWAKE IN THE STUFFY APARTMENT IN SENLIS, hating herself and the situation in which she now found herself.

She had waited until darkness last night and then carefully and quietly broken in through a latched window in the bathroom, sliding silently across the lavatory to the floor, where she crouched, like a cat, waiting to hear anything from Will or the woman.

Everything was on schedule.

She checked the 9mm Glock, quickly, and hand-tightened the silencer one more time. She slid up to the edge of the bathroom door and waited, listening.

She heard nothing, aside from the driving bass line rising up from the floor below, some EuroTrash band rattling dishes and fillings for kilometers around. She realized suddenly and with some embarrassment that she didn't have to be quiet. She carefully crept out into the main room and discovered a double bed festooned with cartoon sheets, a computer system, an older Macintosh model, good memory and CD-ROM, much like her laptop and Paul's massive, state-of-the-art machine, two book racks filled with cycling gear, one dead roach, and an American mystery entitled "Harm's Way" that looked fresh from the printers. An overstuffed chair that didn't look very overstuffed anymore sat silently in one corner.

What a dump, she thought. Just the kind of place for Will and little Miss Crane, both so determined to play with the big boys. She shook her head in disgust and moved the easy chair into a darkened corner of the room for a momentary advantage on anyone who stepped through the door. Then, she resigned herself to a long wait.

A nagging thought kept creeping into the cool and passive demeanor she was trying to build: she was dressed in black, great for working at night, but very, very obvious if the schedule was off and she had to make a break for it during the day. What if her friends decided not to show tonight?

She gave herself until 5 a.m.

When Magda Gertz woke up at 8, she knew she was in the soup. She couldn't wander through Senlis at midday without the possibility of being seen and remembered. She couldn't open a window in the hot little apartment without the possibility of giving away that she was inside, awakening some suspicion in Will or Crane when they did arrive. She couldn't move around the room now that the rock star in the apartment below had turned off his music. And, she couldn't slip away to try again, as her black Emma Peel outfit from the 1960s would attract a great deal of attention from all the workers heading to the office in their wrinkled suits and sun dresses.

Where the hell were they?

Magda Gertz ran the cool of the silencer across her forehead and pondered her predicament. There was, she thought, one out. One easy out. She rose carefully from the chair and walked with as much lightness as she could muster toward a closet door just off the dent in the wall that passed for a bedroom. She opened the door silently and looked over the possibilities that presented themselves in Cheryl Crane's closet.

"OH, I'M SORRY. I PASSED OUT LAST NIGHT," CHERYL SAID QUIETLY AS THE northern reaches of Paris passed the windows of the train.

"Yes, I know," Will said with sarcasm, "I came back to the room and you were dead to the world."

"Sorry. You weren't expecting sex, were you?"

"I always expect sex. I just haven't had anyone to expect it from over the past few weeks."

"I'm sure your little friend would have helped you out," trying to keep the thread of sarcasm out of her voice.

"I dunno."

"Oh, come on...."

"No. You see," he said, his concentration caught for a second by a car wreck that flew by the window of the commuter train, "I never felt that. Not what you saw, anyway. I always felt kinda creepy around her, like a male praying mantis. 'Hey, thanks for the sex, why are you biting my head off?'"

"God, you're so dense."

"That, I am. Denser than the atomic number of lead, I believe."

"Well, Rock Boy, thinking of your friend, when you went out last night did you ever find a computer?"

"No. I bummed a CD-ROM from the hotel. Everything they had was running off this funky EuroSpeak system and the one store I hit sold exclusively Microsoft gear."

"And this...." she asked, pointing toward the disk case he twirled in his fingers.

"This, according to the guy, is Mac. So, we may just have to wait until we get home before we find out what electronic games little Miss Magda enjoys playing."

"That would be a good movie title, 'Little Miss Magda.'"

"I wish to hell it was a movie."

SHE FANNED HERSELF WITH A MAGAZINE.

She wiped herself with a towel.

She focused on a spot in the distance and tried to think herself to a cool, measured place somewhere in the Alps. Nothing worked. Magda Gertz stood and slid quietly over to the bathroom door, where one of Cheryl Crane's dresses now hung on an inside hook. She pulled the door closed behind her as quietly as she could and opened the window, gulping in the last cool breaths of the late morning before the sun began to cook the window sill.

She froze when she heard the door of the apartment rattle and then open. She reached for her gun.

"MY MOTHER WOULD SING SOME DITTY NOW," HE SAID, "HOME AGAIN, HOME again, jiggity jig."

Cheryl paused, waiting for him to continue, before doing it herself, "to market, to market to buy a fat pig."

"Is that how it goes?"

"Something like that."

"I always thought," he said, tossing the bag onto the bed, "that it stopped after jiggity jig." Stepping over and booting up the computer, he stopped and thought for a second, "I guess she just stopped at jiggity jig."

"What are you talking about?"

"Don't know. Don't care." He waited for a moment as the icons lined themselves up across the bottom of the screen and, when his desktop arrived, opened the CD-ROM door. "Oh, shit, Cheryl," he called to the kitchen, where she was throwing open the last of the windows, "could you grab the disk, it's in my bag."

Cheryl stepped out of the kitchen arch and laughed, "you're going to play this for all you're worth, aren't you? By the way … Mr. Fixit … the bathroom door is stuck and I've got to go. Why don't you get settled and then we'll deal with your computer games?"

He slid the heavy cherry captain's chair away from the computer desk, and began a slow duck walk to the bathroom door. He grabbed the door knob and pulled, the door coming open, actually clearing the jamb, but then snapping back, into place as if held by someone on the other side. The next tug moved the door even less.

"Damn, this is odd. Cheryl, you've got to see this."

Cheryl said nothing, but backed across the room, her eyes never leaving the crack in the door where she first glimpsed the heavy black Glock 9mm with what appeared to be a very impressive and efficient silencer on the end.

"Will," she said, distantly.

"Yeah, what? Check out this door."

"Will, I need to get some aspirin at the drug store."

"I might have some in my bag."

"Oh, come on, Will," she whined, trying without success, to get the urgency out of her voice, "the walk would be good for you."

"I just finished walking six blocks, I don't see the good three more are going to ..."

Cheryl stepped quickly to him, grabbed his chin in her right hand and snapped it around, forcing him to look into her eyes. "Now, Will. I need some aspirin."

"What?"

"Now!"

As if on cue, the door burst open, throwing Will back and away, into the arch leading to the kitchen. He twisted himself as he fell and landed on his left side, the elbow exploding into a rainbow of colors, all painful.

Cheryl felt a palm on her chest pushing her away from the door. She grabbed at it instinctively, but felt her hands slide along the tight black spandex until she was clutching at nothing more than air. She fell backward, clipping a small entry table and landing heavily on the edge of the carpet near the front door.

She had a bad feeling about what she was going to see when she opened her eyes.

"Damn," Will squeaked, "the boiler blew or something. I've never had a door swing open like that, Christ, did you see it? Hey, Cheryl are you okay?" Will had not been able to pull himself up, there wasn't enough room to find a grip and do the amazing balancing act it took to pull one fully and one partially frozen leg upright. He crawled along the floor to the open door, blocking his view of the living room, and pushed it closed.

"Man, woo, that was something," he said to the back of Cheryl's head. She was crouched in what appeared to be a very uncomfortable sitting position, with her weight thrown back against the wall. "Hey, you all right?"

He pulled himself up, even with her face, and glanced at her eyes, frozen on a point in the distance. Her silence frightened him for a moment, but without really thinking about it, he followed her gaze away from her eyes, across the room, past the bed toward the easy chair in the far corner. Standing before it, were two legs, dressed in black spandex, followed by two very shapely thighs, a buff and toned stomach, two exquisite breasts, the tops of which peeked out of the top of the jumpsuit, unzipped in the heat, a pale neck and face, streaked with sweat, the makeup of the night before a lost cause, and stringy blonde hair, its body and shape destroyed by a night of humidity in a stuffy Senlis apartment.

"Well, hiya, Magda," he said, lightly. "How you doing?"

He tried to pull himself up, but Cheryl grabbed him by the wrist.

"Don't move."

"What? Why not?" He swung his legs around to the side and began to walk up the wall.

"Will," Cheryl clutched at him, "Will."

"What? Come on, get up." He plucked the cane from the basket next to the desk and turned to face their unexpected guest.

"Will, for Christ's sake," Cheryl pleaded, "she's got a gun."

"Huh?" For the first time, Will followed the trail of black spandex down the right arm of Magda Gertz, where it ended in what appeared to be a black pipe with a handle.

"A gun."

"That's right, Will, a gun," Magda Gertz said, quietly.

"Oh, my," he said, falling against the corner of the wall.

"Where's the disk?"

"What disk?"

"Oh, Will," she whispered, "don't try to hide it or what you did. You know what disk I'm looking for."

"Yes," he said, his voice catching in a tone somewhere between James Earl Jones and Jerry Lewis, "yes, of course. It's in the bag. That one, right there, the parachute fabric one with the Haven logo."

Without taking the gun off Cheryl, Magda Gertz took two steps across the floor and knelt down on the bed.

"Nice sheets."

"Thank you. My mother."

"How sweet."

As Magda's attention, if not the gun, moved to Will, Cheryl slowly moved to her left and readjusted her weight, pulled herself up into a modified crouch, with her left hand grasping the leg of the entry table. It was a light piece of ticky-tacky furniture they had found in an antique shop, but it was the only weapon she had available.

Magda rummaged around in the bag for a moment, unsuccessfully, then waved Will over to the bed.

"Find it. Leave the cane there. Come over here. Find it."

"No problem, Magda, you know I'd do just about anything for you," he said, without a trace of sincerity in his voice. He laid the cane across the top of the desk, the lower end out. It wasn't much and he probably would never be able to reach it, but it was a hell of a club and the only weapon he had available.

Will worked his way back and forth over to the bed and smiled at the sheets. "My mother will be happy knowing," he said, "that I died on her sheets. And that they were clean."

"Just find the damned disk," Magda said, quietly, glancing over to Cheryl. "Don't move, my friend. It will all be over in a minute."

"I know," Cheryl said, her eyes filling with tears.

"Here it is, Magda," Will said, his head snapping back and forth between the two women. "Here's the disk. Sorry about the mix-up." He began to feel a pounding in his neck, as if his blood pressure were going to explode and send his head shooting off into low earth orbit. "Good Christ," he muttered, falling back off the bed and toward the desk, his eyes never leaving the gun.

"Uh-uh. No Will," Magda said lightly. "No more. No closer to your stick, there."

"You know, Magda, we never saw the disk. Whatever's there is there and is still a secret."

"Yes, Will. I realize that now. But the game has progressed a bit too far, hasn't it?"

"No take backs?"

"I'm sorry?"

"Never mind."

She raised the gun and turned it toward Cheryl. "Sorry, dear," Magda cooed. "I like you less and know that you might scream. By the way, before I forget, thank you for the dress. It's my midday get-away outfit."

Cheryl glanced over the right shoulder at the sun dress hanging on the back of the bathroom door.

"Shit," she muttered, "my killer is going to get away wearing one of my favorites, too." Though she knew it was futile, she tightened her grip on the table. Her uncles had always told her that in any given situation where guns where involved, you never knew what was going to happen. Although, they agreed, the worst usually did. Whatever, she tightened her grip and watched for her chance.

"Wait, wait, wait," Will said, frantically.

Magda Gertz paused, but never took the gun off Cheryl.

"Aren't you going to explain your scheme?"

"What are you talking about?"

Will weaved on his two stick legs, trying, without being obvious, to swing himself back near the foot of the cane. "Aren't you guys supposed to tell your victims, like, what was on the disk and what you were going to do and who died and stuff like that?"

"My scheme?"

"Yeah, I suppose so, your scheme."

"You've been watching too many movies."

"It always works for James Bond."

"Yes, but while the villain is talking," Gertz said coldly, "something always happens to get Bond out of danger. Sorry, Will. I was one of those people who sat in the audience telling the villain to 'kill him. Kill him now.'"

"Too bad," Will said.

"I will tell you one thing, Will. As soon as I shoot your friend, here…"

"It's Cheryl. Cheryl Crane, you bitch," Cheryl spat in one last act of defiance.

"… I am going to inject you with my special formula and let you die with a gun in your hand." Gertz reached behind her and pulled out a heavy glass-and-steel syringe, loaded beyond the lines with a heavy, yellow liquid.

Keep talking, Will thought. Keep talking. If you keep her occupied, you buy some time. Buy some time. Buy some time for what, goddamn it? There is no U.S. Cavalry on its way. There is no hero standing outside the door. There is only one last moment to breathe and think and hope.

"Isn't that, isn't that," he panted, "just mucking up a sweet plan? I mean, won't that take longer and maybe I won't die and Jesus, what a mess it would be then, huh? Why don't you just shoot both of us and have done with it?"

"Then it looks like a murder, Will."

"Take something. Make it look like a burglary."

"No. I need a way to make the authorities see how Cytabutasone, in all its glory, made it into the peloton and you are such a good choice. You were right there with Henri. You were right there with Prudencio. You are the perfect choice."

"Won't my autopsy show," he searched desperately for a thought, "won't it show that I O.D.'d on a massive, like, first-time dose?"

"So? What if it does? Will — you'll be dead," she explained. "You'll be dead and so will ..." she paused, "... Cheryl ... and that will be that. Murder/suicide. You killed your teammates, you killed your girlfriend and now you are dead and I am back at Le Tour."

"Ah."

"Simple, no? The police of Senlis will look and think and ponder and then will write it all down and the press will take off with it and before you realize it, you will spend eternity as a killer." She glanced at her watch. "Ooops. I have 40 minutes to catch my train. Best get to work, eh?"

"Woof, well, uhh, me, I'd, uh, call in sick," he said, with a lightheartedness he didn't feel. He realized that one of his last thoughts was going to be that he couldn't control his emotional response in a crisis.

She smiled and kissed the air toward him ever so slightly. She glanced again at Cheryl and raised the gun.

At that moment, the apartment door burst opened, revealing a man that Will recognized, but in the split second that followed, couldn't recognize.

"*Where's my cane, you bastard!*" the man screamed at the top of his lungs.

Magda Gertz turned and fired on instinct.

In the midst of the hollow "thup," all hell broke loose.

CHAPTER TWENTY-SIX:

DUCK AND COVER

Dr. Paul Flacon stared with shock at the red spot that blossomed on his chest, the stain spreading across the dazzling white of the expensive linen of his custom-made shirt. It made a design that reminded him of a small lake he boated on in his youth. As he fell straight backwards onto the landing at the top of the stairs, he had no sense of pain, or falling, or the heavy impact of hitting the floor. His only thought was to his shirt.

"This was new," he said aloud.

The bursting of the door and Magda Gertz's impulsively snapping off a shot toward the intruder had frozen everyone in the room for a split second. Then, Cheryl broke the spell by hurling the table, with all her might, toward the gun and then hurling herself toward the door. Magda saw it out of the corner of her eye and reacted, shifting her weight slightly and shooting, again, in Cheryl's general direction.

The table hit the gun, catching the end of the silencer in a bit of filigree and tore it from Magda's hand, dropping it to the easy chair behind her. The table hit the wall with a crack and fell behind the chair. In a panic, Magda looked to the gun and then back to Cheryl Crane, collapsed at the door.

Magda panted heavily. "Oh, my, Will, but you have been busy. A caller at the door and then your girlfriend trying to escape and then your suic ..."

She heard the heavy 'whoosh' of air as the cane cut the space between them. In his excitement and terror, Will had misjudged the distance completely, coming within an inch of Magda's head, but never connecting. She turned and fell back as Will swung the cane in a frantic arc, back and forth in front of him across the bed. He careened on his frozen legs and shattered the empty air.

Without taking her eyes off him, she felt behind her for the chair and the cushion and the gun that lay there.

"Give it up, Will...." she said, finding the arm and sliding her hand down to the seat and then across to the cool of the silencer. She grabbed it and brought it up to her, the gun pointing backwards. With a bellow of terror and rage, Will bent forward and threw himself across the bed, his right calf screaming in pain, while his left knee twisted itself in an unnatural direction. He swiped at the pistol grip and caught the beak of the eagle in the exposed trigger guard, yanking the gun down and away from Magda Gertz and shooting a hole in the ceiling watermark that looked vaguely like Rhode Island.

As Will fell on the bed, his left elbow hit hard on the bedstead, forcing his left hand open. The force of his fall and the arc of the cane pulled it and the gun out of his hands and sent them both skittering across the floor.

"*Shit!*" he screamed.

Magda Gertz paused in shock for just a moment, then threw herself toward him, the loaded syringe, her last weapon, held high in her raised right hand.

Will tried to roll away, but was caught by the footboard, a six-inch-high barricade of pine slats that hardly seemed worth the name. In desperation, he yanked at the Pocahontas sheets and pulled up a corner between them, catching the hypodermic needle right in the middle of the cartoon heroine's left eye.

He pushed with his right arm, the only part of his body that didn't feel any pain, and rolled over the short footboard, dragging his legs down with a crash to the floor. Without bothering to stand, he crawled frantically to the door, toward the prostrate body of the emergency room doctor who had tracked him down so doggedly over the past week in search of a damned stick of wood.

"See what it got you, you stupid bastard," his mind screamed, "see what it got you?"

Magda Gertz had rolled off the bed in the other direction, away from the window and the chair and the cane and the gun. She pulled herself up and walked toward Will, who was crawling frantically, pathetically, toward the door.

"Oh, Will. Good fight," she said, breathing heavily, "too bad."

She fell to her knees on the floor beside him threw her right leg over the brace on his left, pinning him to the spot. Will began to scream and kick the cast on this right leg, trying in one, last furious effort, to throw her off.

Magda Gertz, took a deep breath, mumbled, "Sorry, my dear," and drove the hypodermic into the back of Will's right leg, depressing the plunger as she did.

"Hey!"

Gertz looked, without thinking, toward the sound.

"Wanna see my impression of Tiger Woods, bitch?"

The cane was already in motion and Magda Gertz heard only the "bi" in "bitch" before feeling a crunch at the bottom of her jaw, her teeth grind together and her head snap back to her spine, her blonde hair pooling on the floor only milliseconds before the back of her skull reached it with a *bang*!

She lay still, half on, half off, the left side of Will.

Cheryl Crane dropped to Will's right, quickly running her hands over his head and his back, reaching down to the hypodermic needle, now partially empty of fluid.

"Oh, Jesus, Jesus Will. Hold on. Hold on, Will. I'll get the doctor. I'll get an ambulance."

She painfully pushed herself up and staggered to the phone, hoping, beyond hope, that they hadn't canceled the service before they left. She picked up the receiver and held it to her ear. Nothing.

"*Damn*," she screamed, throwing the entire phone against the wall.

She began to stagger toward the window to call for assistance.

"Help...."

She stopped in the middle of the floor, just beyond Will.

"Help...." he called pitifully.

Cheryl immediately dropped to his side. "Will, Will, don't worry. I'm gonna get you to a hospital. I'm gonna get you help. We'll get this stuff out of you. I swear it. Hang tight."

"Cheryl," Will whispered, trying to catch his breath, "don't bother. Don't bother."

"Will, stop. You're babbling. Hang on."

She turned to crawl to the window when he grabbed her.

"No. No help yet. Just ... just ... just ..."

"Just what, Will?"

"Just get this goddamned needle out of my cast."

Cheryl stopped, looked and pulled on the silver and glass tube. It held for a moment, then gave, the needle bent at the tip at a 60-degree angle to the true. As she forced the tip from the cast, the bent part of the needle broke off.

"Are you okay?"

Will turned over and pulled himself away from the supine body of Magda Gertz.

"I dunno. Is she dead?"

"No, I don't think so," Cheryl rasped. "She's still breathing … and a house didn't fall on her. Were you injected?"

Will climbed the wall, using his back as leverage. As he did, a few drops of a heavy yellow fluid dribbled out of the toe of the cast on his right leg.

"I don't think so. Not a full dose anyway." He leaned his head back and panted heavily. Cheryl stood and walked over to him, falling into his arms.

"Welcome home," he said, burying his head into her hair.

She chuckled darkly, "Did you like the party, dear? I thought it would be different." They leaned against the wall, supporting each other, afraid to let go for fear of collapse.

"What a sweet scene," the fractured voice said behind them.

Cheryl pushed herself away and looked at Will's face, a face that registered pain and exhaustion, fear and now, perhaps, a touch of exasperation.

"Aw, crap." he wheezed.

Cheryl rolled off him and stood to his left, Will wincing a bit as she pushed herself off his left arm. She opened her tired eyes wide with surprise.

"Damn, girl. How hard did I hit you?"

"Not hard enough, bitch," Magda Gertz declared through shattered teeth, "that was the word you used, wasn't it? Bitch? Now, it is my turn."

"Good lord," Will muttered, "this is like a bad movie."

The Glock wobbled unsteadily in the hand of Magda Gertz. It obviously pained her to raise it and swing it back and forth across her intended targets. She pulled the trigger and sent a shot wide to the left of Cheryl, drilling a hole in the wall. The kick of the shot threw Magda hard in the other direction, off balance and in a struggle to bring the gun back to bear.

As she pulled herself up and turned back to her targets, Cheryl took two steps forward and threw the syringe with all her might at the center of Magda's chest. The heavy metal tube struck her just above the left breast and stuck, the impact driving home the worn and well used plunger and injecting seven cubic centimeters of fluid into the heart of Magda Gertz.

She dropped the gun in a panic and began clutching at the syringe hanging from her chest. As she did, she felt a cool heat course through her veins and a sense of euphoria as the pain began to ebb in her mouth; and a burgeoning sense of power grow as a white-hot kernel in the back of her mind. She looked over at Will and Cheryl and smiled, knowing how easy it would be to kill them now.

She sat back in the chair and reached for the gun which was no longer there.

Cheryl and Will stared at Magda Gertz, collapsed in the chair, her eyes wandering wildly around the room.

"Good shot," Will muttered.

Cheryl kicked the gun to the other side of the room and picked up the cane.

"Why didn't you keep the gun?"

"It only has her fingerprints on it. I'd like to keep it that way. This'll do."

They both looked back at Magda Gertz, who gestured wildly with her hands and rolled her head, mumbling madly through bloody teeth.

"Where do you think she is now?" Will asked.

"I don't know. But she's sure as hell happy about it," Cheryl said.

Magda Gertz grinned and flailed the air around her with her arms.

"I think I'll call the cops" he said, never taking his eyes off the figure in the corner.

"Yeah, you do that," Cheryl said, hollowly, staring along with Will. "By the way, phone's dead."

"Yeah." Will stepped to the window, staring all the while at Magda Gertz, and shouted for help.

THE POLICE HAD BEEN AT THE APARTMENT FOR JUST OVER AN HOUR WHEN Godot arrived, summoned by Will from a neighbor's phone.

Godot stepped over the body of Dr. Paul Flacon, now partially covered with a sheet and stepped into the apartment. It reminded him of a war zone. Will sat on the floor near the bathroom door, his legs straight out in front of him. Cheryl Crane sat next to him, dozing on his shoulder.

Will gave Godot a slight wave and started to move like he wanted to rise. Godot waved him off and walked toward the crowd in the corner, surrounding a figure in a chair.

"Excuse me."

"Get out. We're busy."

He ignored the order and charged ahead, "I'm Luc Godot, formerly with homicide in Paris, now, the head of Security for Haven Pharmaceuticals. These two are Haven employees. I would like to know what is going on here."

Will knew that either his police résumé or the Haven nod would be impressive with the Senlis inspectors, but he wasn't sure which. It proved to be his years with the police.

"Ah, Inspector," a short, sweating man said, "I am Gérard Eteindre, police detective for Senlis. I've heard much about you. Do you know them?" He nodded over toward Will and Cheryl.

"Yes. Yes I do," Godot answered.

"They say they arrived home today and were met by this woman," Eteindre nodded back unemotionally toward the figure in the chair that two doctors obscured with their trauma treatments, "who had broken in and threatened to kill them with this —" he held up a clear plastic bag holding the Glock 9mm, "— and with this." He held up another bag containing the glass-and-steel syringe. It still contained, approximately, three milliliters of a heavy, yellow, fluid.

The Senlis inspector noted Godot's interest.

"We don't know what it is, yet. If you are interested, we will put you on a list for the results." Godot waved him off. He knew what it was already.

"Well, at that time, the gentleman in the hallway made a surprise and poorly timed appearance and was shot to death for his trouble. A fight ensued and this," he said, indicating the mess in the apartment, "was the result. Oh, yes, and her." He pointed to Magda Gertz as the emergency medical technicians stepped away shaking their heads with disappointment.

"What a waste," one said.

"Yes," Godot said, staring for a moment at the ashen gray death mask of Magda Gertz, her eyes forever staring at a point in the distance, a milky white fluid dripping from a corner of her mouth onto the black spandex jumpsuit.

"Did she say anything?"

The technician shook his head. "Not to me. She was pretty far gone by the time we got here. Whatever this drug was, it captured her very quickly."

Godot nodded. "What about them?" He flipped his head in the general direction of Cheryl and Will.

"So far, their story seems correct. The gun is unregistered, but it appears that her prints are on it. We are dusting the bathroom window, that's where she appeared to come in. The body in the hall is a doctor from Lourdes — he has identification — don't know why he's here, but his timing is horrible, as I said. If you can vouch for them, we'll release them for now. We may need them for questioning again. As you can imagine we don't get many cases like this around here."

"No one does. I'll vouch for them."

"Our only question now," the inspector said, holding up the bag containing the syringe, "is what we have here."

Godot thought for a moment, then said, "I believe you'll find that it's a prohibited steroid derivative called Cytabutasone. Eindhoven would have some records on it, I think. They had a case up there."

"Death?"

"Yes," Godot said distantly. "A cyclist. A man named Koons."

The Senlis inspector wrote it down and closed his book.

"My thanks. I'll check."

A noise at the door forced the inspector to turn as the morgue attendants carried the body of Dr. Paul Flacon to the street. The detective stepped away from Magda and pulled Godot with him, "Come along, she's next."

As Godot moved around the bed, he looked at Will and a red-eyed Cheryl and said, quietly, "Get your things together. You can't stay here. You'll stay with me."

Will held up one finger and Godot paused. As soon as the Senlis police detective turned, Will reached behind him and held up a golden computer disk in a clear plastic case.

Without intention, Godot's eyebrows went in the direction of the ceiling.

CHAPTER TWENTY-SEVEN:

THE OLD MAN AND THE SEA

A single lamp illuminated a corner of the apartment, casting a pool of light down and around a solitary figure, dressed in pajamas and a robe, hunched in a chair. He dozed fitfully, snapping awake again and staring with red-rimmed eyes toward the darkened shadows in the center of the carpet, desperately trying to find an answer in the silent gloom that hung like a fog on the edge of morning just before the first streaks of dawn.

Godot listened to the sounds of the apartment.

Isabelle was tossing in their bedroom, turning one way and then the next in her search for his comfort in bed. He thought that he should join her, but every time he laid down, the thoughts of what he had to deal with spilled over into his consciousness. No, it was better to sleep out here.

He turned his attention to the door that led to the small guest bedroom in the rear of the apartment. Will Ross was snoring gently. After the day he had, Godot thought, I'm amazed he could sleep, but, then again, after the day he had, perhaps sleep was his only defense. Block it out, move it away, make it a dream by tomorrow morning.

Cheryl Crane, on the other hand, seemed made of sterner stuff. She wasn't in shock or overly excited about what happened. She said she had seen it all before. Godot shook out the cloud of sleep that was creeping over his brain. I wonder, he thought, I wonder what her story is, for you don't often meet people who have seen this kind of thing before, anywhere.

His eyes shut for only a moment and reopened, then shut again and reopened with a 'snap,' then closed again as he drifted into a warm sea that surrounded and caressed him.

He sank under the surface, drifting in the blue-green comfort, his mind clear of everything and everyone, sliding toward the bottom, the surface and the sunlight falling farther and farther away. And yet, he didn't struggle. He didn't flail for what lay above. He was content to drift away and drown in such luxurious splendor.

He seemed caught by the current now, carried along toward a great, warm nothingness at which he had no desire to look. There was someone else in control, someone else in command, and, after the few weeks he had endured, he was thrilled to let someone else do the driving.

The water began to grow gray and cold around him.

A fish swam by and turned its head in a most unfishy way. It bore the face of Henrik Koons. Another did the same and another and another. And another swam by bearing the face of Paul van Bruggen, which puzzled Godot, for he didn't know what Paul van Bruggen looked like, but he knew this was him. And Bresson swam by, a muscular fish, his fins dark brown from the sun, the rest of his body a pale, sickly white. Godot floated in amazement between the fish as a dark shadow fell over them and with a swoosh of water and bubbles, they disappeared into the maw of a shark he knew to be Magda Gertz without ever seeing her.

The fury and suddenness of the attack surprised him, but still didn't frighten him. In fact, he felt oddly at peace, as if he knew that he could leave the answer there. He knew he could leave the entire disturbance directly in the lap of Magda Gertz, the dearly departed Magda Gertz.

And then, another shadow fell across the sea of his imagination and he knew that one way or another, he was going to have to deal with the situation at hand, with the shark at the core of the problem.

The cool blue-green of the first REM cycle began to fade into a deeper sleep, a mindless, dreamless wall of black. He reached into its forgiving heart and pulled himself in, letting himself drift there, quiet and alone, knowing that whatever he had to face was still two days away, with the answers still locked inside a small golden disk.

His eyelids fluttered, then grew still, as his chin lay quiet on his chest and the single lamp surrounded him in a golden pool of light. Beyond him, through the window, the morning began to dawn in gray streaks of light working their way through the concrete valleys and peaks of Paris.

The city began moving early today.

It was already Friday. Le Tour was due on Sunday.

CHAPTER TWENTY-EIGHT:

IS PARIS BURNING?

Paris had not died in his mind, but it had certainly lost its luster. What had been electric and alive only four weeks before, now seemed cold and painted in false color, like an old woman dressed in mod clothes of the '60s with the garish makeup of a whore.

But, then again, perhaps it was him.

Will hobbled through the crowd, watching Cheryl cut a swath through it just ahead like Charlton Heston parting the Red Sea. Will was Pharaoh, trying to maneuver his clumsy chariot across the gap before the wall of people crashed in and down around him.

He was in a lousy mood.

The heat of the day was sharp, baking the top of his head with piercing points of light. The natural humidity of Paris grew oppressive in the crowd, with sweat and stink creating a wall that Will could very nearly see as a fog before him.

Cheryl was doing a great job in breaking through, but Will kept falling behind. He could bend his right knee, the cast ending just below the joint, but his left leg was braced out straight and he had to swing it, if only marginally, to step ahead. He pushed people aside with the head of the cane as politely as he could manage, but he kept getting his left foot tangled among the legs and the bags and the children and the camera straps that dangled to the ground.

"Whoa! Hey, some assistance," he called out to Cheryl, who turned and worked her way back toward him through the mass of humanity.

"Excuse me, pardon me, please, excuse me, sir," she muttered. Suddenly, in a louder voice, she barked, "Comin' through! *Jeune femme avec un bébé.*"

The crowd parted as if sliced and Cheryl crossed the final two meters with a bound, grabbing Will by the elbow and pulling him along, before the assembled masses realized that there was no lady with a baby and that the grumpy cripple in the middle of it all was to blame.

With a general mutter and a look that would cut cheese, they fell back again along the barricades like a lake once again finding its boundaries.

"Thank you," Will said, trying to catch his breath on the edge of the team enclosure.

"No problem. You could have handled it," she said breezily. "I see you brought your cane. I can tell you from personal experience that it's perfect for getting people to see your point."

"Yeah," he replied with bravado, "but I fear you are but the only one who can truly make it sing on somebody's chin."

"Ooooff," she muttered, turning to the barricade and waving over a security guard, "don't remind me, okay? Even self defense grinds at your soul."

"You know, I had never really thought of that."

"Hey. I'm sleeping. I'm eating. I'm trying to put it out of my mind," she said, quietly, holding up her Haven team pass for the gendarme to see, "but I can't help but think that I killed a person."

"Well, not really though," Will pondered aloud, holding up his pass and stepping through the barricade, "because she was trying to kill us, for one. We defended ourselves, for another. She just whacked that doctor for no good reason and without a thought, that speaks to determination to carry out the deed, I'd think, and, you know, you merely threw the syringe at her. How did you know you'd hit her in the chest or that the stuff would inject and act so quickly?"

"I didn't. By the way, I was aiming at her face."

"I'd say you were close enough."

"You know — where I grew up and with the people I grew up with, you got to know about this sort of thing. Not see it, necessarily, but you heard about it all the time. Burglars or muggers getting whacked by a homeowner or some gun-toting granny on the street, and you never thought about it beyond 'Hey, good for you, man. You got him.' But when it happens to you, you realize that there is a darker hole there."

Will watched her carefully.

"And now," she whispered, "I'm in it."

He swung his left leg forward and reached out to her. She fell into his arms and they both dropped back a step as Will desperately tried to find his balance. Finding it, they stood, silently, two figures in a tight embrace, surrounded by 10-foot-high steel barricades that held back a sea of people waiting for the arrival of the 139 survivors of Le Tour de France.

GODOT MADE HIS THIRD CIRCUIT OF LA TOUR EIFFEL, WALKING ACROSS THE Quai Branly, down the Avenue de Suffren, across on Avenue Gustave Eiffel And back up the Avenue de la Bourdonnais. The moist heat of the day had attached his shirt, under his suit coat, directly to his back. With each swing of his arms, he could feel the shirt pull away, with a cold yank and then reattach itself with a slap.

He pondered the many reasons why he might not survive today. Heat prostration was one he quickly added to the list. He began his fourth circuit of the plaza surrounding the tower and pulled the leather case tightly up under his arm.

He had added the disk to the contents yesterday, after Will had shown him how to access the information by computer. Will had then left, almost as if wanting to remain clueless as to what had driven Magda Gertz to his apartment in a murderous frame of mind.

But Godot couldn't remain clueless, as much as he might want to, as much as he might want to throw the entire case into the darkest, deepest section of the sewers of Paris.

He had to know.

And now, he did. The disk had been the final key, answering the questions that the paper trail had left open-ended. He knew now about BioSyn and Magda Gertz and Biejo Fortuna and Cytabutasone and the end of the Toulouse project and Henrik Koons and everything on beyond that death in Eindhoven.

Magda Gertz had spilled her guts in cyberspace and the answers all led to one place: the second platform of La Tour Eiffel.

❂

LE TOUR HAD GROWN EXCITING.

No doubt that there had been drama and color, triumph and tragedy, all along the way in this edition of the race, but now, it came down to the wire, with three riders within seconds of each other for the third position on the podium.

One of them was Richard Bourgoin.

Will had felt proud and happy for his friend, his teammate, his leader, but he had also felt guilt and frustration. He felt the guilt of having fallen behind and fallen out of the race and the frustration of not being the one who actually got Bourgoin to the podium, of not being the one who would kill himself today in an effort to fling Richard ahead the few seconds he needed to snatch the step away from the other two pretenders.

Will sat in the Haven team area and glanced around. He knew absolutely no one in the Haven area. Everyone he knew, his friends and teammates, and yes, even Miguel Cardone, were entering Paris even now, preparing for the race down the Champs-Elysées, from the Obelisk to the Arc and then the finish.

"Missing it?" Cheryl asked quietly, intruding on his guilt trip.

"Hmm?" He turned to her and smiled, sheepishly. "Yeah, I don't mind telling you that I am."

"Ironic, isn't it? You work all your life to get there, dream of it, train for it, and then, when you're in it, you just can't wait to get it done, but then, if it ends before it is supposed to end, you hate yourself and you hate the world around you and you'd offer your soul to the devil to be dropped back into the mess, anywhere, from first to last to the great unwashed crowd that rides between the two points."

Will nodded. "You're a very wise woman."

"Yes, I am," Cheryl acknowledged. "Yes, I am. Now, if only I could make myself believe that when I'm riding."

They were quiet for a moment, staring off across the team enclosure, now filling with guests and clients and VIPs waiting for the end of the race and the party that was to follow on the second platform of the Eiffel Tower.

Will stared at the scene and then muttered, "You're leaving, aren't you?"

"You knew I was," she replied, quietly, but with a certain underlying force.

"Yes," he whispered, "I knew. Can't say I believed, but I knew."

"Yes, well, that's the fact. Once this is over, I tender my resignation and it's wheels up for the New World."

"When?"

"When what?"

"When everything?"

"Deeds already has my resignation. I get paid through today. I'm supposed to be in Denver on Friday for a ride up to Vail."

"So …" he asked, expectantly.

"So … what?" she replied.

"So, when are you actually out of here? How long do I have to wrinkle your sun dress?"

"This is a great dress, isn't it?" she smiled, standing for a second and pulling the skirt away in an arc, "I'd forgotten I had this. I'm actually sort of glad Magda pulled it out of the closet for me."

"You look great in it."

"Thanks. I've been wearing jeans and shorts and golf shirts so long, I'd kind of forgotten what a dress felt like."

"You've changed the subject," he pointed out. "When — when do you actually leave?"

"Tomorrow. I have tickets on Air France tomorrow."

"Air France? Not United or American?"

She laughed. "No, I figured I'd keep the Continent with me for a few more hours."

"Understood." He looked to the ground again and clasped his hands together, not noticing how much pressure he was putting on his own grip. "Tomorrow," he sighed. "Tomorrow."

GODOT REALIZED THAT HE COULDN'T PUT IT OFF ANY LONGER. HE CROSSED the plaza, stepped underneath the iron framework of the world's most famous tower, showed his pass to the guard on duty who he recognized as a retiree from the police force, chatted a little more than necessary about the weather, then stepped to the stairs.

He took a deep breath and began his climb leading to the first platform.

"*HERE THEY COME!*" SOMEONE SHOUTED.

Will leapt from his depression and the chair and bounced his way over to the observation barricade.

Haven had a prime location along the Champs, just shy of the finish line. Will looked down the broad avenue and saw a burst of color and movement as the peloton shot out of a curve en masse to begin the first true racing of the day.

The final stage had started 126 kilometers before at EuroDisney. It would end some 50 kilometers from now, right here, after eight circuits of the Champs. Until now, the pack had ridden easy, keeping the pace up, but knowing, for the most part, unless miracles really occur, that the race was won. First and second were both sewn up. Only a catastrophe could change either position. The race for third, however, the final step of the podium, was still on and still heated.

Those riders, Will knew, Richard Bourgoin included, had not treated the day like a 175-kilometer parade. The entire stage had been a day on pins-and-needles, watching, thrusting, testing. They had been watching for a mistake, a collapse or a mechanical failure, anything to give them a leg up and the few seconds necessary to win the day.

But the gods had been toying with them all. They all got flats. They all, despite their heightened awareness, made mistakes. They all fell back and recovered and fell back again and recovered again.

They rode into Paris together, all within seconds of each other in the pack. The race would be decided only at the finish.

Will knew the pressures that Bourgoin must be facing, the stress, the fear, the drive, but he also knew that burning in his core was a fire, a fire no one realized was there when you looked at the slim, slight man on the bike.

He looked like hell when he rode, but he rode like a god.

The pack roared toward the 180-degree turn at the top of the Champs Elysées, stringing out and cutting in tight to the left. Immediately beyond the turn, the jockeying for position began again.

A few riders broke away and were quickly reeled back in. The pack was not about to allow an escape, except off the rear.

The pace continued to grow.

Will felt the blood pounding in his neck each time the peloton flew past, each time he caught a glimpse of Bourgoin.

On the second lap, Cardone, leading Bourgoin out, pulled wide and found himself off the pace, his previous spot captured, in seconds, by faster-thinking team lieutenants.

Will barked an oath and felt Cheryl take his hand.

"Relax. It will be fine. They still have six laps yet."

She squeezed lightly and he smiled in return, not believing her for a second.

"He missed the jump. There are four riders jumping and Bourgoin is still back. One of those guys is going for third, I think, too."

Cheryl shook her head. "It's too early. He'll fry and wind up back in the pack. It's Richard and the other guy now. That one up front has just ended his race."

Will knew she was right, but he couldn't help thinking that Cardone was blowing it, letting Richard fall too far behind the leaders. He paced, like a cat with two broken legs, along a few meters of open barricade. He wanted to turn away, but was drawn to the race like a mosquito to soapy water.

This race destroyed me, he thought. So why, oh, why, do I love it so?

GODOT WHEEZED HIS WAY TO THE SECOND PLATFORM, HIS EYES STINGING FROM a wave of perspiration that swept down his forehead and into his eyes. He stood to the side of the sign that said "Closed/Private Party" and pulled off his suit coat, draping it over a filigreed banister.

He took a deep breath and tried, not only to cool, but to calm himself. It wasn't working. His shirt was now a mass of wet wrinkles and his hair, what remained of it, hung limply along the sides of his head.

This, he thought to himself, was the appearance of power. He was dressed for success. He reached behind him to pull the creeping boxers out of the crack of his butt, slung the jacket over his shoulder and stepped into the restaurant.

It had been cleared except for a few tables, set aside with white tablecloths for serving. The most obvious addition were three, huge, big-screen TV systems, now playing the race finale, and soon, he realized, seeing the VCRs below, to be playing race highlights.

Will Henri Bresson be a part of the party, he wondered? Or Prudencio Delgado, still struggling for life in Avignon? Or how about Will Ross, destroying his legs and career stumbling up Mont Ventoux carrying a teammate who didn't care whether Will lived or died?

Would it show all that?

Would it show the face of Henrik Koons or Paul van Bruggen? Or even the face of Magda Gertz? She had as much of an influence on the race as hundreds of others carrying titles and access passes.

Would it show the race or would it show nothing more than the ride?

It would be interesting to see.

Godot glanced to the side and, outside the glass enclosure, saw Henri Bergalis walking the observation platform between the 200-liter drums posted at each corner of the tower.

He straightened his tie and stepped outside to face his boss.

"GOOD GOD, WILL! IF YOU'RE GOING TO BE LIKE THIS, DON'T WATCH."

Will was bouncing and weaving, shouting encouragement and damnation as the peloton passed on each successive circuit of the Champs. Cheryl had watched with fascination for a time, then, with frustration as the race wound down and Will wound up, growing more manic along the barricade.

He screamed at Cardone and Bourgoin each time they passed and hid his face in his hands with embarrassment as the pair fell farther behind.

Cheryl knew what he must be feeling, the race coming down to the wire without him, Richard falling farther behind, but there was nothing either could do but watch and hope and watch some more.

Two laps, just 13 kilometers, remained of the nearly 4000 kilometers of Le Tour de France, two more loops through the heart of Paris.

As the peloton roared toward the team enclosures in a burst of gears and chains and sprockets and sweat, Will pulled himself up over the barricade, took a deep breath and held it until Bourgoin hit the mark directly across from him.

"*Now, Richard! Now! Break aaaawwwwwwaaaaayyyyy!*"

He drew out the last word, trying to overcome the Doppler shift that Bourgoin must be hearing from the crowd. Cheryl shook her head beside him.

"It's too early, Will, it's too early."

"No," he said, quietly, "Richard is falling back. He has to push his pace and overcome whatever Cardone is setting up for him. Otherwise, he'll be sprinting from the front of the middle rather than the back of the front. He's got to pull himself up and have enough left over to sprint with Webster."

"He doesn't. Look at him."

"He'll find it, Cheryl. Believe me, he'll find it." Will leaned forward and watched the rear of the peloton disappear into the crowds and distance along the avenue. As he saw the riders make the hairpin turn around to return, he whispered, "find it, man, find it."

"AH, LUC. I'M GLAD YOU COULD MAKE IT." HENRI BRESSON OFFERED HIS HAND AND Godot took it, letting the younger man squeeze his bones to the point of breaking.

"The weather, I see," Bergalis noted, "has taken its toll on your suit."

Godot looked down at his shirt with embarrassment. "Yes. Yes, it has."

"You know, we could always step inside. It's air conditioned. More comfortable."

"More people," Godot muttered.

"Ah," Bergalis nodded, "I understand. It's one of those talks. One, I suppose, that couldn't have waited until the office on Monday."

"No. It could not wait. Not this. Not this time."

"I see. And what do you have for me?"

From under the jacket draped over his arm, Godot produced the worn leather case holding the research on Cytabutasone.

"Yes," Bergalis said simply. "You told me you had this. I know what is in there. I was a part of the project. Your point is?"

Godot said nothing, but out of the valise pulled a single, gold computer disk in a clear plastic case.

"And what," Bergalis laughed, "is that?"

"It's the key."

"The key to what?"

"The key to you, Henri."

WILL WAS CRAWLING UP THE BARRICADE AND OUT OF HIS SKIN.

"Go-go-go-go-*go!* Richard, *gooooo*ooo!"

"Are your legs all torn up, or is it all an act?"

"What do you mean?" Will asked, never looking away from the peloton.

"You're climbing that barricade like Hillary on Everest. It's all a sham, isn't it?" Cheryl laughed, caught up in the excitement and joy she found in Will's face.

"He's up. He's up, I tell you. Richard has dropped Cardone and he's up. It's gonna be close. This is great."

Cheryl began to weep through her happiness. If only, she thought, if only he had been able to muster this kind of joyous energy on Le Tour. If only he had caught a few more breaks and a little more support. She smiled.

If only, Will. If only.

He leapt up on shattered legs and waved crazily at the passing parade diving into the high turn of the final circuit.

I'll always remember you like this, she thought.

I'll always remember you like this.

She smiled and cried at the same time.

GODOT WONDERED HOW GOOD AN IDEA IT HAD BEEN TO SURRENDER BOTH THE briefcase and the disk when Bergalis had gestured for them. Godot had paused, but a second gesture, a come-on move of the hands, and he had turned them over to his boss, the man who had saved his life, the man he trusted with his life.

Bergalis held the valise open in front of him and riffled through the dried sheets of onion skin and copy paper that were packed within. Some he remembered and recognized, others he did not.

He left the flap of the case open as he peered at the golden computer disk, the sun bouncing off it in reflection and creating a dance of light on the window bchind him.

"So, Luc...."

Godot pulled himself up to his full height.

"What have you found? Or, I might say, what do you *think* you have found?"

Godot had prepared for this moment, laying out a speech and practicing it in his head. The problem was that facing down the man himself was nothing like facing down his own mirror image. Godot balked and his mind went blank except for a few scattered words and phrases.

"I know ... I know ..." he paused, "I know about the project in Toulouse."

"Yes," Bergalis sighed. "I already told you about that, Luc. In Montpellier. It was a government-approved project that, sadly, went wrong. We injected prison volunteers with Cytabutasone. It had the expected results. It repaired muscle damage almost..." he searched for a word "...with miracles. It was amazing, Luc. We had stumbled on a miracle cure, a miracle restorative. The company was very excited."

"But then, it went too far," Godot interjected.

"Yes, it went too far. I was project director. I answered to my brother, Martin, and the board of directors. When we discovered the range of possibilities with the synthetic, then, we found an additional benefit: performance enhancement."

"Without detection."

"Yes," Bergalis said, quietly, "but, you must understand — that particular benefit did not enter into it at that time."

Godot nodded. "When did you notice the first problems?"

Bergalis turned and leaned against the observatory railing, gazing out over the eastern fringes of Paris. "About six weeks after the testing began, we began to notice a rage building in the subjects, along the lines of steroid abuse.

We tried to back off on the dosage, but it was progressive. No matter what dosage we gave, it keyed a rage, great strength, incredible focus and a drive that often ended in death."

"They worked themselves to death, eh?"

"Yes, Luc," Bergalis said, distantly, "exactly. At that moment, I tried to stop the testing, but the government was now interested, as was my brother. He saw a huge potential in it for short-term use. He didn't care that men were dying to test his future profits."

"Convicts were dying," Godot said.

"Men were dying, Luc. No matter how you slice it, men were dying."

"Go on," Godot said, relieved that he didn't have to draw the story out of Bergalis again.

"About then, the leaks began. Other companies found out about Cytabutasone. The tests. The deaths. Some, of course, wanted to feed the press the stories about how Haven had been quietly killing convicts in Toulouse. Others wanted the formula, and were willing to stop at nothing to get it."

"Biejo Fortuna."

Bergalis seemed shocked upon hearing the name. "Wha… well, yes. Him and others."

"BioSyn?"

"Yes. BioSyn. Other companies. Other people."

"Your wife?"

Bergalis stopped cold. He stared at Godot for a long, hard moment. Godot could feel the man reverse his loss of control and re-steel himself toward the conversation.

"Yes, Luc, if you must ask," he said with a touch of venom in his voice, "my wife, my dear departed wife, was involved as well."

"What was she, Henri," Godot asked, "an assistant or a partner in the testing?"

"She was an assistant. We met here in Paris and were married three weeks later. Two weeks after that and we were involved in the Toulouse project. Four months later, we're separated and she's living in a penthouse apartment at my cost and working for my competitors."

"BioSyn," Godot read off a list, "and Biejo Fortuna."

"Yes. Right on both counts." Henri Bergalis wiped a string of sweat beads off the top of his eyebrows and turned to Godot.

"Are you sure you don't want to go inside, Luc? Ten degrees cooler indoors and we can see the end of the race."

"No. No, thank you Henri. I'd much rather stay out here where we can keep this private."

"Ah, yes. Of course."

"You never divorced Magda, did you?"

"No," Bergalis said slowly, "I never did. I suppose there was always a dim hope that we could get back together someday. Magda is a woman you don't easily push out of your dreams, no matter what she has done to you."

"I would agree. There are a lot of people who will never forget her," Godot said.

"It was the effect she had on people," Bergalis said with a shy grin that spoke of fond memory.

Before he had a chance to recover, Godot asked, "Have you ever met Biejo Fortuna?"

"Me? Yes, perhaps, quickly, at a party," Bergalis answered. "But once or twice, perhaps, in 10 years. You don't socialize with a person trying to destroy your company."

"Destroy your company or your brother's company?"

"What do you mean?"

"It wasn't your company then, was it?"

"No. It wasn't my company until this spring."

"Until then, it was run by your brother, Martin Bergalis."

"Yes, my brother who wanted to keep Cytabutasone alive, no matter what the cost," Bergalis said, a trace of anxiety creeping into his voice.

"Indeed," Godot muttered. He turned to go, stopped and turned back to Henri Bergalis, scratching his head. "Henri. Did it ever occur to Martin what you were doing? I mean, he could be mean, but he was also a very smart businessman, not easily fooled. Did he realize that you were trying to undercut him, or was he oblivious? Did he know, or did you and Magda hide your little game so well, your hiding in a mousy, faithful brother facade to fool him while she ran BioSyn for Biejo Fortuna, that he was left in the dark?"

Bergalis shifted uneasily in the harsh sunlight. "How did you get all of that from this?" he asked, holding up the valise.

"I didn't," Godot answered. "I merely asked. A computer disk from an unknown source and a pack of filed papers from a company archive are merely circumstantial. A good lawyer can easily argue around them. But I know. Because I know where these come from. And I know that there are memos missing from that file, replaced by newer copies with different messages: messages implicating your brother, Martin, in keeping Cytabutasone alive. I know. I know that Martin wanted to kill the project because killing your customers is not the way to build a clientele. I know that Magda went on with it, because she believed in it and was still your wife in every way. I know that. Just as I know that you are Biejo Fortuna."

"Now — you are talking like a lunatic, Luc. Nothing here …"

"*Stop it*, Henri! The game is over. There is no more need. Your brother is dead. Your wife is dead. Cytabutasone is dead, because it's deadly. You created a character and a company to undercut your brother wherever possible. You became Biejo Fortuna, to the point where you actually believed the role you were playing. Magda did the dirty work — right down to the point of murder — and you kept the drug alive. How long, Henri? How long did you have to work on it in secret before you unleashed it into the peloton? Did the riders know? The coaches? The team doctors? I doubt it. The best kept secret is secure if everybody who knows about it is dead. How many people who know about it are dead, Henri? How many?"

"It got out of hand, Luc. It simply got out of hand. Sometimes research does that."

"This was not research, Henri. This was greed. You became successful on your own, tripping up your brother as Biejo Fortuna. BioSyn became a success despite a ghost at the helm and a crime at its core. You couldn't give it up because it gave you too much: money and freedom and a power over your brother that you couldn't have any other way."

Bergalis nodded and then looked with pleading eyes toward Godot.

"I suppose," he sighed, "that you have copies of everything?"

"No," Godot answered quietly, "you have the only copies."

"Really," Henri Bergalis smiled, his face showing a mixture of both shock and relief. "Well," he said, "that makes this an entirely different situation, now, doesn't it?"

Bergalis turned and carefully plucked one sheet of onion skin from the case. He lit it with his gold cigarette lighter and dropped it into the barrel. The dry and aged sheet burst into flames and had become ash within seconds.

One after another, the sheets disappeared in bursts of flame, into the barrels, barrels designed to be lit that evening to celebrate Haven's 50 years of participation in Le Tour de France.

"This," Bergalis said, "is taking too long, isn't it, Luc?"

Godot stood at the side and said nothing as Henri Bergalis lit a wad of onion skin sheet and touched them to the igniters lining the base of the barrel. Within moments, the entire drum was ablaze.

"There we are," Bergalis smiled. "Makes life much easier, doesn't it?"

With that, he upended the valise, sending a cascade of paper into the flames. Within moments, the Toulouse project and Cytabutasone were transformed from written into oral history, ever changeable in the telling and retelling.

"Oh, yes," Bergalis said, "and now, the disk. My wife is dead," he questioned, turning his head to Godot as if trying to catch an answer. "Well, that is too bad. She was something to see. Especially nude," he barked, catching a laugh in his throat. "How did she die, Luc?"

"She tried to kill Will Ross and Cheryl Crane. Cheryl stabbed her in the chest with a syringe of your miracle drug."

"Ah, yes. Poetic justice. Cheryl, you say," he smiled, raising an eyebrow, "how wonderful. She's a particularly electric woman. Far too much of one for Will, you know."

Bergalis held the disk in the air and slowly turned it back and forth. "You know, Luc," he said, sadly, "she was going to blackmail me. Magda. Threaten to expose me. And the game. The Biejo game. She was willing to do it. Willing to do," he remembered fondly, "just about anything. So, Luc, I'm glad it was you who came to me with this disk. It's all on here, is it? The Eindhoven research, The Project notes, Biejo?"

"It is. Paul van Bruggen started it. Magda added to it."

"Yes. I'm sure she did. I'm glad it was you rather than her. You would treat this as something important. She would treat it as another payday."

He looked at Godot for a long moment and said, "I won't forget this, Luc."

He tossed the disk into the barrel, the flames pulling it into their core, where the information stored within melted in seconds to incomprehension.

DURING THE LAST LAP, WILL HAD FOUND A BULLHORN IN THE HAVEN TEAM area and positioned himself at the far corner of the enclosure. As the pack began to roar by toward the line, he saw Richard just ahead of his closest rival. Miguel Cardone was nowhere to be seen.

Will raised the horn and waited, watching for the jump of the rider. As they crossed in tight at the 250-meter line, Will saw the twitch, the indication that the Lexor rider was going to jump. He pushed the button, the horn emitting an ear-deafening squeal, and shouted, "Now, Bourgoin!" Richard shot ahead as if electrified. Will hadn't realized that his voice would be so magnified. It caught both him and a number of riders off guard, but not Bourgoin. The leader of Haven bore down and caught the crest of the sprint, putting three seconds between himself and Webster before the other rider knew what had hit him.

Richard split the line, not the winner, but certainly on the podium.

He raised both arms in salute, tears streaming down his face.

Stepping into the enclosure, Carl Deeds leapt into the air and kissed whoever happened to be around, Cheryl among them.

Carl had put a man on the podium. He had proven himself worthy.

Two steps more and he could write his own ticket.

"MONSIEUR BERGALIS, FORGIVE ME — BUT THOSE WERE FOR THE CELEBRATION," the steward fluttered, waving his arms helplessly at the burning barrel.

"That's all right, Maurice," Henri answered. "Just find an extinguisher, put this one out and refill it before nightfall. Everything is under control."

The man in the starched white coat nodded and scuttled off.

"And it is true, isn't it, Luc?" Henri Bergalis said with an air of dismissal. "Everything is under control, isn't it?"

"My resignation will be on your desk tomorrow morning," Godot said, simply.

"Ack! Say nothing of the sort. You've saved me, Luc. I don't forget my friends."

"I don't either. I gave you your life only in return for the life you gave me."

"What, and now you're leaving that life, Luc? I doubt it my friend. I truly doubt it."

"I will. And I must. We are even now."

"How will you live?"

The former police homicide inspector looked slowly over the beauty of the city he had tried to protect for so many years from so many villains and said, "As far as money, I'll survive. How I will live with myself, that, is another question."

"Well, I do not accept your resignation. I am leaving for a week's vacation in Spain tomorrow. When I return, then I will consider it."

"You will find it there, then."

Godot turned and slipped on his suit coat, still heavy and soggy with sweat. Bergalis watched him shuffle toward the door, the weight of the past few days adding years to his carriage.

"Luc. Tell me. You're not thinking of returning to the force are you? Trying to catch me some other way now that you've felt obligated to set me free? Have you become my personal Javert?"

Godot stopped and turned back toward Henri Bergalis, a man he felt he owed, a man he thought he knew. He took a deep breath and murmured, "You have it all wrong, Henri. I am not your Javert. If anything, I am your Jean Valjean. You have your life," he said. "Now, let me have mine."

Godot turned away and shuffled for the stairs leading to the street and the Metro and a small apartment and a bottle of whiskey and a woman named Isabelle.

He felt very old.

In the distance, as he began his march down the steps, he could hear Henri Bergalis saying, "Next week, Luc. We will talk next week."

Godot trudged silently down the stairs of La Tour Eiffel, praying, as his mother had taught him so many years ago, for deliverance from his turmoil and for the strength to look himself in the eye tomorrow morning.

Alcohol would take care of tonight.

CHAPTER TWENTY-NINE:

THE PARTY'S OVER

The awards presentation had been quite a celebration for the Haven team, a celebration of success and failure, drama and tragedy. No one on the team could avoid thinking about Henri Bresson or Prudencio Delgado, or even the man who had been with both when they fell out of the line.

"Hey, Will."

Will turned and couldn't disguise his surprise. John Cardinal actually approached him with his hand extended.

"Great race, man," he said, pumping Will's hand wildly, "great race. You should have been there at the finish. You deserved it."

Will smiled. "Thanks, John. I appreciate that."

As Cardinal stepped away for an interview, Cheryl whispered in Will's ear, "You see? You weren't as hated as you thought you were."

"I was."

"You weren't, you idiot. One person, Cardone, gives you a hard time and you think everybody is against you. Even me. Can you believe that?"

"Yes. Yes, I can."

She hit him on the shoulder, which sent a shiver of pain down his left arm and through his bruised elbow. He opened his mouth in a silent cry of pain.

"Oh, sorry," she said, smiling wickedly. "But you've got to admit, you deserve it."

Will was about to answer when Richard Bourgoin came running up.

"Will, my good friend, Will. Even when you are not behind me, you are yelling in my ear. How did I know it was you on the speakers yelling at me? How did I know?" Bourgoin wheezed.

"It was a bullhorn."

"Bullhorn, bull shit," Richard laughed. "It was the voice of God. I am sure that the day they kill you, you will still come to me in voices, telling me what to do."

Will laughed uncomfortably at the macabre nature of the joke, especially in light of his recent encounter with Magda Gertz. Bourgoin suddenly leapt forward and strangled Will in a bear hug.

"Can't ... breathe ... can't ... breathe."

Bourgoin released him, laughing, and asked, quietly, through his laughter, "Excuse me, Will, but can I borrow your cane?"

Without thought, Will passed to Richard Bourgoin the cane of Charles de Gaulle, the cane that had pretty much saved his and Cheryl's lives, while doing the opposite for Dr. Paul Flacon.

The smiling third-place finisher kept laughing, even though the joke had long passed by. Then, without warning, he twisted his right leg back, planted his foot and drove the heavy brass eagle's head of the cane into the stomach of Miguel Cardone.

Cardone folded at the waist and fell to his knees, the wind knocked out of his lungs. His eyes popped with the strain of trying to breathe and his breath came in rattling, painful gasps.

Richard Bourgoin leaned down to Cardone's ear and hissed, in French, ("You damned near ruined this Tour for me, you son of a bitch. You angled out my lieutenant and you turned the team against him. Then, you moved into his role and you didn't have the knowledge or the legs or the balls to carry it out. It took him — him — standing beside the course to know when to jump. You had gone too early, bastard! You jumped and left me dangling in the breeze without support. But Will — Will had been out of the race for nearly six days and he still came through for me. You were the politician, bastard, but he — he was the rider. You will never ride near me again.")

Bourgoin flicked his hand at Cardone and spit in his face. Then he stood, smiled and handed the cane to Will.

"Thank you, my good friend."

"*Bon ami*," Will drawled in a phony southern accent. "It means 'good friend.'"

"Ah," Bourgoin nodded, missing the joke, "you are finally learning."

The two friends laughed and embraced.

Cheryl, meanwhile, had crouched beside Miguel Cardone. She grabbed his spandex riding pants by the waist and pulled him up into a hands-and-knees position, then, lifted the waist band to get his diaphragm working again.

"Breathe in, breathe out, Miguel. You'll live."

"What," Cardone wheezed, "did Richard say? Why did he do that?"

"Oh, well," Cheryl mused, "I can't really tell you what he said, because torrential French is not my strong suit, but I can give you the general gist of it."

"What?" Cardone gasped and retched. "What?"

"I think he said, 'Don't fuck with me, I'm from Detroit.'" She smiled broadly. "It's a rough translation."

With that, she snapped the waistband and Miguel Cardone collapsed on the ground, throwing up a number of small internal organs that weren't securely attached.

Carl Deeds burst into the crowd, hugging and praising everyone from Bourgoin to the photographer who had slipped past security.

He saw Will leaning uncomfortably on Cheryl and the edge of a folding chair and raced up to them in great good humor.

"I did it. I done-didddly-id it, Godddamn it."

Will laughed at the explosion of good humor coming from a man known only for explosions.

"I'm glad for you, Carl. It's about time. You had a lot of heart on that team."

"Yeah, I did, didn't I? *Damn*! *Yes*!" Deeds bolted and twirled on his one good leg. "Yes, indeed. The team!" he shouted, pointing both index fingers at Will and Cheryl. "The team! Great team! Couldn't have done it without them. Man!"

"Carl, excuse me for asking, but have you been drinking?"

"Yes, Will, I have been drinking. A lot. About a barge of champagne over there and for once, it's good stuff. It's nice to work," Carl bellowed, "for a team that's willing to spend some goddamned money and get me the goddamned horses! Am I right?"

"Whew!" Will waved his hand through the alcoholic air between them. "Don't go near any open flames, pal. Okay? I want to keep you around."

"And I want to keep you around, too, Will. And you, Cheryl." Deeds finger swept the space between them.

"Oh, no," Cheryl declared. "Include me out."

"Oh, come on, Cheryl," Deeds begged. "It was great. And it will be great again. We've still got the core: Bourgoin. You, Will. Delgado. Cacciavillani." He glanced over at Miguel Cardone, still retching on the ground beside them. "Cardone. If he ever learns to hold his liquor. God, we've got it."

"You don't have me, Carl," Cheryl said. "I leave for the States tomorrow."

"Oh, yeah," he recalled, drunkenly. "You're going to ride. What's the matter, don't like us anymore?"

"No. I just can't stand the excitement that continually kicks up around you like Mortimer Snerd in a sawmill."

"Oh, that's all right. But Will, what would Haven be without Will Ross, huh?" Deeds fell against Will's shoulder, sending Will into a spasm of pain.

"Carl, I can't ride. I'm out. I don't know what my recovery will be. I don't know that I can even climb on a bike again."

"Oh, hell. You'll recover."

"Maybe the knee, but not the calf. The damned thing is split from my Achilles to the back of my knee. It's gonna happen again. And again. And again, if I push it. And I need time to decide whether pushing it is worth the payoff."

Deeds stared at Will silently for a moment, lost in a drunken fog. He then lit up, as if someone had goosed him with a cattle prod.

"You don't wanna leave the game, do ya, Will? You can't. You wouldn't survive outside. So stay in!" Deeds clapped a hand on Will's shoulder and bent him sideways.

"I dunno, Carl...."

"Hell, boy. I need an assistant. I need a backup. You know the routine. You know the deal. You know how I train. So, come across. Get into management. It's a helluva lot easier than riding that damned thing." Deeds pointed to the side as Richard Bourgoin, third-place winner at Le Tour de France, who had much better things to do with his time, wheeled a clean and shining Colnago over to Will.

"Take it, friend. It has missed you." Bourgoin pushed the handlebars into Will's hands and stepped back.

Will stood for a moment, admiring the lines, the angles, the technological beauty that was "The Beast," and felt his chest grow tight.

"I thought … I thought I had lost her."

"Well, you left her on Ventoux," Richard said quietly, leaning in close, "which is no place to leave a woman like this."

Cheryl watched the scene and laughed. "Jesus. It's like I'm watching an episode of 'Lassie.'"

"We figured it was the least we could do for you, which is not true because another job with Haven is the least we could do for you. *Ha*!" Deeds alone laughed at his joke. "But, this is thanks, Will. It sure as shit was your day in the barrel this time out. You couldn't catch a bit of luck with an army of psychics."

"What does that mean?" Bourgoin wondered aloud.

"I haven't the slightest idea," Deeds burped. "I've gotta sit down."

As Deeds stumbled off to a chair and a well-deserved hangover, Richard Bourgoin was suddenly surrounded by a wave of reporters. He reached through them to shake Will's hand one more time.

"Think about it, Will. I don't work well without you around." The crowd pulled him away and he disappeared in a sea of bad haircuts.

Will watched him go, his hand raised in good-bye.

A pair of women sauntered past him, stopping for a moment to glance at Miguel Cardone, still desperately trying to catch his breath in a shattered heap on the tarmac.

"What's with him?" the one asked aloud to no one in particular.

Will looked over and muttered, "He ate some bad eagle."

Cheryl chuckled and turned away. "Well, stranger," she wondered, "Who around here could possibly find a drink for a girl?"

Will brightened, puffing himself up with false pride. "I suppose I can. After all, I seem to be a team assistant around here."

"Yes, you do," she said, suddenly distant.

"Congratulations."

CHAPTER THIRTY:

LEAVING ON A JET PLANE

The small Senlis apartment, usually so sunny and warm, was filled with a cold dread this morning, as if the fog and overcast had worked their way indoors and were hovering in the air, determined to affect their moods.

Both packed quietly, lost in private thoughts, while aware of the vague stench of death that still permeated the place.

Cheryl Crane packed quickly, taking two boxes of unwanted clothes and books out to the street. She would leave the kitchen supplies with the apartment. She had arrived with one suitcase three years ago and now was leaving with two and a carry-on. Not bad. She had never been much of a pack rat.

Will, on the other hand, had collected bits of junk like a black wool jacket collects lint. He had four boxes sitting out by the curb now and at least two more to go, but he had finally squeezed everything into two suitcases, a short duffel and a bike box.

"Why are you packing the bike?" she asked.

"I can't ride it. It's going to be in storage, so, why not? Better than having it sit out and get cold."

She nodded, understanding. She watched him tape the box shut and slide it to the corner.

"What time's your flight?" he wondered aloud.

"Fourth time. 3 p.m. Late-afternoon chase-the-sun flight. I should be good and fried by the time I hit Detroit."

"God, no doubt," he answered. "What class did Haven put you in? Here, help me with these sheets."

He pulled the cartoon sheets off the bed and tossed her an end to fold. She picked it up and pulled it tight.

"No class. No class at all. I'm paying for this ticket, not Haven, so I'll likely be in steerage."

Will folded the sheet in half, then again, and walked toward her.

"That doesn't seem fair. What, two years of indentured servitude and they toss you out at your own expense?"

She pulled the half sheet tight toward her.

"Sorry to say, most businesses don't give a damn about ex-employees' flying arrangements."

They folded the sheet into a small square.

"That's too bad," he said, over his shoulder as he walked to the closet. "You should get something out of this. I feel bad that I gave Carl back his credit card at the party last night."

"What did he say when you gave it back?"

"He said he hoped I had a good time with it and he made me promise not to take it anymore."

"And did you?"

Will tossed the folded sheet to the top of the closet along with the pillowcases and knurled his face while he thought for a moment. "Yes and no. No. I didn't have fun. I enjoyed the company — well," he nodded toward the 'death chair,' "some of the company, anyway, but, no, I did not. There is no joy in theft anymore. No joy at all."

"And, yes?"

"Yes, I told him I wouldn't steal it anymore. If he did me a favor."

"What favor?"

"I'll write to you about it."

They both laughed, in muted tones, the atmosphere of the room squelching any outburst of any kind.

"I'm, um, ready," Cheryl said, quietly.

Will looked at his watch. "Ooh. 11:30. Right on time." He slapped his open palms on this thighs in an empty, pass-the-time kind of gesture. "I should get us a cab."

"Yes, maybe you should," she said, sadly, turning to the window and trying to find something outside it on which to fix her stare.

Will walked to the window and paused, then whistled shrilly. Cheryl could hear him speaking softly in the distance. In a moment, he returned.

"He's on his way up," he said.

"Good," she answered. "Is that it, in here? I really want to get out of this place." She shuddered and Will held her close.

"Yeah. That's it."

They silently gathered their bags and carried them to the street, Will trying to balance himself with the carry-on and the duffel, while Cheryl shouldered the suitcases down to the street.

"I'm going to be damned glad when you decide to get your legs back. I feel like a packhorse here," she wheezed as she dropped the two heavy suitcases at the curb.

"Be careful with the bike box, okay? I don't want anything to happen to 'The Beast.'"

She shot him a dirty look.

"Oh, God. We wouldn't want that, now, would we?"

"No," he blurted with mock horror, "we wouldn't."

They walked back into the stairway as the cabby watched them retrieve more luggage.

"HERE," SHE CALLED TO THE DRIVER. "THIS IS GOOD."

The cab pulled in smartly beside the curb and stopped.

Cheryl didn't move for a second, but sat stock still, staring out the side window at the crowds passing the doors of Air France at L'Aeroport Charles de Gaulle.

"Are you sure, Will? Even for just a few weeks?"

"I don't know, Cheryl. And I'm sorry about that. But, they've made me an offer here that gives me new life. I'm No. 2 on the team without serving an apprenticeship. If I do ever get my form back, I'm in a position to ride."

Tears began to well up in their eyes.

"You know how I feel about you, Cheryl. You know that I want to go. You know that I want to support you and your team and your riding, despite the fact that you're riding those damned mountain bikes."

"Will, I...."

"You're gonna put an eye out with one of those things some day, mark my words."

Cheryl laughed. Will smiled an emotional, keep-it-light-or-I'll collapse kind of grin.

"But," he continued, "I've got to ride, too. There ain't much time left for me on the bike. I'm facing an Henri Bresson-kind of season next year. But, somehow, some way, I've got to stay in touch with this team, this company, this sport." He pointed toward the trunk of the cab. "That bike. I've got to stay a part, because it's a part of me. It's what makes me whole. It's what makes me live."

She nodded.

"I know," she said, quietly. "That's how I feel, too. That's why I've got to leave now."

He scrunched up his face and nodded, without saying a word.

Will climbed out of the cab, stepped behind to help the cabby with the bags and pay the fare.

Cheryl Crane sat quietly in the cab, drinking in, for the last few moments, the world that she had built around her. The future was not a comfortable place. The future was filled with new people and challenges and the very real chance of failure.

It felt empty at its core. She stepped out of the cab and toward the terminal doors.

"Come on, the driver's got the bags and a porter to carry them in."

"What? Oh, great. What about yours?"

"I gave him a humongous tip to hang around. As soon as I get you through the customs line, I'll head to Bourgoin's place. He said I could shack up there for a few days until I find a new apartment."

"That's nice."

"That's Richard. Besides, third place in Le Tour and three bottles of champagne do that to a fellow. Makes him expansive."

"It would sure as hell make me expansive," she said, bloating her cheeks.

"Yes, but you'd be the funniest bloated person in the known universe."

Will tipped the man and slid the bags up to the empty Air France counter. "This is it," he asked, "two and a carry?"

Cheryl nodded silently. She stepped to the counter and handed the ticket agent her ticket and passport. She answered the standard security questions while they talked. He nodded and then secured her luggage. He continued to tap away on his computer for a moment, then glanced up at her.

"There has been a change in your reservation, *mademoiselle*."

"A change," she asked, suddenly alert to a problem, "what kind of change?"

"Oh," he said, quickly, "a good change. I think you'll like this."

He tapped the keyboard a few more times and handed her the ticket envelope. "Thank you for flying Air France."

She glanced at her ticket and realized that it was First Class.

"My God," she muttered, turning to Will, "how…"

He stood with a tremendous grin on his face.

"That is a gift," he said, "from me and Haven and Carl's credit card. Have a safe trip." He hugged her for a long moment and reluctantly broke the embrace, as two passengers tried to push past them.

"I thought you gave Carl his credit card back," she gasped, still in shock at the ticket.

"I did." He said, "After I changed your reservation. By the way, you'll notice that your ticket cost more than the airplane itself."

"I see," she gulped.

Will smiled at her. "Have a safe trip," he whispered. "Say hello to your mother."

"She loves you to death —"

"God, not that. Too many people have been doing that lately."

Cheryl laughed and cried at the same time.

"Yeah, that's true."

They began to walk toward the security doors, through which Will could not pass. Cheryl would be locked within the terminal for the next two and a half hours until flight time.

"What will you do?"

"I'll drink. What would you do?"

"I'd drink, too," he said, "but people expect me to be sloppy drunk when I fly the pond. It's a requirement."

She dismissed the thought with a nod. "It passes the time."

"Yeah, it does."

There was a long silence between them.

"Will, there was something you said back at Bagnères-de-Bigorre during Le Tour. Did you mean it?"

Will shrugged. "How could I mean something I said in a place that I can't pronounce?" he laughed.

She sighed and nodded, again. "Yeah." Her head bobbed up and down like the head of a spring-loaded plaster dog.

"Of course. What was I thinking?" She stretched up, kissed him quickly, and disappeared through the security doors.

"Take care," he called out to the disappearing figure. "Call. Call Richard's when you get to Detroit. Be careful. Hey! Hey, Cheryl! Hey!"

She didn't look back.

SHE HAD ALREADY BEEN ON THE PLANE FOR 25 MINUTES, WAITING FOR TAKE-off, when she decided it was safe to steal the seat beside her. She pulled her bag from underneath the seat ahead and dropped it into the aisle companion. She stared out the window at the huge cumulus clouds that had been left behind from the cold and fog of the morning.

In the afternoon sunlight, it was a vivid, beautiful sight. A good way to remember Paris, she thought. And France. And Haven. And Will.

"Excuse me," the heavily accented voice said from the aisle, "but I believe you 'ave taken my seet."

"Oh, sorry," she said, embarrassed. "I'll get this stuff right away." Cheryl scrambled to put her book and a set of unknown keys that had spilled out back into her carry-on bag when she noticed that the legs of the person speaking to her were not what one would call "normal." The right was encased in a blue cast up to the knee, while the left was held stiff by a fabric-and-metal brace.

She looked up past the ratty Haven T-shirt and into the face of Will Ross.

"Isn't it interesting," he said. "When I was a kid, people dressed up to fly. Now, we dress like we're getting ready to clean out the garage."

"Hey, that's my line."

"Yes, I know. But then again, I'm a thief." He tossed two bags of airline peanuts on her lap. "See? I could get 40 in the Bastille for that."

He loosened the straps on the brace and worked himself into the seat, his left leg dangling precariously into the aisle.

"You know, that drink cart comes through and I'm gonna need a cast on this one."

She laughed as she tried to ask, "What … what are you … what are you doing here?"

"I told Carl I'd be back and be his assistant. Next season. But I had some serious ass recovery to do between now and then and I just couldn't do it in the seat of that damned circus wagon Peugeot they call a team car with him screaming at me all the time."

"So…." she asked, expectantly.

"So, I'm going home to see my mama and your mama and to get fed well."

"And get fat," she added.

"That, too. That, too."

She snaked her arms through his right arm and pulled herself in tight to his shoulder.

"I'm glad you're coming," she whispered.

They sat quietly for a moment while electronic bells rang inside the plane, the cabin hatch was closed and the engines of the 747 began their long and beautiful windup.

Presently, he whispered, "By the way, you mentioned something earlier."

"What?" she asked, quietly.

"You asked if I remembered something I said on stage 13. At the start. At Bagnères."

"Yeah," she said, not moving from his shoulder.

"I remember," Will said, the emotion rising in his voice, "I remember very well. And I will remember it as long as I live."

Cheryl Crane stared ahead at the back of the brown leather seat before her and the AirFone that presented itself there. She focused on the words and the colors and the shapes of the seat and the phone and the stitching of the fabric before her. She stared ahead and waited to hear what she hoped to hear. What she hoped he would say in a moment when they were alone, alone with perhaps 196 other weary transatlantic travelers.

"I love you, Cheryl," he said, quietly. "I always have and I always will."

The engines continued to power up as the tug pushed the plane back away from the gate and toward the taxiway. As it did, the plane moved Will away from France and Paris and Le Tour, away from Haven and cycling, away from glory and money and what had been, for nearly 20 years, his reason for being.

It had begun on a strip of concrete at a velodrome, just west of Detroit. It would end only hours from now on a strip of concrete at Detroit Metro, just west of the city.

At that moment, he knew.

Will Ross had never been happier in his life.

His circle was complete.

EPILOGUE

Henri Bergalis felt particularly satisfied with himself as he sank a little deeper into the kid leather seat of the Haven corporate jet and waited patiently for takeoff from Le Bourget.

He adjusted the pince-nez glasses riding low on his nose and read, for the fourth time, another newspaper account of the final stage of Le Tour, as well as an analysis of the drama and tragedy that the Haven team had brought to the event.

He smiled at the picture of Will Ross, standing next to Richard Bourgoin at the podium. Will, he noted, was being hailed for his courage in the Pyrenees despite the hardships he encountered.

"Good for you, Will," he muttered. "Good for you."

But, in truth, Henri's focus was on the figure of a woman just behind and to the right of Will Ross. He could only see a portion of her face, but he knew her well and wanted to know her better.

"Ah, Cheryl, thank-you, Cheryl, thank-you for what you've done for me."

And there would be, he knew, more time to thank Cheryl, personally, in the very near future. He had already left orders this morning to buy the title sponsorship for her mountain biking team in the States. He smiled at the thought: Haven in the States. It was a good business move. Not only would it provide the company with a higher American profile, but it would give him the excuse to visit and woo Cheryl, and, who knows, dispose of Will Ross one way or another.

Too bad Magda never accomplished that. She was so good at so many things, but she never found the key to Will Ross. What was that key?

Friendship? Loyalty? Money? No, not money.

Not the way he lived.

But, no matter. Henri Bergalis would find it. And once he did, he'd exploit it. And once he did that, he'd move in on Cheryl Crane.

Cheryl, dear. You killed the witch. Thank you so very much.

He leaned over and switched on the intercom with the cockpit.

"Why are we waiting?" he asked testily, his patience, a newfound trait, already beginning to wear a bit thin.

"We have an overheat signal on engine one, sir. We thought we might taxi back and have a mechanic look at it."

"Has there been a problem before?"

"Yes, but it was only an indicator light."

"Then I suspect it is only a light again. Let's go." He snapped the intercom off and sat back smugly. It was nice, very nice, to finally have the power.

The jet turned onto the runway with engines powering up and, after a short takeoff roll, fairly leapt into the skies north of Paris.

He sat back and took a deep breath and relaxed in the lap of his company-owned luxury.

"That," the voice cooed, "was a good decision. That was the decision of a manager. That was the decision of a man with 'the power.'"

Henri Bergalis snapped his eyes open in shock and stared at the stranger.

"Who — who in God's name are you?" he demanded.

"I," the stranger answered, sitting on the edge of the opposite seat in such a way as to not wrinkle his turn-of-the-century brown plaid suit, "am the last person in the world you expected to see today."

Henri Bergalis stared at the stranger as the jet continued to climb and was soon swallowed up by the clouds.

Other books from VeloPress

The Cyclist's Training Bible *by Joe Friel*
Now in its third printing! Hailed as a major breakthrough in training for competitive cycling, this book helps take cyclists from where they are to where they want to be — the podium. • 288 pp. • Photos, charts, diagrams • Paperback.
1-884737-21-8 • P-BIB $19.95

Off-Season Training for Cyclists *by Edmund R. Burke, Ph.D.*
Burke takes you through everything you need to know about winter training—indoor workouts, weight training, cross-training, periodization and more. 168 pp. • photos • Paperback.
1-994737-40-4 • P-OFF $14.95

Zinn & the Art of Mountain Bike Maintenance, 2nd Edition *by Lennard Zinn*
Regardless of your mountain-bike experience or mechanical prowess, Zinn will guide you through every aspect of mountain-bike maintenance, repair and troubleshooting in a succinct, idiot-proof format. • 288 pp • Illustrations • Paperback
1-884737-47-1 • P-ZIN $17.95

Bicycle Racing in the Modern Era *from the editors of* VeloNews
These 63 articles represent the best in cycling journalism over the past quarter century: the world championships (road and mountain), the Tour de France, technical innovations and much, much more. • 218 pp. • Paperback.
1-884737-32-3 • P-MOD $19.95

Tales from the Toolbox *by Scott Parr with Rupert Guinness*
In his years as a Motorola team mechanic, Scott Parr saw it all. *Tales from the Toolbox* takes you inside the Motorola team van on the roads of Europe. Get the inside dirt on the pro peloton and the guys who really make it happen ... the mechanics. • 168 pp. • Paperback.
1-884737-39-0 • P-TFT $14.95

***VeloNews* Training Diary** *by Joe Friel*
The world's most popular training diary for cyclists. Allows you to record every facet of training with plenty of room for notes. Non-dated, so you can start any time of the year. • 235 pp. • Spiral-bound.
1-884737-42-0 • P-DIA $12.95

***Inside Triathlon* Training Diary** *by Joe Friel*
The best multisport diary available anywhere. Combines the best in quantitative and qualitative training notation. Designed to help you attain your best fitness ever. Non-dated, so you can start at any time of the year. • 235 pp. • Spiral-bound.
1-884737-41-2 • P-IDI $12.95

Single-Track Mind *by Paul Skilbeck*
This book represents a quantum leap in mountain-bike training guides — the right combination of scientific training information, bike-handling skills, nutrition, mental training, and a proven year-round training plan. • 128 pp. • Photos, charts, diagrams • Paperback.
1-884737-10-2 • P-STM $19.95

Cyclo-cross *by Simon Burney*
A must read for anyone brave enough to ride their road bike downhill through the mud. Expanded from the original to include mountain-bike conversion to cyclo-cross. • 200 pp. • Photos, charts, diagrams • Paperback.
1-884737-20-X • P-CRS $19.95

The Mountain Biker's Cookbook *by Jill Smith*
Healthy and delicious recipes from the world's best mountain-bike racers. The ideal marriage between calories and the perfect way to burn them off. • 152 pp. • Paperback.
1-884737-23-4 • P-EAT $14.95

Barnett's Manual *by John Barnett*
The most expensive bicycle maintenance manual in the world ... and worth every penny. Regarded by professionals world-wide as the final word in bicycle maintenance. • 950 pp. • Illustrations, diagrams, charts • Five-ring loose-leaf binder.
1-884737-16-1 • P-BNT $149.95

Half-Wheel Hell *by Maynard Hershon*
This collection from writer Maynard Hershon gives a human view of cycling and the culture that surrounds it. Hershon explores our perception of ourselves and our sport with humor and sensitivity. • 134 pp. • Paperback.
1-884737-05-6 • P-HWH $13.95

Tour de France THE 75TH ANNIVERSARY BICYCLE RACE *by Robin Magowan*
A masterful account of the 1978 Tour de France, the Tour's 75th anniversary. Magowan's fluid prose style brings to life the most contested Tour de France as if it were yesterday. • 208 pp. • Photos and stage profiles • Hardbound.
1-884737-13-7 • P-MAG $24.95

Eddy Merckx *by Rik Vanwalleghem*
Discover the passion and fear that motivated the world's greatest cyclist. The man they called "the cannibal" is captured like never before in this lavish coffee-table book. • 216 pp. • 24 color & 165 B/W photos • Hardback.
1-884737-22-6 • P-EDY $49.95

Bobke *by Bob Roll*
If Hunter S. Thompson and Dennis Rodman had a boy, he would write like Bob Roll: rough-hewn, poetic gonzo. Roll's been there and has the T-shirts to prove it. If you like straight talk, or cycling, or both, this book is a must read. • 124 pp. • Photos • Paperback.
1-884737-12-9 • P-BOB $16.95

A Season in Turmoil *by Samuel Abt*
Abt traces the differing fortunes of American road racers Lance Armstrong and Greg LeMond through the 1994 season. Revealing, in-depth interviews show the raw exuberance of Armstrong as he becomes the top U.S. road cycling star, while LeMond sinks toward an unwanted retirement. • 178 pp. • B/W photos • Paperback.
1-884737-09-9 • P-SIT $14.95

For ordering or more information, please call VeloPress toll-free: 800/234-8356 or visit our Website: www.velocatalogue.com